Corrupt Goddess

HIDDEN GODS series

April Gaisford

To Kandace.

Sorry about that time I said Kayla wasn't a good name. Kayla is totally cool.
Also, thanks for all your help with the gay stuff.

CONTENTS AND TRIGGERS

Corrupt Goddess contains many triggers and tropes.

Possible triggers:

Sex work, being drugged, Mafia/cartel, Drug trafficking, Childhood trauma, Violence

Possible tropes:

Sapphic, Ethical Non-Monogamy/Polyamory, Boss/employee, Age gap, Grumpy/sunshine, Dark/Mafia, Millionaire, Kink

These lists are not all inclusive. Please read at your own discretion

Contents

Marzanna, Winter Goddess

The winter goddess Marzanna has several guises and multiple names in Slavic
   mythology,
but all of them are evil.
She represents the coming of winter and is one of the three seasonal sisters
   representing the cycle of life and death.
She is also a fate goddess, whose arrival signifies misfortune.
And she is a kitchen goddess, who creates nightmares and mischievously fiddles
   with a woman's spinning.

K. Kris Hirst

ThoughtCo.com, 2019

1 • CATHERINE

"Yes, gods. Fuck," he yells as his body shivers while I thrust deep in his ass.

Brayden visits me weekly. It's not always the same, but our visits usually end with him getting pegged. He loves it, but he also gets paid well for it. I lean forward, lips hovering against his ear. Both hands slide over his hips, his flesh shivering under my touch. I pause, leaving the tip of the dildo just inside him, teasing him. His chest heaves under my own, his knuckles white against my desk he is leaning over.

"It's time for you to come for me like the good boy you are."

My fingers snake around, wrapping over his throbbing cock. Brayden groans under my touch. I slam into him, this angle forcing the toy directly against his prostate. He trembles while my fingers stroke the silky skin of his cock. He yells a curse as his body jerks, cum spurting onto the wood floors in my office. I stroke his back, feeling the muscles tense and settle with his orgasm. That's what this is all about for me. It's never about pleasuring my body. I want control over someone else's pleasure. Seeing their body contort from my touch gives me a high.

I pull out of him slowly, shuffling around my desk to grab the wipes I store in the bottom drawer. Better to stay prepared for any situation. While he cleans himself, I remove the strap-on, wiping it down with toy-safe wipes, not wanting to ruin one of my favorite office toys. I rearrange my skirt and shirt, having yet to remove them for our weekly appointment. I never do. I have no interest in exposing that much of myself to anyone. This skirt is shorter than I prefer, but it's much more convenient for wearing the strap-on.

Once Brayden is dressed, I pass him the envelope of cash. Enrico charges a lot for appointments with Brayden. He is an excellent sex worker. He willingly joined Enrico when he realized how much money he could make working in this field. It's the reason I see him and only him. Enrico has people less willing than Brayden. I could never bring myself to pay for them. Brayden enjoys the attention he gets from his clients, frequently sharing stories with me. I appreciate his company as much as his body. He is built like a damn Greek god. His skin is always a perfect golden tan, a rarity in Kansas City. I run my fingers through his shaggy hair, smoothing it down. The dark brown hair is wavy on top, a few inches long, and has shaved sides. His smile is devastatingly beautiful, with genuine delight shining through.

"Thank you, ma'am," he says, tucking the cash into his pocket. I slip a few more bills into his waistband, hidden from anyone else. Enrico may pay well, but he still takes a cut first. Brayden never argues or pushes back with my desires. Some of the other sex workers grew tired of not being able to see or touch me. Brayden has been around the longest of anyone. In my life, it's easier to see a sex worker than try to establish a relationship.

He nods, leaning back against my desk in a casual stance. His arms cross over his chest, a playful smile on his face. Despite the large age gap between us, I enjoy his playful comments.

"You sure do fuck well for an old lady." He dramatically rubs his ass as I give him a lighthearted exasperated glare.

"If you keep those comments up, I'll cage you again. Longer this time." His eyes raise with a mix of alarm and excitement.

"It'll cost you more. Enrico has been keeping me busy." He pulls a piece of fuzz off his shirt, not meeting my eyes. As much as he enjoys the sex work, he wants more control over his own life. He could branch out independently, but getting out from under Enrico is more challenging than he thought.

"I didn't think there were that many cougars around that could afford you," I tease, not wanting to be too harsh with him. He gives me a sad smile.

"There are plenty of those," he huffs a laugh, crossing his arms over his chest again. "I have some younger women now and a few men." I step up to him, stroking his cheek lightly. Intimacy is a powerful tool for me, but it rarely means more than power.

"If it becomes too much, you tell me." My voice is soft but laced with the threat behind my words. Brayden smiles, his cheek bulging in my hands.

"If I didn't know better, I'd think you liked me, Catherine." We both chuckle. While I do like him, this relationship will never be more than what it is. He is a sweet kid, and I want to protect him, but for purely selfish reasons. His well-being is vital to my desire for control. He lifts off the desk, pulling his phone out as he moves closer to the door.

"When do you want me to come back?" I consider his question, letting my schedule for the next week scroll through my mind.

"What's your availability like next week?" Now, he gives an exasperated look.

"Catherine, you are the only woman crazy enough to ask for a 7 a.m. escort. I'm always available for you." I shake my head, chuckling softly. I always forget he works more during the night. My schedule varies daily, but I always find time for Brayden.

"Come Thursday morning. I have a hectic week and could use you then."

"Got it," he kisses my cheek quickly before leaving the room and typing on his phone. A few moments later, my phone dings. He's sent me a calendar invite with Enrico included. While Enrico has more control over his schedule, Brayden creates some appointments.

I sit behind my desk, closing my eyes as I prepare for the day ahead. Deep breaths, inhaling calm, exhaling chaos. I've used this technique since I was a little girl. Long before meditation was popular. I keep my head level by releasing the tension. I spin in my chair, looking out of my window of the industrial building at the Kansas City skyline. The skyline is not overly remarkable, but it's still my home. My office is bright with morning sunlight. The windows glisten between the metal frames. The exposed pipes running through the ceiling bounce some light around, leaving the space well-lit. My office was industrial chic before that was a trend, too.

New hires are starting today. Marzanna Fashion has been thriving for more than a decade. I last hired new people several years ago. With the fashion industry changing as quickly as it does, it's a smart business move to bring in fresh eyes. Not that I want more people in my building. I don't need them, but I can't deny the benefit of bringing on more designers. Marzanna is mainly dedicated to red-carpet or black-tie events. We have done a few avant-garde shows. I don't care for them, though. My designers sign up for the shows when they want, but their first obligation is our business.

The door opens behind me, interrupting my thoughts. I take another deep breath, exhaling my random thoughts. Turning around, Zedediah is waiting for me with a large black coffee in one hand and a frappe with whipped topping, several sauce swirls, and some crunchy bits on top. He holds my black coffee out, sipping on his frappe. Zed is my assistant, but so much more than that. He's the person who keeps me on track.

"You sure you don't wanna try? It's delicious." His voice rings playfully as he waves his drink in my face.

"If you're trying to kill me, sugar overdose isn't the way to go." The dark liquid burns the tip of my tongue before sliding down my throat, warming me throughout. The fall weather leaves the mornings chilly, with the afternoons sweltering. The coffee chases the chill away. "What's on the schedule for today?"

Zed checks the tablet resting on his arm, scrolling between sips of his sugary drink. His shoulders sway with delight after each sip.

"We have the new designers coming in at nine," he waggles his eyebrows at me, knowing I don't want to meet the new people.

"Who are they again?" He's told me several times, working closely with Helen, my HR manager, to select them.

"There's Maggie, fresh out of RMCAD. Then Vincent from Atlanta. He graduated from SCAD two years ago and has been an intern since. Last is Josephine. She graduated from the University of Minnesota four years ago and has been working in casual design since, but she has phenomenal designs." He turns the tablet around, flipping through some sketches of dresses and suits. They are stunning pieces and will give our shop the edge to stay ahead.

Zed is the most beneficial employee in my company. He has an eye for design and talent but is also perfect at delegating. I deal with the back end of the business while the designers handle the front end. Zed is my go-between. I couldn't run this without him.

"Great. Let me know when I need to meet them."

He takes his cue and leaves, letting me focus on the other work I must do for the day. I have a shipment coming up on Tuesday that I need to prepare for. Marzanna creates the pieces but also ships them. I have a warehouse a few blocks away. All of our pieces are shipped in climate-controlled containers. I have expanded the warehouse to allow other companies to send through us, too. It's an extra income source and networks with many businesses. Scrolling through all my files on my tablet and annotating essential pieces of data, I lose track of time. Buried in my work is my second favorite pastime. Brayden's ass is my first.

A knock on my door draws my attention away from spreadsheets. Zed pokes his head around the door. "It's time," he gives me a shit-eating grin, knowing I don't want to leave my office. I'm not a people person, despite running my own company. Leaving my preferred company of spreadsheets, I step onto the walkway on the second floor. All the offices are along the back wall of the second floor. It only covers a fraction of the space, leaving most of the design floor open. I stand against the rail, taking in the space below me. A couple of designers are focused on their work, keeping their assistants busy with cutting, pinning, or stitching. A group of people gather near the middle, with three new people in the mix.

Vincent is easy to pick out, being the only male. He is tall but skinny, wearing tight jeans and an oversized blazer. A shorter girl stands next to him. She has a tight body suit with a loose crop top. Combat boots with knee-high socks complete the look. She is tiny with dark hair pulled into a high, clean bun. Based on the applications, this girl is Maggie.

The final girl steps outside the ring of people, coming into full view. My breath catches at the sight of her. She's average height but so bright and colorful. Her hair is an unnatural yellow color that fades to bright red. She wears it curled in big ringlets falling around her shoulders. Short bangs frame her delightfully round face. A yellow empire waist dress with a full skirt covers her voluptuous body. The dress is decorated with various red flowers, and I can't help but wonder how often she changes her hair to match her clothing. She laughs loudly with her head thrown back, and my chest tightens.

Josephine spins to the side, twirling her dress around her wide thighs. Thighs I want to bury my face between. Flat red shoes cover her feet with laces that wrap around her thick calves. Laces I want to pull between my teeth away from her in such a slow manner she whimpers with need. Breathe in, breathe out. My thoughts jumped on a fucking rocket ship and shot away from me, but that girl is beautiful.

Zed stands beside me with a knowing look. My face remains stoic. I perfected a neutral mask as a child. Even with my thoughts running away at the idea of licking every inch of Josephine's body until she begs me for release, my face doesn't betray me. The problem is that Zed has been around me enough to recognize the few tells

I have. My white knuckles against the rail, the deep breaths, possibly the length of time I have been staring. Time ceased to exist when my eyes landed on her.

I follow Zed down the stairs, heading toward our new designers. Are my hands sweating? This isn't a normal reaction for me. It's rare to be instantly attracted to anyone, let alone a girl 15 years younger than me. Zed's dark eyes meet mine as we reach the group. He clears his throat and begins introductions.

"Hello, my beautiful little designers. This is Catherine, the owner." He glances at me with pursed lips, teasing my inner thoughts as if he can hear them. "You probably won't see much of her. She focuses on business and only shows her face for shows or exhibits." I give him a quick glare despite the truth in his words. I do not want to be in the limelight.

He introduces Vincent, and I shake his hand. His grip is so loose it sends wildly uncomfortable tingles down my spine. I don't like a floppy fish handshake. Maggie's shake is much firmer. She's young and overzealous, but I hope she will do well here. Finally, I turn to Josephine. Her hand in mine sends tingles through my body, but a different kind than Vincent's. I want to spin Josephine until her body collides with mine, then caress her curves, learning all the places that make her mewl beneath my lips.

"Jo."

"What?" The lust-filled fog breaks in my mind, trying to comprehend what she has just said.

"My name. I prefer Jo." Two letters have never caused such a joyful reaction in my body. I release her hand, again unsure how long I have been lost in my thoughts.

"Nice to meet you, Jo." At least my voice doesn't betray my thoughts. Zed speaks to the new hires about schedules, stations, and all the other things they need to know. One of my other designers draws my attention, showing me some of their work. I turn, glad for the distraction from the magical girl walking to the break room for orientation.

After talking to the designer, I return to my office and immediately begin my breathing routine. My morning routine is designed to start my day, but it also refreshes me when things get too intense.

I sink into my work again, Jo dancing around the edges of my brain all day. The door opens and closes. I see Zed walking in with several containers stacked on his tablet. Ignoring him, I continue my work, scrolling through the pages until I find a good stopping point to give attention to him. He has been with me long enough to know I prefer him to wait until I am ready before he speaks.

"It's been a long time since you worked through lunch," he passes me one of the containers with a salad and fork. I take them, not realizing how late it is. Despite my disdain for socializing, I typically take lunch with my employees to maintain a good relationship. I get along with them well enough, and we have enjoyable banter during lunch. A pang of regret pounds in my chest, realizing I missed lunch with Jo today. And the other new hires. Yes, them too. Not just Jo. All my employees, definitely not just one specific girl. No. I stab my fork into the salad harder than intended, sending several pieces flying onto the floor.

"So, I have a guess, but you have to tell me which one it is." I glare at Zed, angry with how perceptive he is. No one knows me as well as he does. That distance from people is intentional. He shouldn't even know me as well as he does. I let it slide because I need him so much.

"How are they settling in?" I ask, ignoring his statement. He is about to tell me some tidbits about each one. I school my expression, ensuring my face and thoughts don't betray me.

"Maggie," he starts, eyeing me closely, "is off to a wonderful start. She's a little sweetheart that will have everyone wrapped around her finger in no time." He pauses, sipping from his expensive, sticker-clad water bottle. "Vincent is a lot like you." Curiosity spreads across my face. "Quiet, reserved, antisocial." I purse my lips at his response despite the accuracy. "Jo is the exact opposite." His eyes bore into me, but I give nothing away. Frustrated at not getting the reaction he wants, he continues. "She is bright and cheerful and will be best friends with everyone by the end of the week." He shares more details about them as we finish our salads.

"Do you want me to let you know before they leave?" Zed's question is intended to be helpful, but the playfulness is apparent.

"No, I'll be down in time." He nods and leaves my office. I turn to stare out the large window. The sun is beginning its descent. There is still plenty of light, but it will be gone soon. We are heading into the dark days of winter. I sigh, trying to reign in the dirty thoughts raging in my mind. I spend days planning for my time with Brayden, but nothing has ever consumed me like Jo has. I set a timer on my smartwatch to notify me half an hour before the designers leave, then drown myself in my work again. It barely contains my mind. There are many errors in my notes. Anything to keep me from obsessing over the taste of my newest designer's skin.

When the timer goes off, I silence it and stand to stretch. I usually make more rounds through the building, not wanting to sit for long hours. With the upcoming shipment, many things need to be done. I completed most of them today. My dedication certainly has nothing to do with the thought of Jo's legs wrapping around my face.

I make my way down to the floor, plastering a kind smile, another mask I have perfected in the business world. Maggie notices me first, thanking me again for the opportunity to work here. We chat idly for a few minutes before Vincent walks up, expressing his gratitude. Jo hasn't turned around from her desk, buried in her work. I dismiss Vincent and Maggie, letting them pack up their areas before they leave. I step toward Jo, my body lighting up at the closeness.

A citrus scent engulfs me, bright like oranges. My fingers twitch, wanting to caress her back. I take a deep breath, inhaling her scent, preparing to speak to her. My watch beeps loudly, breaking the silence. Jo jumps, twisting in shock to find the sound. I quickly check the watch, realizing I only snoozed the alarm earlier instead of turning it off. My heart freezes with embarrassment at the loud alarm. Her expression fades to a smile as she watches me.

"Ready to go home?" Her words are light, but my mind is fogged over. I cannot give an unsure response again.

"Are you?" That isn't better, but I have acknowledged what she asked. She shrugs, adjusting to sit straighter.

"I was invested in my work. I would have stayed late if your alarm hadn't interrupted me."

"May I see?" She grabs her tablet, spinning it to show me. She is designing a gown with a high neck on one side and a flowing skirt, lifting high in the air as if the model is twirling. Nervousness and excitement knit her eyebrows. Her lip is tucked between her teeth, anxious for my response. All my focus is on not using my thumb to tug her lip away from her teeth.

"Tell me about it."

She slowly starts explaining her design but quickly becomes more excited, mentioning every tiny detail she has put in and wants to add. She zooms in on the screen, zooms out, and slides it around. Her actions become more animated the more she talks. It's a stark contrast to the other new hires today. Her face lights up, sending warm waves through my body. My face remains neutral, taking in each word, each inflection of her voice, each movement of her curvy body. She stops talking suddenly, drawing my eyes to hers. She is filled with doubt and insecurity. I'm filled with rage over why those emotions show in her eyes. Who filled this girl with doubt and insecurity?

"It is stunning." Her eyes rise in disbelief. Her lips part to speak, but I continue before she can say anything. Before I kiss those parted lips just to taste her. "I look forward to seeing the completed design. Then, the process of building it. How long before you are finished?" I nod my head toward the tablet as she fumbles with surprise.

"Another day or two," her voice is small, not meeting my eyes. "It depends on how much time I get for it." She turns her tablet to her chest, holding it close. It is the most precious thing to her at this moment. I hope she understands her worth.

I squeeze her shoulder, unable to avoid touching her any longer. Her arm is soft and plush in my fingers, and I want more.

"I'm excited to see it." I offer a smile before turning to leave. On the way to my office, Zed grins at me, realizing who my thoughts have been focused on today. Fuck. He will not let me live this down.

2 · JOSEPHINE

"OH MY GOD. YOU cannot have a crush on your boss."

"But she's so hot," I whine into the phone.

"Jo! She's your boss. Hold on, I need to look her up."

Sadie has been my best friend since forever. She's my person and always will be, no matter what. She lives in Minneapolis and is unwilling to move to Kansas City with me. I begged her for weeks. She refused. "Her whole family is in Minnesota" she said. As if the eight-hour drive between us would end her world. She is shuffling around to grab her laptop as I listen not so patiently.

My first two days at Marzanna have been amazing. The whole team is terrific, but the icing on the cake is my fucking boss. That saying about a woman having legs for days? Yeah, that's my boss. I've never seen legs so damn long. I could die happy between them. Her dark chin-length bob accentuates her face. God himself couldn't have given her a better haircut. Her strong jaw is perfect and kissable. Catherine is built like a runner: slim, tall, and strong.

"Okay, she's hot," Sadie mumbles in my ear, back from her internet search. "But holy shit, Jo. She's 41! That's fifteen years older than you."

"Sixteen," I correct.

"I always forget you're a fucking baby." I roll my eyes at her comment. I'm only eight months younger than her, but she always gives me shit for it. Rolling over on my bed, I close my eyes, imagining my boss climbing on top of me as I lick her into oblivion. Everything about her is wrong for me. She's older. She's my boss. Hell, she's probably not even gay. I couldn't find any pictures of her with anybody, man or woman. She keeps a low profile on her personal life. No social media. Even magazine articles only focus on her business. Not even a hint at who she is outside of Marzanna.

"You're daydreaming about her, aren't you? Can you at least keep your hands out of your pants while talking to me?" I chuckle at Sadie's quip. This is why I love her.

"I'm not even wearing pants. So, you don't have to worry about that." I roll over, resting against the headboard. I need to get my mind out of the gutter and stop thinking about my boss. It will lead nowhere good.

"What are you doing this weekend?" Sadie's attempt to distract me could be better but still efficient.

"The art museum is having a fashion exhibit this weekend. What about you?" As Sadie drones on about her work as a sports physical therapist, I let my mind wander. Thinking of the fabric that will be on display. The stunning garments wrapped around beautiful bodies, dancing in lights, flowing through the air like clouds in the sky. I don't particularly care for the demands of fashion. It's not about making the next big piece. It's the art for me. The material clinging to a person, transforming them from a simple being to a magical presence. Filling the space with a new aura. Transcending the laws of physics to create beauty where there should be none. An idea strikes as Sadie is winding down her story about a patient she saw earlier. I quickly wrap up my conversation with her, grabbing my tablet to bring my idea out.

I started this design on my first day, but it's missing something. I tinker with the drawing for what feels like a few minutes. I'm lost in my work. Despite the silence in my apartment, my head is filled with swishing material. Steps padding down a catwalk as my dress drapes over the model. My pen moves feverishly across my tablet, shifting colors, lines, and shadows. Putting the finishing touches on the piece.

Once finished, I save it twice to ensure I keep it, then glance at the clock. It's already ten p.m., and I haven't eaten dinner. It's not the first time I've skipped a meal or lost several hours because I was wrapped up in a project, and it won't be the last, either. I grab a cheese stick as I walk through my apartment, locking the door and turning off the lights.

Catherine was impressed when she first saw my design. My initial instinct is that she will love my final design, but anxiety creeps in. It doesn't match the style Marzanna typically showcases. Zed assured me we were hired to bring a new style to the brand. I never thought they needed it.

I have followed Marzanna for years. The designs are always flawless. Marzanna offers a range of options, too. They provide gowns for local, smaller events as well as red carpet functions. Designers occasionally attend high fashion events, even avant-garde events.

One of my favorite things about Marzanna is the outreach program dedicated to the community. They offer internships to local teens. Those kids are taught to design and make pieces they can wear to school dances or wherever. Marzanna offers everything they need: space, equipment, supplies, tutorials, assistance, whatever. It keeps kids off the streets, gives them a head start in fashion, or at least beneficial life skills. All the pieces are donated. I love the company so much.

When I saw the job posting, I couldn't pass up the opportunity. Even though my designs are drastically different, I had to try. To say I was shocked to get the position is an understatement. Despite Zed's constant encouragement, I can't help but feel nervous about sharing my final design. I try to soothe myself. I can always change things if they don't like them.

Standing in line at the cute little café around the corner from Marzanna does nothing to settle my nerves before work starts. Coffee won't help either, but I can never be sure it won't until I try again. Who knows? Maybe one day coffee will soothe my nerves. I'll just keep trying. If insanity is doing things repeatedly and expecting different results, add it to my ever-growing list of descriptors. When will they start making coffee laced with THC? Is that already a thing, and I don't know where to get it?

As my mind tumbles around like a derailed train, someone behind me nudges my shoulder. I turn slowly as I return to reality, only to find Zed behind me.

"Hello, Jo." His tone is far too smooth and happy for this early in the morning. Before I can form words, he points ahead of me where the line has moved several feet without me. I offer a weak apology, stepping up to my spot in line. We chat quietly about the day, the cool weather, and how I like my new job until it is my turn to order. Despite the early autumn morning chill, I order my usual iced coffee with thick cream and caramel syrup. I forgo pastry items today, nerves overtaking me since Zed interrupted my derailed train of thought. I watch as he orders two drinks and moves to wait by my side. My face shows my curiosity because he answers the question in my head.

"I bring Catherine her drink every morning. Large black coffee. No cream. No sugar," he chuckles over her order, and I join in nervously. That bit of information is stored for later. I will definitely be using that tidbit soon.

"How is the design coming along?" My teeth nibble on my bottom lip as my nerves ramp up.

"Oh, um, I finished it last night, but I don't know if it's the right piece for Marzanna." I eye him cautiously as we walk through the doors leading to the design floor.

"Girl, how dare you question your design! We hired you to bring in something different. We need that."

Zed's words comfort me while his tone makes me giggle. He's right, but there's no talking anxiety down. He heads off in the direction of Catherine's office. I settle into my workspace, taking a moment to sip my iced coffee. The cool, creamy liquid hits my throat, instantly reminding me of summer and warm, breezy days. I prefer chilly fall days, with leaves changing and falling, apples blooming, and it being socially acceptable to add cinnamon whiskey to cider at every event you go to. However, I will never stop loving how this creamy drink makes me feel like sunshine hitting my face as I rest on a warm beach.

People start filing onto the floor, readying themselves for the work ahead. I open my tablet, hovering over the link to my newest design. I know it's good, but am I ready to share it? No. I shut off the screen of my tablet and walk over to see what Vincent and Maggie are doing. Maggie is deep in her design, drastically different from mine. It's a stunning dress with high slits that would look amazing on Catherine. Nope, not going there while I'm at work. I compliment her but quickly move to Vincent's station.

Several fabrics are draped over his desk. He is fiddling with some trims, holding one up to the fabric, then a different one. I watch him for a few minutes, but he never notices me. Instead of interrupting him, I walk around the floor, trying to look casual. I have no doubts I fail at that. When I finally turn to head back to my station, I am stunned to see Zed and Catherine waiting. He has a knowing smirk, while she has a neutral, patient face. Did they turn the heat up? Why am I sweating so much? I tug on the hem of my skirt, tucking my hands in my pockets to stop fidgeting.

"Zed tells me you finished your design." How is her voice so steady and clear of emotion? I can't tell if I should be more nervous than I am. My brain decides for me, though, and my anxiety takes over. I nod, stepping to my desk to tap on my tablet. Zed is almost shaking with delight. I am trembling with fear. I try to take a deep, quiet breath but am wildly unsuccessful. Instead, I open the design, turn it to them, and stare at my desk.

A moment passes before I finally look up. Zed's grin is somehow even bigger. Catherine is holding my tablet and has turned away from my desk. She waves her hand out without ever looking up. The head designer, Diane, comes over without further instruction. Their heads are close together for several minutes, whispering and pointing at my design. I brace myself to be fired. At least I made it to day two. That counts for something, right?

"I want you to work with Diane to create this piece. It should be done in time to release with winter designs." My jaw drops. Zed claps cheerfully. My body refuses to function. Catherine gives a tight smile. "Great work." She spins on her heels, her long legs leading her away from me to her office.

Diane and Zed swarm me, along with several other designers. They all pass my tablet around, looking at the newest design to be added to the winter line. People congratulate me, telling me what a huge deal this is. My body begins to function again, grinning over the compliments. The rest of the day passes in a blur as I work closely with Diane to bring my piece to life.

After work, still on a high from the excitement, I change my outfit to go to the art museum. I step into a knee-length, metallic silver skirt. It flows with movement and is my favorite cocktail-style skirt. I pair it with a black crop top with lace sleeves, gold flats, and a diamond-studded boxy handbag. I found the bag in a discount bin at a fast fashion store. It's missing some plastic gems, but I still love it. I pull on a white pea coat to finish the look and keep me warm.

The museum is well-lit, with many people pouring in, wearing extravagant outfits, far louder than mine. I feel out of place, but this is still a standard art museum. This isn't a high fashion runway in New York. I purchase my ticket and wander through the exhibit. Some models are on pedestals, swaying in their outfits. Others remain mostly still, only moving occasionally to show a different side of the piece. Some outfits are on mannequins. I wish I brought my headphones to really get lost in the beauty. Instead, I wander slowly, taking in different materials and colors, drawing inspiration from so many different designers.

I bump into someone as I move around a model on a pedestal. The tall model wears a tight dress with long strips of fabric she waves through the air. I turn to apologize to the person I bumped into but freeze.

"I'm sorry. Oh, hello Jo," a smooth, feminine, shockingly familiar voice swoons.

My body tingles at Catherine's greeting. Of course, she would be here. I don't know why I didn't ask anyone else if they were coming tonight. I should have done that. I'll blame it on being distracted with work.

"Hi," I say meekly. I drive my nails into my palms, trying to calm the raging arousal and anxiety coursing through my body. Catherine is in a sleek floor-length dress with a high collar and dark sleeves adorned with a stitched pattern. Her slim body is displayed, but the dress covers her long legs. As my eyes drag back to her face, where her hair is pulled back away from her face in a twisted bun, mortification sets in. I just ogled my boss. Fuck. A glint in her eyes tells me she knows it, too. Shit.

"What do you think of this piece?" I cough out, turning my back to her to face the model. The model swoops her arm low as I turn, smacking me in the face with fabric hanging from her arms. The only thing left to decide now is whether I should be cremated or if they can shoot my body into space. I'll be dead from embarrassment in 3.5 seconds.

A hand wraps around my elbow, tugging me backward. Catherine has a surprisingly playful smirk on her face. Without releasing my arm, she speaks softly, leaning close to my ear. "I think this piece is excessive." Her eyes turn back to the model, who is now turning in the opposite direction. Catherine's hand tugs me back further, away from the model and her threatening outfit. My heart flutters as my arm warms under her firm touch. What would that touch feel like on my legs, snaking high on my thigh?

A flush spreads on my face as I turn toward Catherine. Her smile is softer now, but her eyes are on me. Can she read my thoughts?

"Are you here with friends?"

"No," I shake my head, trying to clear these perverted thoughts. "I'm alone. Are you?" A single nod confirms her answer.

"Walk with me." Her hand sweeps across the space before us, encouraging me to walk with her. It wasn't a question, more of a command. I'm not about to say no to her. We walk through several exhibits in silence, not speaking. I can barely see anything between my growing desire and fear.

"Would you like to have one of your pieces in an exhibit?" Her question breaks our silence, but I don't need any time to think of a response.

"Yes." That was breathier than I would have liked. I clear my throat, trying to speak like a civilized human. "I've always wanted to see my designs on display somewhere other than our college exhibits." Catherine nods, walking toward the next station. Taking advantage of this time with her, I ask a question now that my mind has settled.

"Why did you decide to go into fashion?" I inquire. Catherine glances at me briefly, then returns to the mannequin before her.

"It's not really a passion for me. I prefer business. I was friends with Diane and found the building for sale. I bought it and made her my head designer. Things grew from there."

"So, you must be loaded then?" Oh shit. My brain is misfiring on every single level. "I'm sorry. That was..." She chuckles at me, waving me off. She leans in close, whispering in my ear this time.

"I am loaded."

My panties are soaked. Catherine's whispered voice. Her words. Her closeness. I'm a goner. She stands and speaks again.

"Would you like a drink?" She motions toward the bar, and I nod my head drastically. Yes. I need a drink. She orders two neat scotches. I'm not much of a scotch girl, but I won't say no. An image of Catherine sitting in a leather chair in a library filled with mahogany shelves fills my mind. In said image, I crawl across the floor to her then bury my face between her legs. Fuck, I bet she has a library like that in her home. Isn't that a requirement of being loaded? I sip my drink slowly, letting the liquid burn down my throat, distracting the wildly inappropriate thoughts of my boss. My much older, richer boss.

"Do you come to these exhibits often?" she asks, then sips her drink, eyeing me over her glass. Her expression is unreadable, though. Is that another rich stipulation, maintaining an unreadable mask?

"Yes, every chance I get. I love to see what other designers are doing. I also love seeing the different fabrics and how they move on a person." Catherine nods at my answer, scanning the area. "Do you come often?" I ask.

"Not normally. Zed encouraged me to come tonight, to be seen in the community." She doesn't roll her eyes, but the desire is there.

"He seems very helpful," I say teasingly. She nods, not quite picking up on my playfulness.

"He is, but very annoying, too." We finish our drinks and walk through the rest of the exhibit. Our conversation remains casual, releasing some of the tension in my chest over being so close to her. At night's end, we retrieve our coats and walk outside. We say goodbye, and I turn to head to the bus stop.

"Where are you going?" Her voice is calm but also concerned.

"I'm taking the bus back to my apartment." Living in town allows me not to drive, which is good because I am terrible at it. One would think learning to drive in Minnesota with all the snow would help, but it did not.

"Come with me." She is a fan of these commands. Nonetheless, I follow. She leads me to a black car with tinted windows. A man in black slacks and jacket is leaning against the door. He opens it when she approaches.

"We're giving Jo a ride home first." He tilts his head, closing the door after we climb in. The leather interior is clean and soft, and the space is roomy for the back of a sedan.

"You really are loaded." I grin, taking in the car around me. She watches me with curiosity on her face. We don't speak again until we arrive at my apartment complex. It doesn't occur to me that I didn't give the driver my address.

"I enjoyed my evening with you, Jo." Her words strike me as I climb out of the car. They feel like there is more to them than professional association. Am I reading too much into this? Sadie would think so. But she isn't here, and I can't stop the words that fall out of my mouth next.

"Some of my friends go to trivia on Fridays. We're short a member for our team next week. Would you like to go with us?" She stares at me momentarily, assessing me with a glare I can't read. My nerves get the better of me as I wait for her to respond, but I can't take the words back now. She responds just as I open my mouth to take back the invitation or offer her a way out.

"Yes."

3 · CATHERINE

I don't go out with my employees.

I don't go to bar trivia.

I don't hang out with young people.

Why the hell did I say yes to Jo? I couldn't have stopped the word if I wanted to. I don't want to say no to her, but I also don't want to be around other kids. I spent my whole weekend debating whether I should cancel this. I was ready to tell Jo I couldn't go on Monday morning. Then she gave me the details during lunch. The giddiness in her body was adorable, almost overwhelming. How could I say no to her?

It's Tuesday night. I sit in the quiet warehouse, waiting for my next shipment. Breathe in, breathe out. This is different from my daytime shipments. During the day, it's all dresses, clothing, fabrics, and the occasional random goods shipment. It's all a front, though. The nighttime shipments bring in the real money. I was desensitized to the darkness of the night a long time ago. It doesn't bother me as much as when I started these shipments.

I was naïve when I started. Like many people before me, I thought I could stop when I wanted to. That's never the case in this line of work. I'll stop when I'm dead. And even then, it won't be enough. The darkness has always been in my life and will stay there forever. There is no beautiful afterlife for me, no happy ending—just more dark.

A car horn rips me from my thoughts. I tell Peter every damn time not to sound his horn. He is an idiot and on my shortlist. His end will find him sooner rather than later, either at my hands or his boss's. He struts into the building, pompous like always. His black slacks and tight turtleneck t-shirt with a gold chain and exposed gun holster reinforce every bad mafia stereotype. He watched one mafia movie and made it his entire personality. He's pathetic.

"Catherine, doll!" I visibly cringe at his greeting as he walks with open arms to hug me. I intentionally show him my disgust. We go through this every few weeks. I hate him. I don't want to be touched. Yet every time, he greets me this way.

"Take another step, and you won't keep breathing." His hands raise in defense, but a smirk rises on his face. I have yet to throat-punch him. He is unwilling to push the threat but treats it like a joke. I want nothing more than to put a bullet in his face. My piece burns at my back, urging me to grab it and make my desire a reality. Tonight is not the night, though.

"The truck is here," he tips his head at the large garage door after checking his phone. Putting aside my desire to give his face an extra hole, I open the door as the semi-truck backs into the warehouse. Only a handful of halogen lights are on, leaving many shadows in the building. The vehicle motion alarm echoes through the building, raising my anxiety. The noise of these shipments is always too loud for me.

Once the truck stops, several men rush out, opening the back of the trailer. The cargo will be unloaded, processed, then placed in another temperature-controlled container before shipping off with a new driver. This part of the process is what keeps me in this business. The men swing the large doors open and step back like they are new to this.

"Get the fucking ramp!" My words are harsh, matching the glare I cast at the men. One cowers, rushing toward the ramp propped against the wall. Another man glares at me but walks behind the other man. I move to the back of the trailer, taking in this week's inventory. It's a smaller shipment than expected, which is concerning.

A couple of large shipping containers are pulled off the truck. A knock from the side door draws my attention. Peter opens the door, letting in four small women with their eyes down. The women are always the same. We know each other at this point, or at least recognize each other. They shuffle toward their assigned workroom. A few more men enter, helping the two from the truck unload the cargo.

Once the shipping containers are unloaded, the men start unpacking them. The material used in our store is placed in carts and will be taken to the shop tomorrow. The bottoms of the crates are removed, exposing the drugs. That's the real business—the drug shipments. They arrive here, are processed by the women, and then shipped across the country. Kansas City is an excellent hub for illegal business. I offer a safe space for the drugs to be processed and moved.

The women begin to strip in the hallway. I hate this part, but the mob demands it. So worried about their product. I've offered to buy surgical gowns, but the men prefer them naked. The women don't seem to mind anymore, so I don't push it. At this point, I'm desensitized to many things that go on around here. Peter ogles the women in the hallway.

"You know the rules, Peter. Fuck out of here." He casts a quick, angry glance in my direction before storming out of the same door he came in. He'll sulk off to one of the strip clubs and return drunk in a few hours. That's fine by me. These women deserve as much of a break as I can give them. He's tried to fuck each of them before, but I won't let him. Not on my watch.

My phone rings, sounding louder in this space than it should.

"Angelo." I don't mask the annoyance in my voice. He's the only one that calls me during this process. I don't always know which crew is coming through. Some of the leaders work directly with me. Others are in rings and have coordinators. Angelo has Peter but stays heavily involved in the process. I wonder if he doesn't trust Peter.

"How is my shipment looking?" Referring to the drugs as a shipment is a safe way to stay under the radar. I strive to maintain a professional appearance to avoid heat. I'm sure the cops suspect me, but no one has ever approached me. Marzanna looks clean and doesn't cause any issues.

"Same as always. Smaller."

"We shipped this one sooner. You'll have another tomorrow night."

"Tomorrow? We never do two shipments in one week." This is a firm rule I have always had. While I run several shipments late at night to obscure what we are shipping, I keep it from becoming frequent. Despite my lack of sleep due to overseeing the shipments, I need to rest eventually. Running shipments around the clock is less suspicious than one or two in the evenings, but I need a break at some point.

"The big boss wanted two shipments. The feds started sniffing around, and they couldn't risk sending everything. They'll be at the same time tomorrow." Before I can object, the call ends. A string of curses falls from my lips. Angelo works in the only international mafia I deal with. His boss always expects me to bend to his will. I have been doing that for decades at this point. The end of that business deal is nearing.

I spend a couple of hours in my office while the women work. One of the men guards the room they are in. He has a gun on his hip but never needs it here. The other men lounge in the garage. They have snacks and drinks and chat among themselves. We leave each other alone. I have little work to distract me because I completed so much during the day. Trying to keep my mind off Jo was difficult, and I finished nearly everything in my attempt. I try not to let my mind think about her now.

I want her body. My desire to control her is overwhelming. The need to take her pleasure, give her what she wants after she begs for it, consumes me. I need to touch her, take what I want, and give her everything. She would beg so sweetly. I can see it in her eyes. She would play well with me. She's so bright and willing. I would ruin her.

Movement in the garage draws my attention, and I leave the office. The women have finished processing the drugs and are getting dressed in the hallway. One man pays them while the other men load the new packages into containers different from the ones they arrived in. The drugs are ready to be sold by foot soldiers on the streets. This order will stay local to KC. Long ago, I stopped considering the effects of the drugs on my community.

Peter returns, rumpled and drunk, smelling of cigarettes and cheap perfume. He is here to ensure the truck leaves the building. He enters in his pompous strut, overly confident I won't put a bullet through his brain. Breathe in, breathe out. He tells the women how beautiful they are, trying to pick one up. I usher them out of the building quickly. I bide my time with his death.

The containers are topped with clothing for sale and loaded onto a truck. The truck, men, and Peter finally leave my building, and I exhale. Despite my time in this field, I am always wary during these evenings. The risk of getting caught is real, regardless of how careful I am.

My cleaners arrive shortly after. The group is paid well for their silence. They take extra care in the workroom, ensuring no traces are left behind. I pay them extra to return tomorrow night. Confusion knits their faces, but they don't ask questions. They pocket the money and get to work. I stare at the wall in my office until the cleaners knock, alerting me of their completion. I escort them out, locking the warehouse behind them.

Everything is set up for tomorrow night despite the last-minute notification. Early communication isn't standard in this business, but I usually get a few days. Never less than 24 hours.

I walk to Marzanna Fashion, which is only a few blocks away. In the beginning, everything was in one building. With so many people working on the fashion side, I quickly realized how much of a risk that was. It was good timing when this warehouse went on the market a few months after I opened the fashion business. I quickly bought this and moved my drug business. The separation has helped remain undetected.

I sleep for a few hours in my office. I keep a change of clothes here for this reason. I don't always want to return to my place afterward. My day is long, filled with exhaustion and stress, but Jo is here. She is wearing a green romper today, which contrasts with her yellow and red hair. Her combat boots and choker necklace give the romper an edgy feel. Despite the heavy shoes, she dances around the floor, streaming materials behind her. The flurry she creates in her wake settles the tightness in my chest. She brings me peace in the days of darkness without knowing it.

I head to the warehouse after work rather than my apartment. A few hours of sleep consume me in my office. Sleep isn't a luxury I get often. Between business and nightmares, sleep only occurs in small bouts. I stretch my muscles, relieving the tiniest bit of tension. It's not enough. It never is.

The car horn sounds again. Peter loves playing with fire. We exchange our usual greeting, his over-the-top welcoming, my violent threat, and his announcement that the truck is here. My body aches at the recurrence of this process. Tonight, the men grab the ramp without my warning. When the doors open, I stifle my shock. My stoic mask is in place, but my mind rages at the site.

The containers in the back of the truck are larger than expected. When Angelo told me his shipment was divided in two, I expected two half-sized shipments. Not one-half and one-triple the normal size. This is utterly unacceptable. The containers are unloaded similarly: legal product first, then illegal. Except the product isn't drugs. It's guns.

The men sort through the guns, putting them together and placing them in different containers. A few go into smaller boxes, covered with fabric, then closed and labeled. I've never shipped guns before. Drugs are one thing; they are smaller and easier to conceal.

"What is this?" I ask Peter calmly, masking the confusion and annoyance. He is fiddling with his phone but glances up at my question.

"Those are AK-47s. A few Glocks in the box over there," he points to another. "I don't think we have any revolvers tonight."

"When did this change?" He shrugs, glancing at the men then back to his phone.

"I'll be back later, doll!" he yells as he exits the building, ignoring my inquiries. No amount of torture will ever satisfy my hatred for him. I debate calling Angelo. Instead, I go straight for the boss. I check my watch, calculating the time difference between here and Spain. It's early morning there. He should be awake.

"What?" The gruff voice barks into the phone. He's never had time for pleasantries.

"Why am I staring at guns?" I don't have time for pleasantries either.

"Ah," he croons, his voice sweeter now. "I wanted to branch out. More money can be made from this. This is good, baby." I have never appreciated nicknames or pet names. I'm glad they don't use my name, but the pet names are unnecessary.

"I didn't approve this," my tone is sharp, angry.

"I know. But you'll forgive me," he explains as fact. I won't forgive him, but I won't fight now.

"It's going to cost you."

"I assumed. Send the bill to Angelo. He will pay." My mind starts churning at the idea as I disconnect without another word. Yes, I will make Angelo pay in more than just money. I've always had issues with Angelo's mob. Angelo is second here in the States. Anthony is the KC mob boss, but he answers to the man in Spain. A man I am intimately familiar with.

When the warehouse is empty, and the cleaners arrive, I change into athletic gear. I run for miles, losing track of time. My muscles scream for a break. My lungs sting from exertion and the cold. My skin tingles from cold sweat. I quit thinking about the impact of the drugs a long time ago. The guns are new. Suddenly, every shooting reported on the news glares in my head. How many of those guns will stay here in KC? How many deaths will the weapons that just went through my warehouse be responsible for? How many will be innocent? I don't know if it matters if they are innocent or not. This is just another point to hyper-fixate on.

I return to the warehouse, dismissing the cleaners when they are done and paying them extra for the change in scheduling. After a shower in the back of my warehouse, I walk a few blocks to my office. It has been two days since I have been home. The amount of work will kill me before someone else does. I collapse on my couch, exhaustion devouring my thoughts and body.

"Catherine?" The soft, masculine voice draws me from my deep slumber. It takes a moment to remember where I am. Brayden stands before me, concern shining in his eyes. My wide-leg pants and long-sleeved, loose chiffon shirt are crumpled from sleeping in them. Worried someone would find me asleep in the office before my alarm, I donned my work clothes before collapsing on the couch.

"Are you okay?" His voice carries the same concern in his gaze. He offers a hand to help me up but doesn't make any other attempt to touch me. I grab a water, my mind catching up to the day.

"Do you want me to leave?" Brayden's words help me focus on the world around me. Do I want him to leave? I'm too exhausted to fuck him, but that doesn't mean we can't do other things.

"No," I respond quietly, taking a moment to fully wake up. "You're going to do everything I say. I don't want a brat today." He nods confidently. I have instructed him before. He can be a brat or an excellent sub. He is a wonderfully willing partner. I spin one of my leather chairs to face the couch and collapse in it. I chug the rest of the water and toss it in the trash. I fill my office with music from my phone, erasing the quiet. Anything to distract me from the visions of the night.

"Strip."

His hands glide over his body as he sways along to the music. The song isn't overly erotic, not something you would expect a strip tease to. Brayden handles it expertly, dancing seductively. My eyes are fixed on his fingers as they trail over his chest, popping each button with a quick glance. He listens so well. Obeys my every command without question. He bites his lip, sending a wave of desire to tug it away with my thumb. I refrain; now isn't the time I want to touch him.

His shirt drops to the arm of the couch, exposing his smooth, tan chest. His muscles ripple, each ab visible down to the v leading beneath his jeans. He kicks his sneakers aside, hands trailing over his chest, down to his jeans.

"Touch yourself."

Knowing me as well as he does, he palms his cock through his jeans. His head tips back, playing up the pleasure. This is an act. He isn't aroused by dancing. That feeds my pleasure, knowing he will do what I say and give a performance while doing it. Despite the act, his dick grows harder under his pants.

"Take them off."

He turns, bending as he slides the jeans down. His tight ass is exposed, round, and beautiful. With a grace only an experienced person could manage, he sways his ass as he steps out of the pants. He is such a good boy, following my rules and giving me exactly what I want. I'm not going to tell him that yet. He has to do more to earn my praise.

He stands naked before me. Smooth skin, free of all hair. His thigh muscles tense and release as he dances to the music. I wave him over, grabbing his cock when he is close enough. I stroke slowly but tightly. My grip is stronger on him than anyone else I would entertain. I don't see anyone else, but I've never used a grip this tight before. He moans under my touch as I slide back and forth slowly. His head tips back, and he curses. He's right where I want him.

"Get the plug. Your choice."

I have a variety of Bluetooth anal plugs. Some days, I choose the size. Not today. I don't care today. This is for him, not me. He returns with the large one and the bottle of lube. A smirk spreads across my face at his choice. He does love the big one.

"Grab your ankles."

Eagerly, he turns and bends in front of me. I stroke his ass, sitting up in my seat. "You are such a good boy. I'm going to give you a little reward." He watches me upside down between his legs. His lip is sucked between his teeth. This time, I do tug it out. My fingers drag up his smooth skin, across his chest and sides, then hips, wasting no time reaching his cheeks and spreading them wide. I lick across his tight hole, eliciting a moan from him. That one isn't a performance. While I've never asked what his preferences are, I have learned anal is one.

I drag my tongue along his crack, sliding back to his opening. His muscles quake, struggling between pleasure and holding this position. This is what I live for. His struggles, his desire, his willingness. This is what I need from a partner. I tongue his hole, circling and pressing against it until he starts writhing. I lean back in my chair, leaving him gasping.

"Wet it."

I hold the toy in front of his mouth as he swallows it. His tongue swirls against his cheek, licking the toy as instructed. I leave it in his mouth, squirting lube on his ass. I work it around, briefly inside, then right back out. He doesn't require much prep.

The toy slides out of his mouth with a pop. I press it into his ass, reaching between his legs to stroke his member. I keep my grip loose this time, teasing him. He squirms, bending his knees to get closer to the toy. I thrust it into him, causing him to place one hand on the floor in front of him. He quickly returns his hand to his ankle, but his eyes are closed tight with pleasure. I tap the toy playfully several times before pressing long enough to turn it on. Before I give his next instruction, I ensure it's connected to my phone.

"Sit on the couch. Touch yourself. I want to watch you come on your stomach. I want you covered in your own mess."

Brayden wastes no time taking the seat directly in front of me. He strokes his massive cock slowly. We've played this game before. He'll fuck his hand at the pace I set the vibrator to in his ass. If it's slow, he goes slow. If it's faster, he goes faster. He knows the rules of this game well. The plug finds a steady pace in his ass as his hand matches it. I leave it alone for several minutes, watching his body tense and glisten with his arousal.

The plug slows to low vibration, and he groans loudly, matching the dawdling pace. I drag the bar, increasing the speed. His hand moves faster, his chest heaving with pleasure. Brayden tips his head back onto the couch, and I stop the toy altogether.

"Fuck," he shouts, slamming his hand to the couch beside him. His angry glare meets my delighted smirk. He was so close to an orgasm. He can't have that yet. I set the toy at a slow pace again, which he matches. He follows these rules so well. I'm lost in this moment. The guns from last night temporarily forgotten. My dark thoughts are only dampened by controlling another person so thoroughly. I guide him through several more denials, his frustration increasing each time.

Glancing at the clock, I see that my time with Brayden ends soon. I increase the speed again, watching his hand glide over his silky dick. The tip is leaking, and his abs are clenching. His chest is heaving again, but his eyes are glued to mine. He is refusing to give me visual clues of his release. Despite not vocalizing, he can't hide his breathing and body tensing.

"Come for me," I whisper, leaning forward to watch. He bites his lip as his eyes roll back in his head, already close to the edge. White fluid spurts from his cock, coating his stomach. His head drops back, his hand slowing over his softening dick. Once his release stops, I turn off the toy, not wanting to prolong this appointment. I hand him wipes, kissing his forehead as he takes them. His skin is wet with perspiration beneath my lips. I don't usually show this level of intimacy to him, but I am thankful for the relief he provides me.

4 · JOSEPHINE

It's finally Friday. Nervousness, excitement, and anxiety have ruled my whole week. I love going to trivia with my new friends, but I have no idea what they will think of Catherine. Or what she will think of them. When I first moved into my apartment a few weeks before I started at Marzanna, my neighbors invited me out. They are fantastic people, and I am so relieved to have friends so close.

The bar has a brewery in the back. They brew their own beers but also offer a selection of other local brews. Pretzels and pub mix are the only food they offer. I should have mentioned that to Catherine, but I could convince her to go out with me afterward. She has been sullen the last few days. Not that I have spent enough time with her to recognize her moods, but that one has been noticeable. I hope to relieve some tension for her tonight. With a fun night. At the bar. Not in her pants.

Headed to the bar. See you there!

My text shows as delivered, then quickly read. I can't hide the grin as the bus rumbles down the side of the road. Catherine didn't reply, but I didn't expect her to. I hope she does show up. She gave me her number earlier so I could send her the information. She rarely texts back more than one word.

Once at the bar, I grab my beer and find my friends at a table in the corner. Despite their willingness to take me in, they are still reasonably antisocial. They don't want to talk to other people. I chat with the announcers before joining my friends. I love chatting with everyone. My mom always said I never meet a stranger. I love hearing other people's stories.

Catherine walks in, looking around the bar. She is wearing long, loose pants, a crew neck top, and a blazer, with unnecessary heels that make her even taller than she needs to be. I step up to her side, speaking to be heard over the chatter and music.

"I don't know why I expected to see you in anything but work wear," I grin playfully. Her eyes rake over my body with an expressionless gaze. I have a pair of geometric patterned pixie pants, a solid-color crop top, an animal print jacket, and low-profile sneakers. My hair is up in space buns to keep it out of my face while drinking. I have a habit of messing it up when I am drunk.

"You look fun." I don't know how to take Catherine's comment. She says it with no inflection. I smile and guide her to the bar, chatting about their drinks and snacks. She asks which drink I prefer, then she orders that one. I grin at her trust in my taste.

We join my friends at our table, pulling up a new chair for her. After introductions, my friends return to their conversations. I turn to Catherine, who still looks stiff in her seat.

"Do you go to trivia?" I ask, sipping on my drink. I never make it to the final round without being delightfully wasted.

"No. I did when I was younger but haven't been in several years." She sips her drink, looking impressed with it. Before I can ask another question, the announcer states the game will start in five minutes, and we must submit our team names. Our team usually plays as Roommates, but they ask whether Catherine wants us to choose a new name. She waves away the question, encouraging us to do what we usually do. Even if she doesn't have fun, she is a great fill-in for us. My friends were originally roommates, picking off the apartments in the building as they became available. Despite each of us having our own apartments, we frequently gather in one apartment to hang out.

As expected, the announcer begins the games, and the first few questions are easy. I get a refill, offering one to Catherine, but she turns me down. Hers is still half full, but I drink quickly at these games. At the end of the first half, our team is in second place, laughing and having fun. Even Catherine has smiled a few times.

The announcer briefly recesses before the final round to top off drinks or use the restroom. I take the chance to grab what will now be my fourth beer. I have a good buzz, but I'm not wasted. That doesn't stop me from sliding my seat closer to Catherine when I sit down. My thigh touches hers. She glances at me briefly. My cheeks are red from the alcohol, and a goofy grin has been stuck on my face for the past fifteen minutes. Instead of admonishing me, she wraps her arm around my back, resting on my chair. She leans in and whispers, "Are you drunk?"

"No," I answer too quickly. "No, certainly not."

"She's wasted!" Ben, who lives on the floor above me, yells out. No one notices, though. Catherine chuckles, her leg bumping into mine several times. My skin heats at the contact. It's probably the alcohol, not my deep attraction to my boss. The announcer says it's time for the final question.

"Who is the first and only cat to go to space, and what year did the trip occur?"

Silence fills the room as every group looks at each other. What kind of question is that?

"Okay, who is the catstronaut?" I ask, giggling at my new made-up word. Catherine leans into the table. My three other friends follow her lead. I lean closer to her, alcohol clouding my judgment.

"The cat was Felicette, and she was launched in 1963." Her voice is soft, so other groups can't hear us, but it sounds so sensual in my ears. The urge to turn and kiss her is nearly overwhelming. My friends shrug at her response.

"I've got nothing. Let's go with it. How many points should it be worth?" Ben asks, glancing at Catherine while he writes. She shrugs, leaning back. Her hand stays on my shoulder, not dropping back to the chair.

"Double our points. That will give us a solid lead even if the other groups guess it."

Everyone in the group stares at her in shock. We only double our points if several of us agree on the answer.

"How positive of this answer are you?" Ben asks, always ready to challenge everyone.

"If the answer isn't correct," Catherine starts, "I'll buy drinks for the rest of the night."

My friends continue staring with a mix of impressed looks and surprise.

"And she's loaded, so she means it!" My whisper is far louder than it needs to be. My friends laugh at me, but Catherine strokes my shoulder. I glance at her to find desire burning in her eyes. That's not the alcohol. She wants me. And fuck, I want her too. My core burns at the thought that she wants me.

"Damn, girl," Amara, the girl that lives in the apartment across the hall from me, starts. "I'm glad you've got rich friends. How long until Jo is that rich, too?" Amara teases and looks to Catherine for an answer while sipping her beer.

"Well, I own the company. So, I suppose when she impresses me enough." Her eyes burn into mine, but Amara chokes on her drink, drawing our attention. She coughs through her drink as we all laugh.

"What the shit? The owner! Jo, I thought she was just a coworker. Holy hell!" My cheeks burn again, this time from embarrassment. Before anyone can say anything else, the announcer speaks up.

"The correct answer is Felicette in 1963. Roommates is the only group to get it correct, and they win by a landslide!" We break out into cheers as the announcer brings our coupons for free drinks. We haven't won first place before and are all ecstatic. Catherine accepts her coupon but passes it to Ben instead. They all head over to get drinks, but I hang back to talk to Catherine.

"You're not going to drink anymore?" I ask, trying to understand why she gave her coupon to Ben.

"No, and you certainly don't need two more." Her voice is teasing and more exciting than the game we just won. I slide off my chair, ready to go to the bar to collect my free drink.

"So, you know a lot about pussies, huh?"

She laughs, wraps her arm around my waist, and pulls me closer to her. Her touch is so warm and comforting. I can't believe my boss is holding me like this. It's wrong to want this as much as I do, but that won't stop me.

"I know a few things," her voice is sultry, and I don't think she is talking about cats. "Go get your beer. When you are done, I'm taking you for food before you go home." Chills run down my body. Yes, I need food, but Catherine is taking me. I'll eat anything she gives me. I hope that includes her. She pulls her arm away from me, giving a slight push in the direction of the bar. I grin, trying not to stumble on my way over. In line, I make up my mind to kiss her tonight. Job be damned. I want her. She is fantastic, and I'm not passing up the opportunity.

We spend another hour at the bar with my friends. As time passes, I lean against Catherine more and more. She keeps her arm casually on my back. I want her to hold me possessively, to claim me entirely as her own, but she doesn't make any further move to do that.

The trivia hosts have cleared out, leaving a space for dancing. A few other girls are already on the floor. We don't typically dance here, but the new Ed Sheeran song blasts through the speakers. I can't resist. I jump up, shouting at all of my friends.

"We need to dance!"

Amara jumps up, waving her hands in the air. Ben groans, rolling his head back, but still stands up. Catherine raises an eyebrow at me. You would think I asked her to fly a spaceship to Mars. Amara is behind me, tugging my waist as I grab Catherine's hands. "Come on, please!"

"I don't dance," her words are clear, but the curl of her lips tells me she just needs a little push.

"You can't tell me you lived through Macarena and Cupid's Shuffle, and you don't dance!" Her smirk grows. Amara catches on to my tactic and joins in.

"Come on, Catherine! We know you were a disco queen back in your day." Catherine looks stunned but stands up from her seat.

"How old do you think I am?" She chuckles but holds my hand as I lead her to the dance floor, Amara still tugging my waist. We join Ben in the small area, bouncing together, laughing, and having a great time dancing. After this song ends, Girls Just Wanna Have Fun by Cyndi Lauper comes on. Amara and I squeal, drawing another loud groan from Ben. Again, he continues dancing with us. As much as he fusses about our antics, he loves us.

"Yeah, Catherine!" Amara yells over the music. "Get it, girl! This is your jam!"

Catherine shakes her head, laughing as we step around her. "I was an infant when this song came out. I am not as old as you think I am."

"But you're older than us," Amara teases. I grab Catherine's hand, bouncing around to the beat of the music. We dance through several more songs, laughing and enjoying our time together. My face is beet red, and my brain is fuzzy from the alcohol. I love doing trivia with my friends, but I love having Catherine here too. After the song ends, we go to the table to finish our beer and head out. It's late.

My friends go to the bus stop and head back to the apartments. Sometimes, we order takeout and gather to watch a movie. Catherine tells me we'll get food, and she'll give me a ride home—tells, not asks. Ben gives me a high five and winks, turning toward the bus stop. Amara gives me a concerned look.

"Are you sure you wanna do this with your boss?"

"Yes, have you seen her? She's smoking." I glance back at Catherine, who is on the phone a few feet away. She's calling the driver to let him know we are ready to be picked up.

"Yeah, but she's also your boss." Amara shrugs, giving me a tight hug. "I would tell you to make good choices, but you won't, will you?" I shake my head at her, and we burst into giggles. She shoves me playfully, waving as she joins Ben. Catherine walks up to my side as her car approaches the curb.

"Ready?"

"Yes."

She smiles, motioning me into the car. I slide in, still overly impressed with this car. I've only owned beaters and typically stick with public transportation over my vehicle. I could definitely get used to this lifestyle.

I'm obsessing over all the buttons and what they control when Catherine reaches her arm around me. I gasp, but she tugs the seat belt around me to buckle me in. I grin bashfully, blood rushing to my cheeks. Her hand rests on my knee as we ride through town, heading to a restaurant she has selected.

"Where are you taking me, Kitty?"

"Kitty?" Her lips purse together. I wonder if she is mad. She's hard to read on a good day. I'm too drunk to read her now.

"Yeah, 'cause you know so much about cats. With the whole catstronaut thing?" Her small laugh isn't enough to indicate her thoughts on her new nickname, but she doesn't say anything else about it.

I'm surprised when we arrive at a small diner. I expected her to choose a fancier restaurant. I prefer this, but I wouldn't have expected her to like it. She doesn't say anything as she slips out of the car, holding her hand to help me. She guides me to a seat in the back of the restaurant. My vision is still blurry from the alcohol. A hiccup escapes as we slide into opposite sides of the booth. The booth is small, and my knees bump hers as I take my seat. I look up to apologize, but the words don't come out. Instead, I start giggling.

She waves the waiter over. Once he arrives, she orders both of us water, BLTs, and fries. She doesn't even look at the menu or ask what I want. If it were anyone else, I would be upset about that. With Catherine, I don't particularly mind.

"You like to be in charge, don't you?" My words are slurred, and the world is spinning faster than usual.

"Do you always drink that much?" Her eyes are serious, focused on me. The weight of her gaze would be intense if I weren't drunk as a skunk.

"No," I hiccup out.

"Put your feet up here." Her voice has dropped an octave, forcing me to obey immediately. She helps lift my feet onto the bench beside her. Her warm hand wraps around my calf, massaging over my pixie pants. I tip my head back in pleasure, just enjoying her touch. She doesn't speak again until our food arrives. I've nearly drifted off, but she softly says my name, drawing my attention.

We eat in silence. Catherine watches me closely but doesn't say anything. I want to talk to her, ask her questions, and get to know her, but the alcohol won't let me consider anything but this fantastic sandwich. I swear this is the best BLT I have ever had.

She leaves a wad of cash on the table, and we walk outside to her waiting car. It must be nice to have someone waiting on you all the time. I buckle myself this time, but my head falls on her shoulder. She doesn't push me away.

This close, I can smell her perfume. It smells expensive. I remember sitting in my mom's bed, flipping through her magazines. We stopped on a page, one of those perfume ads with a folded edge and a sample of their perfume. We sniff and discuss whether we like it, quickly skipping to the next one to compare it. I don't know if Catherine's perfume was ever featured in a magazine, but it reminds me of that.

The car stops just before I drift off, still lost in memories of magazine perfume, and Catherine climbs out. She helps me out again, telling the driver she will return soon. She's walking me to my door? Butterflies bounce around my stomach. She's going to kiss me! Or I will kiss her. Either way, I'm ending this night with a kiss.

She leads me through the hall as if she has done this before. It doesn't phase me that this is the first time she has been to my apartment, and she shouldn't know where it is.

I slip my keys out and turn to face her when we arrive at my door.

"Do you want to come in?" Some of the alcohol has subsided, thanks to the food, but I still have a good buzz. Enough to give me the courage to ask my much older boss to enter my apartment.

"That's not a good idea, Jo." I pout, unhappy with her response.

"But you want to," I raise my eyebrows teasingly at her. She chuckles and shakes her head.

"I'll see you Monday, Jo." That's not a no.

She leans in. My eyes close. This is it. She's going to kiss me. My lips pucker, waiting for the moment hers touch mine. I bet she's an excellent kisser. Firm, demanding, in charge. Warmth spreads through me as her lips brush against my forehead.

Forehead?

It's such a quick touch that I barely have time to recognize it. When I figure out what is happening, Catherine has already turned and is walking down the hall. What the hell? I didn't want a forehead kiss!

5 · CATHERINE

Jo will be the death of me. I can see it all now. Jo makes me want to do things I have never enjoyed. The restraint required to not ravish her after I escorted her to her apartment was unmeasurable. I spend all weekend running from my own thoughts and desires. Outside on the road, inside on my treadmill, I haven't run this much in years. My body shows that now.

The reports for the upcoming weeks sit on my desk, staring at me and reminding me of how unfocused I am. Marzanna participates in quarterly fashion shows. Our upcoming show for our fall line is in Atlanta. Diane already has everything ready. The pieces are done and packed. All reservations have been made for her, two other designers, and a crew of assistants. They leave in a week and will be gone for several days. Things are quiet when designers are gone. The floor will stay busy with our new hires while the others are in Atlanta. Our new designers are working on pieces for the winter show, which is being hosted in Kansas City for the first time in years.

Jo's design is the first piece of our show. It's perfect. Her dress has deep colors and material that magically flutters through the air. She has such incredible talent and a fantastic eye for material and movement. She has been working on her dress endlessly since she arrived. Her dress will be a massive success at the show. She doubts herself, but I don't. She will be amazing. I want to find a way to boost her confidence, but my mind always reverts to sex. While that would help, fucking her over her desk probably isn't appropriate.

My phone ringing breaks my thoughts. The unidentified number flashes across my screen. The problem with the warehouse business is never knowing who calls me. Breathe in, breathe out.

"Hello?" My voice could be more friendly. Zed refers to it as my dark business voice. He's not wrong about that.

"Catherine, love, how are you?" Robert's deep voice has a deceptively playful ring to it. He is my point of contact for a cartel out of Mexico. I haven't met any of the leaders and prefer to keep it that way. Robert is bad enough.

"Fine." It's never a good thing when he calls.

"Catherine, you didn't tell me you allow two shipments now. I want to send a second." I sigh heavily. I knew Angelo's second shipment last week would cause problems for me. I should have refused.

"I'm not allowing extra shipments."

"But Angelo got two last week," his whiny voice grates at my nerves. While many men in the drug business get their position by being domineering, Robert earned his by being pathetically ruthless. Everyone expects weakness from him and is blindsided when he takes out an entire crew.

"Angelo is paying for that."

"Yes, yes. He mentioned that. I can pay too, love. Let's negotiate." These men already pay an exorbitant amount for my services. They can afford it, considering we haven't had much interference from the law. It may be time for a price increase.

"Fair enough, Robert. Five times our current rate."

"Catherine, you know I hate when you call me Robert...did you say five times?" His childlike voice changes suddenly when my words catch up to him. He wants me to call him Bobby. He reserves that name for the women he works with. The men call him Robert. Much like others underestimate him for his childish behavior, he underestimates me for my vagina.

"I did say five times."

"What the hell? I thought we were friends." His voice is loud and angry. Gone is the whiny bullshit. This is who I prefer to deal with.

"We were never friends. You are asking me to increase my risk and my work. That comes at a price."

"It should be double. That's all I'm asking for!"

"It can't be double. I maintain a low-risk business by keeping your deliveries at specific intervals. If I increase yours, I will need to increase everyone's. Which means more risk. If you want to negotiate, we can. But five times our current deal is what I am asking." He pauses, considering my offer. He'll never take it. That's why I chose that number. It cuts too much into his profits. Different dealers are cheaper but don't offer the safety and processing I do. He knows that. I have made a name for myself and plan to uphold that during the daytime business and the darkness.

"Five is too much." I don't respond. I know it's too much.

"What about 2.5 times?"

"Four," I reply casually.

"Three. Final offer." I stay quiet for a beat. I have already considered this. I've been waiting for these calls. Robert has smaller shipments that come through my warehouse. If I increase his, others will ask for the same increase. They always do. Despite everyone having separate, competitive businesses, they all know each other. Some other bosses won't pay more or take on the additional risks themselves. At this point, the benefits of increasing shipments will outweigh the risks.

"Fine. But only what you are shipping now." He groans loudly. He hasn't said whether he knows Angelo shipped guns. I have no intention of continuing with that product.

"I want what you gave Angelo!" That's a hard no. I won't ship guns through my warehouse.

"It's non-negotiable."

"Shit." We sit in silence for several moments while he considers his options: find a new dealer that won't be as safe as me or ship more drugs at a higher price. I have no doubts he is already shipping guns. He's never asked me to ship them.

"Fine. Send over the new contracts. We'll sign them by the end of the week." I stifle a sigh of relief.

"I'll get them to you."

"As always, it's been a pleasure working with you, love. Why don't you let me take you out to celebrate our new deal?" My eyes roll internally at his suggestion as I add a note about his contracts to my calendar.

"No. Enjoy your day, Robert." I end the call before he can respond. Going to dinner with that man makes me want to cringe. He is slimy and looks every bit of it. His hair is greasy, his face oily, and his belly hangs over his belt. Nothing about him is attractive.

I dig around my desk, looking for his contracts. A locked cabinet sits behind my desk, where I keep these forms. The fashion-related agreements are in the top drawer, and the less-than-legal contracts are at the bottom. Once I locate his, I place it on my desk as knuckles rap on the door.

"Lunchtime," Zed grins at me, waving a couple of containers through the door. His smaller office is beside mine. He started bringing my lunch shortly after I first hired him. I kept forgetting mine, and he was running out at the last minute because I was swamped. Eventually, he just started bringing one for me, and I stopped trying to remember my own. Zed is the second highest-paid employee after Diane, my head designer. He's worth every penny. He uses a credit card to pay for the meals. It's easier than trying to give him an allotment.

My thoughts are still swimming with bosses and guns. I tuck the contract into my portfolio, trying not to think about it anymore. I join Zed and he starts chatting about some video he saw. I can't focus, though.

He leads me to a table in the break room; we're the first to arrive. I grab some drinks from the fridge for us, moving on autopilot. New business contracts always leave me on edge, a little raw. Marzanna is one of my few safe places. I won't drop my guard here, but I don't mind letting the dark thoughts flit through my mind. Grabbing a few napkins, I turn back to our table and bump into someone.

"Oh, sorry, Jo." Her bright smile breaks through all my thoughts, offering me peace I'm not used to.

"We have to stop meeting like this," her sultry voice and playful glint in her eyes change my peace to perilous thoughts. I want to grab her throat and claim her mouth, swallowing all the sweet sounds she'll make as I give her the pleasure she wants.

"You've met like this before?" Zed's confusion is written on his high eyebrows.

"Yeah, I bumped into her at the art exhibit several weeks back." Jo's chuckle breaks my growing desire enough for my body to function again. I take my seat, passing Zed his drink. A devious grin spreads across his face as the other employees enter the break room.

It's a small space, but enough for all employees to sit comfortably. Several round tables spread through the area with metal chairs around them. A counter with a sink, stove top, and fridge line one wall. A wall of windows similar to my office exposes the street beyond and hosts a bar for extra seating. Decorations and small plants finish the industrial chic feel of the entire building. The break room is also where we hold all our meetings. It's the perfect gathering space, located directly under my office, at the end of the design team's floor.

Soft chatter fills the area. To my dismay, Jo is at a table with the other designers. Her profile is in my direct line of sight. Her soft face fills my vision. Her round cheeks are perfectly kissable. Her cherry nose is delightfully centered. Her throat, long and exposed due to her hair in buns today, is begging for my lips.

Vincent says something that causes Maggie to cower and Jo to cringe. Jo snaps back immediately, pressing her chest out, asserting power. Before I can get involved, Vincent throws his hands up, backing down from her. He stays quiet but keeps a distasteful eye on Jo the whole time. She doesn't let him upset her again, not that he tries after her assertion.

An elbow in my ribs draws my attention. Zed nods his head ever so slightly toward Diane. She is discussing the upcoming trip that I should be focused on. A glint in Zed's eye confirms he knows my every thought about my newest designer. He is more perceptive, part of the reason I hired him. He notices things many other people don't. This is an unfortunate skill for me at this moment.

Diane discusses the trip next week. They fly out Tuesday night and will return the following Monday. All the details have been finalized. After doing this for many years, we have found a routine that works well for us. We rarely have hiccups; when we do, they aren't catastrophic. A few events were ruined initially, but we've learned and adjusted to make most of these trips go smoothly.

Everyone disperses slowly when lunch break is over. The designers head back to the workspace, working on their pieces with their assistants. I walk through the floor, looking at all the work. Vincent and Maggie are still working on their designs but are not as far along as Jo. Vincent positions the material and then draws his thoughts. If it works, I won't stop him. Maggie has a primarily complete design, just adding the finishing touches. Jo is already cutting pieces to put together. Some things are draped over the mannequin, but it's far from finished.

Diane walks with me to our warehouse, ensuring everything is ready. We both know it is, but these final checks are part of our process. We discuss potential problems and then walk the few blocks back to the design room. She is a chatterbox, keeping the conversation flowing easily between us. She knows the topics I willingly discuss and those I shy away from. I'm not shy, but I don't want to discuss many topics. This is why she is one of my closest friends.

In my office, Zed is waiting with his afternoon coffee and my tea. I drink water throughout the day, except in the morning and after lunch, when I have coffee and tea, respectively. I sip my warm tea, letting the temperature calm the chill from the autumn breeze outside. Zed eyes me as I open my portfolio, remembering the contract I need to update.

"Jo is quite exquisite, wouldn't you say?"

I give him an unimpressed look, returning to my contracts. "Yes," I respond coolly, "you have built quite the design team here." His playful smirk shows we both know that isn't what he meant. He turns his attention to his tablet, knowing he planted her in my mind. Thoughts of the contract are buried under thoughts of her body. Spreading her like a buffet, waiting for my mouth to devour every square inch of her curvy body. I've never had a specific type of body I am drawn to, but fuck if Jo doesn't do it for me.

Zed's cough draws my attention. The playful smirk is still on his face as he stares at his tablet. I swear that fool knows me too well. I sip my tea, waking up my computer to update these contracts. I would much rather daydream about pinning Jo to her bed and making her scream in ecstasy. Work needs to be done. These contracts must be sent before Robert can sneak a shipment past me. He would be the one to do that, especially now that he knows Angelo was successful at it.

When closing time hits, I watch the design floor pack up and leave the building. Jo bends at the waist, grabbing her bags off the floor. The desire to cup her ass before burying my face between her thighs overwhelms me. My nails dig into my palm as desire fills my entire body. Breathe in, breathe out.

"Maybe you should schedule extra sessions with Brayden," Zed teases as he walks past me on his way out. I glare at him, clenching my jaw. "Have a good night, Jo!" His voice rings across the floor. She pauses near the door, turning back with a soft smile. She raises her hand to wave, but her eyes lock on mine. My face is hard, still reeling over Zed's comment. She freezes, but it's hard to distinguish her emotions from this distance. Our gazes remain locked, each trying to read the other through the distance. Zed's steps down the stairs break our concentration. Blood rushes to her cheeks, visible from here.

"Night, Zed." Her voice is soft and timid. She slightly waves in my direction, tightening her jacket before walking outside. I have more running in store for me tonight.

6 · JOSEPHINE

THE DESIGN FLOOR IS quiet, with the team away at their show. I can't wait to go to one. The winter show is here in November, but I want to travel. I want to see other cities and how fashion looks amongst their people. The people of Kansas City are not the same as those in LA or NYC. I want to visit their museums and see the shops where other people work. I want to be inspired by the buildings, landscape, and people. I sigh dreamily in my workspace. It'll be my turn one day.

My piece is so close to complete. It's even better than I envisioned. We changed the material at one point. Diane suggested it. The fabric differs from the one I had in mind, but she is right. It looks so much better. The dress looks like colored light shimmering on a wall. It's wonderful. Some moments, I can't believe I ever doubted my design. It's drastically different than the pieces the team took with them. I thought that wouldn't be a good thing, but seeing the diversity in our pieces is breathtaking.

Zed is making his daily rounds. He usually visits at least twice a day, sometimes with Catherine and sometimes without. I haven't been able to spend time alone with her since we went to trivia. I catch small moments around the shop, but people are always around. We never have a private moment here. I'll get that soon enough, though.

"This piece is just amazing, Jo," Zed praises as he walks around my dress. I preen under his praise, always a sucker for it.

"Thanks," my bashful voice betrays my confidence, but I can't help that. Vincent and Maggie walk up, also looking at my incomplete piece.

"Have you ever used plus-size models for exhibits?" Vincent scoffs at my question. Zed eyes him suspiciously before answering.

"We haven't thus far, but that's not to say we can't. Is that something you want? This dress would be amazing on anybody." I grin, excitement coursing through me. Vincent's eye roll brings me back a step, though.

"Yes," I say, not as giddy as I was but still confident. "Plus-size models would be amazing for this piece, especially if Marzanna is looking to truly diversify."

"Fat models are just promoting unhealthy lifestyles and shouldn't be given a platform." Vincent's stare is aimed directly at me. I'm bigger than many plus-sized models. My social media presence is limited because of hatred like this. Initially, I posted some designs for plus sizes but quickly backed off due to the disgusting comments. Now, I just share with people I work with. I'm not inexperienced in body shaming, but I'm not immune either. His comment cuts deeper than I want it to. Before I get a chance to respond, Zed speaks up.

"If that is your attitude toward models, you may want to consider a career change. Hatred will not be tolerated here. This is your first warning." Zed turns on his heel, stomping off toward Catherine's office. Vincent turns his nose up, looking down at me. I puff out my chest, holding my ground. He walks back to his station, not saying anything else. Maggie squeezes my arm before returning to her own work.

I clear my head by walking over to the outreach program area. Some of the teens are already here, and I love watching them work. A separate team of designers and teachers is available to the students who come over after school. I didn't get a program like this in my school, but I would have loved it. It's such a great opportunity for those who want it.

In the afternoon, Vincent is called into Catherine's office. He stays in there with Zed for nearly half an hour. When he emerges, he keeps his head down. He tries to look confident, but his shoulders slump in defeat. I suppress the grin, trying to break free. He deserves to be taken down a peg. He hasn't shown enough talent to be as cocky as he is.

Catherine walks around the floor shortly after their meeting. She observes Vincent's work, giving him a firm stare, not saying anything. She chats with Maggie, maintaining a friendly demeanor. She chats with the other remaining designers before making her way to me. My body tingles with anxiety and excitement as I watch her walk around. I value her opinion, but I also want her to like me.

"How are you today, Jo?" Is that a twinkle in her eye? She looks happier to see me than anyone else. I'm not projecting that. Though I am more delighted to see her than anyone else.

"Good. Zed mentioned the possibility of working with plus-size models. I would absolutely love that." I try to tamp down the excited heart eyes I feel rising, but I can't suppress my joy over the chance. She nods, the corner of her lips turning up. I'm not the only one working to hide excitement.

"Yes, he mentioned that. We're working on it. It's an excellent idea." Vincent scoffs from his position, rolling his eyes again. Catherine glares at him, and he quickly turns around. She leans close to my ear. Her nearness sends warmth down my spine, landing securely in my dampening panties. "If he continues bothering you, tell me or Zed. His behavior will not be tolerated," she says with a low voice. Why is that such a turn-on? A shiver runs down my body. Her breath is warm against my neck.

"Yes, ma'am," I practically whisper, swallowing hard. She stands up, a full grin on her face. Gods, it should be illegal to be that beautiful. She is in a black mini-skirt today with those legs that stretch for miles. I could get lost exploring each leg before I ever find the center. Her oversized shirt hides her upper body, but I already know that is amazing. She has worn tighter outfits that display her perfect breasts. Without another word, she walks away from my station, heading back to her office. Meanwhile, I'm left dripping between my legs.

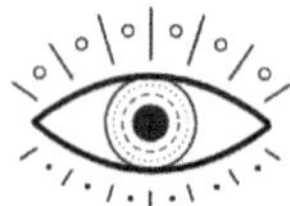

I'M GOING TO A bar with Maggie and Vincent tonight. I don't like Vincent, but Maggie invited us both during lunch. I didn't want to seem like an ass with new coworkers, so I agreed to go. His comments rubbed me the wrong way. I haven't figured out if he has something against me or if he is just an asshole. I plan to give him the benefit of the doubt, but that won't last forever.

I slip on my favorite pair of overalls with a long-sleeved shirt underneath. Ankle booties complete the look, ensuring I'll be comfortable but not get too wet from the damp fall weather. It's not the same as the Minnesota weather I grew up with, but it still has that perfect fall feel. I slip on headphones as I ride the bus to the bar we are meeting at.

During the ride, I turn up the music and let my mind wander. Diane mentioned Catherine rarely travels with them to shows, but she has occasionally. I want her to travel with me. We could go to LA and show one of my designs on a plus-size model. We would walk down the beach at sunset, watching all the colors dance across the sky. I would be swept away by some new design, spending hours absorbed in my tablet, drawing, erasing, and drawing again.

I would only stop my work when she crawls between my legs, spreading me wide for her. She would toss my tablet to the side, giving me that wicked grin. She already knows how wet I am from that simple action. I'm always wet for her. My knees drop open, my body image long forgotten. She knows how to make me feel beautiful. She can silence the voices in my head. Her hands slide over my calves, my thighs, heading straight for my cunt, whispering praises.

"Hi, Jo! How long have you been on the bus?"

To say I'm startled would be an understatement. Those are not the words I was thinking of. My eyes focus on my surroundings. Maggie is sitting beside me on the bus, destroying my perfect daydream. Not that I haven't had that exact daydream eight million other times, but she killed this particular moment. I tug my headphones off, asking Maggie to repeat herself. My brain cannot comprehend the words she said to me.

"Oh, a few minutes or so. Do you live near here?" Maggie has told me where she lives, but I'm not familiar enough with KC to know where everything is. As the bus rumbles down the road, she tells me about her apartment building and what hers is like. We chat briefly about our new homes, neighbors, and neighborhoods. She announces this is our stop, and I follow her off, thanking the driver as we exit.

Maggie leads me into a building with a corner door. A neon sign reads "Drinks & Books" in the front window. Maggie always has a book with her. I read occasionally, but I prefer a different pastime. Inside, the bar has a hipster feel. It matches the chic appearance of Marzanna but has a younger crowd. People sit in leather chairs or metal and wood barstools at tables that look like the tree was cut in half, coated in resin, and thrown in the middle of the room. The exposed brick is decorated with minimalist drawings, books, and plants. So many succulents. An entire section is dedicated as a bookstore. It feels adorable. I can see Maggie spending hours here.

I'm drawn to more modern places. Less brick, more light grey walls. Less plants, more abstract art pieces. I enjoy being with friends, especially when they find somewhere that fits their personality well. We head to the bar, checking out the menu. Just before we order, Vincent arrives and appears to be under a storm cloud. He is hunched over with his dark trench coat collar pulled up around his neck. I envision his ideal setting as a basement with a coffin for him to sleep in.

Maggie greets him warmly, hands him a menu, and chats about this bar. I nod casually, trying to reign in my disgust with him. I'm trying to be friendly, for Maggie's sake, for Marzanna's sake. I'm trying hard. He focuses on the menu, ignoring Maggie. I listen to her. She knows so much about this bar, having researched it heavily before she suggested it. She has that type A personality. She has everything heavily researched before she commits to it.

Vincent smacks the menu on the counter, waving the bartender over. I give him a disgusted look, unable to reign it all in. He doesn't need to be so rude. We order our drinks and pay separately. I leave a huge tip, unsure if Vincent will leave anything. Once our drinks are made, we find a small table near the wall and settle in. I chat with Maggie about her degree while Vincent sulks in his chair.

We order new drinks, and Maggie tries to engage Vincent. He talks for a few minutes, then abruptly leaves, walking to the bathroom. I roll my eyes at his behavior. He's such a creep.

"I don't particularly like him," I tell Maggie once the bathroom door closes behind him. She sighs and sips her drink.

"I don't either, but I didn't want him to be excluded." She looks down at her hands, sadness showing on her face. "I don't have many friends yet." Her statement shocks me. Maggie is so friendly and nice; I'm surprised she doesn't have a dozen friends already.

"Really? You're so wonderful, though." She looks up with a sad smile on her face.

"The people in my apartment complex are mostly older families. They're nice enough but are only interested in me for babysitting," she rolls her eyes quickly. "I've always been close to the people I became friends with. The real world isn't the same as college." I chuckle at her statement.

"No, it isn't." I rub her shoulder, trying to lift her mood. She's such a sweet woman. She deserves so much happiness. "I've got great apartment mates. Why don't you come out with us sometime? We usually get shitfaced, then go back to our building and drink and eat takeout. You can stay with me, so you don't have to worry about getting intoxicated and taking the bus home." She perks up, smiling at me.

"Okay," she nods excitedly. I grab my phone to send her the details as Vincent walks up with a fresh round of drinks. He places the tray on the table between us.

"I got drinks for all of us," he waves at the tray, not offering a smile or looking at us.

"Thank you," I say, surprised by his kindness. A small voice in my mind tells me to be cautious. The larger part is excited for free drinks. I shoot off a text to Maggie with the details for trivia, then grab a fruity cocktail with a fancy stem poking out of the side. Maggie spots some board games on a shelf and grabs one for us to play.

The night has taken a pleasant turn. Maggie and I take turns buying rounds for all of us. We laugh as we play random board games for which we don't remember the rules. Vincent is being surprisingly friendly. He keeps glancing at me with this weird look in his eye, but he hasn't said anything awkward or rude. The atmosphere is pleasant in the bar. People laugh randomly, sitting in small groups like ours. Some people read or discuss their books. Others are just chatting. Some people shop at the bookshelves. Music plays softly in the background, making it easy to converse.

At this moment, I can see my future here. Hanging out with Maggie at this little hipster joint. Maybe I'll start reading more. Maybe I'll bring my tablet to draw while Maggie reads. Bar trivia and takeout nights at my apartment with my friends. Working endlessly on designs at Marzanna. Maybe I'll snag Catherine and find her in my bed most nights. Or perhaps I'll find someone else that makes me feel as hot and bothered as she does. I haven't found that before her, but who's to say it won't happen again?

Vincent breaks my daydreaming as he rises after slapping his thighs. "I'll get the next round." He's being shockingly friendly tonight. What was in the bathroom when he went earlier? Drugs would not surprise me in the least. He looks like he could be on drugs. The sudden mood shift would support that theory, but if it makes him friendlier, more power to him. I won't knock something that makes someone better to be around.

"Oh, no thanks," Maggie waves her hand to stop him. "If I drink too much, I won't be able to find my way home," she giggles, leaning back against her seat. She clearly doesn't have a high tolerance for alcohol. These drinks are good but not overly strong. I've got a nice buzz, but I can still take the bus.

"Maybe you should take an Uber instead of the bus," I suggest, slightly worried about her getting home now. I have no clue which stop is hers, so I wouldn't be of any help.

"Yeah, Maggie," Vincent interjects. "One more, and I'll call an Uber for you."

"You shouldn't go home with Maggie," I speak before she can say anything else. Her wide eyes stare at me, clearly not even thinking about Vincent wanting to take her home.

"I prefer the company of men, not wasted girls," he responds sassily. "Besides, I live in the opposite direction and have no desire to drive all over the city. I was offering to ensure she gets home safely." Maggie watches the face-off between me and him. His insult doesn't get past me, and I won't stand for him bullying her. I'm also not comfortable with him getting her address, but that's not my call to make.

"It's okay, Vincent," she grabs his arm, drawing his attention to her. "I can get my own ride instead of the bus. I would like another round if you are still offering." She looks up at him with these doe eyes that would have anyone caving to her. He nods at her, casting me an evil stare. He walks to the bar to order drinks for each of us. I watch him for a minute to see if I need to order my own. Once he places the order, I turn my attention back to Maggie.

"I would feel better if you take an Uber, Mags." A wide grin spreads across her face.

"My best friend always calls me Mags." She waves her phone at me, showing an app already open. "I'm getting a ride for 15 minutes from now. I will definitely get lost on the bus." She giggles again and rises to go to the bathroom. I chuckle, shaking my head at her. I've only known her briefly, but I can already tell she will be a good friend.

"Where's Maggie?" Vincent's angry words break my thoughts of my new friend. I lift my head, hiding the scowl I want to show.

"She went to the bathroom. She ordered an Uber and will be leaving in 15 minutes."

"Fine," he sits the tray down and hands me a milky drink. He says nothing else as he pulls his phone out. I thank him for the drink, taking a sip of it. It's sweet and tropical and has some coconut in it. I'm not the biggest fan of coconut, but this drink is delicious. Maggie returns a moment later then grabs her pink drink. She sips and moans in delight.

"Oh, this one is good." We chat for a few more minutes as we finish our drinks. We discuss the drinks and the likelihood of returning to this bar together. I agree we should, but I want to avoid coming back with Vincent. I've been friendly enough, for Maggie's sake.

"My Uber is about to arrive. I need to go," Maggie stands, reaching over to hug me.

"Yeah, mine too," Vincent replies, standing also. I didn't realize he ordered one, but that's fine. My bus won't run for another ten minutes or so. Maggie hugs each of us. I stick my hand out to shake Vincent's, but he gives me a floppy fish handshake. It's so awkward. Why can't he grip my hand? I shake off that feeling as they leave the building. My vision is starting to blur. I didn't drink enough to be this affected. Maybe the last drink was a double, and I didn't realize it. I gather my things, heading toward the bookshop. This drink is hitting me harder than I expected. It takes work to walk straight.

I decide to sit at the bar. I'll order a soda to help settle my rolling stomach. After I order one, a brilliant idea pops into my head. I should call Catherine! I wonder what she is doing now. I bet she could use some company. I could use some company. Man, my head is really spinning. The bartender delivers my soda and asks if I'm okay. I nod at him, asking what he put in my last drink. He tells me it's just soda, but the confused look on his face doesn't match the tone of his voice. He is more concerned than confused. I try to clarify that I'm referring to the drinks Vincent ordered, but my words are too slurred.

Another couple walks up to order drinks, so the bartender steps away from me. I don't understand why it is so dark in here. I try to look around, but turning my head makes the room spin at double time. The spinning also happens in my stomach. I cannot vomit at the bar, but I also cannot make it to the bathroom in this state. I'll just rest my head on the bar. I just need a moment to get my head to stop spinning. If someone would turn the lights back on...

7 · CATHERINE

WEEKENDS ARE ONE OF the few times I get to relax and rest. It's not every weekend, but I treasure the time I do get. Tonight, I am lounging on the couch in boy-short panties and a loose crop top. Being at home is the only time I wear more revealing clothing. No one can see my body; I don't give anyone access to that much of me. I have one of my favorite movies, but I'm not paying attention. It's just background noise. Sometimes, I'll sit silently, but I don't want that now.

Instead, my mind wanders. Thoughts of work and shipments darken my thoughts. Jo pops up, brightening the darkness. She's such an enigma to me. I've never had feelings like this for anyone. I don't get crushes. I'm not drawn to people that way. I use people to fill my needs, and that's it. I don't need a deep personal connection, but I want that with her. I want to be close to her and fulfill her needs. It's about more than power, unlike Brayden. This need to care for Jo is new.

My phone rings, breaking my thoughts. I glance at the screen, an image of Jo filling it. I snapped a picture of her at the fashion exhibit when she wasn't looking. She was engrossed in the dress in front of her. It's a side view; her perfect profile stares at the fabric like something she has never seen before. Her eyes shine with intrigue, looking up at the model on the pedestal. She is glowing in the image. Despite my skills with technology, that glow is natural and not something I added. This is my favorite picture ever.

"Jo," I say in a deep raspy voice. She is calling me late at night on a weekend. There's only one thing she could want. The last time I saw her outside of work was trivia night. The risk of having her in my life is too significant, but I can't turn down a call from her.

"Um, hi. Is this Catherine?" Why is a man using Jo's phone, and why does he know who I am?

"Who is this?" I demand, sitting up on the couch.

"My name is Donovan. I'm a bartender downtown." His pause angers me. While he answered my question, I clearly need more information.

"Where did you get this phone? Why are you calling me?" I don't mask the anger in my voice. Where is Jo?

"Right. So, this girl has been at the bar for a few hours. Her friends left, and she walked over to the bar. She's had a few drinks, but now she's passed out. I'm not sure it's from the drinks, though. She had her phone open to your contact. She needs help, and I thought I would try you first."

My mind is racing at high speed. She isn't a lightweight. She had a lot to drink at trivia and didn't black out. What could be wrong with her? Who was she with? I need to get to her to help her.

"Okay, what bar are you at?" He tells me the name of a bar downtown. I put my phone on speaker and search the bar. It is close to me. I haven't been there before, but I know the location. I send out a text to my driver while I continue talking to Donovan.

"Can you keep her safe until I get there? I'll be there in ten minutes." The bar is ten minutes away. It should be closer to fifteen with the added time of getting ready to leave, but I'll make John drive quickly. Speed limits don't matter when my girl is in trouble. My girl. I don't stop to think about that.

"Yes. She's at the bar, so I'll keep an eye on her until then." I disconnect the phone and run to get clothes on. I meet John in the front of the building. He already has the address and knows to get there quickly. Having a task pushed the racing thoughts back. Sitting in the car, the thoughts rush back in. Who was she with? Who left her alone in this state? Why is she in this state? Will she need to go to the hospital? Before I can dwell on those questions, we arrive at the bar. I rush inside, leaving John to keep the car running.

I scan the area, trying to maintain a calm façade. Inside, I am on high alert. I finally spot Jo slumped over the bar, only held up by her awkward position. I rush over to her, pushing her hair out of her face to check her breathing. A tall, blonde man walks up to me.

"Are you Catherine?" I nod at him, gently shaking Jo's shoulder. She doesn't react.

"She's been like this for about 20 minutes. She seemed fine with her friends, but after they left, she fell into this state within minutes." That's too fast for alcohol. She would have shown signs before if it were just alcohol. I scan the building briefly, spotting several cameras around the room.

"Do you have access to those cameras?" Donovan glances at them and nods at me.

"Can you give me the footage?" He cringes slightly, informing me he is uncomfortable with my question.

"No, but once we close, I can check and share some of it with you if I find anything." That's not what I want to hear, but it will work for me. I need that information to know what happened to her. This will not go unpunished. I will end whoever did this to her.

"Fine," I grab my business card from one of my pockets, along with a few bills. Keeping cards and cash on me is beneficial for situations like this. I hand him the card with the money beneath it. "Thanks," I mutter, wrapping my arms under Jo.

"Jo, can you walk?" She mumbles something. Her head rolls onto my shoulder. Her eyes stay closed, but she lifts her body. I wrap my arms around her, glad for the touch but angry it's in this state. My girl deserves better than this. She leans against me, her large body resting on mine for support. I practically drag her as she stumbles to the street. John jumps from the vehicle to help me get her in the backseat. I let her lie down in my lap as we drive to her apartment. Mine is closer, but that's another thing I don't share with people. Jo will be more comfortable in her own space.

During the ride, I stroke her hair gently. She groans a few times, rolling around the seat. I try to keep her still, not wanting to upset her more. The concern she will get sick racks my nerves. I don't have issues with people getting sick, but it will go all over me. That's not something I want. I whisper soothing words to her, ensuring we are almost there and she is safe now. Relief washes over me; I understand this situation could have been far worse than it is.

John helps me get her to her apartment. I could carry her myself, but I am thankful for the extra help. I dig her keys out of her bag. Nervousness and excitement swirl through my body as we enter her space. I want to be here so badly, just not like this. She should invite me in to do filthy things to her body. Not be on the verge of unconsciousness.

I dismiss John and carry Jo to her room. I undress her, again angry at this situation. I forgo putting her in other clothes, not wanting to jostle her more than necessary. She collapses on the bed once her clothes are off, leaving her in underwear. I position her in a more comfortable spot on her side. After rummaging for a few extra supplies, I settle on her bed by her back.

My hand runs soothingly over her shoulder, arm, and curvy sides. She is so beautiful, even in this state. She's also wrong for me, but I can't keep my hands from her. Not in a sexual way. I won't take advantage of her like this. Offering her this small comfort is all I can do at this moment. I lie to myself; it doesn't mean anything. I'm just providing comfort to someone who needs it. No deeper feelings are lurking just beneath the surface. I don't need to know what lies beneath her clothes. I don't need her taste on my lips.

I take out my phone, needing to distract myself from her body. She sleeps next to me. The groaning has stopped. She looks peaceful now. I should let her rest. My needs aren't important now. Several new messages pop up on my screen. Donovan did what I asked him to do. I open the messages, glancing at Jo. She didn't deserve this. Rage swirls through my chest again, watching her sleeping form. I didn't want to spend my first night with her like this. Not that I should be spending the night with her, but I won't leave her alone now.

The files from Donovan are pictures of the computer he watched the video on. The original is clear, but mine are a bit blurry. He sent multiple images, all with time stamps in the bottom corner. The first shows Jo arriving with a girl. It looks like Maggie, but I can't be sure. The following image shows Jo sitting with two other people, laughing and having a good time. Now, I am confident it's Maggie. The other figure is unmistakably Vincent. What happened that she was left alone in this state? They will both be fired if they left her like this.

The following few images show them taking turns buying drinks for each other, still having a good time. They are all in chronological order, and before the point, Donovan called me. An image shows Vincent buying drinks, then Maggie and Vincent leave together. The last two are Jo going to the bar and collapsing. My chest clenches at the last images. Her demeanor is so different in the last two. She looks unable to hold herself up. I can almost hear her slurring in the picture. Rage fills my body. Breathe in, breathe out. I need to figure out what happened. I'm missing something.

I scroll back through the pictures to the one of Vincent buying drinks. He is glancing over his shoulders, looking back at Maggie and Jo. At first glance, he seems to be checking on them. I zoom in on the drinks. His hands hover over one of the drinks. He could have add something to it, but I can't be sure. I send a message to Donovan, asking for more images. The urge to go find Vincent is increasing at an alarming rate. I have no desire to ask him questions at this point.

Jo rolls over, her arm flopping over her face. She is so young and innocent. I tug her arm down so she doesn't suffocate. She is safe now. I won't let anything bad happen to her. My fingers brush the hair off her cheek, unable to resist. She moans softly, turning into my hand. I jerk back; that's not the response I want now. A shameful pleasure fills my soul that she responds to me that way. In time, baby girl. I'll get that response when it's time.

My phone dings with a new message from Donovan. This time, it's a video. His message reads, "Should I call the cops?" I type a quick no, already knowing what is on the video. I'm going to deal with this myself. I rarely get involved with the cops under any circumstance. I won't let them deal with any situation involving Jo.

I take a deep breath before opening the video. I know what I will see. That doesn't make it easier to watch. Vincent takes the drinks from the bartender and pulls them close to his body. Donovan walks away to serve someone else. Vincent glances at the girls, his hands moving over a milky drink. There is a certain deniability in this angle. He could claim he is stirring the drink, gathering them to carry, whatever excuse he can come up with. Maybe other cameras could show a better angle in the bar, but I'm convinced he's the one who drugged her. Did he plan to come back for her later? She was alone for at least 20 minutes before I got there. Why did he drug her and leave her alone?

My vision turns red as I watch the clip over and over. Vincent takes the drinks, waves his hand over one, then delivers it to Jo. The video is 20 seconds long. Thoughts race through my mind of all the things I could do to him. For the second time, I have visions of torturing someone. I've been around plenty of torture, but it's not something I've ever done. It's too messy, too risky, too long. But this video drives my desire to fuck all those excuses and beat Vincent with my bare hands. Chop his own hands off and beat him with them. How dare he think he can do this to my girl?

My girl. She isn't my girl. She can't be my girl. I'm too dark for her. My life is too dangerous. She's too soft and sweet. She deserves someone who can give her everything. I find myself pacing in her kitchen. I don't remember walking in here. It fits her well, though. The cabinets are sleek and white with black finishes. The stove and fridge are along the wall, with an island and a sink. She doesn't have a table, just a high-top bar behind the sink with a few stools. The kitchen opens to a comfy living room. Digital art decorates her white walls, with modern furniture filling the space. She has tastes similar to my own.

A stirring from the bedroom draws my attention. Jo rushes to the bathroom. The door is cracked, and the light is on. I don't know if she is aware of my presence. I don't want to scare her, but I want her to know I am here if she needs anything. I step to the cracked door, knocking softly but not peeking around.

"Jo," I keep my voice soft, "do you need anything?"

She doesn't say anything for a moment. The toilet flushes, and she steps to the door cautiously. Her eyes are glazed over, and she is still unsteady. She gives me a small smile when she sees me.

"Are you really here?" I can't stop the laugh or smirk spreading on my face.

"I am," I say, taking her arm to guide her to the bed. "Do you think you can take some medicine and water?" She nods softly.

"It's in the kitchen. I have sports drinks in the fridge, too." She tries to step past me, but I stop her.

"Sit," I motion to the bed. "I'll get it." My smile stays on my face, pushing down thoughts of slicing Vincent's neck open. In the kitchen, I find medicine and a drink for her. She's sitting on the bed, swaying when I return. She's barely awake but takes the meds and sips on the bottle. It's not enough, but it will do for now. I urge her under the blankets, wanting her to be comfortable. The lights are already dim, but I turn them off completely. I plan to wait in the living room since she is improving. I'm not leaving until she returns to normal, but I don't need to hover either.

"Lay with me?" Her voice is childlike and makes me weak. My heart sings to give her what she wants. Cuddles won't be a problem. I can hold her, comforting her the way she needs right now. That's all this is. She's not feeling well and needs a friend. Nothing else.

I climb into the bed and wrap my arm over hers. Jo lifts her head, letting me slide my other arm under hers. Her body relaxes as she sighs against me. I hold her tight, her back against my chest. Her hair is in my face. I take a breath, inhaling her scent. I have good self-control, but I'm not that strong. It smells like honey, different from the citrus smell when I first met her. She must have changed her shampoo. My fingers draw tiny circles over her hand, savoring the smooth feel of her skin. Her breathing slows and steadies as she drifts off to sleep. I don't know how long to stay here, but I want to keep her safe.

I fall asleep at some point, waking later to realize I'm still holding her. I have never slept with someone this way. It's warm and comforting in ways I never expected. As soon as those thoughts hit, discomfort swamps me. I've never been this close to anyone for this long. I slowly shift away, needing to distance myself before my heart shatters for her.

It's only been a few hours since I brought her here. She'll probably sleep for a few more. I won't. I never sleep much. Instead, I dig through her cabinets to see what kind of food and pans she has. I only cook occasionally, but I'm not too bad at it. I find all the ingredients I need for my favorite breakfast bars. It'll take a bit of time to prepare. They can be served cold or reheated quickly. I begin the process of baking, letting my thoughts focus on the steps instead of the beautiful girl a wall over. Time passes more quickly when I have something to do with my hands.

"I didn't know you could cook." Jo climbs into one of the stools on the high top. She is wearing shorts and an oversized band tee. Dark bags are puffy under her eyes. Her skin looks pale. Her yellow hair is tied back into a messy red bun at the top of her head with stray strands all around. She is sipping the drink I gave her last night. Without responding, I put a couple of bars on her plate. I made different flavors, unsure what she would prefer since she had all the ingredients in her fridge.

"How are you feeling?"

She pulls the plate closer, picking at one of the bars with fruit. She shrugs, not making eye contact. Dark, intrusive thoughts fly around my brain. All involving Vincent's hands detached from his body.

"Like shit, but I don't remember what happened." She finally looks up at me, and fear fades into confusion. "Why are you here?"

"Before you blacked out at the bar, you opened your phone to my contact. The bartender called me." She nods, accepting this answer. She glances over my body, cheeks flushing. I suppress the grin at her response. "Eat," I instruct, take a plate, and sit beside her. We eat silently for a few minutes.

"Fuck, Maggie was with me." She hops off her seat, stumbling to her room. While she has regained most of her control, the drugs have not worn off completely. She returns with a charger and her phone. I didn't think to plug in her phone last night. She opens Maggie's contact, dials, and presses the phone to her ear. A groggy Maggie answers.

"Where are you? Did you get home?" Jo's voice is filled with fear and worry. I place my hand over hers. Her free hand is on her lap. I am vividly aware of how close to her thigh my fingertips are. Less than an inch, and I could stroke her inner thigh. Her voice breaks my filthy thoughts.

"Did Vincent go home with you?" Her voice is tight now. She has yet to say whether she is aware of what really happened. She is concerned with Vincent's actions. My hand tightens over hers on reflex at his name. She glances at me, but her face relaxes when Maggie responds.

"You took the Uber by yourself. Yes, I remember that now." She hangs her head and pulls her hand from mine to rub her forehead. I take my hand back, unsure how else to comfort her now. "No, I'm fine. I just drank too much last night and couldn't remember how we all got home." Her chuckle is weak, thinly hiding the pain she is feeling. Maggie seems to buy her deceit, though. The call ends, and Jo buries her face in both hands. "What happened?" Her voice is soft and fearful.

"You were drugged." Her head jerks to look at me, a small gasp escaping her lips. "I got to you before anything happened and brought you here." Relief washes over her. She settles in her seat, returning to pick at her food. She is taking small bites. I would like her to eat more, but something is better than nothing. She doesn't say anything else until her food is gone.

"I need to lay down again." I nod, taking her plate and mine to the sink.

"I'm staying here until you are better." I rinse the plates in the sink. I didn't ask permission. I don't need it. I'm not leaving her alone until I am sure she will be alright. She looks at me with an unreadable expression.

"I have a TV in my room if you want to watch a movie."

She turns without another word and goes into her bedroom. I clean all the dishes, put them away, then walk to her room. She is on her side, facing away from me again. A plush chair sits in the corner with a few fluffy pillows and a blanket on the back. I could climb into the bed with her again, but I no longer feel comfortable now that she is doing better. She didn't invite me into her bed this time.

I settle in the chair. Her eyes open, watching me. A book with a receipt sticking out is on her nightstand. I grab the book, noting the half-naked man on the front. I give her a playful smirk, opening the book to the page she has marked. Her cheeks flush, but she closes her eyes, tugging the blanket tighter over her shoulder. I scan the words, unconcerned with the actual story. I quickly realize this is a favorite scene of hers. The pages are worn down from frequent touching. A small tear is on the bottom as if she turned the page and ripped it.

This is a sex scene. My girl likes to read her porn. I don't even correct myself for thinking 'my girl' this time. She is mine. I'm going to do everything I can to protect her.

8 · JOSEPHINE

SOFT GOLDEN SUNLIGHT SHINES through the window in my bedroom. The afternoon light rouses me from my sleep. My body is achy, but my head isn't pounding anymore. The medicine and food from earlier did wonders for pushing away the hangover from the drugs. The thought sends chills down my body. Last night could have been so much worse. I was drugged. I should be concerned about how or why I was drugged, but I don't want to think about that. I'm safe here.

Catherine is in the chair in front of me. Her eyes are closed; she's sleeping. She protected me last night. She is the reason nothing terrible happened to me. I try to suppress the rising delight at that thought. I would have preferred to learn she wants me without being drugged, but I'll take what I can get. She's here, in my room, watching over me. I could get used to that.

I rise quietly, draping a light blanket over Catherine. My apartment isn't frigid, but who doesn't like a blanket when they sleep? My head spins a bit, but nothing as bad as last night. I need a shower. The warm water will soothe my muscles and help wash away the disastrous night. I take my time in the shower, not in any rush to get out. Catherine said she will stay until I'm better. Part of me is giddy that she's here; part of me is nervous. She's my boss and a lot older than me. This is so crazy.

The shower is refreshing, but thinking of Catherine the whole time only makes me horny. I want her so bad. I bet she is terrific in bed. She looks like she knows how to please someone. Shit, I need to stop thinking like that. The deep ache in my core makes it hard to stop. I left the door to the bathroom cracked. If I had closed it, I could masturbate quickly without worrying about her knowing. She will hear me with the door open, though. I've never been good at being quiet or inconspicuous when it comes to sex. I sigh, resigning myself to being aroused until she leaves and I can get to my battery-operated friend.

I dress and leave the bathroom, pausing by my room. She made brunch, so I can make dinner for her. I will ask what she likes, but she is on the phone with her back turned to me.

"No, I don't want to go there." Her voice is tense. This isn't a conversation she wants to have.

"That's not my problem." She pauses, staring out the window. I can't hear the other person. I'm too far away.

"No, I don't want to think..."

"No, you don't need to buy me tickets. I'm too busy for that."

"Fine. I'll come next year. Will that work?" There is a long pause now. I'm snooping; I shouldn't be listening to this conversation. As much as I want to stay, I walk into the kitchen to prep dinner. I'll make enough for her; if she doesn't stay, I can save it for lunch. I wonder who she is talking to. I never hear her that tense. Not that I listen to her on phone calls much. She stays in her office most of the time. Was that a business call? It's 4 pm on a Sunday. Why would they be calling at this time? Maybe it's a vendor trying to set up an exhibit.

I shrug off the thought, gathering chicken to cook. I don't know what she likes, but I like chicken stir fry. I cut the vegetables and put some rice in the cooker. It's such an easy meal. I make it frequently enough that I am primarily on autopilot.

I usually have music blaring while I cook, but I won't do that while she is on the phone.

"Do you always dress like this when you have company?" Her voice is low, a few feet away from me. I gasp, spinning around, startled by her sudden appearance. I'm wearing a spaghetti strap crop top with short cotton shorts. It's my typical attire while I am home alone. I did not think about the fact that my super hot boss, whom I shouldn't be attracted to, is here. I should have worn less revealing clothing, but it's too late.

"Only for you." Oh shit, why didn't my filter stop that? Well, it's out there now. Her grin is devious, sending a wave of need through my body.

"Is that so? What do you wear for your friends?" Her deep voice sends tingles straight to my clit.

"Pants and a sweater." My voice is so breathy.

"So, you are showing off for me?"

"Yes, ma'am." Why does that feel so good to say? Her eyes are pure desire. Carnal lust is oozing from her body.

"Your food is going to burn, Jo." The way she says my name turns my insides into a puddle. I can't even process the other words she said. She's stalking toward me. I gulp, backing up a step. I bump into the stove, feeling the heat coming off it. I spin around, ready to turn it off. My hand reaches for the knob when her front brushes against my back. Her hand grabs mine, guiding it to the spatula I have out.

"Keep cooking, Jo."

"Yes, ma'am." There is no other response I could give her. My body is on fire, and it's not from the stove. She is touching me. Her body is pressed against mine. I can't think through the cloud of desire in my mind. She guides my other hand to the sliced chicken, encouraging me to grab it. My body manages to function enough to add the chicken to the pan. Thankfully, I seasoned it before she walked in. I can't process anything now. We would've had bland chicken.

She takes a deep breath, sliding her nose up my neck. My head angles, giving her more access. Fuck, why is that so hot? I add the chicken and stir it around. I can't differentiate the pan's sizzling from my body's sizzling. Everything is hot. As I stir, her arms wrap around my body. Both arms land on my stomach, her fingers exploring every bit of my skin. Anxiety creeps in; the self-doubt I harbor inside rises. I'm self-conscious about my body. I'm not small like her. Many people love to remind me of that.

I push the chicken around the pan as her hands get bolder. One hand caresses the bottom of my breasts, the other moving to the waist of my pants. If she had any qualms about my body, she wouldn't be touching me, right? I repeat this as the hateful words clash with my growing arousal. The arousal wins. My head tips back on her shoulder as her fingers dip under the hem. She's not even touching anything erogenous, and my body is burning for her.

"Don't burn my dinner, Jo."

Fuck. Her dinner. I'm making dinner for her. I groan as her hand wraps around my breast, squeezing it. I force my eyes back to the pan. I have to keep cooking. But oh, her fingers are pinching my nipple through my shirt. I groan, shoving my ass back into her. She chuckles against my ear, sending pulses through my clit. I am so wet right now. Her hand is moving lower into my pants.

"Did you forget your panties? Or was that just for me, too?" She's onto me now. I don't even care if she keeps touching me like that. Her fingers are just above my core. I need more.

"For you."

"Mmm, I like that, baby girl."

I've never had anyone call me baby girl. Coming from Catherine, it's the only thing I want to be called for the rest of my life. I want her to call me that until the day I die, then etch it in stone. Her sultry voice makes those two little words sound like pleasure incarnate. I will do anything to keep those words on her lips.

Her fingers slip lower, brushing against my clit. Just the tiny touch is overwhelming. I nearly double over, arching to get more while the rest of my body clenches in desire. Her arm tightens on my chest, holding me up from collapsing on the stove. I can feel her grin against my neck. She's enjoying this as much as I am.

"Turn off the stove, baby girl."

"Yes, ma'am." I don't say 'yes, ma'am' to anyone. Or 'yes sir' for that matter. It feels right with Catherine, though. She deserves that title. Especially if she keeps lighting my body up with her touch. I regain control of my body, lifting myself upright again. Catherine twists to the other side of my neck, kissing the column. Her hand returns to squeezing my breast. Her finger grazes my clit, sliding over my wet opening. I can't hold myself up. Pleasure is wracking my body. I tip forward again, trying to hold myself up but overcome with need.

"I can't..." I huff out. "I can't stay up. You can't..." My eyes shut with embarrassment at the thoughts in my head. Catherine may be strong, but I'm not a small girl. How can she support my weight when I'm crumpled over like this?

Suddenly, her arms tighten around me. My feet are off the ground as she spins me to the counter. My feet contact the floor as my arms land on the counter, caught off guard by what she just did. She lifted me and spun me around. Apparently, she is stronger than I thought.

"You don't say negative things like that. I can and will control your body." Her words have an edge as if she is mad about my thoughts. Chills roll through my body at the bite in her voice. Without another word, her hand shoots down my shorts. She slides her middle finger inside my aching core while her hand presses against my clit. My body crumples at the delicious feeling. Before I can slump against the counter, Catherine's other arm wraps over my chest, hand resting at the base of my neck. I've never done any breath play, but I'm not opposed to it now.

"I've got you, baby girl. I won't let you fall."

Her voice is back to the sultry one again. I moan, sinking into her hand to get more from her. She chuckles, deep and smooth against my neck. Her voice, her breath, and her sounds on my neck and back send pleasure rolling through my whole body. From the top of my head to the bottom of my toes, everything is heated. I haven't had total body arousal in so long. I need it.

"Your sounds are so good. Give me more."

She slips a second finger inside me, sliding smoothly in and out. I tip my head back, groaning loudly. Her hand caresses my extended throat, then slides down to my breast, squeezing and stroking my nipple through my shirt. Catherine drags her teeth along my neck, causing my pussy to clench around her fingers. She chuckles again. I bet I could orgasm just from that sound alone.

"Your body is so beautiful in my arms, baby girl. Is your orgasm just as beautiful? Will you show me?" Oh, dear gods. Oh, Jesus. Oh, any god out there listening, please let me come and give this woman everything she wants. Her fingers increase their speed, pounding in and out while her palm keeps pressure against my clit.

"Yes..." I start to reply, but she strokes my G-spot. "MA'AM!" I scream as my orgasm crashes through me. My body burns as stars fill my vision. Her arms tighten around me, holding me up while my body convulses in her arms. Fuck, she's so strong. Her fingers keep up their pace expertly. Her teeth press against my neck, not in a bite, just applying pressure. It sends my mind soaring even higher. I suck in a deep breath. A silent scream escapes my lips as my body finally crumples onto the counter in front of me. The stove would have burned me if she hadn't spun me around. Her move was as much for my safety as to prove me wrong. That thought swims through the pleasure coursing through my body.

Catherine slides her arm around to my back while her fingers are still inside my cunt. Her hand caresses my back and ribs soothingly. I've never felt such calmness from a partner's touch after an orgasm. She slips her fingers out of my pussy, avoiding my sensitive clit.

"Fuck, Kitty." I spin quickly, noticing the surprised look on her face. My lips crash into hers in a brutal kiss as I throw my arms over her shoulders. It takes her a moment to relax and get into the kiss. Her arms settle over my waist casually, as if she didn't just give me an earth-shattering orgasm. The kiss is almost awkward, with my rough passion and her lackadaisical enjoyment. It works for us, though.

She pulls back from the kiss, placing her hand on my face. Her thumb strokes over my cheek.

"You are so beautiful."

I blush, lowering my gaze at her comment. I'm not used to receiving such compliments, especially after sex. Usually, there are a few giggles, but one of us always leaves quickly. I clearly have been with the wrong people. My arms drop, sliding down hers and wrapping around her waist. Now, it's my turn to touch her. I get to make her feel as glorious as I do. As wonderful as she just made me feel. My fingers tighten on her small waist, ready to explore under her clothes.

"Why don't you finish dinner now?"

Catherine presses her lips against my forehead, then steps to the side. Her hands trail my body as she walks around the counter. I watch her leave me, confused about why she stepped away. Maybe she's just famished. We haven't eaten in a long time. I take a breath, tamping down the confusion, settling my body after the orgasm. I turn the stove back on, unsure what else to do.

My rice cooker goes off as I add the vegetables. My mind is spinning, but the thoughts aren't complete. As soon as one starts, another forms halfway. Doubt, excitement, insecurity, and desire all wrack my brain in such a conflicting manner. I manage to finish dinner without burning anything and plate the food. I slide them across the island, grabbing two bottles of water. I sit next to Catherine, finally looking at her.

Her eyes are filled with lust and want, but why did she stop me? I could have finished dinner after. Her hand on my thigh breaks me from my trance.

"Eat." I take a few bites, pleased with my meal. It's tasty and seasoned well, especially considering the distraction I had. I blush at the thought.

"Why are you blushing, Jo?" Her voice is teasing, but desire is laced underneath. My cheeks burn with embarrassment now.

"Do you fuck all the girls while they make you dinner?" I ask playfully. It's not meant to be jealous, but I can hear that when the words come out of my mouth.

"No, baby girl," she whispers close to my ear. Her hand slides up my thigh, not reaching the place I want. "I only do that for you. You're special." She leans back over to eat, leaving me heated. I don't believe her. I want to, but I don't know her well enough. She's skilled with her fingers. This isn't the first time she's done this, but it doesn't mean it happened the same before. Maybe she learned from hookups. I shake my head, eating the last of my food. These thoughts are crazy. I have no right to be jealous.

"Are you feeling better?" Catherine's voice sounds so typical, shifting faster than my mind can.

"Yes," my response is quiet and forced out on a breath. Arousal is still coursing through me. Despite the orgasm she just gave me, I want more. I want to touch her. Pleasure her the way she just pleasured me. I want her to do that to me again. I never want it to stop. She chuckles at my response.

"Food and orgasms are always good for your health."

She rises, carrying her plate to the sink. I watch the way her body moves. She is so in control, so smooth. Every inch of her body does exactly what she wants it to. She knows what she wants, and she takes it. Our eyes finally meet. She wants me, and she's going to get it. I won't deny her. She rounds the counter, stalking toward me. I can't breathe. What is breathing? Who needs that in her presence?

Her hands stroke my cheek, my jaw, my neck. I suck in one breath and another, my lungs on fire with my entire body. One side of her mouth tips up. Her lips are so gorgeous. I bet they know how to work a pussy too. I bite my lip, thoughts of her lips on my pussy swirling through my brain. Her thumb tugs it down. My eyes lift to hers. Desire glares back at me, but something darker, too. I can't place the other emotion.

"I need to go home now. I'll see you tomorrow, Jo."

She leans in and kisses me lazily again. It's so casual, so unhurried. I'm thrown off by how she can change emotions so quickly. Maybe it wasn't that quick. I did eat my entire dinner.

"Okay, Kitty," I finally muster. The smirk on her lips doesn't quite match the odd expression in her eyes, but she doesn't say anything else. She leaves my apartment with me still in my seat, lost in everything that happened.

I finally move, still trying to figure out Catherine. Her fingers and voice were so demanding and claiming. Her kiss was casual, though, like she didn't have a care in the world. Everything is hers for the taking. She has taken me, that's for sure. Someone bangs on my door, pulling me from my thoughts.

"If you don't open the door now, I will shout your secrets for the whole building!" Ben is yelling through the door. I'm guessing most people in the building know what I was doing. I was nowhere near anything that could be considered quiet. I open the door, laughing at him as he walks in. I grab a couple of sodas as he settles at my high top.

"So, I saw a certain older woman in the hallway. Unless Amara is trying to steal from you, I'm guessing someone got lucky?" He waggles his eyebrows at me, causing me to giggle.

"Yes, she was here with me. Wait, you could tell she's gay?" He waggles his blonde eyebrows. I throw a dish towel at him, telling him to shut up. He glances at his watch before speaking.

"Not really, but she is into you. Last night must've been pretty great if she is just now leaving. Or did you ruin a dinner date, and she left early?" He gives me an expectant look as if I always go around ruining dates. I'm better than that. I gloss over his comment about her being into me. I can't focus on that now, or I'll become a giggling pile of mush again.

"She stayed last night, but it wasn't like that." I am not about to tell him my boss just fingered me into the best orgasm I've had in years just feet from where we are standing. "I was drugged at a bar Friday. She found me and brought me home. I'm better now." Ben's eyebrows are as high as they go. I sip my drink, allowing him to process what I just said.

"You were drugged? How did that happen? Who did it? Are you okay?" His genuine concern warms me, and I am glad to have someone who cares about me. I have been growing closer to the people in this building and consider them friends. I've only lived here for a month or so, and it can be challenging to form close relationships during that time.

"I'm fine. Nothing happened. Apparently, I was trying to call Catherine when I blacked out. The bartender called her, and she picked me up and brought me here." That's all he needs to know. He doesn't need the details; I am still processing them myself.

"Who drugged you?" I shrug at him. Catherine didn't tell me, and I didn't ask.

"You don't know? Don't you think you should find out? If for no other reason than to avoid them." That's a good point. I hadn't considered that. I just wanted that night to be over. I should know if it could happen again.

"I'll ask Catherine if she knows tomorrow. I didn't think about that." He nods, then starts hounding me for more questions about what Catherine did with her time here. I shove him from my apartment, not wanting to kiss and tell. After he leaves, I clean the kitchen and drop into bed with a comedy on the TV. I do my best to stay focused on it and not think about everything that has happened in the past forty-eight hours.

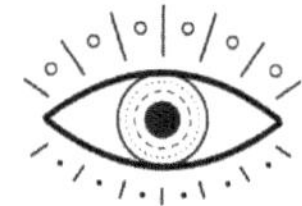

I WAKE UP MONDAY morning, ready for the day ahead. I'm working on my dress. It's coming together nicely. I have a few ideas for the next piece, but I'm not putting a lot of effort into that right now. Everyone is back today, and I'm excited to hear how the exhibit went. I must get in early to speak to Catherine before the others arrive. Zed usually gets her coffee in the morning, but I messaged him earlier. I asked if I could bring it in since I need to chat with her. He agreed and sent a winky face emoji back. I hope he doesn't realize I am attracted to my boss.

I stop by the café close to work, ordering a large black coffee and my preferred iced beverage. I haven't taken a sip yet, nervous about showing up early with coffee for Catherine. She didn't say anything when she left. What if she doesn't want to see me? Maybe it was just a one-time thing. She didn't sleep much at my place. She could have been exhausted and not thinking straight. I try to push the doubt away. She wouldn't have come to the bar for me if she didn't like me. There is something between us. I know it.

I climb the stairs, taking deep breaths to settle before entering her office. I don't bother knocking; I just let myself into the room. I freeze at the sight before me.

A man about my age is bent over Catherine's desk, completely naked. Catherine is behind him in a short skirt and long-sleeved top. She has a strap on over the skirt with a dildo shoved up the man's ass. It's clear he's close to orgasm by the pained expression on his face. Catherine is also frozen, staring at me with shock and horror. Yeah, that's a mutual feeling.

"Jo," Catherine starts. Her voice jolts me into action.

"I, uh, brought you coffee...s." I hold them up, showing both. I place them on the opposite corner of the desk. The man's expression changes to a soft, playful look. He observes me. He is beautiful, with tan, smooth skin, well-defined muscles, and, holy hell, a cock that goes on for days. It's so big. Why is my mouth watering? I audibly gulp, quickly returning my eyes to his then Catherine's. My cheeks are burning, and my body is a thousand degrees hot.

"Jo," Catherine tries again, but her hands stay on the man's hips. I've never pegged someone or received anal. I'm guessing you shouldn't jerk out suddenly, though.

"I'll... speak with you later." I turn on my heels and rush out of her office empty-handed. Oh gods, I can't believe I just walked in on that. As I reach my desk, what happened comes crashing down. She is fucking a man. Maybe that's why she wouldn't stay or let me touch her last night. But why would she touch me if she's with someone? And why is she seeing him here and not at her place? Why bring him into the place where she works? My mind swirls, and questions and doubts crash through my brain.

I don't know how long it has been when the man stops at my desk. He watches me for a moment. His smile is knowing and youthful. I can see why she likes him. He's gorgeous. His dark hair is wavy and looks like he just crawled out of bed, or maybe that's his just fucked hair. Oh god, jealousy burns through me. I don't think I even have a right to be this jealous. It's not like she asked me to be her girlfriend. She just fingered me in my kitchen. And called me baby girl. And saved me when I was drugged. The ice rattling in his coffee draws my attention back to him. He sips the coffee I bought for myself, giving me a once over.

"She's obsessed with you, ya know?" His statement surprises me. What does that mean? Why would he say that to me? He pulls something out of the pocket of his shirt and holds it out to me. I take the business card he offers. "Brayden," he nods, sipping the drink I gave him. He walks away before I can say anything. I'm left staring after this real-life Adonis that my boss was just silicone balls deep in. I can't help watching that ass as he walks away. That man knows what he has and how to work it. He leaves the building as Zed walks in. They greet each other in a friendly manner.

What the fuck is happening? Am I still on drugs? Nothing makes sense right now. Catherine saved me from the bar and stayed at my apartment. She made me brunch and took a nap with me. Then she fucked me in the kitchen and left without saying anything. Now, I've caught her pegging the hottest man in Kansas City, probably all the Midwest. And he is friendly with Zed? No, the simulation is obviously glitching, and the alien overlords have messed up my life. This can't be real.

I look down, remembering there is a business card in my hand. It's black with gold lettering. It's simple and sleek. Brayden is in the center. No last name. Underneath, it reads "Escort". His phone number is beneath it. I turn it over, seeking more answers. The backside is entirely blank. He carries around a business card with two words and a phone number.

It slowly dawns on me that he is a sex worker. Catherine pays to see him. Questions crash into my brain again. My head sounds so loud. I don't know how to process this information. I have yet to have coffee today. Because I gave it to Catherine's hooker. Oh gods. When I left Minnesota to pursue my dream job, this was not what I had in mind.

Zed greets me with a smile, but I'm too frazzled to respond. Catherine calls my name from the landing in front of her office. I glance back at her, then turn and run out of the building. I'm so fucking glad I wore boots today instead of heels. I'm not running from her, but I need more time to process what happened. And I need coffee. Okay, I am running from her, but not forever. I still need answers. I just need coffee and time first.

9 • CATHERINE

WHAT FRESH HELL IS this? No one but Zed ever comes in this early. Watching Jo run from me is devastating. I sigh heavily as Zed looks between the door and me. I could run after her. Explain the situation. How do I explain why I was pegging Brayden a day after touching her?

Her body is so exquisite. I could think of nothing all night but her sounds, her skin, her pussy clenching tightly around my fingers. I forgot Brayden was coming today. When I saw him, I needed to release so much steam. I fucked him hard and fast until Jo walked in. She was clearly aroused by what I was doing. The way she ogled Brayden and me made me more desperate. Maybe my girl is a little depraved like me. Perhaps she'll understand, even be interested. That's too much to hope for.

Zed's footsteps up the stairs break my thoughts. Jo's phone and bag are still on her desk. She must be replacing her coffee. If not, she'll have to come back eventually. The thought of grabbing her things and bringing them to my office so she is forced to come to me crosses my mind. I need the chance to explain myself.

Before I can move, people start walking into the building, getting set up for the day. Zed and I walk into the office.

"What was that about?" Zed asks.

"Fuck, Zed. It's been a long weekend. Please watch for her. I need to speak to her today. I also need to speak to Vincent right away. He's done." Zed's face spreads in shock.

"He has one strike against him. What did he do over the weekend to cause you to fire him?"

I shuffle some papers around my desk, debating how much I should tell Zed. He already knows I am attracted to Jo. He probably even knows her feelings for me. She's more conspicuous than I am, not that it's glaringly obvious, but nothing gets past Zed. I sip my coffee, looking back at him.

"Why was she here with my coffee instead of you?" He shrugs casually.

"She texted this morning and said she needed to talk to you. Guess you two have lots of talking to do." His chuckle and teasing words earn a glare from me.

"Vincent drugged her Friday night and left her in a bar downtown. She tried calling me but passed out before she could. The bartender filled me in." His mouth forms a perfect o as he gasps, eyebrows near his hairline. Any more surprises, and he may lose them to his hair. He collapses on the couch, processing everything I just told him. I tuck a couple of photos into a paper folder. "Once he is here, I want him brought in. You can start the paperwork whenever, but he isn't staying here."

"Shit," he groans out. He takes a sip of his coffee then walks to the window. "He's here now. Are you ready for him?" I nod, not needing to say anything else. "And Jo is back." He winks at me, walking out the door before I can respond. Relief rolls through my body, relaxing my tense muscles. I can still salvage things with her if she is back.

I wait at my desk, typing on my computer. Vincent finally walks in. His dark, baggy clothes hide his small frame. He doesn't look like someone who would drug a girl, but he also doesn't look innocent. I motion for him to take a seat as I finish typing. It's just an email I'm sending to my aunt. It's not essential and could wait. I don't even need to email her. I want to make him sweat for a moment. He has already been here for causing problems. He thought he could get away with something on the weekend. He underestimated me.

"Good morning," I start, rising and walking around my desk to stand before him. He looks up at me, anxiety shining through his face. His shoulders are curved, and his fingers are fidgeting. He doesn't say anything, so I continue with this meeting. I grab the paper folder I put photos in earlier. I debated a manila envelope at first, but it felt so cliché. I considered forgoing a cover for the images but realized keeping the truth discreet is necessary. Plus, it adds a bit of tension as the person opens the folder and realizes what I have.

I hold the folder out for Vincent to take, saying nothing. He looks at the folder then up to me, trying to figure out what is happening. He'll know as soon as he opens it. I nudge it toward him, tired of how long this takes. I use this tactic to keep some mafia men in line with the shipments. Some of them love the mafia movie vibe it gives off. I'm willing to play the game. He grabs the folder and opens it. Inside are copies of the images Donovan sent me. I watch as Vincent's face falls briefly, then hardens.

"What was your plan?"

He bristles, sitting up straighter. He glares at me but says nothing. I don't need the why. It won't change my decision. I wanted it for purely selfish reasons.

My fingers twitch with the urge to punch him. I dig my nails into my palm, trying to suppress the desire. I roll my head, looking at him from an angle. I lean in so I am next to his ear. My voice is soft but laced with anger and violence.

"You will take your things, only your things, and leave. Do not stay in Kansas. I don't care if you go back to Georgia or fall off the fucking earth. Do not stay here." I lean back, cross my arms, and speak normally. "You have 48 hours." He pales but assesses me. His eyes are searching my face, not finding any answers.

"What happens in 48 hours?" I don't speak. I'm not going to admit to the harm that may befall him.

"Are you threatening me?" While his voice is loud, the fear is unmistakable. Again, I stare momentarily before I turn and walk to my seat.

"You can keep those photos. I have the originals." He rises, watching me as he walks toward the door sideways. At least he's smart enough not to turn his back. I wouldn't do anything in my office, but he recognizes the threat. He leaves my office, stomping down the stairs. I open the security cameras from my computer. Like the scared little chicken shit he is, he does exactly as I asked, keeping his head down. I don't know what he has against Jo, but my business won't tolerate his actions.

Zed walks in and informs me he has started the paperwork for Vincent. He rattles off a few more things on our agenda. We have a meeting this afternoon to discuss the upcoming winter show. I'll have Diane choose another designer to cover whatever Vincent would do. The new hires are designing two pieces each for the show. We'll need others to create the two designs Vincent was responsible for. We must also decide whether to replace him or rely on Maggie and Jo for newer ideas. Jo's ideas are good enough to carry us. Maggie also has extraordinary ideas. I don't think we need to hire anyone else now.

A slight knock on the door interrupts Zed's agenda. Jo is standing on the other side. My heart rate increases when I see her. Zed opens the door, turning to let me know he'll be back later. She came to speak to me. I can salvage our relationship, whatever it is. She looks nervous as she sits in front of my desk. She hasn't made eye contact with me. I can't be sure what she is thinking. Did she come in here to quit? That isn't an option. I won't lose her over this situation. Before I can even think of something to say, she starts talking. Of course, she had a plan when she walked in here.

"I know I'm not as attractive as Brayden. I can understand why you would want to see him. I shouldn't have tried to call you Friday. Thank you for what you did for me this weekend." She pauses, finally looking up to meet my gaze. She glances back down quickly. "I would still like to work here and will keep things professional. I won't call you on the weekend again." Her fingers pick at the material of the sweater dress she is wearing today. It's a deep green and looks beautiful against her skin, making the red in her hair pop. I hate that she doesn't see how gorgeous she is.

"I have a standing appointment with Brayden." I pause, looking into her eyes as she lifts her head. "I meet with him because he chose to go into sex work. It's easier for me to avoid a relationship because of my work." Her face twists, pursing her lips. Fashion isn't so complicated that I couldn't have a relationship. The mob work that she doesn't know about is dangerous. She won't know about it. She's too innocent and happy to be wrapped up in that. I can occasionally see her at work and her apartment without risking too much. It's probably not what she wants, but we can have fun until she meets someone who can give her more. I'll hate that person for the rest of my life, but she can be happy.

I rise from my chair and move to stand before her like I did Vincent. Instead of intimidating, I relax into a more casual position. Her cheeks blush from our closeness. I reach out and stroke her cheek. Anyone could see if they walked by my office. Windows are on both sides of the door, but with Zed's office on one side and nothing on the other, few people have a reason to be up here.

"You're not leaving me yet, baby girl." She shivers at my words. I lean in, my lips next to her ear. I whisper, "Invite me to your apartment this weekend."

"W..will you come to my apartment this weekend?" Her voice is timid, but she follows instructions very well.

"Yes, baby girl." I blow against her ear. A low grumble sounds from her chest. It would have been a groan if she wasn't holding back. "Tell me to bring dinner and an overnight bag." Her breathing is shallow. She is giving me the reaction I want, and I love it. I thrive off this. She interfered with Brayden this morning, but this... This is much sweeter than what he gives me.

"You...bring dinner," she swallows before continuing. "And an overnight bag," her voice isn't confident, but I'll accept it. Before I respond, she clears her throat. "And you'll make this up to me. Make me feel special." A huge grin spreads on my face. I chuckle against her neck.

"Anything for you, baby girl." I press my lips against her neck. My fingers trail up her arms. Her breathing is so shallow now, cheeks even redder than before. I lean back, smirking down at her. I haven't smiled this much in a long time. She does something to me that I haven't felt before. She makes me feel things I don't usually feel. I cup her cheek with my hand. I stroke my thumb over her face.

"You follow instructions well. You're a very good girl." Her eyes go wide, and she wiggles in her chair. I'm playing with fire here. I can't wait to get her alone in a consensual setting. All I can think about is her body. Her cunt will be so warm and soft, her body so responsive. Oh, this weekend will be fun.

ROBERT'S FIRST SHIPMENT FROM new contracts for the Mexican cartel is coming in tonight. I wait in the warehouse, thinking of all the devious things I can do to Jo. She won't have any body issues when I am done with her. I plan to worship every single inch of her body. I want her to come so many times she begs me to stop. Then I'll take one more from her. She will spend Sunday recovering again but in the best possible way this time.

The truck outside sounds its motion alarm, pulling me from my dirty thoughts. I raise the garage door, finding a sedan near the truck. Robert climbs out then walks toward me. Shit. He didn't tell me he was coming. I'm not too fond of it when bosses arrive unexpectedly, especially the bosses for the cartel. The Mexican cartel I work with checks in more frequently than the others, but it is still annoying when they show up unannounced. The truck backs in while Robert walks over to me. He looks incredibly gross tonight.

Robert's suit is surprisingly nice for such a disgusting man. It's tailored well, dark grey with a crisp white shirt. The top buttons are undone instead of wearing a tie. The suit is high quality but still looks wrong on him. His hair is slicked back with tar or whatever product he uses to get that effect.

"Catherine, love! How wonderful to see you tonight. You look radiant." Even his words feel slimy.

"Robert," my reply is curt. "I didn't expect you tonight."

"No. I just thought I would pop in. It's been such a long time since I've been here."

I don't respond; I wait as the men open the back of the truck. Robert follows me over to watch the process. His men are more competent than Angelo's. The truck is unloaded as the women walk into the garage. They head straight down the hall like always, stripping outside their workroom.

He watches the women like a wolf on a hunt. This is why I don't have bosses here. They act like they are entitled to the women. Despite the women's job to process the drugs, the men want more from them. Robert is a sleaze. He could ruin the bit of safety the women have here. I don't allow anyone to harm them while they are in my warehouse.

Robert has tried to use them before. When he started shipping through my warehouse, the room with couches and a shower had just been installed. I use it myself or offer it to women or drivers. Robert took one of the women into the room, only to emerge half an hour later. The woman hurried into the workroom without saying anything. Robert walked out with a cocky expression and zipped his pants. To my knowledge, he didn't force her. I doubt she consented willingly.

"Robert, come with me. Let's have a celebratory drink." We both know what he wants, and there is no denying that. I can lure him into a false sense of security by not bringing it up. He follows me through the warehouse to my office. However, he keeps his eyes on the women, scoping out his next victim. I've often wondered how many women he has raped, how young they were, how close to him. I don't focus on that. It will consume me entirely if I do.

In my office, I grab two tumblers and a bottle of scotch. I turn, placing both on the desk in front of him, and pour the drinks, giving him a double. I pass the tumbler to him. He swirls it around but watches me to see if I will drink. We need to be cautious to get ahead in this business. I raise mine to him in salute, then take a long drink. The liquid burns down my throat, warming my insides. I allow myself one drink in these situations. One never has a concerning impact on me. I can keep my head about me with only one.

"Business seems to be booming around here," he says after taking a long drink. He drinks more while waiting for my response.

"It is," I nod. "Yours must be, too, if you want to double your shipments."

"Yes, yes," he drinks again, emptying his glass. I lean over to refill it. Robert always has several drinks. He doesn't usually get sloppy drunk, but enough that it's obvious. He nods his appreciation. "The feds were down a few weeks ago, but we got them out without any incidents."

I already knew this. I keep tabs on all my clients. The feds were sniffing around him under the guise of tax evasion. My clients are smart enough to control their legal businesses. They maintain low sales, just enough to stay in business, but not raise alarms. The feds learn about their other activities but have difficulty connecting the different businesses.

He talks for several minutes, bragging about how clean his legal business is. He operates a shoe store. It's a good front for maintaining frequent deliveries. I only half listen as he starts complaining about the manager he hired to run the store. He has some issue with her and is whining. I hate his whiny voice. It grates my nerves. I sip my scotch, biding my time with him. I glance at the watch. He has been in here for twenty minutes. That's twenty minutes of listening to him bitch and moan. Any minute now, this should end.

He takes another drink, spilling half of it down his shirt. He starts to speak, but his words slur. I hold a towel out for him over my desk. He reaches for it but tumbles off the chair. He rolls on the floor for a moment. I finish off my drink, in no rush to deal with him. After a few minutes, he is still and quiet. I walk around to look down at him. He is blacked out, sprawled out on my floor. Perfect.

Is it hypocritical to fire Vincent for drugging someone in the same week that I also drug someone? Maybe. Do I feel bad about it? No. The difference is I drugged Robert to stop him from raping someone. Vincent drugged someone so they would be assaulted. He didn't give me a reason why he drugged Jo. I don't think he would rape her, but that doesn't mean he wouldn't hurt her in other ways. The rage that usually fills me thinking about Vincent ebbs. Robert lying on my floor brings a calmness I shouldn't feel.

I move to the cabinet I keep in this office. This cabinet is also locked, specifically for my nighttime deliveries. I open a drawer, pulling out tiny, lacy panties. I slip the panties into Robert's pocket. When he wakes, he'll think he blacked out drinking after banging one of the girls.

Tonight isn't the first night I've drugged one of the men here. It happens frequently enough that I keep a specific set of tumblers just for this situation. I have a tumbler coated in the drugs. One tumbler has a tiny chip on the rim. That's mine. No one ever notices. Overfilling their drinks ensures they drink enough and don't suspect drugs. They wake up the next day, hungover with undergarments tucked in their pockets.

The worst part of this plan is I now need to sit in here for an hour or so. If I leave too soon, the drivers and bodyguards will suspect something. If I hide in here, it's more believable that the man over drank. I put on my headphones to listen to a new podcast I found. It's the easiest way to kill time while keeping an eye on Robert, not that he'll wake up anytime soon.

When the podcast ends, I leave the office to check on things. Men are moving around the space, loading the drugs the women processed. Robert's bodyguard and driver are standing against the wall, watching my office. Fuck.

I walk into the room where the women work and ask one to accompany me. They don't question me. They glance at each other briefly before one removes her gloves and masks and walks with me. I lead her back to my office. We step inside, and I close the door behind her. She doesn't speak, but her eyes are wide on the man on the floor.

"He won't wake up for a while. I need you to stay here for twenty minutes or so. His bodyguard will believe he fucked you. He won't touch you. He'll stay out for at least another hour." She eyes me suspiciously but seems to understand what I am saying. I raise a letter opener that looks like a small dagger and place it in the middle of the desk. "To help you feel safer, but you won't need it here."

I leave the room alone, closing the door behind me. The driver and bodyguard watch me, but they know their boss is in there with a girl. They won't go in. When she leaves, precisely 20 minutes later, she returns to work. She keeps her head down, managing to look upset about this situation. I'm glad she followed through.

I sigh loudly in my office and then inform the driver and bodyguard of their boss's state. They carry him out of my warehouse. Shortly after he is gone, the truck is loaded and leaves. I should feel guilty for being relieved the night occurred without incident, but this is the life I live. It will always be dark.

10 · JOSEPHINE

It's Saturday night, and I'm freaking out. Catherine will be here any minute. I've texted her several times this week, but she doesn't text much. She still uses her phone to actually call people. She really shows her age sometimes. She's coming tonight for dinner and will stay overnight. I don't know what her plans are. I have hopes and ideas, but I don't know what she's thinking. She hasn't said much since she told me to ask her.

I've never been crazy about following directions, but I love it when she bosses me around. I'm drawn to her in an unexplainable way. When she's around, I feel calm and aroused. She makes me feel sexy and gorgeous. I can't say I've felt that from partners before. Women make me feel more attractive than men, but they leave so quickly.

A soft rapping on the door draws my attention. I stand up, straightening my short skirt and tank top. I didn't know how to dress. I've been so nervous. Two days ago, I went to a salon and had everything waxed. I've never done that before, but I want to be prepared for whatever happens. If nothing happens, at least I can enjoy my smooth skin.

Catherine stands in the hallway holding a paper grocery bag. Fuck, she is stunning. She's wearing high-waisted pants with a plain t-shirt tucked into them and a blazer over it. She could easily kill someone with the pointed heels she is wearing. Her body is slim and looks so damn good. My eyes rake over her, heat rising on my neck and cheeks. I could stare at her for hours. Probably experience an orgasm or two from just looking.

"You should invite me in, Jo."

"Hm?" I chuckle nervously, "Come in." I step back to let her in.

She enters my apartment with an air of confidence. She knows what she is doing. I've never experienced confidence like that in my life. To watch her is astounding. Her ass looks fantastic in those shoes and pants. I hope she takes them off, and I can see what it looks like underneath. Her bag jostling on the counter draws my eyes away from her ass. She doesn't look at me but has a knowing smirk. I'm not going to hide my desire at this point.

I walk to the counter, looking at the packages she is taking out. She brought grilled chicken, a salad, and ice cream. I didn't expect ice cream. I chuckle as she puts it in the freezer.

"Is there no whipped cream?" I tease.

"Why whipped cream?" She asks in a sultry voice. "Ice cream is more fun."

Moving through my kitchen like she owns the place, she plates our dinner. She slides me a plate and a glass of water. I'm surprised she didn't bring wine. I hop down from my seat and walk into the kitchen.

"I have some wine that will go well with this." Before I reach it, she grabs my hand, stopping me.

"No wine." Her thumb strokes my wrist, sending a flame of desire through my body. "You'll want a level head for what I have planned after dinner." Her gaze roams my body, desire blazing in her eyes. She releases my hand and walks around to sit at the bar. My body is hot, bothered, excited, and nervous about what she has planned.

"Oh, are we playing Monopoly? That can be hard when we're drunk," I say innocently.

"We will be playing a type of monopoly," she says after considering my comment. "Come sit, baby girl. Your dinner will get cold." My body moves instantly at her command. I don't put any effort into sliding into the seat beside her. I don't need to think when she commands me. She cuts my chicken into small bites, then her own. Once she's done, she drops the knife, placing her hand on my leg. Zings go straight to my clit under her touch. I breathe deeply, working hard not to groan under touch. I eat in silence, consumed with what she will do later. She doesn't say anything. She never says much.

"So, a type of Monopoly, huh? Like one of those spinoff versions?" My voice is weak, overwhelmed with arousal. Catherine chuckles, her fingers sliding over my thigh. She slips under the hem of my skirt, caressing my skin. My mind is so clouded with desire.

"No, baby girl. Not one of those." She's so mysterious, driving my desire even higher. I don't say anything else as we finish eating. It's quiet; only soft music plays in the background. Catherine doesn't say anything else; she finishes her food quietly. The silence increases my anxiety. Her fingers so close to my pussy sends surges of heat through my body. She drops our plates in the sink and grabs the large weekend bag she brought.

"Now, I'll show you how I play Monopoly." She pulls out a small gift bag, holding it for me to take. "Go into your bedroom and put this on. Only this." Her eyes burn into mine, heat flaring in her stare. "Turn on those LED lights to whatever color you want. Turn on your speaker so I can connect to it. Tell me when you are ready." She leaves no room for questions. She is thorough in her instructions.

I take the small bag, nervous about what could be inside. I hope it's manageable because I can't think through something like that now. I hope it's the right size. I hate it when people buy me clothes. The sizing is always so awkward. What if she didn't get the right size? If it's too small, I can't face telling her. But if it's too big, that will hurt worse.

My mind spirals. Catherine approaches me and places her hands on either side of my face. She leans in, pressing a soft kiss to my lips. My brain instantly calms under her touch. It will be fine. She won't judge me. She is here of her own free will, after all. She invited herself. Butterflies swarm through my stomach. Catherine releases me, and I walk to the bedroom in a daze.

I start the lights and the speaker. Those are easy enough and don't run the risk of not fitting. I set the lights to purple, my preferred choice in my bedroom. Soon, a playlist of sensual songs streams through my speaker. I smile at the music filling the room. I can get down to this. Feeling more confident, I grab the tiny gift bag, ready to face what's inside.

A soft silk fabric is in the bag. I tug out a large piece of material, flipping it around until I recognize it. A black silk robe unfolds. It's simple, no frills. A thin waistband laces through a couple of loops. It's large enough it will cover me easily. Pleasure surges through my body. This is the perfect gift for me. It will fit nicely.

I slowly take off my clothes. Even though I'm alone, I enjoy the act of removing them. I slip my tank top over my head, letting my fingers graze my skin. My hands slide over my ass as I slide my skirt over my hips and down to the floor. I stand only in my thong and bra. I'm wearing a matching set and feel disappointed that she won't see them. She said nothing but what was in the bag, but this lacy black set matches so well. Plus, it offers more coverage when the robe comes off. I decide to leave them on.

I slip the robe over my shoulders. It glides smoothly across my skin; goose-bumps spread over my arms. My body burns, wondering what Catherine will do. Maybe she'll eat me out, then after my orgasm, I can finger her into one. I bet her cunt is warm and tight. Her legs are so long they could wrap around my body. She could straddle me while I touch her. Or maybe she brought her strap-on, and I can fuck her with it. If not, I also have a few toys I could use on her. The possibilities are endless.

The door creaks open as she steps in. She removed her clothes from earlier. She now wears high-waisted panties. Tight straps run across her stomach over the bottoms. She has on a long-sleeved top that slides under the panties. I can't see any of her body, which is disappointing. It will be so much sweeter when I get to uncover it. I can tug that material over her legs.

Oh my god, her legs. They look long in pants and skirts, but hell, they are that long. And muscular. Her legs are defined and strong. Of course, Catherine would take care of them. She moves closer to me, each leg flexing and relaxing as she walks. I'm mesmerized. What will it feel like to run my fingers over her legs? My mouth waters at the thought of her legs on either side of my face.

Her fingers graze my chest, just under the collar of the robe. I groan under her touch. My body is so hot I may explode at any moment—my eyes close while I enjoy her touch. I gasp when her lips land on the place her fingers just were. She leaves small kisses across my chest. Her fingers glide over my arms, then across my belly. I almost jerk away from her, but her touch feels so good. Her lips trail up my throat. I stretch my neck, giving her more access. The touch sends fire rolling through my body.

Her fingers undo the robe, letting it drop to the floor. I'm left standing in my bra and panties in front of her. I don't open my eyes. I don't want to see the look in her eyes when she sees my body for the first time.

"What is this?" Her fingers slip under the shoulder strap of my bra, popping it against my skin. I look down, finding her staring at my body. It's not the dissatisfaction I expected to see. Her gaze is filled with lust and fire. No one has ever looked at my primarily naked body like that. Damn, now I kind of regret not watching her when she first dropped the robe. I should have watched her first impression if this is how she looks now.

"I said nothing but the robe."

I bite my lip, unsure what to say. Should I tell her I was nervous about her seeing me? Before I can decide what to say, her thumb plucks my lip from my teeth. Her intense stare increases my breathing.

"I'll just have to make you pay for your disobedience."

Am I a sub right now? She never said anything about being a domme. Is she going to spank me? I haven't been spanked as a punishment before. I like it sometimes when I'm getting railed from behind, but I don't know if I'll like it otherwise. She grabs my waist, spinning me around. She sits on the edge of the bed with me in front of her. Her hand roams across my stomach, touching every little bit. It feels awkward initially, but her hands are warm and soft. The touch is sensual. I love it. I want it everywhere. I want her to go slower and go faster at the same time.

I watch her hands wrap around to the back. My bra droops before I realize she unhooked it. She leans in close. My breath hitches, thinking she will go for my breasts. Instead, she bites the bra, pulling it back. She didn't even touch me. The moisture between my legs tells me she won't ever need to. Her hands stay on my waist as she removes my bra with her teeth. I shift my arms, letting the straps slide off. She releases the bra. Her eyes land on my breasts, taking them both in. She's practically eye fucking my breasts. They burn to be touched. I want her to bury her face there.

Catherine leans in, blowing air across my breasts. I groan, biting my lip as I watch her. I want to tip my head back in pleasure, but I don't want to miss her worshipping my body like this. No one has ever made me feel this way. Her hands glide around my stomach, waist, and back. Her touch is so soft, so sexual. It leaves a burning trail around my middle. Her tongue flicks my nipple, causing me to gasp and clench. Her fingers tighten and glide across my waist. Her touch feels divine.

She flicks her tongue on my other nipple. I'm ready this time and enjoy the touch. She nips the soft skin just above my nipple, then kisses the tiny hurt. I stroke my hands over her shoulders, up her neck, and tangle in her hair. She's being slow and methodical. I've never experienced something like this. Sex is always rushed and hard, needing to get to the orgasm as quickly as possible. Her hands cover my breast as she leans back to look up at me.

"Have you ever had someone control all of your pleasure?" I think for a second, but the answer is undeniably no. Sometimes, there is a mix of sharing the pleasure, but usually, I find ways to get my own. I shake my head. She leans in, sucking one of my nipples into her mouth. I close my eyes, enjoying the warmth of her mouth until she pops off.

"Lay down," she nods her head back toward the bed. I crawl onto the bed and lie down facing her. She stands on the side, her eyes roaming my body. My cunt clenches in anticipation. She's going to drag this out. My breath hitches at the thought. Do I want that? My body is on fire. My core is already clenching, and she's barely touched me. How long can I last while she is doing this?

"With your consent, I'm going to take you to the edge of desire, then bring you back. That is your punishment for not following my instructions." She leans over the bed, propping one knee on the edge. Her fingers trace under the hem of my panties as she speaks, but she stays focused on my face. I don't know how to react to that. "When you are squirming with desire, burning with need, so desperate you want to cry, that's when I'll give you what you want. I'll take your pleasure, leaving you sated in the best possible way." Fuck.

"Yes," I whisper. I don't need to think about that. I've never been edged before or denied an orgasm, but I'm not scared to try it with her. I've heard it is incredible. Her fingers grip the thong I am still wearing, sliding it down. I lift my hips to help her. Catherine glides her fingers along my skin down to my ankle. She leaves a trail of burning need on my legs. My breathing is shallow. Her eyes stay on my face; a slight smirk shows her enjoyment.

Catherine tosses the panties onto the floor, rising to her full height beside the bed. Her eyes exude desire as she gazes over my body. She uses a hair tie I didn't realize she had. I'm not paying attention to those small details. My body is filled with arousal. I only want one thing. Her hair is pulled back away from her face.

She doesn't usually pull her hair back. Her neck, like her legs, stretches for days. Her strong cheekbones are more prominent, with her hair away from her face. Everything about this woman is beautiful, and none of it displays her age. She takes care of her body.

She climbs over the bed, over me. Catherine's body reminds me of a cheetah on the hunt, slinking through the brush. Her eyes laser-focused on her prey, on me. Tingles erupt through my body, anxious about her next move. Her shoulders and hips shift in slow motion. My cunt burns with need. She won't be able to deny me an orgasm. It's going to happen before she touches me.

"Kitty," I whisper. When I first called her that, I was unaware of how fitting it would be for her. A wicked grin spreads on her face. She has me right where she wants me. She can hear the desire in my voice. She can see the lust in my flushed cheeks. She can feel my burning skin. Her fingers lift to trail my legs, pushing them apart. I feel so exposed like this, but so fucking beautiful too. Her eyes drop to my core and glaze over. I have never felt this desired.

Catherine kisses the top of my thigh, and then her fingers touch, gliding across the top. She kisses the other side and places her fingers there. She massages my thighs as I watch. She searches my body, looking for the next place she wants to claim. My chest rises and falls quickly. She leans in, heading straight for my core. This is it; she's going to lick me. My breathing is as fast as my heart beating out of my chest. I struggle not to thrust my hips closer to her.

Her lips kiss on top of my pubic bone, and I groan, twisting with disappointment. Catherine places her hand on the spot she just kissed. A huge, wicked grin covers her face as my pussy clenches relentlessly with need. She rests her body next to mine and props up on her side. Her head lifts above me, but her hand is still free to touch me. Her fingers graze over my nipple, drawing a low moan from my chest. Her fingers massage the top of my hips, never connecting where I need her to.

I squirm under her. She smiles as if this is the best thing in the world. I am the only thing she wants. She wants me squirming beneath her touch, and she has it.

She is ecstatic. Her fingers finally slide lower, but they split, only stroking either side of my opening. I groan, pressing into her touch. I have never been this worked up by another person. Once, I was masturbating, and my toy died. It was a similar feeling to now, but far less intense.

Catherine drags one finger over my opening, just across the slit, then circles my clit. I cry out, twisting my head into her arm. She kisses my forehead, whispering against my skin. "You are so perfect, baby girl." Her finger makes the laziest circles around my clit. I said I wanted the denial and edging, but shit, I think I was wrong. This is so intense. My body is burning; I'm so on edge. I could die in this moment.

"How are you doing, baby girl?" Her finger doesn't stop, just continuing the slow touches over the most sensitive area of my body.

"I...I..." How am I doing? I feel like I'm going to explode. I need her to release the pent-up arousal in my body. I'm so close to an orgasm but so far away. She kisses my forehead gently again. Her finger presses harder against my clit. Yes, yes! That's what I need. Her movements are still slow, but I can come from this. I'm so close. My body is right on the edge. My breathing is quick. I groan as my orgasm builds higher. I'm going to come.

Then her fingers are gone.

I gasp, eyes flying open. I whine, jerking under her as my body calms down from my missed orgasm. I am so frustrated. So in need. I want to cry. My breathing hitches several times with disappointment. Catherine's face is filled with pleasure, with wide eyes and a huge grin. She is loving every second of my disappointment. I will never disobey her again. I can't stand this denial. As my body settles beneath her, she finds my lips in a lazy kiss. What is it with her being so slow? Her control is impeccable. I would have given in and fucked hard and fast to get that orgasm by now.

"You are lovely." She kisses my forehead gently as her fingers caress my stomach. "Now I'll take care of you, baby girl. I'll give you what you want."

"Yes, please," I beg. I need to come.

She slips her fingers behind my head, guiding my mouth to hers—her other hand slides down my body, aiming straight for my core. I tense in anticipation. My desire is almost where she left me, instantly filling with need. Her kiss becomes more intense, claiming me as hers. Her tongue swirls with mine. I want her to do that on other parts.

Catherine finally reaches my pussy. I groan into our kiss as two fingers slip inside my tightening core. Her hand pulls on the back of my neck, keeping me securely against her mouth. Her fingers thrust in and out of me. She presses her thumb against my clit. My head pushes back as I scream out.

"Fuck yes."

She increases her pace in my pussy. My body burns with desire and need. My skin tingles with lust. I'm going to explode for real. My body will disintegrate with arousal. My breathing is so fast. I can't get enough oxygen. I whimper as she drives me closer. I've never whimpered from need before. I've never felt this desperate, either.

"Come for me, baby girl," Catherine whispers. It's my undoing. My body soars through planes I didn't know existed. My mind goes silent as pleasure wracks my clenching body. I'm floating on the ceiling of the room, watching my body convulse beneath Catherine: my eyes close tightly, and pulses of fulfillment roll through my body. I fly through worlds that only know the most carnal joy.

As my body begins to settle, Catherine's finger grazes my body. A calmness I have never experienced settles over me. I can't open my eyes. I can't move my muscles. I am relaxed into a state of bliss. My fingers relax their tight grip on my bedsheets. I didn't realize I had grabbed them so hard. I take back everything I said about denial. If this is the orgasm I get from denial, I want it every time. I want nothing but this experience every time for the rest of my life.

My eyes crack open as Catherine drapes a blanket over my body. She brings over a water bottle with a straw, encouraging me to drink. I take a couple of small sips. She puts the bottle away then crawls into the space beside me. Her body is so warm, so welcoming. I curl into her as my mind returns to reality. I don't know how long that orgasm lasted, but it's definitely a personal record.

I move my hand over to Catherine, but my movements are jerky. My hand lands on her waist, and she chuckles at me. She doesn't stop me from touching her, but I'm not as smooth as her.

"Baby girl, just be still and relax. You did wonderfully for me. Enjoy that." She tugs me onto my side, wrapping her arms around my back, soothingly caressing my body. I drift off, unable to fight the calm settling from complete satisfaction. This is my new favorite place to be. In her arms, post-earth-shattering orgasm, that's my heaven.

11 · CATHERINE

Jo is absolutely amazing. No one before her has given me the control I desire. Brayden does well for me, but something about Jo is different. Watching her confidence bloom under my words is breathtaking. Her willingness to please me and follow my instructions fills my soul, even with some deviations. She is so perfect. I can see myself falling for her. I need to be careful. I can't drag her into my life.

Soft light is peeking through the curtains from the window. Gentle raindrops tap on the window outside. The clouds block most of the sun, darkening the room more than it should be despite the open curtains. The grey curtains tie the room together in a sleek aesthetic. Her style is similar to my own: clean, modern, minimal. Photos of her friends and family are propped on flat surfaces. She has more personal touches than I do. I keep my space clear to decompress. I don't have people I want to think about while I'm at home.

She shifts in my arms, stretching as she wakes up. I loosen my grip, pressing a kiss on her forehead. Sleep eludes me most nights, but waking up next to her wouldn't be bad. She mumbles something unintelligible and snuggles into my chest again. A soft chuckle escapes as I caress her back. She sighs contentedly.

"Do you always wear long sleeves?" Her words are muffled, and her fingers trail over my arms.

"Yes," I respond—the long sleeves cover secrets I don't want to share. I don't want her to know the secrets etched on my body.

"Does anyone see your body?"

"No."

"Not even Brayden?" Her voice is soft. She's hiding her face in my chest. She must not register how close to my breasts she is. I'm surprised she hasn't made a move for them. I grab her chin, turning her face up to mine.

"No, not even Brayden." Her eyes fill with something akin to relief, but she bites her lip, nibbling with worry. I tug it away with my thumb, stroking her cheek to calm her.

"How often do you see him?"

"Once a week." Very few people know about my appointments with Brayden. They help me clear my head, especially during crazy weeks. It's easy to remain disconnected from him. He provides a service and is paid well for it. He offers what I refuse to find in relationships. That is, until I met Jo.

She nods, snuggling against me again. Her body is tense. She still has more questions but isn't asking. I wait patiently, unsure if she is thinking about what to say or nervous to voice it. I kiss her forehead, unable to avoid the intimacy.

"Do you see him when you are in a relationship?" Her words are soft and unsure. She doesn't sound jealous but anxious over asking.

"I don't have relationships."

"Oh," she nods, pulling away from me. It hits me how that sounds to her. I grab her wrist, not letting her leave the bed.

"I haven't had a relationship. I..." I pause. Do I tell her the truth? That my life is so dangerous any partners would have targets on their backs. That being associated with me could put her at risk. That my business could be ruined at any moment by mobs, feds, or any number of people. I can't tell her all of that. I stroke her hand, thinking through different options to tell her.

"I have secrets. Secrets I don't share. I don't get close to people to keep them safe." She sits on the bed next to me. I push up to join her. She keeps her hand in mine, staring at where we connect.

"Will you get close to me?" Her voice is so meek it crushes something in my soul. I don't want to get close to her. I don't want to risk her safety. But can I honestly stay away from her? No. I cannot do that. I need her like I need air. I can keep a low profile with her if we go out in groups or only meet in her apartment. Entering her building without her will be less noticeable. I could be here to see anyone. I can see her at the office, too. I keep a set of toys there. She could come in early like Brayden. Or late. I could make that work.

"Yes." My breathy response causes her to jerk her eyes to mine. The corner of her lips turns up slowly, delight brightening her face. She's ethereal when she's happy. Her yellow and red hair creates a halo of fire, adding to her magical feel. I lean in and kiss her cheek. She squeezes my hand in response.

"Could I play with Brayden sometime?" Her sudden shift sends my mind spiraling. I'm not used to feeling this stunned. This question is coming out of left field. I don't know where that came from, but visions of her and Brayden following my instructions fill my mind. We could have a lot of fun together.

"Is that something you want?" Her cheeks blush, but she doesn't break my gaze.

"Maybe. Do you treat him the way you did me last night?" I chuckle. This girl is fantastic.

"Not exactly the same. I give him instructions, but I tend to be more hands-off." An idea strikes suddenly. "What do you think about playing with him two weeks from now? I need to check with him, but I have an excellent idea for us." Her eyes light up as a grin slowly rises on her face.

"Um, yeah. Okay." She nods enthusiastically. "I think I would like that." She pulls my hand to her lips, kissing gently. She's so sweet and delicate. "I'm going to make you breakfast now since you made dinner last night." She tries to crawl out of bed, but I hold her hand tight, not letting her leave.

"Before you do that, I need one thing from you." Confusion knits her eyebrows together, but she doesn't argue. "Put your robe back on." Her face scrunches, but she does as told. She side-eyes me while I grab a new toy from my bag. I settle on the edge of the bed, waving her over to me. "Do you know what this is?" The flat round toy has two bumps with ridges in different areas, like a plate with small hills.

"Um, I'm not sure." She looks between the toy displayed in my hand and my face. She's still perplexed, but a hint of excitement sparkles in her eyes. I press a button on the bottom of the grind pad, which vibrates briefly then stops. I place it on my thigh, looking up at Jo. Her eyes are wide as she realizes what this toy is for. Her chest rises and falls quickly, excitement coursing through her body.

"You are going to make yourself come on my thigh, baby girl."

I reach up to her cheek, stroking her thumb as I pull her face to me. My lips meet hers gently, rubbing my tongue along her lips. She tastes like the first crisp spring morning when everything is new and fresh and full of life. Her hands grab either side of my face, deepening our kiss. I slip my tongue in her mouth, making lazy circles around hers. She thrusts her tongue, wanting more from this kiss. She's so desperate for me, but I won't give that to her. I'm not going to drag this out like last night, but I won't rush it either.

My hand slides out to her thigh, stroking up to her core. She is far away from me, bending over to kiss me instead of lowering over my leg. She widens her stance as my fingers glide over her inner thigh. I slip one through her core. She's so wet and excited. Her responsiveness fills me with undeniable pleasure. I force my finger deep inside her, hooking it and pulling her closer to me. She moans, breaking the kiss as I pull her in.

"Baby girl, I already told you what to do. Do I need to repeat myself?"

Doubt covers her face. She doesn't think she can sit on my thigh. I grab her hips with both hands, squeezing her tightly.

"Have I given you any reason to doubt me?"

She doesn't say anything. Jo shakes her head after a moment. I pull her down onto my lap, letting her get comfortable. One arm wraps around her back while I grab the remote with the other. She settles over me, wiggling her ass. My hand drops to squeeze her. Fuck, she's perfect. I click the button, setting the toy to vibrate at a low speed.

"Oh fuck, Kitty."

Her head tips back, and I lean in to kiss her exposed chest. I trail my fingers over her back, tugging the material. The bottom of the robe rises over Jo's ass while she grinds against my thigh. Her hands rest on my shoulders, stabilizing herself while she moves. She swirls her hips around, letting the ridges of the toy hit different areas of her cunt. Shit, I need to see that.

I untie Jo's robe, letting it fall open. A small patch of hair presses against my leg. The pink toy peeks through as she rocks over it. I love using this toy, but I almost hate that it's not my hand bringing her pleasure. Almost. Her face twists with her impending orgasm. I grab her side, squeezing her curves. Her skin rolls beneath my fingers, jostling under her movements. She grabs the back of my head, shoving me between her breasts.

"Bite me. I'm so close. Please, Kitty."

Very few people force me the way Jo just did, but I won't deny my girl when she asks nicely.

"Anything for you, baby girl."

I sink my teeth into her breasts, increasing the speed of the toy. She yells out, jerking erratically. It's not an orgasm, but she's very close. Keeping one hand on her back to stabilize her, I press my lips over the spot I just bit. I kiss her breast several times, increasing the speed once more. She groans loudly, tipping her head back in pleasure. I watch her for a moment, then chomp down on her other nipple. She screams, but the sound quickly stops. She lunges forward, landing on my shoulder as her body shakes through the waves of her orgasm. Her hips jerk wildly as the toy vibrates under her.

She moans when another wave washes over her. Her body tenses and relaxes. Jo buries her face against my neck and whimpers. "Rise up, baby girl." I guide her up just a few inches, slipping the toy from under her. I shift my leg, placing both between hers. I tug her hips, encouraging her to sit on my lap. I don't think she would if she wasn't so overwhelmed with ecstasy right now. Her body molds to mine. Her head rests on my shoulders, chest against mine, thighs perfectly wrapped around my own. It's like she was made just for me. She's meant to be here, against my body.

I hold Jo tight, not letting her go as her body calms down. I stroke her back, soothing her. She giggles against my neck. I pause my touch, worried I've tickled her. That isn't my intention.

"Is it always that good?" She leans back to look at my face. Her body is exposed, and the robe is still untied. Both breasts hang out, resting against her stomach. I drag my eyes back to her face, where I find glazed eyes and flushed cheeks.

"Yes," I whisper and lean in to kiss her. This date has been better than I imagined. I don't even mind considering it a date at this point.

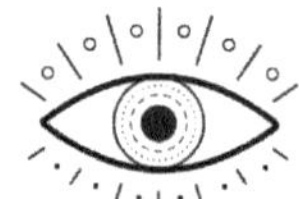

It's been four days since I was with Jo—four days of riding a high I have never experienced before. I've lost track of time, missed conference calls, and haven't run since last week. I'm not an avid runner. I use it as a tool to decompress after long days or stressful events. I haven't felt the need to run in the past few days.

Brayden slips his jeans over his ass. He has a perfectly round ass. I hate seeing him cover it, but it looks phenomenal in jeans. I didn't touch Brayden today. I let him pleasure himself while I gave instructions. I don't need to take from him like I usually do. I'm content just watching. He doesn't mind. He's so malleable.

"What would you think about having another person with us next week?" His eyebrows raise over his shoulder, surprised at my question.

"Is it the girl from last week?" I nod. He considers as he ties his shoes.

"Sure. I'm good with that."

"Perfect. Come here."

He walks around the desk to stand in front of me. His waist is right in front of my face. I tug the belt loops, lowering his jeans briefly.

"What are you... oh, not this again!" He groans, tipping his head back as I pull out the metal cage.

"You know I won't put it on you if you don't want it." His weight shifts from foot to foot as he considers. He knows it will be worth it; we have played with a cage before. I have already cleared all of this with Enrico. Despite Enrico's position as a pimp, he is uneducated in many sexual actions. I had to explain the cage the first time I used it. Even this time, I had to remind him how it works so he could adjust Brayden's schedule accordingly. I paid extra for the cage and again to have Jo participate with us. It'll be worth it, though.

"Yes," he sighs. "Yes, Catherine. You know I want to do it. I hate the week, but the payoff is always worth it." I grin, sliding my fingers over his soft cock.

"Good boy." I kiss his stomach, drop the cage on the desk, and grab the lube. He tips his head to the ceiling as I smear the gel over his flaccid penis and the cage.

"Don't get hard. Don't get hard. Don't get hard." Brayden's whispers make me chuckle. His job is to get hard. Staying soft while I manipulate him, even after an orgasm, can be a challenge. The cage locks in place, and I grab a wipe to clean my hands. He tugs the pants up, adjusting so the cage isn't as noticeable in the tight jeans. "Shit, I'm gonna have to go change pants now." The cage itself isn't apparent, but his package bulges more than before.

"This girl better be worth it," he teases.

"She is."

He kisses my cheek, and I hand him two envelopes. One contains the money for Enrico, with extra for the cage and Jo. The other is a tip nearly triple what I normally give. He deserves it for putting up with my antics. He walks out of the door with a nod as my phone rings. It's Harpo, my hacker. He lives in San Antonio. I met him before he moved down there. He starts speaking as soon as I accept the call.

"The party is Saturday night. Did you see the location?" I tap on my tablet, opening an app he set me up with. He can share secure information with me, including locations.

"Yes. I have it. What intel do you have?"

"Surprisingly little security outside. The product is in the basement." I scroll through the details of the building, making notes of the layout.

"Can you get me a car?"

"Working on it now."

"And what time does it start?" Jo is standing outside my window and knocks against it. I wave her inside, knowing this conversation is almost over.

"Eight, bidding starts at eleven."

"Perfect. I'll be in Minneapolis this weekend, then." The phone disconnects as Jo sits in the seat across from my desk. I click a few more things on my tablet, finalizing plans for this sudden trip.

"Did you talk to Brayden?" She is unsure of herself again, but I'll fix that again soon. I can stay with her tomorrow night before I leave.

"Yes. He's willing. We'll see him next week. I planned for Tuesday, but I need to push it back to Wednesday. I'm going to Minneapolis this weekend." Jo wiggles to the edge of her seat. Her fingers fidget in her lap. She won't look at me, instead biting her lip. She wants to go with me but is scared to ask. I place my tablet on the desk, rolling my shoulders back. I tighten my lips, stopping the grin from spreading.

"Ask me, Jo." Her eyes shoot up to mine. She hesitates, looking around the room. I give her a look, begging her to defy me. I wonder how many orgasms I could get out of her before work starts.

"Could I go with you?" She asks calmly, but the next part comes quickly, rushing to get the words out before she loses her confidence. "I can stay with my parents. You don't have to get me a room or anything. You can even leave me in the hotel lobby, and I'll take an Uber to their house. Then I can meet you back at your hotel before we go home for the weekend. You could probably come to have dinner with them if you want. Or maybe I could cook for you while they go out. I can pay for gas and snacks for the drive, too. I just haven't been home and don't have a car, and it's expensive to fly." Her shoulders droop when she finishes speaking. I can't suppress the smile any longer. This girl is something special.

"Yes, you can come with me, Jo. You can stay with me instead of your parents. I have a condo there. I don't need money for gas or snacks. I have plans Saturday night, but I will do whatever you want the rest of the time." She grins, bouncing in her seat. This woman is literally bouncing in front of me. I don't know how she can be that excited about traveling to Minnesota. I never enjoy these trips. Maybe this time it will be an enjoyable experience for me, too.

"Really? You don't mind?" Her face is full of hope and excitement. She's so adorable.

"No, I don't mind." I wink at her, grabbing my tablet. "Anything for you, baby girl." She giggles, swooning under my words. She loves being called my baby girl, and I love treating her like mine.

12 · JOSEPHINE

STANDING IN THE LOBBY of my apartment complex, I bounce from foot to foot, waiting for Catherine to show up. I have everything arranged for this weekend. Sadie, my bitch of a best friend, is out of town this weekend. I'm seeing one of my friends from college on Saturday. On Sunday, I'm spending the day with my parents. They are going to a show that evening, so I'll make dinner for Catherine while they are out. It'll be a great weekend.

A sleek, black, old-school muscle car parks in front of my building. I half expect Dean Winchester to climb out and rush inside, looking for demons or something. As I'm swooning over that thought, Catherine steps out of the driver's side and opens the trunk. Catherine. She's the one driving this tantalizing vehicle.

Fuck, she looks every bit the owner of it too. She has dark pants with a leather jacket and hair pinned back from her face. She leans against the car, crossing her arms and ankles. She's phenomenal and knows it. Catherine oozes power and money. Suddenly, I feel out of place in my cotton pants and hoodie. I dressed for comfort for the seven-hour drive. Catherine looks like she belongs on the cover of some car magazine. Or even a fashion magazine. Gods, I would go into debt buying those magazines.

My brain starts calculating the amount of debt I would acquire purchasing said magazines with this woman on the cover. She's stunning. Everything about her is power, sex, money. She raises her hand to push a stray hair back from her face. No, wait. She's waving at me. Oh hell. I've been staring this whole time. Of course, she wouldn't have stray hair. My body jolts into action as I walk out to the car. My cheeks burn. I want to blame the chilled air, but that's a lie. The tingles between my legs prove that.

"Good morning, baby girl." A smile creeps over her face. Even her soft words promise seduction and orgasms. "Is it too early for you?" She's teasing me, and I want more of it.

"Coffee." I blurt the single word from my lips. It's not early. This is the time I usually go to work. I shouldn't be this unfocused. Catherine laughs, tossing my weekend bag in the trunk and slamming it. The sudden sound causes me to jerk. Her hand lands on my back as she kisses my cheek.

"Anything for my baby girl. Slide in." She guides me into the passenger seat and shuts the door behind me. So chivalrous.

After a quick stop at my favorite coffee shop, she drives us onto the interstate. This car is sleek and sensual. Everything about this car screams sex. The bench seats are black leather, probably Italian. The paint is shiny; it looks like you could slide across the hood smoothly with a bare ass. The only thing I can think of is starring in my own Whitesnake video. How mad would Catherine be if I climbed out of the window while she's traveling 80 miles an hour?

"I didn't think you'd be the type to drive a car like this."

Catherine glances at me briefly, keeping her eyes on the road. She's a very diligent driver.

"I originally bought this car for John. He likes to fix old cars. He mentioned wanting a Chevelle. So, I bought one. I use it on occasion, but he's the one that put all the work in." Damn. My heart flutters at her kindness. She bought a car just for her driver.

"Why isn't he driving?" I haven't seen her drive. I assumed she didn't.

"I gave him the weekend off. I don't take drivers on these weekend trips."

"So, you have the grey sedan for driving around and this Chevelle for your driver. Any other cars you're hiding from me? A Porsche? Some other foreign imported car?" I know nothing about cars. That's probably obvious as I slide my hand over the dash, taking in all the knobs and buttons.

"I have two others." Her playful smirk tells me the other two aren't vehicles I would expect. "I have an electric vehicle and a Harley." Yep, didn't expect that.

"A Harley? Like the motorcycle?" Her laughter is full of delight.

"Yes. A motorcycle."

She reaches over, unbuckling my seatbelt. Before shock sets in, she tells me to slide over next to her. I obey, pressing into her side. Her hand slides over my leg, causing my body to tingle with anticipation. She glides over my knee, down my calf, leaving heat everywhere she touches. The disappointment when she hands me an auxiliary cord is unprecedented.

"Start some music, baby girl." Dismay is written across my face. Here I was, expecting some road sex in this car that drips with salacious intent. Catherine has had a smirk on her face since we left Kansas City. I plug in my phone, starting my favorite playlist with various songs.

Catherine places her hand on my thigh. My expectant body betrays me with arousal. Her hand slides slowly across my leg, with enough pressure to make her touch ambiguous. Is she being friendly? Am I going to get some road sex? I chew on my lip as I watch the small hills roll by. Rock structures splattered between fields. My body tingles under her touch. I try to focus on those stupid rocks instead of the growing ache in my core.

"Baby girl," her voice is husky, almost a whisper, "did you think I wouldn't take care of you?"

Her hand rises higher until she reaches the apex of my thigh. I moan and slink down in my seat to spread my legs for her. The gear shifter is on the floor, so I don't have much room for my legs. I stretch one into the passenger side, twisting just enough to give her access. Catherine strokes my pussy over my pants expertly. She uses just enough pressure to arouse me but not to bring me to orgasm. Her hand slips away, reaching into her jacket pocket.

"What good is a long drive without an orgasm or two?"

I huff at her comment, unable to use any words. Her face is beautiful. Relaxed but stoic. In charge but teasing. This woman is perfect. Catherine lifts my shirt, slipping her fingers into my waistband. She makes the awkward move look like the most natural thing in the world. Is this something she does a lot? She said she doesn't have a lot of partners, but damn, that was smooth.

Before the doubt sinks in, her finger finds my cunt. She rubs the outside, torturing me thoroughly. She knows exactly how to touch to create the effect she wants. She has a mastery of my body that I don't even have. She caresses my lips, slipping one finger in between. My core tingles as she explores my opening. Her eyes stay on the road, seemingly unaffected. I, however, am a puddle of need beside her. Melting into the seat, liquified by desire. Barely avoiding humping her hand.

Another finger slips through my soaking core. I close my eyes, savoring the touch. Her fingers glide between my wet lips like fish in the sea. Just as I settle into her hand, the vibration sends a shock through my body. I nearly jolt out of the car.

"Son of a biscuit-eating shit bag!" I cry out as my pussy clenches around her fingers. Her eyes dart to mine, watching with concern and excitement. "I didn't know you had a toy." My voice is breathy like I've just run ten blocks. That smirk spreads across her face as her hand swirls the bullet vibrator against my clit.

"Fuck, Kitty." I moan, pleasure rolling through my body. I stare at the black fabric roof, but my mind is shrouded in arousal, buried in a sea of Catherine's touch. Her arm creates pressure across my body. Her fingers work inside my cunt while her palm keeps the vibrator against my clit. I turn my face into her arm, clutching it with both hands. I'm scared my body will slip away, float into the sky of Missouri, then land in some fucking cornfield.

Catherine leans closer, her fingers pushing in deeper, the toy forced harder against me. She whispers, "Come for me, baby girl." Holy hell, I love it when she calls me that. It erases all my doubts about her abilities and previous partners. I'm hers. She will take care of me.

My body tips over the edge. I tremble with pleasure as she draws out every last bit and then some. Never satisfied with just one orgasm, she works me relentlessly until my body is uncontrollable. I'm giggling. I'm screaming. I'm soaring with delight. My body is shrouded with pleasure.

Catherine removes her hand, slipping it into her jacket, before wrapping it over my shoulders again. I adjust my clothing, settling into her side. She kisses the side of my head, and I swoon under her. The world around me slowly returns. We're close to Iowa now. From here on, there are only bare corn fields and silos. It's the worst stretch of this drive.

"So, you haven't had many partners?" I ask, wanting to know her better. We still have at least five hours on the road.

"Not romantic partners. Plenty of play partners." She glances behind her before shifting lanes. So serious while driving.

"Play partners like Brayden?" She gives a slight nod, speeding up to pass a truck.

"Have you had many partners?"

"Four," I reply.

"All women?" She spares a glance at that question. I sit up, moving closer to her height.

"No, actually. One woman, one man. A nonbinary person and a trans woman."

"Hm, quite a diverse background."

I didn't go into the relationships with the intent of dating diversely. I just found interesting people I wanted to be with. I'm still friends with all of them except the man. I learned a lot from each relationship, glad for the experience.

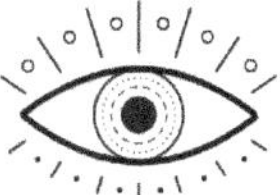

"YOU DON'T HAVE TO go to lunch with me. It's just a friend from college. I know you have your party tonight. That I'm not invited to." Catherine laughs at my ramblings while I slip into skinny jeans and a sweater in her bedroom. She won't tell me anything about the party other than it won't be fun, and I'm not allowed to go. I don't particularly appreciate being told I can't do something. But she told me I could order whatever delivery I wanted. I've never had unlimited access to delivery. I plan to take full advantage of that perk.

"I want to go with you. I still have several hours before I need to meet my friend for the party. I want to spend that with you," Catherine replies. Be still my heart. She's still my boss and still way older than me. I shouldn't fall this hard or this fast.

We walk down the street, crisp air hinting at the looming winter ahead. The first snow may fall in a couple of weeks. In Minnesota, it could snow in October or not until January. It's anyone's guess. It's still cold outside, regardless. I huddle close to Catherine as we walk close to the building, trying to fight against the chilly wind. I repeat the Midwest motto: it wouldn't be so bad if it weren't for the wind. Stupid wind.

The bar I'm meeting my friend at is a local brewery filled with hipsters in thick-rimmed glasses and classic Minnesota moms, the kind that makes a dozen different hot dishes to bring to a potluck. Nostalgia settles in my body, glad to be back in my home state. I don't realize how homesick I am until I spot a dad with khaki pants and those classic white New Balances.

"Josie!" My friend calls, waving me down from the back wall. I lead Catherine to her table. Catherine raises her eyebrow at me as my friend rushes to meet me. In college, everyone called us Josie and Rosie. It's the only time I've ever gone by that nickname.

Rosie's short stature and long brown wavy hair flood me with memories of that time. Despite very different degrees, we shared a dorm room. She introduced me to a group of friends that became my own. Even after she graduated and settled down with her partners, we stayed in touch, getting together frequently. We hug tightly, an embrace to make up for the missed time.

"Rosie, this is Catherine. She's my boss. Catherine, this is Rosie. We were roomies in college."

"Nice to meet you," Rosie says, reaching to shake Catherine's hand. They shake hands, and Catherine guides me into a chair beside Rosie's.

"Take a seat, and I'll go grab some drinks." I settle next to Rosie, slipping my coat off.

"Oh my god, Rosie. You have to tell me everything. You've been MIA on social media since your dad was arrested. What has been going on?" She chuckles, rolling her eyes.

"Things have calmed down a lot. My father is serving several years in prison. We worked things out with James after his article about Martin broke out. James struggled with knowing his article led to my father's arrest. Things were rocky for a bit." She sips her beer, clearly thinking about her relationship with her boyfriend. A couple of years ago, she started dating a journalist. He wrote an article about a business owner breaking all kinds of laws. Neither of them realized it was Rosie's father, Martin, until it was published. I notice she is calling him both Martin and Father. It must be a difficult transition to settle on what to call him.

She shakes her head, telling me about the rest of her partners. "Addy is still working, saving to buy the bar she works at. Megs is getting top surgery." An excited shock simmers through me. Megs is nonbinary. I knew them in college, but they always stayed close to Rosie or Addy. Megs is shy and socially awkward. It's why Rosie loves them. Addy has been Rosie's best friend since childhood. They have a relationship similar to mine and Sadie's. Only I don't have sex with Sadie.

"Oh, really? What made them want to do that?" Rosie shrugs, sipping her beer before answering. Catherine sits next to me, placing a beer in front of me. I give her a quick smile then turn my attention back to Rosie.

"Megs has worn binders for a long time. I think they just realized having their breasts removed is an option. They're working on getting enough money to pay for it. Addy offered her savings, but it's expensive. James was sad over it but still supportive. Megs won't take Addy's savings, but we're all pitching in to help." I love their relationship. It gives me all the warm fuzzies. I lean to Catherine.

"Rosie is in a poly relationship with three other people." Catherine smiles appreciatively.

"I haven't met someone in a relationship like that. Is it more difficult than monogamy?" I didn't expect Catherine to be rude, but to be inquisitive fills me with giddiness.

"I don't think so," Rosie shrugs. "It's nice that there is always someone around. Different opinions to seek. Different personalities."

"I'm surprised Addy is willing to share. I didn't think she'd share you with anyone." Addy was possessive of Rosie in college. Megs was the only other person Addy would let get close to Rosie. She chuckles at me. The three of them have been together since high school. James came into the picture a couple of years ago while hanging around Addy's bar.

"I don't think she would have a long-term relationship with anyone other than James. He's special." Her eyes glaze over. I can see little hearts floating around her. I'm so happy for her. She deserves all the happiness the world has to offer.

We chat about everything else going on. Where her parents are. How Marzanna is working out for me. Which is obviously great since not only is the boss with me, but I've got my first design in a show soon. What Kansas City is like. How Rosie is handling being a grade school teacher. It's so easy to talk with Rosie. That's how we became such good friends. Catherine gets several texts throughout our conversation but still stays focused. I don't know how she divides her attention like that. I'm all or nothing in one conversation.

Her phone rings, and she hits the button to answer it. She kisses my cheek and whispers she'll be right back. I watch her walk away. She has a power strut. Her long legs and tall stature prowl through the room, slicing through the crowd with ease. My body cools with her absence. Her arm was around my shoulder or on my thigh possessively.

"Josie, how old is she?" Rosie's scandalized whisper draws my attention. I can't help the schoolgirl giggle I have over mentioning Catherine.

"Sadie asked the same thing. She's 41." Rosie smirks, shaking her head.

"Are you sure you want to do this with your boss? Is that a good idea?" I laugh loudly.

"Am I known for having good ideas? Have you seen her legs? Fuck." We both laugh as Catherine walks back.

"You sound like Addy," Rosie chirps. Addy is the overly sexual one in her polycule, always making lewd comments. That's why I love Addy. I agree with Rosie; it's a true statement and something Addy would say. I shrug while Catherine grabs her jacket, and Rosie slinks to the bathroom.

"I need to leave, baby girl. I'll be back late tonight. You'll have the condo to yourself. Do you want me to call an Uber for you? I can give you a ride before I leave." I grab her shoulder.

"I'll be okay. I'm a big girl." She eyes me suspiciously but kisses me. I return the kiss. It feels different than other times. This isn't a lazy one. She's connecting with me on a different level.

"Be in bed before I get back." I roll my eyes at her.

"Yes, mommy." I tease seductively. She stares at me warily but kisses my cheek before leaving. I've never been into kinks, quite content with mostly vanilla sex. Clearly, I should have been learning kink the whole time. I've tapped into something based on the warmth spreading through my body.

13 · CATHERINE

Liam is one of my best bodyguards. He doesn't need to be told how to do his job. I can't leave without saying it, though. He will do everything he can to protect Jo, but I don't want to take risks. I have never had someone who wasn't involved in my efforts accompany me on these trips. I can't afford to worry about her tonight. With Liam, I won't have to. He will ensure her safety for the rest of the evening.

I meet Harpo in a small, seemingly abandoned building on the east side of Minneapolis. His nickname is short for Harpocrates, the Greek god of silence, secrets, and confidentiality. He's good at his job, and that's all I need. He is tech-savvy and my favorite hacker. He set up this building in a dummy corp that won't be traced back to me. Harpo helped me set up most of the equipment and how to process the needed information.

"Is the car ready?"

"Yes," he replies, nodding over his shoulder, where a sedan is parked. I glance at it as I pull on my black skinny jeans. Usually, I never wear jeans, but they are more practical for tonight. I also have a black hoodie and black combat boots. Jo would thoroughly enjoy my outfit tonight. She has commented on my outfits before, especially my more casual ones. I layer my clothes to create more bulk and distort my figure. The bulletproof vest also adds bulk and offers protection. I hope I won't need it tonight.

Harpo is surprisingly muscular for a hacker. Before I met him in person, I expected a skinny guy with acne and bad posture. He's the opposite. He works out to counteract the hours he spends on his computer. He also wears black, even though he will be in the car the whole time.

This building doesn't have any street cameras pointed near its entrances. It makes for stealthy arrivals and departures. Harpo verified that when I bought it and checks every time we use it. I don't know how he manages to hack all the cameras, but I don't care. I leave my Chevelle here, using the black sedan with fake, covered license plates to drive to the party.

Harpo rides with me, updating me on the security situation. He has been monitoring this event, but things can always change at the last minute. He will wait in the car while I take care of business. We leave the building and drive down a highway with car dealers and expensive buildings on either side. The scenery slowly changes from business to private property. Gates and manicured lawns grow more prominent the further we travel. Wealth grows exponentially as we drive up the side of the hill surrounding a lake.

The party is located at a mansion on a lake. The backyard is expansive but is covered by trees on the sides. Thankfully, the elite enjoy their privacy. The house is lit up; they are clearly hosting a party tonight. It doesn't look nearly as nefarious as it is. Money buys a lot of things, including seclusion. After Harpo drops me off and parks down the street, I slink through the trees, keeping an eye out for guards. A few walk around with guns attached to their hips, not nearly as many as there should be. Another thing money affords is complacency in illegal activities.

I reach the back corner with an entrance to the basement and huddle near the side to watch the guards for a few minutes. From my spot, I can see the room where the guns are stored. Angelo has kept this shipment hidden since it came through my warehouse. Some of the bigger guns will be auctioned off at the party tonight, while the rest are sold in bulk. Typically, sales occur at the street level. This shipment was different, though. It was intended for high-end buyers. The mafia boss in Spain spent a lot of money to ensure the success of this party.

The guards' rotation allows me a few minutes to sneak into the basement. This place will be crawling with elite criminals in another hour or two. My work needs to be quick. I tiptoe through, ensuring my hood stays tight and my black mask covers my face. This grows harder with age. I stay active to ensure I can do this, but it is still hard on my body. I'm not as young as I used to be, and my knees and hips often ache. Not tonight, though.

The only door in the hallway is locked but easily picked. I step in quietly, close it, and lock it behind me. Most guns are on a table, while some hang on the walls. My task is simple: disassemble the weapons, remove the firing pins, put them back together, and leave. Easy enough. I've practiced in my free time at home since I formed this plan with Harpo. Angelo will pay, just as I promised.

I work through the guns. They are all well-maintained and ready to be inspected. This works well for me because they are easy to break down and put back together quickly. I'm a little over halfway through the guns when a key enters the lock on the door. Fuck. No one was supposed to come in here. The room has already been secured.

I abandon the gun and pad to the side of the door. I dig in one of my pockets. I laced a rag with chloroform just in case this happened. It wasn't supposed to, but it's better to be prepared. I'm not at a great angle when he opens the door, but I have the element of surprise. I grab his mouth with the rag and tug him away from the door. It takes longer than I would like, but it goes unnoticed. The man falls limp, and I guide him to the floor. I lock the door and return to my work.

I don't have much time left. With the guard down, someone is likely to notice his absence. I just need to get out of here with my bag of firing pins. I grab a gun, remove the handle, get the firing pin, carefully reassemble it, and move on to the next. I repeat this as quickly as possible, trying not to think about the man lying on the floor near me.

I finally reassemble the last gun. I shove the bag of firing pins in my jacket pocket, ensuring everything is where it is supposed to be. I must return to Harpo unnoticed before anyone finds the guard I took down. No big deal. Breathe in, breathe out.

I peek in the hallway and don't see anyone. No one will notice me; it's dark enough here, but the door is across an empty, brightly lit living space. I watch for a moment, trying to find any other guards. I don't see anyone and decide to make a run for it. I rush to the door and pull it open. I run around the corner, pausing to scan this area. A guard stands at the corner, but they won't spot me if I creep.

I creep along the wall, quiet and crouched, and watch the yard. Static breaks through the silence as a man speaks over the guards' walkie-talkies.

"We just found Brad down in the room! Watch for an intruder!" Damn. The guards search the area. I huddle lower and creep closer to the edge of the house. When I reach the front yard, I make a run for it. Harpo is waiting for me in the car. As long as I can reach him, I'll be fine. I see the car now. I'm so close.

A hand lands on my shoulder and spins me around. Two other guards are behind him, rushing toward us. One man runs into the street, firing his gun at the car. He either has terrible aim or is firing too erratically because he misses by a mile. The tires squeal as the car rushes away. This is our backup plan. Harpo will drive about half a mile away, and I'll make my way to him. It's more important that he get out safely to cover our tracks.

The guard in front of me swings his fist, but I duck. While down, I grab the knife from my boot, thrusting it into the man's abdomen as I rise. I tug as hard as I can, ripping through his intestines. Blood sprays from his midsection, showering me in a hot stream of copper-smelling liquid. He screams and wraps his arms around his stomach. He topples to the ground, curling into the fetal position. He'll be dead soon. He will bleed out before anyone will try to help him.

Another guard is approaching me. I need to get away from these men quickly. Behind me, the guard with the gun is aiming toward me. Running to either side puts me in danger of being shot in the back. I'm trapped at this point. The guards are shouting, trying to call for backup. If this is my end, I hope I go quickly, but I know I will be tortured. My only wish is that they don't find Jo.

Well, this event has gone from bad to worse. Shots have already been fired, so it's time for my last resort. I grab my gun from my waist. I don't use it unless absolutely necessary. Guns are too loud. I fire one round directly at the guard running at me. It hits him square in the forehead. Brain matter sprays from the back of his head as his body crumples to the ground, surrounded by a quickly growing pool of blood. I don't have time to marvel at the amount.

I spin, firing at the guard behind me. He is quicker, already aiming at me. His gun blasts. A searing pain rips through my left shoulder, my shooting arm. My hand drops with the pain burning in my flesh. I nearly drop my gun but recover it with my other hand. The guard is running toward me, thinking he will apprehend me. Not on my watch, buddy. I raise my right arm, firing several shots. One goes wild. A second hits him in his chest, the third in his neck. He falls, gurgling as he bleeds out.

More guards run from the house, but still far enough away. I sprint down the roads, darting through a backyard on the other side of the street. I studied the maps relentlessly before this trip. Situations like this are always a possibility. Occasionally, Harpo and I will ruin a shipment of drugs. Those don't take as much time, but we are always prepared for shit to go sideways.

My arms pound, pain radiating through my chest, but adrenaline keeps me moving. Harpo's sedan is at the corner we agreed on. None of the guards were able to keep up with me. I may be getting older, but I'm not weak. Harpo opens the front door, and I dive inside. He stomps on the gas hard enough the door slams behind me. I adjust in my seat, sitting up straighter and breathing heavily.

"Drop me at the building."

"Are you sure?" Harpo glances over me, taking in my bleeding shoulder. I'm covered in a staggering amount of blood, but it's not all mine. We have a doctor on call who will help us, but I am ready to get away from this. The shoulder wound isn't deep. I can stitch it myself later. I don't want to spend time waiting for the doctor. I nod to Harpo, wincing at the tug on my shoulder. Adrenaline is still coursing through my body. I do what I can to hold it together. Now isn't the time to break down.

Harpo drops me on the street before my building, and I head inside. It's been years since I have done a mission in Minneapolis. I only do a couple a year to keep the heat off me. The risk of being caught is too significant. The information we track will go to other groups closer to the final deliveries. I work with a group in Minneapolis to deal with the drugs, but they don't deal with the guns. This is a new beast for me.

A text chimes on my phone from the bag I left here. I pull my phone, toss the bag in the front seat of my Chevelle, and check the messages. I have a few texts from Jo and one from Harpo. I reply to Harpo first, letting him know I am safe and will check in later. We may not be overly close, but we always check in when we work these missions together. I like working with him.

I check the texts from Jo next. She told me she got to the condo safe. Then she sent a photo in a fluffy white robe with a bottle of vodka. I keep the condo stocked with various liquors. Vodka isn't one I drink, but it's nice to have on hand. The Minneapolis condo is one of the few places I allow others to visit. Several other photos follow the first, each with less clothing and more provocative than the previous. I close the chat, unable to respond or garner the emotion to react. My body is still numb, high on adrenaline and cortisol.

Like every other mission, the vast emptiness of the trip home is filled with dark memories. Like smoke filling a room, my mind darkens as my traumas replay. My body moves on autopilot, driving through the city to return to my condo.

"No, Don. You can't play in my house." My doll kicks her boyfriend out of her fancy house for the second time this evening. Isabelle doesn't need a man in her life.

I toss the Don doll on the floor, placing Isabelle on her couch to watch a movie with her other doll friend. The door downstairs opens and slams loudly. I start at the sudden sound. Mama didn't mention any guests coming tonight. Not that they tell me. I'm only eight. Why should I know who's coming to visit after dinner?

The yelling isn't normal. Mama screams as glass shatters in the room. I should go to the safe room. That's what Daddy always says. "Go to the safe room if you are scared." I'm definitely scared now, but Mama could be in danger. What if it's just a game, and I get stuck in the safe room? Last month, Daddy's guard, Gabriel, got locked in the room for hours. The lock broke, and they couldn't open the door. Daddy was angry and said the company rigged it to malfunction. He said they were working for the other family.

I'm not stupid. I know my Daddy is in the mafia. He thinks I'm stupid and don't know anything. But I'm not. Secret passages are part of this house. Hidden in the walls behind wood panels. I found them when I was still little and playing hide and seek. Now, I use them to spy on Daddy.

I don't hear Daddy's voice downstairs. Mama screams again. Feet shuffle on the floor while men yell at her. I sneak through the hallway, slipping into one of the secret tunnels that will take me downstairs. I walk through the tunnel that leads to our dining room. This room has a slot with a sliding door to peek into the room. Daddy has meetings here sometimes, and I listen through this slot. No one has noticed before.

The men drag Mama into the room, shoving the large table to the side. Another man throws the chairs across the room. One crashes into the wall not far from me. I gasp, covering my mouth with my hands. If Mama is in danger, I will be too. I don't think they heard me. They force Mama into the chair and tie her with rope. She spits at one of the men. He punches her in the face. Tears blur my vision. Mama glares at the man.

"Where is Giuseppe?" Mama glares at him but doesn't respond. He slaps her with the back of his hand. She cries out. When she lifts her head again, her lips are bleeding.

"Where does he keep the guns?" Mama just glares. He slaps again. This time, her nose bleeds.

"Where are the drugs?" Silence. Slap. Blood.

"Where did he take Marco?" Stare. Smack. Drip. Why isn't Mama answering? Tell the men what they want! They'll let her go, and we can tell Daddy. He'll fix this. He always does. I wipe away my tears with the lace collar. I hate wearing these stupid dresses. Mama says I look beautiful in them, but they are stupid.

The man punches Mama in the stomach, and she bends over. Tears are streaming down my face. I can't stop them. She raises her head to the man, spitting again. Blood splatters across his face.

"Fine. You can deliver a message for us if you won't tell me."

The man pulls a knife from his waist. My breathing stops. He doesn't need a knife for Mama to deliver a message. She can get a pen and write it down. A tiny part of my brain knows what is about to happen and that I am powerless to stop it. I am frozen in place, watching with horror.

The man pulls his arm back and sinks the knife into Mama's stomach. Then again, in her chest. And again. And again. I lose count of how many times he stabs her. Mama is silent, head drooped toward her lap. The men yell about searching the house and leave the room. Once they are out, I rush from my hiding spot. I stand in front of her, my socked feet now soaked with her blood.

She lifts her head slowly, weakly. Her eyes find mine, but it is hard to see through the tears.

"Go to the safe room, Kitty. I love you."

"I love you, too, Mama."

Her head drops heavily as she exhales. Her chest doesn't rise again. Footsteps are approaching. The men are coming back to the room. I rush back to my hiding spot, tugging the hidden door behind me. I turn around and realize my mistake. Tiny red footprints lead a trail straight to my hiding spot. They'll know I am here. I rip my socks off, running as hard as possible through the tunnels to our safe room. The men chase after me. I worry I won't make it before they catch me. Will they tie me up and stab me like Mama? More tears blur my vision as I reach the safe room.

I rush in and slam the door as voices and footsteps grow louder. I push in the four numbers, the year I was born, to activate the alarm. Daddy will get a notification. He will make all of this better. He will come to save me. Daddy will know what to do.

14 · JOSEPHINE

HAVING THIS CONDO TO myself for a few hours is amazing. Catherine left her credit card with me so I could order food. I debate going crazy; she does have a ton of money. Ultimately, I settle on Thai food. And doughnuts. And more alcohol. I slip into a robe and cozy up on the couch to watch TV. After the first episode, all I can think about is Kitty. She said she was at a party. I could tease her a bit while she's out. I grab a bottle of vodka for some liquid courage and take a few sips.

I snap a few pics in my robe. One, I'm fully covered; the second, I'm less fully covered. I slip into the lingerie I bought for this trip and snap more pics to send her. I pose on the bed in front of a mirror, bending and twisting to hide my stomach. I feel sexy, but it doesn't always translate to photos, in my opinion.

My body is warm and tingly and wants more than just the scandalous pictures. I didn't bring any toys, but knowing Kitty, some are stashed around the condo. I bet she hides toys the way mafia men hide guns. One is always within reach. Her messages are still on delivered. Would she be mad if I masturbated while she's out? Probably. She wouldn't let me come for a long time. Is that worth it, though? Yes.

Snooping around the condo for toys, I start in the closet, but nothing's in there. I check the dresser, but again, empty. A few sweaters are tucked away in the drawers. I didn't expect her to be a sweater person, but it does make sense in Minnesota. Maybe she keeps the toys in the living room. I search through drawers and cabinets. Nothing. Does she really not keep toys here?

I'm just being nosy, sifting through drawers and the pantry. The ache in my core decreases with each new drawer, each new potential of finding something scandalous. I tug open the drawer closest to the door. A handgun sits next to two full magazines. That thought about the mafia men was more accurate than I expected. Why am I able to find a gun before the toys? I'm familiar with guns, but I'm not super comfortable. I slide the drawer shut, ambling slowly back to the living room.

Catherine hasn't checked her phone. Dazed by the gun, I drop absently on the couch. I can continue watching my medical dramas for now. Why would she have a gun here? We're in a nicer part of the Cities. The condo is located on the top floor of the building. Would someone honestly break in here? She is loaded, but she's not obvious about it. Besides, there is nothing in this apartment. Though, a robber wouldn't know that. The TV show plays in the background, but I don't pay attention. I eventually drift to sleep, thoughts of guns and robbers filling my mind.

The door closes, startling me awake. My first thought is an intruder is here. A tall person in dark clothes moves through the apartment into the bedroom. They don't notice me on the couch. I stand up to grab the gun, ready to deal with the intruder. I've never shot a living thing, but I probably can if my life is in danger. Adrenaline surges through my body. All of my senses are heightened. This could be a dangerous situation. How far away is Catherine? Could she get here in time to help?

Before I reach the drawer, the shower starts running. Why would a robber be taking a shower? It's a great shower, but that's an odd way to start a theft. The shower is fabulous and massive, with multiple nozzles. I wouldn't break into the apartment to use a shower, but I'm not a criminal. Is it illegal to break in to shower? I guess it's still breaking and entering. I grab the gun and creep toward the bathroom.

The intruder is removing their clothes. I hide in the bedroom, my breathing heavy. Peeking around the door, I watch the person. The lights are still off, but my eyes adjust to the darkness quickly. They peel off a black hoodie and toss it to the ground. Another one after that. Then, a thick vest clanks on the tile floor. The tall, slender frame appears as I look at their face.

"Kitty?"

She turns to look at me, but her eyes are glazed over. She sees me, but she doesn't at the same time. She continues undressing without acknowledging me. Leaving the gun on the dresser, I walk toward her slowly. My heart rate is slowing down, but I'm still on edge. She's moving in a trance, not speaking to me.

Her clothes are on the floor, and I notice red splattered around the pile. I grab the hoodie from the bottom, holding it up. It's soaked, but that tangy metallic smell is undeniable. Blood covers her jacket. My breathing hitches. She places something hard down on the counter. I watch as she drops another handgun, two knives, and several magazines beside the sink. The once pristine white granite counters are now covered in droplets of blood.

What kind of party did she go to? Was it some sort of animal sacrifice? Is that better than the alternative? Did she kill a person? Or multiple people? I don't know how much blood comes out of a person. Her hoodie and jeans are soaked. I blink several times, realizing Catherine is covered in blood and wearing jeans. What in the fuck happened? I don't know this woman at all. Fear surges through my body.

Catherine pulls out her phone, checking it before adding it to the weapons on the counter. Her laugh starts small, catching me off guard. It grows louder as she steps into the shower. She doesn't even close the door behind her. Not that she needs to. It's large enough that water won't splash far onto the tiled floor. Her back is to me, red droplets rolling down her face and body.

I step slowly, quietly, to her phone. She is still laughing, growing louder every minute. Confusion and fear rage through my body, unsure of what is happening and what I am supposed to do in this situation. She didn't lock her phone. That's strange in and of itself. With everything else, I don't know what to think. A text chat is open. Someone Catherine has labeled as Harpo sent a message.

> The party is pure chaos! Heading back to TX. Will update later this week.

What in the hell? A choked sob sounds from the shower. I spin around. Catherine is hunched over, hands over her face as her body shakes. I walk closer to her. My heart isn't beating as fast, but my body is still tense with anxiety. I reach the door. I open my mouth to say her name, but her body crumples, dropping to the floor. Despite my confusion, despite all the concerning actions and items, I rush to her. I don't know what's happening, but I still care for Catherine. Even if I feel differently tomorrow, I don't want her hurt.

She is somewhere between sobbing and laughing and mumbling. She is muttering about getting them all. Water falls over her body, which feels so tiny at this moment. Catherine is slender but not small at all. She's tall and built well. But here, in my arms, she feels little. Her arms wrap around my shoulders, burying her head in my neck as sobs wrack her body. My heart twists for her. Confusing emotions swirl through my mind. Why is she covered in blood? Why does she have so many weapons? How do I help my sobbing boss in the shower?

I tug her gently, shifting her into a better position to support her. Her head drops into the water spray. She's still wearing clips to pin her hair back. I adjust one arm to remove them. I don't know what's happening, but I will help her. She's seen me through a terrible situation. I can do the same for her before I get answers.

Her hair falls into her face as I pile the clips in the corner of the shower. Red runs down my arm, streaming from her hair. I stifle a gasp at the sight. I've never been covered in blood before, let alone someone else's. My stomach twists with nerves and disgust. I swallow the lump growing in my throat. My chest rises and falls with heavy breaths. I need more air to get through this. My eyes are closed tight, fighting off the nausea.

I take several deep breaths, turning my head away from Catherine. My body settles at the same time as Catherine's. I realize she is completely naked in front of me. She told me she never lets anyone see her body. Her arms and lower back are covered in American Traditional tattoos. Birds with thick outlines. Women's faces and skulls. Roses and a tiger decorate her arms. Bold colors and thick black lines. Her shoulders are covered with snakes wrapped around butterflies and knives with interspersed stars and dots.

The only place not entirely covered in tattoos is across her shoulder blades. Three rows of small identical knives stretch from one side to the other. The third row has fewer than the top two. I bring my hand to count each row. I tap the first knife, wondering if it means anything. It seems too organized and intentional compared to the rest of the tattoos. I count ten before Catherine tugs away from my arms. She leans back slowly, lifting her eyes to mine. Her eyes are still cloudy, but it seems to be lifting. She can see me now.

Catherine's fingers trace my cheek then slide over my ear. She pulls me slowly. I watch, confused but not fighting, as she pulls my face to hers. She kisses me gently. The kiss is so at odds with all the other times she has kissed me. It's not desperate. It's not possessive. Her kiss is soft and gentle. Intimacy that's not remotely sexual. Her lips are smooth and delicate. Despite my confusion and concern, a brief sadness pangs in my chest when she pulls away. She rests her head on my shoulder. I hug her tight.

My own body is tense with anxiety, but I hold her anyway. In this new position, I can see her chest. Like her back, her breasts are mostly blank. A tiger is stretched across her stomach, surrounded by flowers and butterflies. I avert my eyes quickly, not looking below her navel. Matching knives are mirrored across her collarbone. A tiny bit of skin is left uncovered at her throat. Wearing a crew neck or high-collared shirt would easily cover all of this. I don't understand why she hides it. The artwork is impressive. She may come from an older generation that considers tattoos unprofessional, but they aren't seen that way anymore. Nearly all of her employees have visible tattoos.

Two giant eyes are inked on her chest, just above her breasts. I can't help but wonder if they mean anything. The knives on her back remind me of people who keep a body count in prison when they tattoo tears drops, or something. Does Catherine have a body count? Could my mafia comment be more accurate than I thought? No. Catherine couldn't possibly be in the mafia. That's an absurd thought. Women don't get involved, right?

Catherine stands, holding her hand down to help me up. Her eyes are clear, but she still appears distracted. I take her hand, rising beside her. Blood is running down her chest and back. She shouldn't still have blood on her. I skim her body and gasp when my eyes land on her shoulder that was tucked into my side. A bleeding gash cuts through a tattoo of a flower.

"Catherine! You're bleeding!" Her fingers touch the edge of the wound. The only indication she is aware of it is a slight twitch of her lips.

"Got shot. I'll stitch it later." What the hell? Can she do her own stitches? My stomach flips over, twisting into knots. Fear and discomfort swirl under my skin. Scars across her body become apparent. Small circles, long slashes. She isn't covered in scars, but several decorate her stomach and sides with similar ones on her back.

Uncertainty keeps my own body tight, ready for an attack. She steps under the water, rinsing her hair until it runs clear. I stay back, hovering in a second stream. I wrap my arms around my body, unsure what else to do. Realizing I am still in the lacy lingerie from earlier, I remove the clothes and toss them into a corner. They land with a heavy flop, soaked and covered in blood.

Catherine washes her hair then rinses. She grabs more shampoo, though. My forehead scrunches with confusion as I watch her step toward me. Her hands rise slowly, allowing me time to back away. I stand still, indecision controlling me. My breathing becomes shallow by the time her hands reach my head. She massages the shampoo into my hair, creating a sudsy crown. If she is affected by the pain in her shoulder, she doesn't show it. Tension melts away as her fingers apply just the right amount of pressure. I close my eyes, sinking into the relief she is creating. I don't know if I should feel this relaxed under her touch, but I can't help it.

She rinses my hair and adds conditioner to both of us. She pours body wash on a loofa and slowly cleans my body first. We remain silent as she moves. I'm frozen with toiling emotions: fear and anxiety over her entrance, concern for her sudden shift in moods, and warmth and intimacy evoked by her actions. She guides me under the shower, rinsing my body and hair.

Her arms wrap around my shoulders, pulling me tightly against her chest. Her cheek presses into my head. Catherine doesn't say anything as she holds me. Soon, I lift my arms, holding her tightly. Something settles in my chest. I don't know what happened at her party. Things didn't go well, but she is here and safe. That is enough for now.

"I'm sorry," she whispers, then pulls me from the shower. She doesn't speak while she wraps a towel around me. As she moves around, I watch her body, the elusive skin she hasn't shown anyone. I don't understand why she hides it. She is gorgeous. Blood trickles across her tattoos from her injury. Standing in front of the mirror, she pulls medical equipment from a drawer and starts poking at her shoulder. My stomach flips, unable to watch this process.

I dry off and get dressed. Anxiety races through my veins. My muscles are tense. I'll be sore tomorrow. Not as sore as Catherine. I've been so head over heels for her, so caught up in her beauty and sexuality. I don't know who she is at all. Showing up in jeans, covered in blood, with a gunshot wound. This version of Catherine is so different from the person I thought I knew. I watch as she slips into a loose shirt and a pair of boy shorts. Her legs are stunningly long, more so with so much of them exposed. Despite my uncertainty, I can't deny what her body does to mine. Desire clouds my judgment as I watch her legs shift, flexing and releasing.

Those legs are moving toward me. My eyes snap to hers, realizing she knows I've been staring. The smirk on her face says she isn't upset about that. Her hands wrap over my cheeks as she kisses me again. Hell, her kisses are amazing. She knows exactly how to move, touch, hold, to elicit the exact emotion she wants. This kiss is possessive and reassuring. She is fine, and she owns me. And that doesn't upset me as much as it should.

"ARE YOU SURE? I can stay with you. I can tell my parents I don't feel well or something."

Catherine is shoving me out the door to spend the day with my parents. That was my plan, but that was before Catherine came back covered in blood, laughing hysterically, and sobbing naked in front of me. We slept wrapped around each other all night. I feel better today, but that doesn't dampen my concern over her state. Nor does it answer any of my questions from last night. She hasn't said anything about it. I haven't worked up the courage to ask. Or figured out where to start.

"I need to take care of a few things. I'm a big girl. I can take care of myself, baby girl," she mocks. I chuckle, shaking my head at her. I pull out my phone and open the Uber app. I was hesitant about everything this morning, unsure of what this meant. She assured me everything is safe, and she will explain it all soon.

"Okay, well, you're still coming over at 6, right? My parents are leaving at 5. So, we'll have the place to ourselves. Mom is making the best dessert for us." We have a long drive home tomorrow. I can ask her questions then. Resolve sets in. I'll ask her tomorrow. That will give me time to process my own thoughts and emotions. It's not like I could easily return to Kansas City on my own anyway. She grabs my phone and closes the app. I give her a weird look. She doesn't have her driver with her; how am I supposed to get over there?

"Yes, I'll be there at 6. Take the Chevelle. I'll Uber later." She drops the keys in my hand. My mind goes silent. She wants me to drive the Chevelle? "You know you want to drive it," she teases. Yes, I do want to drive it. My body itches with a desire to drive that car. My mind, however, is saying no. Stupid mind.

"I shouldn't," but my fingers close around the keys anyway. "Am I going to get arrested for some nefarious crime I know nothing about?" I raise my eyes to her, genuinely concerned about that possibility. She laughs loudly, grabbing her stomach. She is back to her long sleeves and pants today, though they are simple cotton lounge clothes.

"No, you won't get arrested." She kisses my cheek and slips my phone into my pocket. I'm not convinced yet. "There's nothing to worry about from last night. The law won't be involved," she kisses me deeply, a reassuring kiss that soothes some of my concerns. She swats my butt as I move slowly toward the door.

"Go before I decide you must be punished for not listening." Tingles creep down my body with excitement, betraying my confusion. I take a deep breath, trying to settle the desire for punishment. Despite everything, I still want her. I pull the handle, but Catherine's arm appears by my head, forcing the door closed.

"I haven't forgotten those pictures you sent me last night." Her chest is pressed against my back. Burning heat rages between our bodies. My breathing is suddenly very shallow. She's going to give me asthma at this rate. Can you get asthma from arousal? Before that train of thought continues, her teeth glide along the outer shell of my ears.

My knees are weak, and I drop an inch. Her teeth close over my ear. She presses her waist against mine, wrapping her other arm around my front, fingers teasingly tracing my lower stomach. I'm trapped between her and the door, and my body is burning with desire. I may be a strong, independent woman, but I'll let her capture and control me any day.

Catherine releases my ear, replacing it with a quick kiss, and then she is gone. Frozen in place, I take several deep breaths, unable to cool my heated core. I'm molten lava inside, regardless of everything that has happened in the past twelve hours.

The elevator ride to the parking garage below does nothing to quell my ache. The Chevelle is parked at the end of the garage, away from other cars. A quick glance around tells me no one else is here. Catherine backed into the spot. The sleek hood stretches out in front of me.

An urge to dance against it crosses my mind. Another quick glance informs me I am still alone. I drag my hand across the hood, then quickly twist, dropping my upper body backward in a sexy pose. One leg props on the bumper while my arms fan out around it. Music sounds in my head, electronic and sensual. How hot would it be for Catherine to claim me like this, spread out on the hood? Images of making a video with 80s music playing while she feasts on me appear when the elevator dings. I roll quickly, slinking off the hood in the most ungraceful manner.

I don't think the other person saw me, but I buckle up and start the car quickly, driving out of the parking garage just in case they did. All thoughts empty as the hum of the car takes over. It vibrates through me, making me feel powerful. I can see why people like these cars. Newer cars are soft and quiet. This is all bark and bite. Driving through the cities, heading toward my parents' quiet suburb, I feel on top of the world. My cockiness grows the longer I'm behind this seat. I'm ten feet tall when I finally pull into my parents' driveway.

Their house is on the property, surrounded by large, bare maple trees. Their yard would have had gorgeous orange bursts a couple of weeks ago. The ground is covered in shades of brown leaves and wet with dew and ice. The leaves crunch under my feet as I walk to the front door.

"Honey, I'm home!"

I yell as soon as I walk in, stomping to knock off the leaves and water. We've always made that joke when we come in. It's not even funny anymore; it's more tradition than a joke now. Rustling comes from the kitchen as my parents rush to greet me. We all start speaking at once, a loud greeting of excitement and love. We hug each other, and then I tug off my coat. All three of us are asking questions and trying to answer each other instead of patiently taking turns.

"Okay, Jo. Phone in here."

Mom pulls out what she refers to as her phone bucket. She's always had a rule that certain times were not meant for phones, and we have to put them away during those hours. It was specific hours when we were teens. Now that my sister and I have moved out, we're considered visitors and not allowed to have them at all. I'm not always stuck on my phone, but that doesn't mean I want to give it up. What if Catherine needs me or the Chevelle?

"Mom, no. I'm an adult now. I can keep my phone on me without it being a distraction."

"No, honey. You know the rules. Into the phone bucket it goes."

She's the stereotypical Midwest mom. Her 'o's become 'oo's. Her hair is short, and she wears flannel like no other material exists. Today, she even has a puffy vest on top. Dad is also wearing jeans and a flannel. They could be a pair of lumberjacks. I try to argue, but she shushes me, thrusting the box in my face. I finally concede, dropping my phone in it. She adds hers and Dad's, then I follow her into the kitchen.

Dad gives me a cup of coffee and starts lamenting the season the Vikings are having. Next year will be their year; I'll see. I laugh at his comment. It's always the same. I believe every Minnesotan is required to say it at least once during the football season, or they get kicked out of the state. Mom starts in with her gossip around town. Dad complains about the drivers. It's a pleasant familiarity. While I miss my home, I wouldn't trade what I have in KC for this.

Mom starts pulling out baking supplies. I take my place next to her. Even though we're cooking together, the most I'll do is hand her an ingredient or spatula. I don't mind the lack of tasks, though. Less work for me.

"Oh my god, Josephine!" my father yells from the living room. Mom and I look at each other stunned. Before we can see what he is hollering about, he walks into the kitchen. "You didn't tell me you bought a Chevelle. Is that a 68 or 69? Did you find it in that condition? It must have cost a fortune! How are you paying for it?" I snicker at his rapid-fire questions.

"It's not mine; it's Catherine's. She let me drive it today. I don't know what year it is. I'll ask her later and let you know. She didn't get it in that condition, but her driver is the one who repaired it." I pop a pecan in my mouth as Dad whistles, walking back to the living room to stare out the window.

"So, Catherine, she's a good friend?" Mom asks with a hint of suspicion.

"Yes, Mom. She's a good friend." I didn't really tell them anything about her. They don't know she's my boss, fifteen years older than me, or in a sexual relationship where she calls me 'baby girl.' That's not essential information for them. Mom suspects there is more to our relationship, but she hasn't, and won't, outright say anything. Minnesota Nice is really just passive aggressiveness. She'll hint and poke until I break, but I won't.

"It sounds like you two are close." I hum at her. Not gonna break today. "Well, I'm excited to meet her tonight." I choke on my coffee. She isn't meeting Catherine. She is going to a show tonight. That's the only reason I invited Catherine over. We're not in a 'meet the parents' kind of relationship.

"What? No. You said you were going to a play." Mom waves her flour-coated hand at me.

"We rescheduled. We can go anytime. We want to meet your friend." She says 'friend' with a wiggle of her eyebrow. Oh, hell, this is going to be bad.

"Fine, but I need to let her know." I take a couple of steps toward the door to get my phone.

"Oh no. You know the rules. No phones while you're here."

"Mom! I can't have her come over without knowing you'll be here! That's unfair."

"Pfft, I'm sure she can handle it. If she's your friend, she should know to expect surprises. And your sister will be here too!"

Oh damn. This is going to be bad. So very, very bad.

15 · CATHERINE

I DON'T KNOW HOW to explain last night to Jo. She hasn't asked about it, but she has questions. She has been more reserved than usual. Shock and disbelief led to me forgetting she was in my condo. I would have used more caution if I remembered. I typically change at the empty building. Perplexity prevented me from behaving in my usual manner last night.

I check in with Harpo before cleaning the bathroom. He's still driving to his home in San Antonio and likely won't answer his messages for a while. Hopefully, my disguise was enough to keep out of any inquiries the mob made. Angelo and the people at the party will search for whoever messed with the guns. They'll likely get new firing pins quickly and easily, but it is still a huge hit. Their credibility is shaken. They'll lose millions from last night, not counting the millions I already charged them to ship through me. I told them they would pay.

Cleaning the bathroom is cathartic. Removing the blood and clothes releases tension and worry about this situation. The repetitive motions free my mind to focus on other things. I wish I could say those other things were beneficial, but they are not. I only replay the events from last night: what I should have done differently, what went wrong, and how I can change things for next time. The afternoon melts away in silence.

An alarm on my phone chimes, breaking my concentration. It's time to go see my girl. I still don't have a plan to explain last night. Maybe she won't ask. That would be ideal. If I could keep her out of it, I would feel better. I don't want her involved in this life, this darkness. She's too sweet and loving. She doesn't deserve this evilness.

Jo said her parents would be gone tonight, so we'll have her house to ourselves. The room she grew up in, her own space, will be ours. I'm going to claim her on every surface in her room. She only moved out a few months ago, but she told me it has stayed the same. Thoughts of her soft body fill my mind. I long to touch her, make her tremble under my fingers. I need to be in complete control of something.

I don a mesh long-sleeved crop top. I didn't have the intention of showing her my body. Now that she has seen it, I don't need to hide it. I don't want her asking questions, though. The top has snakes and flowers across it. Despite being opaque, it still covers my tattoos reasonably well. I slip into a pair of high-waisted boy shorts. The waist overlaps the crop top, providing more coverage. It's shiny red leather and compliments the black top perfectly. My breasts are visible, with my hardened nipples poking through. This little exposure is more than I give anyone, but Jo isn't anyone. She's special.

Due to the cold outside, I slip into wool trousers and a pea coat. Knee-high boots fit under the pants, easily hidden until I am ready to expose them. She said dinner would be prepared when I arrived. We both need to release the tension of the past day. I don't plan to make it past the foyer before claiming her. The Uber driver doesn't say anything as I dream up all the things I'm going to do to her body. I want to feel her melt under my fingers, beg for more, tell me she is mine.

The house is a typical Midwestern home, precisely what I would picture for her family. My Chevelle sits in the driveway, looking out of place in this middle-class neighborhood. Nothing about this area matches Jo's style or mine. It's cozy and warm, a family neighborhood. I shudder at that thought. I'm not interested in having a family like that. I like my peace and solitude.

It's precisely six o'clock. Light shines through the windows, inviting and friendly. I ring the doorbell, adjust my clothes, careful of my injured shoulder. I plan to pounce as soon as the door opens. I shift my position as footsteps shuffle behind the door. It sounds like more than just Jo. She didn't mention a pet. Maybe her parents adopted a big dog in her absence. The door jerks open suddenly.

"Hello! You must be Catherine! Come in; get out of the cold!"

Shock strums through my body as an older woman guides me inside. I school my face quickly, offering a smile and a friendly greeting. Jo is huddled beside her, a cringe on her face. An apology is written across her face as she tries to push past her mother. The similarities are striking. Their eyes are the same color and shape. Jo has her mother's jaw. Their noses are different, but that's about the only thing. They could be sisters. Her mother starts tugging at my coat, trying to remove it.

"Here, let me take that for you, sweetie." She's only a few years older than me, not enough to refer to me as sweetie. I cannot let her take my coat, though. Not only is my top revealing, but it is very clearly dominatrix wear. With the red leather shorts and my breasts exposed, there's no doubt what it is.

"I'll keep it on for now, thanks. The driver didn't have the heat on, and I'm still chilled." Her mother gives me a curious look as Jo finally steps in front of her.

"Mom, why don't you give me a minute with Catherine? She wasn't expecting you to be here." Her mother eyes us suspiciously. I don't know what Jo has told her about our relationship, but there will be no doubt if I don't get a moment away with her. Her mother finally nods and turns around to walk to the back of the house. Jo rushes close to me as soon as she is around the corner. Her scent hits me, soothing my tension. I wrap my arm around her back.

"I'm so sorry," she whispers in a hurried tone. "Mom canceled her plans and didn't tell me until I showed up and..." I interrupt her.

"Jo, do you still have clothes here?" Her eyebrows knit together, but she nods.

"Take me to your room." She stands up straight, forehead crunched adorably in confusion. The urge to kiss away her concerns is strong. Not knowing how much her family knows is the only thing that stops me. She guides me to her room, and I close the door behind her. She starts apologizing again.

Instead of silencing her, I slip off my coat and toss it on the bed beside her. I unbutton my pants, and she stops talking. Carefully tugging them over my boots, the pants land on the coat. She stares at me, startled, but lust fills her eyes. She scans me from top to bottom, then up and down again. She lands on my peaked nipples. I am still cold from the ride despite the warmth of this house.

She's frozen in place, watching my body as I stalk toward her. I grab her cheeks, turning her face to mine. Excited fear dances across her expression. I love that I can always read her.

"I was told no one else would be here." Her face drops at my menacing words.

"I know. Mom didn't tell me she changed her plans." I tighten my grip on her neck, bringing her closer to me. Her face is an inch from mine. I can feel her breath on my face.

"Why didn't you tell me?" Her breathing quickens.

"Mom has a no cell phone rule. She took it when I showed up and hasn't returned it." I tsk at her response.

"That's not good, baby girl." That excited fear dances across her face again. "Now I'm inappropriate for a family dinner."

"Are you going to punish me?" Her words are breathy, arousal swirling in her gaze.

"Oh yes. That's too many misdeeds." I bring her hand to my face. "The photos you sent me last night." I tap her pointer finger. "You questioned me this morning." Middle finger tap. "Now, I'm here, all dressed for you."

"I'm sorry," she whispers. The grin on her face says that's a lie.

"No, you aren't," I whisper against her cheek, "but you will be." A soft moan sounds in her throat. My lips connect with hers. I kiss her deeply, claiming her, warning her of her impending punishment. I step back quickly, removing myself from her. She gasps, biting her lip.

"I need a sweater." She nods slowly, lost in a whirlwind of arousal. "Now, baby girl."

"Right." She turns quickly as I chuckle at her. I love teasing her like this almost as much as watching her melt under me. Nothing is as sweet as the way she is affected by me. She darts to her closet while I sit on the bed to remove my boots. I've been in enough Midwestern homes to know they don't like wearing shoes inside. I don't wear mine past my door, either. I can leave the boots here, not wanting to leave the tall leather boots in the foyer for everyone to see. Jo returns with a thick cable knit sweater. It has a turtleneck and will cover the sheer top I have on.

"Jo, everything okay up there?" Her mother yells from the first floor.

"Yes. We'll be down in a minute," Jo calls back.

"What do they know about our relationship?" I need to know how to behave, whether I can tease her for a couple of hours or need to keep my hands to myself.

"Just that you're a coworker."

"Do they know I'm also your boss?" She shakes her head, looking down at her feet.

"Oh, my naughty girl." I step to her again and lift her face to mine. "You really do want to be punished, don't you?" I kiss her gently, not the passionate kiss she wants. She whimpers against me, grabbing my back to pull me closer. I break the kiss and whisper, "Not now." I step back to let her guide me out of the room. She thinks about throwing a fit but eyes me warily. She'll add more to her punishments if she keeps that attitude. She finally takes a deep breath, centering herself before walking out of the room and to the kitchen.

"Mom, Dad, this is Catherine." She motions to both of them, who turn toward me. "Amy and Jeff." Jeff reaches out to shake my hand, nodding but not saying anything. Amy steps around the island, holding her arms out.

"Oh, come now. You can give me a hug." I am wildly uncomfortable with this level of physical touch from strangers. I give her a quick hug then step back quickly. "Would you like some wine?"

"Yes, please." I would have brought a bottle as a gift, but a certain girl of mine didn't tell me about this. Amy fills three wine glasses as Jeff pulls a can of beer from the fridge. She hands me the wine, waving her arm at a thought.

"You need to put your phone in the phone bucket."

"Mom, no. She's a guest," Jo whines with more attitude than she shows me. She is very much a child complaining to her parents. A chuckle bubbles inside me. Before it breaks free, an old shoebox is shoved in my face.

"It doesn't matter, Jo. Rules are rules. No phones allowed during visits." I smile at her. I, too, have a penchant for rules. I pull my phone from my pocket and slip it into the box with a nod.

"See, Jo?" Amy starts, "It's not that difficult. You'll get it back when you leave." Jo sighs heavily, covering her face with her hands. I sip my wine to hide my blooming grin. Jo is so adorable. The wine is decent but of lower quality than I am used to. I should have brought a bottle to share with Jo.

"So, Catherine. Jo mentioned she works with you. Are you a designer, too?" I glance at Jo in time to notice her jaw clench.

"No," I start, watching Jo for another moment. "I don't have much of an eye for design. I'm better at selecting great designers." If Jo said I'm a coworker, she doesn't want her parents to know I'm her boss. I'm just going to overlook the part where Zed is actually the one who picks the designers.

"Is Jo a great designer, then?" Her father asks from where he leans against the counter. I can't tell if it is a dig or not.

"Absolutely. She was the first of our newest designers to complete a gown. Her piece will be featured in the winter show in Kansas City. We don't normally let new hires show pieces so soon, but Jo's was too amazing not to showcase." I offer her a reassuring smile as a blush creeps across her face. I want to kiss her cheeks. Stop her from cowering under compliments. She deserves every bit of it.

"Oh, that's so nice," Amy coos, pulling a dish from the oven. "I hope you're hungry. I made hotdish."

"I've never actually had hotdish before." Despite my time spent in the Midwest, it's not something anyone has ever made around me. I understand the concept; I've just never tried it.

"Oh, well, you're in for a treat then!" Amy places a huge, steaming casserole dish on the counter. Tater tots cover some creamy filling. It looks questionable, but it doesn't look like it will give me food poisoning.

"It's Brittany, bitch!" A woman younger than Jo bursts into the kitchen with a loud voice. Jo sighs again, rolling her eyes. Amy glares at the woman with that motherly, unimpressed look. The new woman laughs, finally turning to me.

"Oh, you must be Jo's 'friend.'" She uses air quotes and winks wildly at Jo. Jo groans as the woman sticks her hand toward me. "I'm Brittany, the sister." I take her hand to shake it. I knew Jo had a sister, but she was away at college in South Dakota. I didn't expect her to be here, too.

"She came in when she heard I would be here." Jo groans, slouching to make herself smaller. I offer her a reassuring smile.

"I'm not gonna miss a chance to meet my big sissy's new friend." Again, she uses air quotes and an exaggerated wink.

"What is this, Brittany?" Jeff waves his hand between his two daughters, picking up on the not-so-subtle hints Brittany is dropping.

"Nothing, Dad. Let's go sit down." Jo answers quickly, grabbing my arm to pull me into the dining room. I step behind her, pressing my lips behind her ear briefly.

"You're adorable, baby girl," I whisper and pull away quickly, taking the seat in front of me. Jo's cheeks turn a deep shade of red as she sits beside me. She's so flustered and out of her element right now. This might be more fun than what I had planned. Not as erotic, but still fun. Her parents walk in with the casserole dish and a pecan pie. Plates and silverware are already on the table. Brittany grabs the serving spoon, scooping a heap of hotdish on her plate.

"Our guest should have gone first, Brittany," her mother admonishes.

"I am a guest, Mom. Remember? I live in South Dakota now." Her mother huffs, taking her seat. She encourages me to serve myself next. I scoop a spoonful and place it on my plate. Vegetables and what looks to be ground beef are coated in a white creamy sauce with crispy tater tots on top. I have no idea what to expect of this meal. Steam rises from the pile on my plate. I wouldn't call it appetizing, but it does smell good. Jo plops a spoonful on her plate and then dives in. She takes a huge bite, then starts huffing over the food. Her hand waves in front of her mouth.

"It's hot, Jo." Her mother sighs, rolling her eyes with a playful smirk. "She never learns." Amy shakes her head at me. The exasperated look that follows is the exact reason I never want children. I like people who can follow instructions well; children aren't well-known for that ability.

I slide my fork into the side of my pile of hotdish. I raise it slowly to my mouth, blowing gently before eating it. It's certainly a simple meal, but I can see the appeal. It's warm and comforting. An excellent choice for a cold night. It's not a dish I'll add to my regular meal rotation, but I don't hate it.

The rest of the dinner progresses with laughter and banter. Brittany teases Jo relentlessly. Amy gives more exasperated sighs at her daughters than I can count. Jeff says very little, eating his food and drinking his beer, blocking out all of the conversation. The familiarity is comforting. Growing up, I never had meals like this or any kind of relationship like this. It's interesting to see how other people connect.

After dinner, pecan pie is served. While I have had this pie before, Amy's is phenomenal. I'm pretty sure her secret is just more sugar, but it tastes spectacular. Jo becomes less embarrassed and more alive with her second glass of wine. It's very different from the Jo I am used to seeing. She's witty, confident, and so happy. I can't help but watch her with adoration.

"What is this?" Brittany breaks the current conversation, waving her fork between Jo and me. "Friends don't look at each other like that." The nervous, embarrassed Jo is back. At this moment, I hate Brittany for doing that to my girl.

"I'm sorry you don't have friends that look at you like that. Everyone deserves friends that adore them." Brittany's jaw drops. Jo snickers at my thinly veiled insult, covering her mouth with her hand.

"Brittany!" Amy scolds. "Help me clean up this table."

"We should go, Mom. We need to leave early to drive home tomorrow." Jo rises from her chair, collecting our plates.

"Are you sure, honey?" Amy asks while I assist in clearing the table and move into the kitchen.

"Yeah, I'm sure."

Her mother nods. Jo guides me back to her room to gather my coat and boots. I sit on the bed to tug my boots on. While I'm bent over, Jo steps in front of me, forcing me to lean back to look up at her. She looks like she will say something but bends down instead. Her lips meet mine. I wrap one arm around her back, using my injured arm to grab her thigh and pull her closer to me. I deepen our kiss, taking control of what she started. Her thumbs stroke my cheek, an intimacy I don't let others have. Her fingers feel electric against my face.

Jo means so much to me. I've shown more of myself to her than to anyone else. I never meant for things to get this serious with her. My life isn't safe for her. I'm generally not targeted because I maintain a low profile. It's a feeble mask at best, though. Any bosses get wind of my interference, and I will have a target on my back. I shouldn't let her affect me this way, but I can't stop it. Jo is different. My life would be so empty without her. I can't live without her, but I shouldn't fall for her.

16 · JOSEPHINE

DINNER WITH MY FAMILY was the most awkward thing I have ever experienced. No other family meal has been that cringy. I'm going to hire an assassin for Brittany's birthday. My parents now suspect there is more to my relationship with Catherine. I'm not ready to tell them anything about that. I called her mommy this weekend. That's not something I want to disclose to my actual mother.

Catherine didn't say anything about the horrible dinner but didn't punish me. Unless the punishment was not touching me. In which case, it worked. Unease courses through my guts as I shove everything into my bag. I'll be in my apartment tonight. I have a bottle of tequila somewhere in my kitchen. I'll drown my sorrows and be good to go tomorrow. As long as my mind doesn't remind me of the most humiliating dinner.

Catherine and I pad to the Chevelle, leaving her condo's clean, quiet solace. I could stay there, but it's too close to my parents now. Even Kansas is too close. I shudder at that thought as the elevator dings. Catherine grabs my bag as we near the Chevelle. I walk toward the passenger seat, rounding the hood. I try to suppress the memories of my attempt to dance on the hood yesterday. It didn't feel awkward then, but my mood of the day is embarrassment.

"Wait," Catherine calls from the trunk. I wait as she walks to stand in front of me near the center of the hood. She stands pressed against me, chest to chest. Her gaze is filled with excited desire. It's not a look she has often. It sends butterflies through my stomach. Her hands grab my thighs, lifting me up. She steps to the car, placing me on the hood. I'm stunned, but don't miss the wince from her shoulder. I open my mouth to say something, but she stops me.

"Did you know there are security cameras down here?" Oh fuck. I glance around, trying to spot them. "The residents have access to the videos." She leans over me, hands caressing my body. Arousal is buried under intense discomfort. A video exists of my attempt to Whitesnake on the hood of Catherine's car. I'm definitely going to die of embarrassment now. What in the fuck was I thinking? Of course, there are security cameras in a place like this. Catherine positions her face in the crook of my neck. "Don't worry, I removed the video clip. No one else will see it." I sigh a deep breath of relief. Catherine still saw it, though.

Her hands slide up the inside of my thigh, leaving tingles in her wake. "You like my car, huh?" I tip my head back, not responding to her question. She nips at my neck, sending a shiver across my skin. "Do you want me to fuck you here?" Her fingers reach my apex. My thighs spread open wider for her.

"Fuck yes," I moan, leaning back to give her better access. She continues kissing my neck and ear. My body is warm. I need to take my coat off. I need to take all of my clothes off. My eyes roll back in my head as her fingers press into my clit. All at once, she steps back, jerking her hands off me, leaving me gasping.

"Get in the car." Her head nods toward the passenger door as she walks to the driver's side. Fuck, I'm hot and flustered, just the way she wants me. Oh shit. She's going to keep me like this for the whole ride. That's my punishment. This is going to be a long ride. I toss my coat into the backseat then slip into the passenger seat.

"Over here." Catherine taps the seat beside her. Yep, I'm in trouble.

She keeps her hand on my thigh between shifting gears. The touch isn't arousing, but that doesn't stop my body from heating. She stays silent as we drive. Her hand is still on me through the ride out of Minnesota and into Iowa. I remain silent also, eventually drifting off to sleep.

I could ask her about the blood and wound. I'm not positive at this point, but I want to know. She's never been violent to me, and I don't want to be an accomplice in a crime. It was the first time I saw her like that. I may be misreading the entire situation. Talking about it now doesn't seem like a situation I want. She'll tell me when she wants. It was probably just a wild game of Russian Roulette. That's a real thing, right? Totally normal to get shot with a gun on a weekend. In Minnesota.

She wakes me gently when we stop for gas. She pumps and tells me to come inside with her. I need to go to the bathroom anyway, so I follow her instructions. After doing my business, I open the stall door, but Catherine shoves me back in. A devious glint in her eyes has my apex tingling. She pushes me back to the wall. My chest heaves against her as her fingers cup my cunt.

"You didn't think I'd let your misdeeds go unpunished, did you?" I shake my head, staring at her face. Excitement and fear course through me. Of course, she wouldn't let that happen.

"You sent me dirty photos, doubted me, didn't tell me about your parents, and danced on the hood of my car for anyone to see." Her fingers stroke up and down my wet core. "No one else gets to see you like that." Her possessiveness shouldn't give me butterflies. It's a huge red flag. A red flag that makes me horny. She pushes her body against mine, squishing me against the wall. She feels fantastic on me like this. All the alpha men who like to take control have nothing on Catherine.

Her lips are trailing kisses and nips across my neck and jaw. My eyes close, enjoying the sensation. Neither of her hands touches me, but with her body pressed against mine, it doesn't register. She tugs on my thigh, raising my foot to the toilet. Her kisses distract me from how awkward that is.

Then, her hand slides down the front of my pants and panties. Her fingers slip through the patch of hair I keep trimmed. She reaches my folds, spreading them apart. Something slips inside me, larger than her fingers, but not a dildo. It starts vibrating before I can process what it could be. She slides it up and down my core, gently fucking me with whatever this thing is. A thin tube rests just over my clit. It doesn't vibrate like the part inside me. It reverberates what is happening on the other end, a slight tingle. Enough to arouse, but not enough to cause an orgasm.

Once she is happy with the toy's position, she slides my leg back to the floor, stepping away from me slowly. She holds her phone up. The screen shows a circle and a wave bar. Without saying anything, she adjusts the circle. The vibration in my cunt increases, sending the wave bar higher, too. Fuck, she has a Bluetooth toy I have to wear for the rest of the drive. We aren't even halfway yet. Based on the size and placement, there's no way this toy will lead me to an orgasm. She's going to deny me as a punishment. I should have seen that coming.

Catherine kisses me deeply, passionately. Her hand caresses my neck, thumb stroking over the front of my throat. I've never been into choking, but I can see the appeal. Her tongue swirls lazily against mine. Her kiss is filled with quiet power. She knows she has control and will keep it; nothing threatens that. She moves back from me, a devious grin across her beautiful face. Her short bob makes her look more menacing than she is.

The toy remains off while she merges back onto the highway. Catherine has a mount on the opposite side of the steering wheel. I'll be able to see her reach for the app to control the toy but not see her adjust it. She's a big fan of Bluetooth toys.

Nervousness and anxiety course through my veins. When will she turn it on? How long will she tease me? My thighs clench together, wanting some sort of sensation. She notices the slight movement. Her face doesn't show any emotions, though. She's excellent at hiding her thoughts while I wear everything on my face.

She strokes my thigh, just enough pressure to tease me. I bite my lip, watching as her fingers stretch toward the phone. The toy wasn't on long enough in the gas station. I have no idea what to expect. The vibrations start slow. A deep ache in my core builds an endless pit of desire. I'm already desperate to be fucked, and she's just getting started. The vibration picks up. I groan, tipping my head back on the seat.

Catherine's fingers stroke my jaw, tugging my face to look at her. My eyes are hooded, cheeks burning with arousal. She drags me over, taking her eyes off the road long enough to kiss me. It does nothing to bring me back from the edge. The vibrations increase again in my pussy. I moan, twisting in the seat. I need to be fucked so badly. She played with me Friday when we got to the condo but hasn't fucked me since then. God, I will come so hard whenever she finally lets me.

I'm a moaning, writhing mess when the toy stops. I whine, thrusting my hips to release some tension. It does nothing. I'm on a cliff, and only an orgasm can save me. I'm teetering the line between pleasure and torture. Catherine controls both, expertly working to keep me where she wants me instead of letting me have what I want.

She laughs as my body settles down. I want to cry. I'm so desperate, so unful-filled, so aroused. I've never experienced anything like these denied orgasms be-fore. At this moment, I never want to upset Catherine again. I will do everything to keep her happy and keep my orgasms.

She must do this a lot to be this good at it. Maybe I'm just weak and would have this reaction to any teasing, but this feels different. I've been teased before, but it always led directly to an orgasm. It wasn't prolonged or snatched away at the last second. Pleasure was always given freely to me. Now, I have to work for it. I have to earn it. She came to my parents' house in a leather and lace outfit. What would she have done then?

"Are you a dominatrix?" She glances at me. A smirk spreads on her face just for me. No other person would get that reaction. She's giving me more of herself than anyone else. I see how she acts with my coworkers. She's friendly enough but keeps her feelings hidden. She isn't giving me her whole self, but I get more than most.

"Not in the way you think." My eyebrows knit together, unsure of what she means. "I don't do sadomasochism. I'm more of a pleasure domme." I consider this for a minute. I know a little bit about BDSM from Rosie and the internet. I may have stumbled on some porn a time or two, but I didn't look into it more than that. Rosie tells me about some of the things her polycule does but doesn't go into specifics.

"What does that mean?" Her hand rests on my thigh as her fingers stroke up and down. Up and down.

"I don't use pain devices to get what I want from partners." I glance at her, considering her answer, but still not fully understanding. "I want your pleasure. I want to watch you squirm with desire. When you are so desperate, you are whining and begging; that's what I enjoy." Of course. She always gets me to that point. The amount of time I'm there varies. Today, I'm going to be there for a long time.

"Do partners get to bring you there?"

"No." That was a hard and fast answer. No wiggle room. Absolute and not up for debate.

"Why not? You don't like orgasms?" I tease to hide my desire to know.

"I do not." The toy starts at a low buzz. My brain starts to fog over. She's trying to stop me from prying too much. The cloudiness wants me to stop. To sink into this feeling, let the desire surround me in the hope of release. The rest of my brain realizes what she is doing. I want to get answers.

"Don't distract me with your games, Kitty." Oh, that ache is back, though. "Why don't you like orgasms? Surely you've had plenty if you are a domme." The toy is relentless in my cunt. She bumps it up higher. I have to stay focused. I'm not giving up this conversation to arousal. But oh, that feeling...

"I don't like to lose control." Her words are soft but laced with anger and certainty. The hidden message is she doesn't trust anyone. Even my lust-addled brain can pick up on that.

"Could you one day?" My voice is breathy. Muscles tighten with need. Catherine eyes me before setting the toy to the highest level. Her fingers reach my cunt, viciously massaging, bringing me back to that cliff faster than I ever thought possible. I moan, thrusting into her hand, searching for release. It's so far away. The sensations aren't in the right place. I need more. Her fingers, the toy, I can't get off from them. I wiggle, trying to adjust into a better spot, but it's not working. Her fingers stay away from the place I need them. She knows what she is doing.

Catherine's hand leaves as the toy stops. My body jerks violently against the seat. I cry out in agony; unfulfilled lust burns through my veins. My tense muscles almost hurt. My core is clenching around the still toy, nowhere near enough to give an orgasm. A wicked gleam covers Catherine's face. This is what she wants from me, needs from me. I'll give it to her, knowing she'll give me what I want. Eventually.

"I don't know." Her words are soft and apologetic. It takes me a minute to process what she is saying. She is answering my question, not letting me forget with her distraction. A tiny hope flutters in my chest. Maybe I could give her an orgasm one day. Maybe she'll trust me enough to lose herself in me. That brings me more joy than it should. I want to be the person she trusts that deeply. I want to be that connected to Catherine, to be that close to her. I can be that for her. Through whatever she has going on. It would be worth it. I want to be her person. I want her to be mine. This may have started as lust for my older boss, but it's so much more than that now.

She sends me on edge four more times before we make it to Kansas City. My panties are soaked; my body is exhausted and jittery. Catherine takes my bag from the trunk and walks me to my apartment. I'm glad she's walking with me. I could not carry my bag without stopping on the stairs to rub one out. I lead her inside, and she drops my bag in my living room.

"Come here," she speaks gently, tugging me to the couch. Finally.

She kneels in front of me, pulling my pants down slowly. I watch, loving the angle of her kneeling beneath me. She's a kid in a candy store, ready to claim the item she's been pining for. I want her to claim it, too. I keep my hands by my sides, not wanting to do anything to stop her. She won't let me come if she thinks I'm trying to take control.

Catherine leans in with my pants around my ankles, breathing my scent deeply. I want to be embarrassed. I find myself aroused instead. She tugs my black panties over my thighs, letting them fall to the floor with my pants. I move to step out of them, but she grabs my leg, holding me in place. I relax, keeping an eye on her. She will need more room if she's going to eat me out. My thunder thighs block access to my pussy. What is she doing?

Her hand slides between my damp thighs. Her fingers grip the toy and pull it slowly out. It drops with a trail of fluid and a groan from my chest. She buries her face in the patch of hair above my thighs.

"You're so wet, baby girl." Her fingers slide up and down my thighs. "You did so well today." She kisses the apex of my thighs, nowhere near my clit or opening. Concern floods my body when she stands before me, worried she won't give me what I so desperately need. Her grin is devious, promising her own version of torture.

"I have a surprise for you." Her hand grabs my cheeks and peppers my face with little kisses. I'm frozen in place. Fuck, I hope the surprise is a giant monster strap-on, and she's about to fuck the life out of me. "But you have to wait for it." I stomp and whine like a petulant child. I was just denied yet again. I don't feel bad for my behavior.

"Wednesday, we play with Brayden. You can't come until then." I cross my arms over my chest, angered and more frustrated than I thought possible.

"This totally unfair." My inner brat is coming out, and I'm going to let her. Catherine chuckles, pleased with my anger.

"Do you want to play with him?"

"At this point, I want the goddamned crackhead on the corner to get me off." Okay, I'm not quite that desperate. I don't think.

"Oh, baby girl." Catherine chuckles, planting kisses on my face again. "I promise it will be worth it for you." She leans in close to my lips, hovering over them. Electricity zings between us. Five centimeters separate our lips. I want her to kiss me almost as much as I want her to fuck me. "I will know if you come." I gasp, leaning back to see her face. How could she possibly know that? My dildo has been screaming at me since we walked in. She won't know if I fuck myself.

As if reading my mind, she drops my face. "I've been working you for hours and likely will tomorrow, too." Her statement is far too casual for the state of alarm I feel. "When I let you come on Wednesday, it will be epic. Life changing. Explosive. But if you come before then, it won't be." I bite my lip. I want that kind of orgasm, but can I wait that long? "You'll be okay until then. I promise." She grabs my face again, kissing me deeply. I sink into the kiss, trying to calm my raging body. I can make it until Wednesday. It's only 36 hours. How hard can that be?

17 · CATHERINE

"My entire shipment is ruined."

Angelo is pissed. He just lost out on millions of dollars and a few guards. I'm not entirely sure why he is calling me. I tamp down the nervousness. I need to hear him out before jumping to conclusions.

"How did that happen?"

"Some fucking idiot came in and fucked with my product." I laugh internally. His anger pleases me.

"Who would do that?"

"I don't know. We have a few leads, but nothing is panning out. That's not why I called you."

"Okay. Why did you call, Angelo?" Finally. Let's get this call over with. I have more to do today.

"I want extra shipments this week. I can secure the load. I need to ship it quickly."

"That's not in our contract. You already broke our agreement before." He broke it with this specific delivery. I won't mention that, though. He has yet to say which shipment was messed with, and I would give myself away by mentioning a certain one. I don't make mistakes like that.

"I have angry buyers. I need to make them happy."

"I don't care about your buyers. I care about my own. If you bring another shipment, it increases the risk. I'm not doing that again."

"When was the last time you had any heat on you?" He has a fair point. I haven't had much heat on me. I've maintained a low enough profile that I don't typically come up in investigations. It's also helpful that I am just a middleman. I'm not actually buying or selling. It was a challenging job to step into, but knowing the right people helped.

"The risk is the problem. If I increase shipments, I increase visibility. If I get heat, it could end my entire operation, and you're back to driving cross country and needing days to get the shipment and have it prepared. What I offer you isn't worth the risk of ruining it." He harrumphs on the phone. He expected me to cave to him. Who does he think I am?

"I'll pay extra."

"Of course you would."

"Five times the normal shipment cost." That makes me pause. I may be in this job for altruistic reasons, but it's hard to say no to that kind of money. I don't need it, but it could return to my business. I could expand. Am I really considering this now?

"You're being quiet. Are you going to take the offer?" I shuffle some papers around, checking my schedule for the next few weeks. Angelo already has one shipment this week and next. I have a different boss on the schedule next week, and another is asking for an earlier shipment.

"If I give you two this week, one is five times the normal amount, and the other is our standard price. But you don't ship one next week. We get back on track, and you tell no one." Now, it's his turn to process the offer. Silence fills the phone, and

Jo walks to my office, waving at me. I glance at my watch; it's still early, even for our planned meeting. I wave her in, waiting for Angelo to answer.

"Fine. But these shipments will be the product I need." I don't want to ship guns. It's risky. But is it really worse than the drugs?

"Get me the numbers, and I'll adjust the invoice appropriately," I say coldly. The line disconnects. I'll have a new message within the hour. I don't particularly like this option, but it could work out for me in the long run.

Jo is sitting in the chair expectantly. I have yet to tell her I changed our meeting with Brayden. She won't be happy about that. I haven't had a chance to talk to her. She is a fan of texting, but I don't like the trail it leaves. I do not like phone calls, but they are a necessary evil. Jo waits patiently while I organize my papers and put them away. I stand in front of her, crossing my ankles. She is such a good girl for me.

"Our meeting is pushed back to this afternoon."

"What? Why?" The anger and confusion that shroud her face is adorable. She's anxious to finally get an orgasm.

"I don't want you to work after what I do to you." Arousal tints her cheeks, blood rushing through her. "I have an idea." She perks onto the edge of her seat.

"What is it?" Jo is so eager, so ready to please. She doesn't know how happy that makes me.

I have been thinking about this since I rescheduled our appointment. She'll come beautifully for me this afternoon, but I can have fun with her until then. I pull the device from my pocket. I put it there this morning, confident Jo would want it. I reach to grab her hand. The motions pull at the stitches in my shoulder. It's been a long time since I had stitches. I keep forgetting they are there. I'll need to be careful this afternoon.

I drop the pink toy into her waiting hand without saying anything. Jo eyes it curiously, trying to figure out how it works. She finds the power button. It vibrates once, indicating it is turned on and connected. My favorite toys are all Bluetooth, but this particular brand is my favorite. It has an app that can control the device from anywhere. She can be at her workstation, and I can start it. She can be at the coffee stop down the street. She can be anywhere, and I still control her pleasure. What better toy for someone like me?

I grab my phone, and she notices the movement.

"Oh fuck," she whispers. My girl is smart. She knows where this is going. I open the app and turn up the vibration. I stop the vibrations, not wanting to prolong this anymore. I need more of her pleasure.

"Take off your pants and sit on my couch." I nod my head, but she hesitates.

"Kiss me first?" Her words are soft like she's scared to ask. Given that I have been edging and denying her in the name of punishment for the past four days, she should be nervous. I won't hold this over her, though. She has done so well, taking my acts with grace and delight. I lean down, giving her what she wants. I keep the kiss soft, but she is desperate. Her tongue drags across my lips, wanting more from me. I don't kiss people like this. I definitely don't let them take charge if I do kiss. It's hard to deny Jo like this, though. Orgasms are easy to deny. She'll get her pleasure eventually, but this kiss is different. I grant her the access she wants.

She moans against me, and my possessiveness takes over. I pull her to stand, bringing her against my chest. I need her to make those sounds. I need to claim them. Her sounds are for me. No one else gets them. Suddenly, the thought of sharing her with Brayden isn't as appetizing. This is the first time I've had problems with sharing. In fact, I preferred it. Easier to keep my distance if more people are involved. Jo is different. I'm possessive over her. I want to protect her and take care of her. She is mine.

I break the kiss, not wanting to get too carried away in her. She settles against my chest, wrapping her arms around my back. This intimacy throws me off. This isn't part of my plan, but I can't stop her. Her body is so warm against mine. So comforting. She molds perfectly against me as if she were made for me. Which is absurd. I don't believe in true love or soul mates. It's all garbage someone made up. In this moment, though, it's hard to hold onto my beliefs.

"Sit." I push her back, nodding toward the couch. My voice is softer and less confident than usual. This girl does something to me that she shouldn't. I don't know why she has this effect on me.

She follows my instructions, removing her pants and sitting on the couch. Her legs spread open, exposing her glistening pussy to me. I've never been big on oral. I'm content with fingering and using the strap-on. I've given and received oral before. It never was my preferred method. I planned on fingering Jo for a bit before placing the toy in her panties, but seeing her cunt open, exposed, ready, the desire to taste courses through me.

I kneel in front of her, placing the toy on her side. Her gaze burns for me. She likes me down here as much as I enjoy her pleasure. When I kneeled in front of her in her apartment, the look in her eyes gave me more satisfaction than a single look ever has. She has the same look now. Every inch of my being wants to damn all the work I've built up and make her come on my tongue right now. I press her knees, spreading her legs wider for me.

"Move closer to the edge."

She doesn't hesitate this time. Moisture is gathering between her lips. I wonder if that is from this or the build-up of the past few days. Either way, the response excites me. I lean in slowly. My tongue spreads against her, drawing a thick line from the bottom to the top of her opening. She moans, tipping her head back. I want to capture that sound and listen to it on repeat.

Jo's cunt tastes like a warm summer day. I slide through her lips, dragging into her depths. Fuck, if I thought watching her come was good, eating her out is a whole new level. She's so responsive, clenching around me. My hands rub her thighs. She moans, thrusting her hips into my face. I lose myself in her pussy. Her taste, her softness, her pleasure.

"I'm gonna...I'm gonna," Jo moans between heavy breaths.

Reluctantly, I lean back. If she hadn't said anything, I would have kept going. It would have ruined her time with Brayden. It would have been worth it, though. Next time, I will finish her on my tongue. Maybe that's what I will do this afternoon. It isn't part of my plan. I plan to finger her while she plays with Brayden, but now I'm rethinking that whole thing.

Jo sits on the couch, breathing hard. Her eyes are closed tight, and her lip is between her teeth. She is exquisite. I grab my phone, snapping a picture of her exposed cunt. I capture her face, twisted with pleasure. I don't have any pictures in my apartment, but I want to print this one out and frame it. I'll hang it above my bed so it's the last thing I see every day and the first thing I see in the morning. The picture is perfect. It captures her essence in the best way.

"Did you just take a picture of me?"

My eyes snap to hers. I didn't ask permission. I should have for such a profoundly private photo. Asking would have ruined the moment, though. I needed to capture her in the heat of the moment, not a recreation of it. Like the photo of her in the art museum, I want her candor. If I ask, it will break the spell. Jo is so beautiful in these moments, lost to the real world. Buried in her own intrigue, pleasure, her own world.

"I did." I should offer to delete it, give it to her, show her how exposed she is. Would she see the same beauty I see? She can be self-conscious; would this upset her? I hold the phone near my chest, unwilling to risk giving it up. The image may be burned into my head, but I want to look back on it to examine it more thoroughly. I want it to be my dirty little secret, hidden on my phone for only me to find.

"Okay," she says softly. A gentle smile spreads across her face.

That's my girl. She likes this as much as I do.

"Stand up." I slide back, giving her room. "Your cunt is beautiful." Unable to resist, I drag my finger through her wet lips. Her cheeks are stained red, and her lip is between her teeth again. I slide her thong up her thighs, kissing each one gently. Her skin pebbles beneath my touch. So reactive.

I place the toy against her pussy and instruct her to hold it. I glide her thong the rest of the way up. I hate to cover that delicious cunt, but this isn't the end. I turn the toy on, setting it to a low level. I watch her reactions, ensuring the toy is where I want it. It shouldn't cause her an orgasm today. That would be easy enough with this toy, but that's not what I am after. She groans, shifting into my fingers. Perfect. It's teasing her. That's where I want it. I clip the magnet on to hold it in place and turn it off.

I pull her pants up then stand in front of her. I kiss her deeply, needing more from her. This woman is everything I want. I shouldn't be with her for a multitude of reasons. She's fifteen years younger than me. I'm her boss. I lead a dangerous life. She's too bubbly for me; I could ruin her. I will ruin her. Despite everything, I can't stay away from her. I'm a kid in a candy store, told to pick whatever I want. She is what I want. She is my life.

I pull back from the kiss. I'm in too deep with Jo. Do I end it now? Keep going until it explodes? Because it will. The real question is whether I can honestly give her up. That answer is no. No reason will convince me to leave her at this point.

"I got the rose from you this morning." Her words confuse me.

"I didn't send a rose."

"Oh, one was left outside my door this morning. I nearly stepped on it. It was just a single rose." She shrugs, considering something. "It was probably just Ben. He likes to pull pranks like that." She smiles, kissing my cheek before leaving my office.

My mind is already racing. Her apartment doesn't have any cameras on the inside; I already checked. Jo may not be concerned about a single rose at her door, but that is a signature trademark in my family. Why would they know about her? Could they? Are they watching me? Of course, it's possible.

Zed walks in, breaking my thoughts. He settles in the chair, opens his tablet, and sips his coffee. He didn't bring me a coffee this morning. This is unusual. He doesn't say anything while I'm frozen in place. Too many thoughts are racing through my mind.

"People are going to know something is up with you two." He doesn't even look up as he says that.

"They won't know." This pulls his attention to me.

"It smells like sex in here. She is here early and has been several days." He gives me a pointed look.

"Well, I'm the boss. I can fuck whoever I want. I don't have a policy against fraternization."

"No," Zed starts slowly, "but Jo is quickly proving to be one of the best designers. If you keep this up, people will begin to talk." I open my mouth to respond, but he waves me away. "Her designs may speak for themselves, but that won't stop the speculation."

I release a hard breath. He's right. Of course, he is; that's why I keep him so close. A few years ago, an office relationship ended with firing one of them. It was fine while they were dating, but when they broke up, things went sour. We had to escort her from the property. It wasn't pretty. That isn't Jo and me. Things won't end like that. Things won't end. Fuck, that thought hits hard.

"Just be careful." Zed knows my feelings as well as I do. He knows I can't give her up now. After today, I'll save our trysts for her apartment. I don't need to claim her here. I can find somewhere else. I'll do anything to keep her with me.

18 · JOSEPHINE

"HELLO! I'D LIKE TO order a large iced...oh." My panties start vibrating. What in the hell is that woman thinking? At the coffee shop? She watched me walk out of the office. Catherine knows I'm getting coffee right now. And she chooses this moment to tease me? Of course, she does.

I complete my order and grab my phone. I don't care if I get punished. I'm giving her a piece of my mind. She can't just turn it on like that while I'm in public! I open our chat and realize she messaged me earlier. She needs coffee, too. Zed didn't bring her one this morning, and I didn't get the notification. Well, that's one way to get my attention. I giggle and add her drink to my order. The vibrating stops when I tell her I have her coffee.

I just have to make it until this afternoon. Then I finally get the orgasm Catherine has been building since the weekend. To say I'm excited is an understatement. I'm so worked up; I need release now. It has been so hard to focus. I spaced out so often yesterday that Zed started hovering near me to snap me back to my work. I will focus today despite the constant threat of teasing lingering in my panties.

As if on cue, I grab a pair of scissors to cut material, and the tingles zoom through my thong. She's going to kill me. I cough to cover the moan. Fuck, I hope that wasn't too obvious. Blood is rushing to my face and neck. I grab my phone and open our chat.

> Oh my god! Are you trying to kill me?

> This has surpassed teasing and is now considered mal-treatment. I would like to speak to HR.

> Zed and I are HR. When would you like to set a meeting?

> Never mind.

Gods, that woman is infuriating. I still like her, though. Now, I'm starting to question if it's more than that. I thought it might be before I saw her covered in blood with a gunshot wound. That night really threw me for a loop. We still haven't talked about it. Her actions since then are back to normal, or what I know as normal. On a regular day, Catherine is the person I am in love with, but how do I reconcile that with the person I saw in the shower? Who is that woman? I'm happy living in this fantasy world for now. I'll deal with the fallout later.

The rest of the day goes by exasperatingly slow. Catherine teases me during lunch and afternoon break, and it's been on and off every couple of minutes for the past hour—at different levels and lengths of time. My panties are ruined. I'm surprised the toy is still working at this point. The company says it's waterproof. It really is.

"Hey, Catherine wants to see you before you leave," Zed mentions before he walks out for the night. I nod and walk toward her office. My body was already tingling, but now excitement courses with the arousal. I knock softly on her door then enter. She's waiting for me, leaning against her desk, oozing sex and power. She removed her blazer. Her sleeves are pushed up a few inches from her wrists, giving me that little bit of herself she doesn't share.

I stand in front of her, butterflies fluttering around my stomach. Catherine strokes my cheeks. I can't help but lean into her touch. I need the touch. I want to be reminded that I'm not alone in this desire. Her fingers tug me gently. She kisses me sweetly like she hasn't been torturing me for five days. I melt into her. My arms wrap around her back, holding her closer to me. Leaning against her feels like my own special heaven. This is where I want to spend eternity.

Another knock breaks our kiss. Catherine calls him in, pulling her sleeves back down. I sit on the couch, perplexed by her actions. I thought Brayden would get to see more of her, being he's a sex worker. She said no one gets to see her that way, and she meant no one. I assumed there were some exceptions. I guess that exception is me. Giddiness fills me as I stare off into space, caught up in my newest revelation.

"What have you been doing to her?" Brayden's words break my trance. A huge, goofy grin spreads as I find Catherine's. Her look is more subtle, but she knows what I am thinking.

"Just some light teasing."

"Light?! LIGHT?" My voice is louder than it needs to be, but holy hell. "If that was light, what the hell is heavy? Strapping me to the bed with a sex machine for a month?" My outrage is both fake and real. Seriously, light?

Brayden chuckles, standing beside Catherine. They would make a good couple. He is a beautiful man who looks every bit like a man born with a silver spoon in his mouth. Catherine, beside him, looks like a trophy. People would be surprised to learn she is the one with the power and money. They would disregard her as arm candy, treating Brayden with all the respect—until Catherine swoops in and destroys them with some business move.

"That's a good idea." Catherine sits in her armchair with a smirk on her face. Damn, now I've given her an idea. A terrible, exciting one. Brayden watches the two of us for a moment but doesn't speak. With him here now, I feel nervous. I've never done this before. Is there a discussion? Do we jump straight into it? Do we get a drink? Can I get a drink? Shit, that would make things better.

"Are you nervous?" Brayden asks calmly. His neutral tone isn't judgmental or expectant. I glance between him and Catherine before nodding. Catherine watches with her intense, emotionless gaze. Shouldn't she take control and tell us what to do?

"Have you ever done this before?" He questions. A nervous laugh bubbles from my chest.

"Which part? The threesome, escort, or part where Catherine has been teasing me for days on end, promising a grand orgasm." Brayden's chuckle is soft and comforting. "No, on all accounts," I respond.

"Come here." Catherine holds her hand out for me. I walk over to her, glad I'm not in charge here. When I reach her, she pulls me down onto her lap. My instinct is to jump up. I'm too big to sit on people's lap. Her hands grab my waist. She's done this before, held me on her lap. I don't know if she would tell me if I'm too big for her, but she wouldn't let me feel bad for it. I try to relax in her lap, but nerves roll through my body.

"Strip." Catherine nods at Brayden.

"Music?" he asks softly. Catherine shrugs. Brayden digs out a speaker and streams sensual songs through it. I watch as everything happens around me. Catherine and Brayden are so comfortable in their elements. I feel out of place here. The thought of a threesome and an escort has always excited me, but now I'm just nervous.

Catherine's hand slides across my side, applying just enough pressure to be enjoyable. Brayden is slowly unbuttoning his shirt, swaying his hips to the music. He is good at this. The toy in my panties starts vibrating again. Catherine drags her other hand around my waist, rubbing my sides and back.

"Relax, baby girl." Catherine's soft words soothe me. Brayden removes his shirt, exposing his defined, tanned muscles to us. I first called him Adonis. This is an understatement. He is more beautiful than any god, except maybe Thor. He's a dark-haired version of Thor.

Catherine slips her fingers under my shirt, caressing the soft skin of my sides and belly. My eyes close, enjoying the feel of her fingers, the vibration in my core. I am wearing high-waisted pants and a crop top. I wanted to wear a dress, but it's nearly freezing outside. I didn't want to deal with stockings. She unbuttons my pants, fingers still exploring my body.

I open my eyes to see Brayden remove his pants and shoes. I gasp when he stands up straight, a cage around his cock. He smirks as Catherine's warm hand slips under my bra to grasp my breast. A quick breath escapes, my mind clouded with arousal.

"You're not the only one she's been torturing," Brayden chuckles. He leans against her desk and crosses his arms across his chest. His legs are just as strong and defined as his chest and arms. This man is all tanned muscle. Glorious, powerful muscle. His penis is covered with a metal cage, but even in the cage, it's obvious he's massive. I've used some big toys before but never been with someone as well endowed as him.

I twist to look at Catherine. She gives a casual shrug. The toy starts vibrating more in my panties. Her hands caress my body. She pushes my shirt over my head. My nervousness forgotten at this moment. Cool air hits my breasts as I realize she has removed my bra, too. I didn't even notice that. Her fingers are there, squeezing, rubbing, caressing. God, her touch is so exquisite.

My eyes crack open. Brayden is still against the desk, but he is rubbing the cage. Lust burns in his gaze. I don't know if he can fake that, but it's there. I don't feel quite as embarrassed by this situation now. He probably knows all the ways to make women feel wanted and valuable. That's his job, right?

"Come here," Catherine instructs, and he walks. He follows instructions well. Is that because it's his job, or did she train him to do that? Does she tease and deny him like she does me? I bet she does. That's what she likes.

"Do you know how to remove the cage?" I shake my head, but Catherine guides me through each step. My fingers shake at first, but I feel more confident when the cage is off. I don't look at Brayden's face, though. I don't want to see what he feels.

"Stroke him." I bite my lip, reaching out to take his dick. It's so soft, already half erect. I slide up and down, feeling him grow beneath my fingers. His cock has serious girth. I lick my lips, fingers stroking the length. Catherine's hands are on my breasts, but it barely registers.

"Do you want to taste?" I glance back at Catherine, unsure if I can. I nod at her. She gives a subtle nod at the dick in my hand, a silent approval. I finally glance up at Brayden. He is staring with an intensity I'm not used to seeing in a man. I've also never seen a man caged for a week. Perhaps it's a standard look in that situation.

I bring the tip to my mouth, wrapping my lips around it. Brayden moans, a bit of pre-cum leaking into my mouth. This drives me crazy. I take more in my mouth, swirling my tongue around his length. Before I get going, Catherine pulls me back.

"Go sit on the couch," she instructs Brayden. Like a good boy, he reacts instantly, following instructions with precision. Sitting on a couch is not hard, but I'd have difficulty leaving a warm, arousing mouth. "Stand up," Catherine swats my hip, and I rise before her. My chest is exposed to Brayden. He slowly strokes himself on the couch across the room. The image of him staring at me while touching himself will forever be seared into my brain. I don't care if he is a sex worker. That's hot and encouraging.

Catherine tugs my pants down, leaving my still vibrating thong in place. Her hands caress my hips. Brayden watches her with intrigue but doesn't change the pace of his hand. He is enjoying this as much as I am. Catherine tugs the waist of my thong over my hips. I gasp, realizing I am fully naked in front of Brayden. He is also fully nude, but it feels weird now. My hands move to cover myself, but Catherine catches them. She pins them at my side as her mouth kisses my lower back and ass. Again, my mind swirls with arousal, leading me to forget all other concerns.

She pushes me forward a couple of steps and walks toward the couch. She pulls over an ottoman. Catherine is still wearing all her clothes. She'll keep them on the whole time. Seems a little unfair for her to be dressed entirely while Brayden and I are butt-ass naked, but whatever. She is paying for the session, so she gets what she wants. Does that mean she'll pay me, too? I'm not a sex worker, but I won't say no to cash, either.

Catherine guides me to the ottoman she just positioned. She has me kneel on it, then bends me toward the couch.

"Suck him." Okay. I don't need to be told twice.

I wrap my lips around the tip again, and he groans. His noises make all of this worth it. It feels awkward, with my ass in the air, head down, wrapped around his cock. It's a glorious cock, though. Entirely worth the awkwardness. One hand wraps around the base. I need to hold it in place because I can't swallow the whole thing. He is far too big for that. I take in what I can, swirling my tongue and stroking my hand over the rest. I pull back and lick the slit, eliciting a glorious grunt. I slide back down, taking more in my mouth.

Catherine drags a finger through my open, exposed cunt. I moan around the cock in my mouth. Brayden cusses, rubbing his hands over my shoulders. I love that reaction and swallow more of him. He shifts, thrusting his dick closer to me. Catherine's hands are caressing my backside. She squeezes my ass while I nearly bottom out on Brayden. I didn't think I could take all of him, but my own arousal drives me to take more.

A tongue swipes across my core, broad and intentional. I groan, pushing my ass back, wanting more of that sensation. Brayden's cock jolts against my tongue as Catherine makes another pass across my pussy. This feeling is unlike anything I have ever experienced. A cock in my mouth, a tongue on my cunt, more arousal than I knew possible. Maybe this is how I should spend my eternity.

"Come at will, Brayden," Catherine instructs from behind me. What about me? I don't get to come at will? Because I am ready for that now. She knows that. That's why she is only making wide passes. She's winding me up more as if she hasn't already done that. My cunt clenches, wanting so much more. Needing more. The licks are great, but I'm getting desperate now. Her hands tease over my ass, my hips, my inner thighs. I swear to god, if she doesn't let me come, I'll do something. I don't know what. Maybe I'll give her other shoulder a matching wound. I'm not a violent person, but all this teasing and denial has snapped something inside me. I'm desperate in an entirely new way.

I bring my focus back to the member in my throat. I cup his balls, rubbing them gently between my fingers. I've figured out how to take him to the back of my throat. His balls start to tighten in my hand. He's closer than I am. Catherine drags a single finger across my pussy, and I groan around Brayden's cock. He moans in return.

"Fuck, I'm gonna come." I suck harder, maintaining my pace. He groans as hot fluid spurts into the back of my throat. I'm not a huge fan of the taste of cum, but I want it in this moment. I pull back just enough to swallow, then take him in. He is groaning loudly, wiggling beneath me. Catherine pauses her actions, letting me focus entirely on Brayden.

I suck up the rest of his release, licking him clean as he goes soft. When I stop, his head is on the back of the couch, staring up at the ceiling. His eyes are closed, cheeks flushed with pleasure. It feels good knowing I brought him to this state. He is such a beautiful person, and knowing I gave him this feeling gives me more confidence than I need.

Catherine pulls me back against her chest. Her arms wrap around me, fingers finding my clit. She strokes it slowly, but after all this time, it's enough that my body is tensing. Tingles course through my tightening muscles, so close to my orgasm. Then, her fingers still.

"Look what you did to him."

I look down at Brayden. His head is still on the back of the couch. His body is completely relaxed, chest heaving. He looks so peaceful, so happy. His eyes lazily meet mine, a gentle smile spreads across his face. Post orgasm Brayden is somehow even better than regular Brayden. I see why Catherine has a standing appointment with him. He adjusts to sitting up on the couch.

Catherine grabs my hips, spinning me around quickly. I would fall if she didn't hold me. She kisses me deeply, passionately. I can taste myself on her. My pussy is beyond tingling now. It's dripping down my thighs. Every inch of my body is tingling, burning, itching for release. Being in her arms brings me comfort but not release.

She breaks the kiss, glancing at Brayden. I can't decipher the look. Maybe it's a silent command. Maybe she is just checking on him. I'm glazed over, lost in lust. Suddenly, she hoists me up against her chest, grabbing my thighs. I gasp and grab her shoulders to stabilize myself. I wasn't expecting that. As soon as I grab her shoulders, I remember her wound and jerk my hand back. She hasn't mentioned the injury, but there's no way it's had time to heal completely.

Before I can say anything, Catherine lowers me onto Brayden's chest. I've never been handled like this. No one picks me up. No one carries me around. I'm a big girl and have accepted that. I never expected a partner to lift me. I was okay with that, but now... how will I go back to not being lifted? No one will ever be as good as Catherine. She's everything to me.

Brayden grabs under my knees, pulling my legs wide apart, exposing me to Catherine. She kneels in front of me, hands rubbing along the inside of my thighs. Damn, that feels so good. My eyes roll back in my head. I savor the touch, tingles under her fingers, zings through my core. My stomach clenches, aching for release. Brayden's grip tightens on my thighs, holding me securely.

Catherine leans in, kissing my pussy several times. I moan, head rolling back against Brayden's shoulder. His nose trails my neck, leaving tiny kisses and nips. Goosebumps spread with all the sensation. My hips shift uncontrollably into Catherine's face. I can't even stop. I've lost control. I can only feel pleasure and touch. Nothing else exists in my life right now.

Her tongue slides through my opening, circling my clit. She sucks it into her mouth, and I nearly explode. Two fingers swirl my entrance without entering, and

I whine. I'm so close but still so far away. My body aches and screams for release. My core clenches, pulling my body, bucking against Brayden. He holds me tightly. Not letting me move at all. Those muscles aren't for show. He is strong.

"Look at Catherine," Brayden whispers in my ear. I manage to lift my head. She's kneeling in front of me, buried in my cunt. Her tongue swirls around my clit, sending a shudder through my body. A tiny thought in my mind tells me this isn't a normal position for Catherine. She doesn't kneel for anyone. She's always in charge, leading things, but she's kneeling for me. Worshiping me. Tasting me.

"Be a good girl and come for her." Oh fuck. I didn't think I had a praise kink, but I want to be a good girl. I want to come for her. For me. For the past few days, she's been teasing me. At Brayden's command, Catherine shoves her fingers deep inside me. Her mouth tightens around my clit, pulling it roughly, almost to the point of pain.

My body explodes. It's not even fireworks. Bright white consumes the room. A feeling like I have never experienced courses through my veins. It feels like lightning in the best possible way. Everything is light. It's all-consuming. Delight tingles across my skin. Everything else has faded away. Pulses of pleasure seize my body. My muscles clench and release. Time doesn't exist. Life doesn't exist. This is the afterlife. Did I die? Am I still here? Who am I? What is happening?

Fluffy white clouds surround me. Beating wings flutter by me. No, that's the beating of my heart. It's loud and erratic and elated. I'm flying through the air. Is it air? Sensations zing across my skin. This isn't the best orgasm I've ever had. No, this is heaven. This is every good feeling multiplied by infinity. This is a warm, sunny day in March. This is the first crisp apple of the season. This is a first kiss. This is life.

As the feeling slowly subsides, my surroundings come back into view. I hate that. I want to stay in pleasure purgatory forever. My mind drifts slowly back to reality. I'm lying on the couch on my side. I don't know how I got here. Catherine and Brayden are moving around the room. I can hear them, but my eyes refuse to open. A blanket is draped over my tingling shoulders. A sigh escapes as my reality begins to slip into slumber.

"She's pretty special, huh?" Brayden asks from across the room. Catherine strokes some hair from my face but doesn't say anything.

"Are you dating her?" Brayden questions. I fight off the looming sleep. Are we dating? Will Catherine answer if she thinks I am sleeping? Does she know me well enough to know I'm still awake? My eyes are closed, and I have a steady breathing pattern. I am fighting off sleep. Is my current state passable as sleep? Catherine isn't speaking. She's silent again. Am I not special? Are we not dating? Is this just a good time for her? Doubt courses through my mind. I'm swept up with her, but she doesn't see me the same way.

"Do you even know how to date anyone?"

Catherine sighs, "No." Her response is quiet and full of doubt. She's said she doesn't have many partners. I try to silence my mind, worried I will start crying from doubt. Brayden's chuckle is soft, almost impossible to hear.

"It's not that hard. Take her out to dinner. Treat her well. Talk to her." Catherine chuckles at him now. I don't know the full extent of their relationship, but this feels friendly. I'm curious how much of his concern is genuine or paid for. That's why I couldn't have a long-standing sex worker. I think things are real. Like I do with Catherine.

"Does this mean our appointments are over?" Brayden is moving around and getting ready to leave. For a man who was in a cage for a week, he is in a better state than I am after four days of edging.

"Yes, I think so." My heart clenches at her words, but that isn't the answer I want.

"No," I mumble in a soft, sleepy voice. I don't want her to see him every week, but I don't want him to go away for good. Catherine huffs a laugh, strokes my forehead, and kisses me.

"You sneaky, dirty girl." Her thumb rubs across my face. I can't open my eyes, but my lips curl at the edges. It's the best response I can muster now.

"I'll keep you on retainer but won't schedule regular appointments." She rises and moves away from me, chatting with Brayden in hushed tones. I could make out the words if I wanted to, but sleep is tugging at my body. It's hard to fight it any longer.

Catherine wakes me. It's completely dark in her office now. I've been asleep for a while. "Hey, baby girl. I wanna get you home, okay?" I nod, sitting up slowly. My body feels heavy and tired, but still so good. She helps me dress, not focusing on making everything neat.

John drives us through the city to my apartment. Catherine sits beside me, holding me in her arms. She hasn't said anything to me since she woke me. Only a few instructions here and there on what I need to do. She knows I heard what Brayden asked. She didn't answer and hasn't addressed it. I still don't know anything about what happened over the weekend. Insecurity rolls through my mind. I'm tired and want to go to sleep. I don't feel as good as I did a minute ago. I want to cry now.

I pull away from Catherine, unsure why I suddenly feel so sad, so uncertain. Aches spread through my muscles. Probably from all the tensing and pulsing that happened. Tears threaten to spill. This isn't normal. I've never felt like this after an orgasm. Sex is supposed to make you happy; why am I so sad right now? Negative thoughts swirl in my mind.

I sniffle, fighting hard against the tears. We're only a couple of blocks from my apartment. I can rush inside and hide whatever this is from Catherine. I can sort it out tomorrow. Shit, I still have to work tomorrow. Maybe I'll call in. I can't work if I'm feeling this upset. Maybe it'll pass after some sleep. I just need a good rest. I'll be fine in the morning.

"Baby girl?" Catherine wraps her arms over my shoulder, trying to pull me closer. I don't budge. I stare out the window, watching the lights on the street pass by. One more block. I'll make a run for it. I bite my lip, holding off the sadness as best I can. A tear slips down my cheek. Hell, if I wipe it away, Catherine will know I'm crying. It's dark enough she won't notice. Hopefully.

My luck isn't that good. Her thumb wipes the tear away. I can't explain all my doubts to her. If I speak, the wave I'm barely holding in will crash. I won't be able to stop. I can feel it in my bones. A colossal sob-fest is growing inside me. I may not even be able to sleep tonight. I'll spend the whole time crying into my pillow, alone, swallowed with uncertainty and sadness.

"What's the matter?" Her question is soft, laced with concern. John stops the car on the sidewalk.

"I'm sorry," I whisper. I shove the door open and race into my building. The tears flow faster than I expected. My vision is completely blurred. I rush up the stairs. I don't want to stop and wait for the elevator. Choked sobs break from me. I fumble around for my keys, slowing once I reach my floor. I can't see my bag and have to feel around for the keys. I finally grab them but drop them. A loud sob escapes me, exasperated over this whole situation. I don't know what's happening to me.

I bend to grab my keys, barely able to see them through a fresh wave of tears. As my fingers reach them, I bump into another hand. I glance up, finding Catherine's face staring at me. Of course, she would follow me. Why didn't I think of that? She wouldn't let me run off alone in this state. Whether or not she cares for me as a partner, she cares for me as a person.

She lifts my keys, opening my door for me. She steps inside and allows me to walk in with her. Tears pour down my face. I feel like an idiot right now. How could I fall from such a high just a few hours ago? I drop my bag on the floor and kick my shoes across the room. I don't care at this point. Catherine drops my keys on the stand beside my door and wraps an arm around my shoulders.

"Let's get you into comfy clothes, then I'll get some food for us."

I nod, unable to say anything or argue. Even if I wanted to, I can't think of the words. She guides me to my room, and I shuffle through my drawers, pulling clothes and throwing them on the floor. I don't care about the mess. Catherine watches me for a moment, then pulls out her phone. I don't know what she is doing. I can't find the energy to care. I finally come across some fluffy pants and a loose shirt and change into them.

"You're feeling depressed? Sad? Maybe angry?" I glare at her for a moment, then nod. She walks over and wraps her arms around me. I don't want her comfort, but I cry more against her shoulder. She rubs my back and my hair, gently shushing me.

"It's normal, baby girl. You experienced a huge surge of endorphins. With that gone, your body doesn't know how to regulate. It's called sub drop." I lean back, sniffling as I look at her. Is this a normal feeling? It even has a name. "I'm sorry I didn't mention it before. I should have known it would happen. I've been pushing you a lot the last few days." I nod and collapse on the edge of the bed. Catherine walks away and returns a moment later.

She kneels in front of me, a wet rag in her hand. She wipes my cheeks, cleaning my face of the tears. When she's done, she pulls me into the living room. She puts me on the couch, covers me with a blanket, and hands me the remote. I watch her move through my apartment with ease and grace. A contrast to everything I feel at this moment. She returns with a bottle of water and tells me she ordered delivery. Catherine settles next to me, pulling me against her chest.

"Are we dating?" My voice is weak, and I hate that. I need to know, though. We've been together for a couple of months. If this is just casual, I want to know. I need to reign in my feelings if it is. I've been letting them run free for a while. She takes a deep breath, pressing her cheek against my head.

"I'm scared of hurting you."

19 · CATHERINE

I WASN'T READY FOR that question. It's not an unreasonable question and not unexpected. We spend a lot of time together. I put a lot of energy into fucking her. I can't stay away from her. Even if she quit Marzanna and moved back to Minneapolis, I would follow her. I would stay in my condo. I could run Marzanna from there. I would do it for her. She means more to me than any person ever has.

How long until someone realizes what she is to me? How long until she is in danger? Holding her in my arms makes me both anxious and calm. This is where she belongs, but how do I protect her? She fits against me so perfectly, lying in bed together. Her head is cradled against my shoulder. Her arms draped over my waist. Jo is perfect. She breathes deeply, asleep in my arms.

I brought her to bed after dinner and tucked her in. I didn't plan on staying with her tonight. When I saw she was crying, I couldn't leave her. She tried to run from me. The hurt that tore through my body was unlike anything I had ever experienced. As frightened as I am of her getting hurt by someone else, I'm equally scared of hurting her myself. I don't know how to be in a relationship. I've never seen a healthy one, a successful one. Relationships in my world are used for benefit, power, or temporary pleasure to be discarded quickly.

Jo mumbles, twisting in my arms so her back is to me. I stay wrapped around her. Despite all my fears, I'm not letting her go either. That settles it. I have to find a way to make this work. To keep her safe from others and me. I have to learn how to have a relationship. I can do that for her. I have to. She is mine, and I won't accept anything else. Scenarios course through my mind over what could happen, what could go wrong, and how I need to prepare. I eventually drift off into a fitful slumber.

Beeping wakes me up. I startle and tighten my arms around Jo. She groans, slapping her hand on her nightstand. The sound eventually stops, and she settles against me again. I don't know what time it is, but I don't want to get up. It would be too suspicious if we both call in today, but it's a tempting thought.

"There's only an hour before I go to the office," Jo's voice is heavy with sleep as she stretches in my arms. I curse under my breath. I don't have time to go to my apartment and make it in on time. It's too late for me to sneak into the office first. Someone will be there by the time I arrive. Plus, I need a shower. Fuck it, I'll just be late today. I'll say I had a meeting. I'm the owner. I can do that.

Jo twists to face me. Her vibrant red and yellow hair splays around her, brightening her round face. Her eyes are still puffy with sleep, cheeks stained with tear streaks. She's stunning. I trace my fingers up her arm, over her shoulder, neck, and cheeks. They are perfectly plump, soft, and oh-so-precious. I lean in and gently kiss her full lips. It's a light kiss, a good morning kiss. This is how I want to wake up every day. In bed with her, beautiful and soft, staring at me like I'm her whole world.

"I want to take you on a date this weekend."

Her face lights with excitement. That's all the response I need.

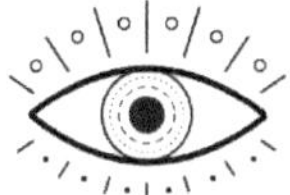

I'VE REFRAINED FROM SPENDING every day at Jo's. I want tonight to be remarkable. She deserves romance and to be treated like a princess. I have every intention of doing that for her. The problem is we're in Kansas City. This location is perfect for my legal and illegal business. Larger cities would be better for fashion, but we make this work and have made a name for ourselves locally and nationally. Many great restaurants serve the area but none are quite fit for a princes. Instead, I settle on something Jo will enjoy. A jazz bar.

Zed found the restaurant and made a reservation for us. I don't think I will share that detail with Jo. She doesn't need to know that. I pull on my favorite pair of high-waisted pants and pair it with a loose top and a leather jacket. I grab my overnight bag. I didn't tell her I plan to stay over, but I'm not passing up the opportunity after I've stayed away all week.

I gave John the night off, telling him I plan to take the electric car and he can use whatever he wants. He's been wanting to go out in the Chevelle. He won't ask for time off unless it's pertinent for him to be away. I give him extra days from his schedule for that reason. He's such a good employee; I want him to stay happy.

Jo is waiting in the lobby when I pull up. She rushes to the car before I can get out. I lean over and push the door for her. I would prefer to open it from the outside, but I can't beat her now. She jumps in the car, huffing with a huge smile. She adjusts in the seat and reaches for the seat belt, but that won't do. I lean over and grab her face. Her breath catches as I pull her to me, crashing our lips together. I kiss her like I've never kissed anyone. I'm dying of thirst, and she is a never-ending fountain of water. I need her.

"Hi." Her greeting is breathy as I pull away.

"Hey, baby girl." A blush spreads across her face as her lips curl into a smile. She's adorable like this. She buckles in as I drive away. She looks fantastic in a dark cocktail dress with colorful leggings and chunky boots. I'm glad I settled on the jazz bar. Her style will fit perfectly there. I place my hand on her thigh. She is staring around the car, taking it all in.

Her fingers lace with mine. I've never held hands with anyone like this. It's one of those experiences normal kids get, but I've never been normal. Her skin is smooth under mine. It shouldn't feel this intimate, but it does.

"You look beautiful tonight." My words are soft, but I don't glance at her. I don't drive frequently enough to be confident in taking my eyes off the road for long.

"Only tonight?" She's teasing me. I raise my eyebrows, giving her a quick glance.

"Do I need to keep a count again?"

"Gods no." She giggles, squeezing my hand. "I loved the orgasm, but I need time to recover from that." That was an intense experience for her. I hope she'll let me do it again, but I won't push it if she doesn't want to.

"Alright, baby girl. I'll take care of you in different ways." I bring her hand to my lips. She bites her lip then stares out the window with excitement dancing in her eyes. She loves the ways I take care of her. I will gladly do whatever she wants. As much as she loves being on the receiving end of my affection, I love giving it to her. Something about Jo stirs a place deep in my soul that didn't exist before I met her.

We are escorted to a small table with a couch inside the restaurant. A band is setting up on the stage, which is near our spot. I sit on the end of the sofa. Jo sits politely beside me, but that won't do. She needs to touch me. I want her close. I wrap my arm over her shoulder, pulling her into my side. She adjusts easily, melting into me. I drag my nose along her neck, taking in her scent, the sweet smell of citrus.

"You belong here, beside me." I place one soft kiss on her neck. She shivers beneath my touch. Jo drapes her arm over my thigh, hand landing on my knee. No one has ever been this comfortable with me. I keep everyone at arm's length. She drives me to hold her in my arms. A deep need to keep her close swirls through my entire being. She is mine, and I am hers entirely. I push down a growing fear. Anxiety swirls inside me. Jo speaks, pulling my attention away from the cloud of fear.

"What if I slide back?" She's being sassy tonight. She said she doesn't want the denied orgasms, but that doesn't mean I can't find other methods of punishment. Denial is my favorite, but I have others. I wasn't planning on doing that, but I will if she keeps pushing me.

"I won't let you. I'll punish you for trying." Red spreads across her cheeks. Her chest heaves a time or two. My girl wants that. "I don't have to deny your orgasms. It might be more fun if you had one here, in front of everyone. That seems like a good punishment for a girl that wants to act out." Her head turns as she scans the room, taking in all the people and the lights. The gears are turning in her mind, figuring out how it would work.

I drag my fingers up the inside of her arm. A feather-light touch can make any spot erogenous. My fingers trail her bicep, across her shoulder, over her exposed collarbone, then pause at the base of her neck. Her skin is flushed with red patches, and her chest rises and falls rapidly.

"Seems like an appropriate punishment. An orgasm where you are acting out." I nip her ear, pulling back just enough that it doesn't look like I'm going to fuck her on this couch, but not enough to let her think that.

"You don't have a bag. You have toys hidden in your coat?" Her words are soft and husky. I'm not sure if she's testing me or genuinely curious, so I give her the benefit of the doubt this time.

"Come on, baby girl. You know me better than that," I whisper. "I have half a dozen in the car." A muttered curse slips out from her. She is still scanning the restaurant. More people file in and taking seats for the band performing tonight.

"What does John say about all those devices?"

"He doesn't ask, and I don't tell." I shrug casually. All my toys are in a bag with spare clothes and other items I keep on hand. I doubt John has ever gone through the bag. If he has, he didn't say anything. His discretion is top-notch. "We could walk to the car together. I could slip the device inside you in the parking lot. You could come during dinner. Again, during dessert. When the band plays their finale. You want more than that?"

Jo bites her lip, turning to look at me. She doesn't say anything. She doesn't need to. She wants that but is also terrified. She can be loud during orgasms and certainly can't be still and inconspicuous. She is considering how much she wants that when the waiter walks up. I pull away from Jo a respectable amount and order drinks from the waiter. She still stares at me, wondering when I will drag her to the parking lot. That's not my intention tonight. I genuinely want this to be a regular date. I don't think this is date conversation though.

When I don't return to her neck, her eyebrows knit together.

"So, you're not going to make me orgasm in this restaurant?"

"Not tonight, baby girl." I leave that option open for later. "This is a regular date. Not a sex date."

"Oh," she laughs incredulously, "A regular date, huh?" She shifts in my arm, turning to look at me. "So, where do you work?" A joyous laugh erupts from my chest. Jo was so quiet and reserved when I first met her. She has opened up to me in the past couple of weeks. I love seeing her personality come out. She is showing me who she is now.

An overwhelming emotion I can't place fills my chest. It almost hurts, but when I look at her, it doesn't feel like pain. This feels like heaven. It feels right. I trace my fingers along her jaw, bringing her attention back to me. She was watching the band. I didn't realize they started their set. I am consumed with Jo. Nothing else matters. I pull Jo to me with a delicate touch, kissing her gently. Her hand tightens on my knee. A soft, calming, centering kiss.

Jo pulls away with a knowing smile on her face. What does she know? She stares at me for a moment, waiting for me to speak. When I don't, she turns back to the band. She thought I was going to say something to her. I haven't spoken that word to another person in decades. The last person I said that to died before I left the house. It dawns on me what this feeling is.

Our food is brought over while my mind rages with fear, anxiety, nervousness, and an all-consuming feeling I won't name. It dances through me, but I can't give it the power to take over. My jaw clenches. I force it to relax, only for it to tense again.

Jo shifts away from me to grab a bite of her food. She turns back to me. I'm frozen in place, watching her move. Fear and excitement war inside me.

"Hey," her voice is soft, grounding. She kisses me, holding my face like I held hers earlier. She tastes like joy and ecstasy and happily ever after and buffalo sauce. She's perfect. "Your food is going to get cold."

My laugh is boisterous, exploding from me in a torrent of delight. I kiss her cheek, focusing on the present. I'm here with her now. I don't need to worry about what I'm feeling. I can sort emotions out later. Tonight is about the date.

The band is good, playing various songs, from sensual to rowdy. Jo enjoys the music, bopping along on the couch. We split dessert. Conversation flows easily. We talk about the band, her upcoming show, the chance of snowfall. Being with her is the easiest thing I do. If only it didn't fill me with a sense of dread. As soon as I settle into a comfortable state, my mind becomes enamored, then encased with apprehension. I struggle to find a balance. Jo is my anchor. When I return to her, I gain my control.

We leave at the end of the set, heading back to her apartment. I park the car in front of her building. We are lucky to have found a spot near the door. I turn the engine off but stay in the seat. My battling emotions overwhelm me. I hate this feeling. I am always in control. This feels dangerous.

"You coming in?" Jo's holding the handle, angled to get out. She's so sure of everything. I wish I had that confidence in this relationship.

"Yes." My response is breathy, unsure, but I get out, taking my bag. I know what I want. I just have to stop the anxiety to get it. Breathe in, breathe out.

Her apartment feels familiar and comfortable. I've been here; I know the layout. My mind centers as my body relaxes. She drops her purse on the counter and checks her phone. I approach her, spinning her around and crashing into the counter. My lips find hers in a searing kiss. I've held back all night for the sake of a regular date. It's exhausting. I want my control back now, and I plan to take it.

"I have something for you. Wait for me in the bedroom."

Excitement dances across her face. She practically bounces to the bedroom. I chuckle at her, heading to the bathroom to change clothes. The clashing emotions tear through me again, crippling doubt and rapturous warmth. I focus on my task, changing into the lingerie I brought for tonight and securing everything where it needs to be. I carry a small bag of toys into the room.

Jo is relaxing on the bed in the robe I bought for her. Her skin is smooth and luscious. The robe covers everything but leaves enough exposed to make my mouth water. Her curves are hidden beneath the silky material, but I'll get to those soon enough. She sits on the bed, scanning my body from head to toe.

I ordered new lingerie pieces to wear just for Jo. I have used the same pieces for years now. Bodysuits or high-waisted pants paired with long sleeves to cover my body. So many secrets are inked on my chest, my back, my arms. I don't share that with anyone. Even though Jo unwittingly saw me, tonight I am giving that to her. Most of it. I found a corset with a lace midsection and no straps or sleeves. Boy shorts, my preferred style, have a built-in strap for a toy. Tonight, I am giving her more of myself than anyone has ever had.

She rises slowly, walking toward me. Her steps are slow and measured like one would approach a scared child. She's giving me time to run, to change my mind. But I won't. I want to share myself with her. She realizes the weight of my actions. The warmth spreads through my body, but the anxiety doesn't follow this time.

Jo stands before me, taking in my chest, shoulders, and arms. All the exposed skin I am giving her. As exposed as I can manage. Her fingers rise at a snail's pace.

I take a deep breath and close my eyes as her fingers land on my skin. I try to think of the last time I felt a touch like this, but I can't remember. She traces the ink on my shoulders. She pauses at the scar, still bright red. It's healing well but will leave a huge scar. I've always struggled with stitching myself.

She walks to my back, gently tracing my shoulders. "You have new tattoos." Her fingers glide near my recent additions. Another column of knives. She looks up to me. "Will you tell me what they mean?"

"Not tonight." Not ever if I have the option. It's the secret I don't want her to have. The part of me I'm scared of for her. She nods her head, tracing over my other tattoos.

"Get on the bed. Take off the robe."

A wicked grin grows, shading her face with desire. She steps around me and unties the robe. It slides over her shoulders effortlessly, creating a black pool at her feet. She watches me as I take in her body. Every inch of her is perfect. Her round stomach, wide hips, a perfect dip for her waist, spreading up to her large breasts. Before I take a step toward her, she moves backward. When her legs bump into the mattress, she sits, sliding back to the headboard. Her legs spread, flashing her glistening pussy. Hunger fills me, eager to rush in and claim her.

I control myself; I have a plan I want to stick to. I move to the bedside, keeping my gaze on her. I dig in the bag for a dildo that fits in these boy shorts. Jo watches, desire and curiosity burning through her. I fit the toy into the harness and place a bottle of lube within reach. Her legs spread wider for me. I knew she would be eager, but I didn't expect this level of willingness.

I crawl across the bed, taking a spot between her legs. I want to taste her. Just a taste. I haven't been able to get her out of my mind since I last had her on my tongue. I lick her full length. She tips her head back, moaning loudly. I dip my tongue deep inside her. She curses, covering her face with her arm. I usually wouldn't let that slide, but I do for now.

She's so wet, so ready for me. I lick her again, closing my mouth around her clit. She jerks beneath me. So eager. Unwillingly, I leave her delicious pussy, placing a few kisses across her stomach and breasts. Her arm drops, and she watches me. I keep my eyes on her body, hungry for every inch. I lick and kiss her skin, soft under my lips. I finally reach hers, kissing her deeply.

I squeeze a tiny bit of lube on my fingers as our tongues dance in a passionate kiss. I stroke the dildo, ensuring it's ready for her. I debated what size to get. Too small wouldn't be pleasurable for her, but too big would detract from my intent. I don't want her to be overwhelmed. I settled on one slightly longer but not as much girth as others.

I drag my fingers across Jo's opening, pulling back from the kiss to watch her. She keeps her hands on my face, focused on me. It's almost overwhelming. The excitement from earlier is still there, but it's mixed with more profound emotions now. Unable to resist, I plant a quick kiss on her lips as I notch the dildo in her wet cunt. She shifts her hips briefly, lining up for me.

Slowly, I push inside her until I bottom out. My hips flush against her. Her breathing is heavy, eyes rolling with pleasure. Her hands drop to my shoulders, then my sides. I pull back slowly, getting a feel for where the dildo ends. I use a different one with Brayden and have to adjust for this. I slide back in, and Jo's hand clenches my sides.

"You okay, baby girl?"

"Yes, gods, yes. Please fuck me."

Her hands slide down to my ass. I'm not going to deny her. I thrust in deeply, pulling out and shoving back in. She groans as I move in and out. I lower myself over her, finding her lips again. Her legs wrap around my back, heels digging into my ass. Her hands are on my back, holding me close. I continue to thrust in and out, bringing her the pleasure I want her to have. My own body tingles over her.

I massage her breasts, kiss her neck, nibble her ears. She groans beneath me. Her hands roam my exposed skin, holding me close. Being with her like this is different from my ordinary experiences. This isn't about controlling her. This is intimate. Emotions are involved in this. While I am in charge, she has equal power in this moment. This is deeper than my typical sessions.

"Fucking hell, Kitty," she moans. I slide my hand down her body to find her clit. I circle the little nub several times. Jo squirms beneath me, overwhelmed with pleasure.

"Come for me, baby girl."

I shift just enough to watch her face. I've seen her orgasm before, but not like this. Not this close. Not this personal. Pebbles break out across her body as her muscles tighten. Her face scrunches as she cries out. Her body shakes beneath mine as I continue to pound into her. I circle the nub under my fingers faster and harder. She whimpers, almost calm before another wave crashes over her. Jo opens her mouth in a silent scream, her body arching with overwhelming pleasure. She is the most beautiful person I have ever seen.

I slow my thrusting when she bursts into giggles. I kiss over her shoulders and cheeks. She comes so beautifully for me. Nothing fills me with more satisfaction than watching her fall apart. Seeing it from this position is the best thing I have ever done. I refuse to name the emotion rippling through me, but I know what it is. I remove the toy, tossing it aside to clean later. I pull Jo tight in my arms. The look on her face implies she also knows what the emotion is. She doesn't say anything, though. Just kisses me deeply. Smart girl.

20 · JOSEPHINE

TOMORROW IS THE FASHION show. I'm nervous and excited and not at all concerned about being judged in a new area for my work. Everyone at Marzanna loves my dress, but that doesn't mean anyone else will. I'm heading to the warehouse to check on it. I know it's fine. We ensured everything was perfect during work today, but I can't sleep. I might as well double-check everything.

Things have been fantastic with Catherine. She loves me—I know it. I think I'm in love with her, too. This feels so different from anyone else I have been with. Catherine is amazing. The way she treats me is unlike anything I have experienced. She takes care of me in everything. She treats my body like the most incredible pleasure there is. I've never felt more confident in my plus-sized body than with her.

Catherine hasn't been naked around me. Her lingerie is getting more revealing, but she's not there yet. From what I understand, she hasn't been entirely naked around anyone in decades, aside from the night in Minneapolis. We've both just been avoiding a conversation about that. It hasn't happened since then, that I am aware of. I don't think I want to know at this point.

We decided to make our relationship known tomorrow at the fashion show. With everyone busy and distracted, it will take some of the awkwardness out of the situation. Zed already knows and agrees it will be a good opportunity. He expects we will need to meet with everyone on Monday to fill them in. I don't want to do that, but it does need to be done. We're also hoping that my piece will stand on its own. That will help dissuade people from favoritism. They'll still suspect it, but hopefully, it won't be as bad. Catherine will be there to support me. She doesn't always go to shows but is going with me.

Christmas is just around the corner. I've spent so much energy thinking of a gift for Catherine but always come up empty. She has enough money to buy whatever she wants. She's a minimalist. I can't exactly buy her a little trinket or anything. She has access to me any time she wants. Trying to give her sex wouldn't have an impact. I'm running out of time to come up with something. At this point, I'm considering going home to avoid getting a gift. I'm sure she'll come up with some fantastic gift to give me while I give her a box of saltwater taffy or something ridiculous. Ugh, just the thought makes me uncomfortable.

The ride to the warehouse takes longer than expected. Who would've thought city buses run less frequently on a Thursday in the middle of the night. The air is crisp. Winter has arrived. A light dusting of snow coated the ground earlier this week. Now, it has melted, leaving the ground wet. Everything is slippery. My winter shoes can handle it, but I still have to walk carefully. I waddle like a penguin to avoid slipping on black ice.

I stomp my feet off on the rug in the warehouse. I use the front door because I have access to that one. Everyone at Marzanna has their access code, but most of us only use the front door. The building has more doors, but I don't bother with them. Moving through the entryway, I hear people moving around the space at the back. Catherine explained that beds and showers are installed there for truckers. However, the sounds of feet and hushed voices are more than a few drivers. Maybe there is a party?

I sneak carefully through our crates. Only two are packed for tomorrow. Our team has several boxes and bins. Since this is a local show, we don't need as much as a show further away. We're taking a delivery van instead of a large truck. Many empty crates fill the area. The lights are off where I am, but dim lights are on in the back of the warehouse. It's different from the standard bright lights we use.

The crates keep me out of view, and I can maneuver around them to see what is happening. Four or five men sit around a table playing cards. A table along the wall is set up with snacks and water. No music is playing, though—just grunts and occasional yells from the men. After a few minutes, the rolling door on the far end opens, and a truck backs in. A few small women emerge from a hallway, pulling on clothes.

The women stand along one wall, and the men around the table clamber up. They walk down the hall the women just exited. They return a moment later carrying bags and boxes. The smaller boxes are the ones we use for shipping small items. The bags are loaded into a larger crate. A small, hidden section on the bottom is open. This is the first time I've noticed that. The bags are canvas and relatively small.

I don't understand what is happening here. A man with a clipboard climbs out of the cab. He and another man open the back of the truck and lower a ramp. Catherine emerges from her office, watching everything. She constantly monitors and scans, ensuring everything is going according to plan. She surveys the area I am in but doesn't see me. I'm in the shadows. She couldn't see me even if she knew to look for me.

The crates and small boxes are loaded onto the truck while others are still being packed. One of the small canvas bags is dropping. The contents spill out onto the floor. It's filled with tiny Ziploc bags with white powder inside. Another man yells, and then one of the women joins in. My mind is too frazzled to process everything. He just dropped a bag of drugs. The woman is shouting about work and payment and effort.

A man starts yelling at the woman. Both are erratic, waving arms and shouting at each other. The man who dropped the bag is scrambling to pick it up. Another woman bends down to help him. The first woman who shouted grabs the woman's shoulders and tugs her back against the wall. The angry man doesn't like this. He slaps the woman. She jerks away, but I can see the blood spilling from her lip. The women take their spot against the wall, remaining quiet and still.

The bags of drugs are secured in their canvas bag, then placed inside one of the containers. The men load the truck with precision. This isn't their first time loading these containers in this warehouse. The last container is loaded, and the back is closed. Two men climb in the cab and drive the truck out of the large garage doors. The women, with their heads down and shoulders slumped, are escorted out by the rest of the men. They are shoved once or twice, but no one is slapped again.

Catherine closes the rolling door and walks back to the table where all the food is. She collapses in a chair beside the table, dropping her face in her hands. She looks stressed, almost heartbroken. She's a drug dealer. I can't think of any other explanation for what this is.

Does she sell to these people? Does she find people to sell them on the streets? Is there a whole network of people in Kansas City that run drugs for Catherine? How many containers move through this warehouse on any given day? I don't know much about drugs or amounts sold at once, but that was a lot of bags and containers.

She rises and picks up some of the trash left behind. I walk toward her slowly, worried about her reacting to me. Does she have a gun on her? She has several, but how often does she use them? How frequently does she carry them?

Catherine turns in my direction at the sound of my steps. I'm in the light now. When her eyes meet mine, a small inhale indicates she is startled. We stare at each other for what feels like an eternity. Questions roll through my mind, demanding to be answered. Fear keeps me rooted in place. Catherine is frozen in shock, disbelief, and uncertainty.

"Jo," she starts slowly. She never calls me by my name. It's always 'baby girl'. This is serious. My heart pounds in my chest. "How long have you been here?"

"Just," I have to cough to clear my dry throat. "Since before the truck came in."

She takes a deep breath then steps in my direction. I don't think I want her close right now. I need to keep her at arm's length. I can't let this go without answers. The gun and gunshot wound from Minneapolis could be kept in the dark, written off as a one-time thing. Not now. This isn't a one-time thing anymore.

Before she reaches me, a side door slams loudly. A man in dark pants and a dark turtleneck with a gold chain around his neck walks in. He moves like he owns the place. He has some sort of power here, and he knows it. Catherine tenses but doesn't look away from me.

"Well, doll, that was another successful load. Angelo will be happy with that." He finally spots me. He quickly draws a gun, aiming it at me. I jolt and cover my head. A little voice sarcastically says that won't save me, but I don't know what else to do. I've never had a gun pointed at me. I've never been involved in illegal activities. The only illegal thing I've ever done is smoke cannabis before it was legal. I'm not a lawbreaker.

He cocks his gun, and the sound pierces the empty warehouse. If cocking it is that loud, what would a gunshot sound like? Probably a train rolling through while blasting its horn. I hope, for many reasons, he doesn't fire it. One of those reasons is how loud it sounds. You know, after the fear of being shot and killed.

"What is this, doll?" Why does he keep calling her doll? She hates it when people give her nicknames. I'm pretty sure she only tolerates me calling her Kitty because she loves me. I watch him between the crack in my arms. He is walking toward me but has lowered his gun slightly. "You don't let us fuck the women. Is that why you have her here? Or is she a buyer? Angelo didn't say anything..."

A gunshot blasts through the room. I was right. It's loud as fuck. My body tenses more than it already was. My eyes are closed tight, swelling with tears. I'm not a big crier, but this much stress makes me cry. A body collapses on the floor, and I finally look up. I wasn't shot. He didn't fire his gun at me. Instead, I find Catherine lowering hers. She turns her head from the man to me. I meet her for a brief moment before looking at the man.

He is unnaturally crumpled on the floor. A pool of blood is spreading around his body from a gaping hole in his head. The blood is shiny, contrasting with the light floors in the dim lighting. It's hard to breathe. Something bubbles in my chest, and then a scream erupts from my mouth. I'm terrified. I've never felt fear like this. I've lived a spoiled, cushy life. I'm not an outlaw. I'm a good girl. I continue screaming, my body unwilling to react any other way. Catherine starts toward me. A murderer is moving in my direction. I'm in love with a murderer.

My body finally begins to function. I turn and run. I run as hard as I can. As fast as I ever have. While my winter boots are called sneakers, they aren't suitable for running, but I keep moving. My apartment is several miles from here. Even with the adrenaline, I'll never be able to run the whole way. I don't really need to. I just need to run faster than Catherine. But she runs for exercise. Shit, I need to hide.

A taxi drops someone off at the curb. I push my body harder and rush to the cab. When the other person is out, I dive into the seat and rattle off my address.

"Please drive. I'm in danger."

Thankfully, she listens and pulls off. Tears stream down my face. I don't bother stopping them or wiping them away. I focus on the last bit of control I have on my body. I just need to get home. And lock the door. And put a chair in front of it. Maybe the fridge, too. Then, I can fall apart and think everything through. Or just fall apart.

The ride goes by quickly. The driver asks if I'll be okay, and I assure her I will. She offers to drive me to the hospital or call the cops. I consider the offer. Would I turn Catherine in? She killed a man and had drugs in the warehouse. But does that make me an accessory to murder? Would I go to jail? I don't know how murder charges work. I don't want to go to jail. I'll think about that tomorrow. I decline the offer and move through my building on high alert.

I collapse on the kitchen floor once everything is locked and a chair is shoved under the handle. Great, heavy sobs take over my body. I roll into the fetal position, propping my head on my bag. What the hell is going on? I went to the warehouse to check out a dress I had made. Instead, I witnessed drug trafficking and murder.

Catherine told me her life was dangerous, but I never expected that. Who would? How many people has she murdered? What else is she in? Does she work for a cartel? Is she in the mafia? How did I not see this? What is my life? Who would have thought coming to Kansas City would get me tangled up in this kind of mess?

My parents will be so disappointed. I can't tell them. I can't tell anyone. I was there. I saw everything and didn't even try to stop it. I froze. I didn't help that woman. I'm no better than Catherine. Am I a felon now? Should I go on the lam? Will Catherine? Tears stream down my face. It's easier to breathe now, but I'm no less tense.

A knock on the door startles me. I jerk up, hiding behind the counter. It won't stop a bullet, but it offers me a false sense of protection.

"Jo? It's me, Zed. Can I come in?" Why is he here? Did Catherine send him to kill me? To tie up the loose ends?

"What do you want?" I'm surprised by the conviction in my voice. I certainly don't feel that.

"I want to talk with you."

"That's what they all say before the guns start blazing." Or at least that's what happens in the movies.

"Jo, I don't," he pauses, then continues in a lower voice. "I don't even own any guns."

He doesn't seem like the type to own guns, but Catherine doesn't seem like the type to murder someone in cold blood. I don't want to let him in. Will he go away if I don't?

"I'm going to stay until you let me in. But at a certain point, Catherine will replace me."

I stand quickly. Zed is better than Catherine right now. If I'm going to be forced to talk to someone, I would rather it be him. The chair drags across the floor as I pull it away. I unlock the deadbolt and handle, neither of which feel sufficient anymore. I crack the door open, peeking out at Zed. He opens his coat, showing me he's not wearing guns in a holster. I've seen enough TV shows to know that's not the only place people keep guns.

"Do you want to pat me down?" Yes. Do I trust him not to have guns right now? Is that a risk I should take?

"Can I?" He nods to me. That makes me feel better. I step back and let him inside. I don't close the door as I pat his arms, chest, and legs. If he has a gun, I need a way to escape. I tap his lower back, not feeling anything. I assume a gun would stand out, but what do I know? I guess I need to learn these things now that I'm a criminal.

I close the door. Zed removes his coat, hanging it on a hook. It occurs to me that I am still wearing mine. I didn't notice. I remove it, and my body shivers. I'm covered in sweat, and the cool air makes me cold. Or maybe that's a stress reaction. I can't tell the difference at this point. I kick my shoes off and walk to the kitchen. I stare at my fridge for a moment. I have wine and tequila. Catherine left a bottle of scotch on the counter. We don't drink often, but she'll occasionally have a glass with me.

Fresh waves of tears and indecision overcome me. Zed walks behind me with heavy steps—he's not ordinarily heavy-footed—but he's doing it, so I know where he is. He steps into my view, holding his arms out to guide me to the chairs. He doesn't touch me, though. I'm thankful for that right now.

"Come sit down. I'll grab a drink for you."

I wish I had better control of my mind, my body, my emotions. I don't want him to do that for me. I'm fully capable of making myself a drink, just not right now. Instead, I nod and do as told. I'm good at following instructions. That's something I can do. I'm not cut out for a life of illegal activities.

Zed walks over with a sports drink and a single shot of scotch. He knows that bottle is Catherine's. Why he's giving me that instead of my tequila, I don't know. I also don't understand why he is only giving me one shot. Did Catherine not tell him what happened? Oh shit, is Zed involved in it too? Does he help her find the drugs?

I take the shot, letting it burn down my throat. I close my eyes, savoring the pain. It's the only thing I can feel at this moment. Everything else is cold and numb. When I look up, Zed watches patiently, waiting for me to speak first.

"What did she tell you?" My voice is meek again. This is who I am. A good, quiet girl.

"Nothing. Just that something happened, and you'd be upset." That's true. Though, upset is an understatement. What is the right word? Terrified? Horrified? Overwhelmed?

"What do you know about her? Outside of work?" Maybe he can tell me something.

"Not much," he shrugs. I'm not even surprised. "She has other business ventures outside of Marzanna but keeps those to herself. She's reserved and doesn't get close to anyone." I sigh. This isn't helpful. I knew those things. I take a sip, unsure what else to ask. If he doesn't know anything, asking questions won't do any good. I don't want to drag him into whatever this is.

We sit in silence for several minutes. My body calms, almost to the point of fatigue. I don't know if I could sleep. I imagine as soon as I lay down in bed, my mind will start racing, and terror will strike. Maybe I'll just sit on the couch and watch a movie. Hell, maybe I'll just start using crack. That'll keep me awake. Will Catherine give me some? How do I even use it? Can I Google that? Was that even crack in the warehouse? I don't even know what drug it was.

"Why don't you get some rest? We need to leave for the fashion show in a few hours," Zed breaks the silence.

The what? Oh fuck. I forgot about that. Watching a murder will do that to a person.

"I'm not going to the show. I can't be around her. Or anyone." I take a deep breath, the next step clear in my mind. "In fact, I'm leaving Marzanna. I'm going to Minnesota for a few days, then somewhere else. I can't stay here."

"Jo," he says sympathetically. "Catherine isn't going to the show. She will give you space, but you need to go to the show. You've worked so hard on that piece. You deserve to show it off."

"I can't, Zed." A fresh wave of tears streams down my face.

"I know it feels like that now. Whatever Catherine is in is deep. But you can't give up on this because of whatever happened." I huff a laugh. Pretty sure I need to give up if I want to stay out of jail.

"Look, go to the show. Flaunt your work. Then rest. Take a couple of days off. I'll complete the paperwork if you still want to leave after that. Don't make a rash decision in this state." He is pleading with me. "Please," he adds desperately. I've never known Zed to beg. He gives orders, much like Catherine. It's what makes them good businesspeople. They know how to get what they want.

He's not wrong. I do deserve to show my design. What good would staying in my apartment or running to Minneapolis really do? It just further proves my guilt. Guilty people run. I didn't do anything wrong, not really. I just watched. That's not really illegal. Is it? God, I feel so naïve. I don't know anything about the law. I'm a basic Midwest girl. I like flannel, saying things like "doncha know" and eating hotdish. I don't go around being an accessory to murder.

Catherine won't be at the show. I can go if she's not there. My heart breaks. We were going to announce our relationship this weekend. She was going to support me. I sob again, unsure how any tears are still left. Zed wraps his arms around me. I cry into his chest as hard as I have been, seeking any bit of comfort I can get. I can't do this. Everything hurts. Physically, emotionally, legally. My life is shattered into a million pieces, and I can't talk to anyone.

21 · JOSEPHINE

It's been three months since the fashion show. The show was terrific, and my piece did well. It won the Best Overall Design award. No one questioned Catherine's absence or my reserved attitude. So many people applauded my dress. I was riding a weird high, ecstatic about my dress but also devastated over the events of the night before.

After the weekend, I couldn't imagine not going back to Marzanna. I took a few days off but had to go back. It's been my dream for years. I can't give up on that now, illegal business or not. I have avoided Catherine. I haven't spoken to her, not even in passing. My stomach is suddenly upset when she does group meetings, and I need to go home. No one says anything. Zed covers for me. She doesn't eat lunch with us anymore. She doesn't try to talk to me. I wouldn't say things are great, but the stress I feel going into work has decreased. I haven't been back to the warehouse, though. No cops have shown up. I guess that's a good thing.

I have yet to create another piece as good as the first one. Everything is dark or red. Whenever I see red silk, I flashback to the warehouse. One of the pieces I designed was a black dress that had a red train. It pooled like blood on the floor. It would have been a good design if I hadn't paired it with a one-sided red silk veil dotted with blood-red pearls on strings. It was too gory for any show other than Halloween, and that's long since passed.

I did go home for Christmas. I couldn't fathom staying here alone. My friends from the apartment invited me to have dinner and swap presents with them, but I needed to get out of town for a few days. Catherine sent me a present. It was on my doorstep when I returned. I still haven't opened it. It sits in the spare room. It's out of sight, so I frequently forget about it. Every now and then, I spot it and remember it's there. Curiosity swells inside me, but hurt and anger usually win, and I leave it alone.

Catherine hasn't texted but has sent me a few other cards and gifts. They also sit on the bed, unopened. I don't want to hear what she has to say. All the gifts have been left at my door, not my mailbox. I imagine she is sending Zed or John to deliver them. I don't know if they are knocking when they drop it off. I find something on my doorstep when I open the door.

It's Wednesday morning. I'm heading into Marzanna. I have an idea for a new design that isn't dark or red. Though less enthusiastic than when I started, I'm excited to get to work. I'm still anxious about going to work. Catherine has done a good job of avoiding me and giving me space, but that doesn't mean there isn't a chance of bumping into her. I don't see her every day, but she's there.

I didn't check the mail yesterday, so I grab it on the way out. I sit on the bus, turning up some music on my headphones. I flip the envelopes, mostly junk mail. A small Manila envelope sticks out, so I rip it open. I don't check the sender. I don't remember ordering anything, but there's always a chance I did and just forgot about it. I do that, especially when I'm emotional. I have a breakdown, and a package arrives a few days later. It's always a pleasant surprise from Past Me.

I slide the items out and flip them over. It's a couple of photographs. It takes me a moment to place them. The first one is from when Catherine took me to the jazz bar. We're cuddled on the couch, her face buried in my neck. My heart swells, then burns with anger. Did she send this to me to remind me of the good times? The next photo is us at the grocery store, buying food to cook at my apartment. The third photo is us outside Marzanna. We hadn't been able to spend time alone for a few days, and she kissed me in the alley. Now I know she was busy trafficking drugs.

Did John take these photos? The Manila envelope is blank, with no sender or address. Why is she sending them to me now? I burn with rage at the implications. Does she think I'll come back with a couple of photographs? I haven't spoken to her since that night. It's time to break my silence.

At the office, I drop my bags at my workspace then glance around the floor. Catherine isn't down here. The lights in her office are on. Zed is moving around, chatting with the assistants. I grab the envelope and walk toward Catherine's office. I want to stomp and make a ruckus but hold back. She won't see me, but everyone else will. Making a scene isn't for their sake; they don't need to know what happened. Or that anything happened. I'll release my anger on Catherine in her office, behind closed doors. I take a deep breath, trying to settle the rage.

I don't knock when I get to her office. She is turned sideways and doesn't see me walk by the window. I slam the door behind me. I can't resist that urge. She is on the phone when the sound reverberates through her small, empty office.

"I need to call you back." She lowers the phone, and muted protests come from the receiver. She hangs up anyway. I breathe deeply, trying to calm everything I'm feeling. I'm angry, hurt, nervous, scared, and still, my body tingles with desire. How long will she have this effect on me? She doesn't speak, watching me with a calmness I may never achieve.

I toss the envelope down on the desk in front of her. I try to keep some distance between us, scared she'll read every emotion and play on the ones she chooses. She knows how to work me to elicit the feeling she wants. She glances at the envelope but quickly looks back at me.

"What the fuck is this?" My voice is all but a yell, laced with anger and annoyance. She grabs the envelope, only looking away from me long enough to get it.

"Did you think I'd come crawling back if you sent me a few photographs?" The pictures slip into her hands as she takes them in. She examines each one as though she's never seen them before. I turn away, more outraged by her audacity to act surprised.

"Where did you get these?" Her voice is soft.

"Don't act like you didn't send that shit to me to win me back. I haven't opened any of the other gifts, Catherine. Slipping this into my mailbox was sneaky. If I wanted your shit, I would have opened it. I'll bring everything back tomorrow. I don't want it." My words are harsh, laced with all the negative emotions I feel.

"Jo," her use of my name still stings. I'm not her baby girl anymore, but it doesn't hurt any less. We had something real. The way that it ended will take more time to recover from. I bite the inside of my cheek to stop the swell of tears. Her voice is soft when she speaks again. "Please keep the presents. I sent them to you. I know you don't want to hear anything, but let me explain things," she pauses, glancing at me with uncertainty. "Meet me Saturday. I'll tell you everything."

"I don't want to know anything, Catherine!" I start yelling but quiet my voice by the last few words. I haven't made a scene in the office; I don't want to start now. She stands, walking around her desk toward me.

"Please just give me a chance to explain."

"No," I say sternly. I'm not listening to any of it. "Stop sending me shit."

I turn and storm out of her office. I'm not staying to listen to anything else. I walk to my desk, shuffling through my bag. Zed stops by my desk, pausing like he will say something. I glare at him. He nods and walks away. He has been understanding about this whole situation. I don't know if that will run out eventually, but I'm not talking to him right now.

I leave the building to get coffee. I already had coffee at home but need fresh air and a break from Marzanna. I'm overwhelmed with emotions, and tears threaten to spill. I'm constantly on the verge of crying and hate being like this. I call Sadie to get her to distract me. She can only talk for a couple of minutes, though. She tells me about some new client she has at work. We're off the phone by the time

I return. I feel more calm than I did when I left. I didn't get to say anything but didn't need to. Just hearing my best friend's voice was enough.

Zed asks me to follow him to a meeting room. I'm positive this is about Catherine, but sometimes, we discuss specific client needs. I give him the benefit of the doubt and follow him. He closes the door behind me, motioning to the chairs. I don't really want to sit. I stare at the chair for a moment, then sit cautiously. My body is more tense than I realize. I relax in the seat more than I anticipated.

"She wants you to meet her Saturday at 4." He slides a folded piece of paper across the table. I open my mouth to object, but he speaks up instead. "I don't know what this is," he taps the paper. "I have an idea. If it is what I think, you should know no one else has this. She uses a P.O. Box for all business forms. Even her tax forms. I'm pretty sure only she and the realtor have this. I also suspect she used an alias so no one knows who she is." I huff at that. She has a lot of secrets to keep. How many aliases does she have? I cross my arms over my chest, unwilling to look at the note.

"I don't know what happened between you two. It's clearly tragic. I'm going to say one thing, then I'll drop the subject," Zed takes a deep breath before continuing. "I've been with her for eight years now. She has many secrets. I know that. One thing I know for sure is she doesn't date anyone. Ever. She's never gotten close to anyone, and it's not for fear of breaking up. She has been distraught since things went down. She's missed appointments, meals, and phone calls. She's made errors I've never seen her make. She cares deeply for you. And you cared deeply for her. Talk with her this weekend. If for no other reason than finding some closure." He pushes the paper a few inches closer to me and then leaves the room.

I stare at the paper, unsure what to think. I'm surprised to learn Catherine's been distraught. I hadn't thought about how this would affect her; I didn't care how it would. I knew she loved me, even if she didn't say it. I assumed she hid her feelings about this split like she does everything else. To learn that she is slipping up makes my heart twist. Am I angry? Sad? Empathetic? Glad?

I open the paper to see what she wrote. It's an address. No name. I look it up in my maps app, and curiosity gets the best of me. It's in the nicer part of town, but not too far away. I could easily take a cab or even the bus. John's name is written next to a phone number. She's offering to let me call him for a ride. While that's tempting, I want to use something other than her driver. I'll find a way there on my own.

That thought lands heavily in my stomach. I guess I'm committed to going to see her. Zed does have a point about closure. What will she say? What will I say? Do I have to say anything? I will finally get some answers.

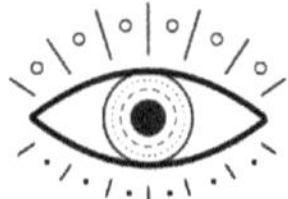

IT'S TEN TIL FOUR. If I'm going to make it to Catherine's place on time, I should have left fifteen minutes ago. I've been staring at my bag for twenty minutes. I'm going to go. As soon as I can make myself move. She can wait for me. I packed all the gifts to take back. It's less noticeable if I take them to her place than to the shop.

I finally leave my apartment to catch a bus that will get me close to her building. I'm stressed and nervous. My stomach hurts. I might vomit. I might cry. I brought a pack of tissues just in case. Not because I'm sad but because I cry when I get too stressed. This is definitely a high-stress situation.

Her building is so tall. It's mostly glass, with a few balconies scattered around. Some have chairs, but most look empty. I enter the lobby and realize she didn't give me an apartment number. I think she owns a whole floor, probably the top one. I pause, debating what to do. I could call her, but I could also leave.

"Jo!" a man calls my name. I turn to see John walking toward me. Catherine made him wait down here instead of telling me which floor she was on. I guess she can't give me everything.

"She has a private elevator in the back. You need access to get to it. She doesn't have extra cards yet." He motions behind his back and turns for me to walk. He said 'yet.' Do they expect me to take her back? To need a keycard to get to her apartment? Rage pierces through me as I follow John. He scans his card and guides me on the elevator. Only three buttons are on the panel for the top three levels. John presses the top button but doesn't join me. He gives a nod as the doors close. I don't know what I'm walking into. Who will get shot this time?

The elevator dings and opens to a small foyer. One door is across from me. Bare white walls surround me. This is it. I could still turn back. I could leave the presents by the door and return to our life. Our complicated, painful life of avoiding each other. But I've come this far already. I deserve answers and closure. I take a deep breath and knock softly on the door.

"It's open," she says from the other side.

I didn't think Catherine would be the type to leave her door unlocked, even with other security measures. She's so guarded all the time. I suppose a drug trafficking murderer should be. I open the door and step inside slowly. Her apartment is designed similarly to mine. Sleek modern furniture and appliances, few decorations, white and black lines. She has a couple of paintings that add a small amount of color. It could be an operating room. It feels cold and empty.

She is standing next to an island in the kitchen. She is wearing a sheer crop top and low-waisted boy shorts. Catherine is a big fan of the boy shorts. Her sheer top does little to cover her breasts. My betraying body reacts with arousal at the sight of her breasts. I can't deny my attraction to her, but I don't need that now.

"Thank you for coming," her voice is soft, unlike the confident woman I am so used to.

"I'm only here for answers." She nods and motions to a chair near her. Thankfully, there are several chairs, so I don't need to sit beside her. I kick my shoes off, set the bag of gifts on the counter, then sit closer to the opposite end. She peeks in the bag and recognizes the gifts but says nothing.

"Do you want a drink? I have wine or whiskey. Soda or the sports drink you like." I instinctively roll my eyes at her having my favorite drink, but something in my backstabbing heart clenches. She thought to get what I wanted. I want to hate that. I need to hate that. I can't let my stupid, broken, but desperate heart control things.

"I just want answers." I insist again.

"It's a long story, Jo."

"Fine," I grit out. "Give me a shot and a drink."

She moves through the apartment with grace I've never had. She's still beautiful and powerful, even in her subdued mood. I watch her muscles tense and release as she walks. Her tattoos are exposed beneath the sheer top. The low-waisted shorts reveal more tattoos across her stomach and lower back. It's all the same style, the thick lines from the American Traditional style.

A gun and a fox poke out from her underwear. I didn't notice those before. I tried to keep my eyes above her waist when she was in the shower. It didn't seem right to stare at her when she didn't intend for me to see her. She's showing me that now. Or more of it. The broken bits of my heart clench, wanting to come back together for her. I refuse to let them.

She slides the drinks to me and returns to the island's end. I take the shot, gritting my teeth as the alcohol burns down my throat. That pain has brought me back to reality too much recently. I won't take more than two shots, but the burn is oddly comforting. Some days, it's the only thing I can feel. I refuse to make eye contact, waiting for her to start talking. I fidget with the drink.

"I never wanted you to be involved..."

"I just want to know about the trafficking and murder." She pauses when I interrupt her. I'm generally not this rude. I'm not usually in the same room as a murderer.

"Do you want to know how I got into it or explain why?"

"Tell me why." Her fingers tap on the counter, the only sign she is nervous. This is the only time I have ever seen her break her confidence. I finally look at her. She is tense, staring down at her fingers instead of me. This is hard for her, too. She doesn't know how to open up to someone, let alone explain her illegal activities. "Why is Marzanna involved? Who are you involved with?"

"Marzanna Shipping is my way of keeping the law away. Everything looks legitimate. I have contracts with everyone."

"Contracts." A humorless laugh sounds from me. "What, you write up how many dime bags they can ship through your warehouse?" My sarcasm is heavy, but Catherine doesn't react.

"Yes. We call them units instead." She actually looks upset about that. Is she upset because I caught her? I want to believe she genuinely doesn't like it, but I can't. "The contracts detail how much they can ship and how frequently. It's vague enough to have deniability but strict enough to keep the bosses from taking advantage of me."

"Who are the bosses?"

"A variety of people. Cartel, mafia, rich and powerful. Some are only in drugs, some have other businesses."

"Do you ship anything else? Are there guns in the warehouse? You transporting stolen goods? Let me guess, you have a couple of nuclear bombs in there that are going to China?" Catherine shakes her head, taking my attitude in stride. I'm not going to cut her any slack right now. I'm too far beyond caring.

"No. Just drugs." The way she says that... It's both confident and heartbreaking as if she knows it's wrong, but it's still her truth. I hate it so much.

"How long have you been doing it?"

"I started looking for ways in when I was 18. I worked my way up and got my first client 15 years ago. I expanded enough to start Marzanna ten years ago."

"So, Marzanna is just a front for your trafficking business?" Disbelief shrouds my question. My chest squeezes. My dream job is just a scam for drugs. My eyes burn with the tears I knew would come.

"Not entirely. Marzanna Fashion is still a legitimate business. Diane is in charge of the fashion side. I'm only on the business end."

"Ha, so you can funnel all your illegal activities without anyone knowing?" She nods at me. A tear strolls down my face. My life is a lie. My dream is crashing around me. "Why fashion?"

"I was friends with Diane and saw how talented she was. She was struggling at the company she worked for. She had mentioned starting her own line, so I gave her that. I fronted the money, and we started the business together. I realized the shipping would work well for my other ventures. The large containers for clothing, climate-controlled shipping, and frequent shipments of large items are innocent enough to not draw attention."

Innocent enough, I sigh at her words. My chest clenches. Everything hurts. I don't want to hear any of this. I want to go to sleep. I want this to not be my life. A thought slams through my heart like a sledgehammer.

"The outreach program for the kids?" My voice breaks on the last word. I don't want to think about the kids that come to the shop after school to work. I stay on the fashion floor and don't deal with them much. They have different spaces, but I see them occasionally when they walk to our side of the building. It's one of the reasons I love Marzanna so much. The program gives teens a safe and healthy outlet that is away from drugs. Or it should be.

"It's a front for the money. Easy to launder the cash." Catherine pauses but adds, "They still get the benefits. I fund it with drug money." I choke out a sob, tears spilling down my face. We are silent, aside from my soft cries, for several minutes.

"Who was the man?" It's nearly a whisper. I can't manage more than that now.

"He was a mid-level capo in one of the mafias. He was terrible at his job."

"Oh, so he deserved to die?" Sarcasm oozes from me. I can't control it anymore.

"Yes." That's a fair response, I guess.

"What about the party in Minneapolis?"

"Jo," Catherine takes a deep breath, dropping into the seat beside her. A chair remains between us. I'm glad for the space. Any closer, and I would consider strangling her. "I'm not telling you to garner favor with you. If I explain my past, it would be clear." As if she could say anything at this point to make it better.

"Just tell me about that night."

"A few weeks before the party, I had a shipment come through with guns. I've never shipped guns." I cringe at her words. I didn't see any guns in the warehouse. Guns would take up a lot of space. "The guns were snuck in without my approval. I tracked the shipment once it left the warehouse. It stopped in Minneapolis. The weekend we were there, the boss hosted a party to sell them." I suck in air. I don't want to hear this. I don't want to know what happened next. She came back with a gunshot wound and covered in blood. Did they practice with the guns on each other? Was she there to buy more?

"I worked with a partner to get intel. He drove me there and waited while I snuck in before the party began. I removed the firing pin from each gun, rendering them ineffective and potentially ruining the dealer's reputation. One of the guards caught me. I subdued him long enough to finish the job, but he was found before I was off the property. They pursued me. I only got away after a fight."

Wait, what?

I stay silent for several minutes, trying to process what she said. She ruined the guns? Why wouldn't she fucking lead with that? How do I know that's the truth? Sure, her story lines up, but that isn't proof. She's good at keeping secrets. She could be good at lying.

I take her in, trying to figure out if she is lying. Her shoulders are slumped. She stares down at the table. She feels terrible about this situation. If she ruined the guns, does she do that for the drugs?

"Do you interfere with the drugs, too?"

"Not often."

"Why not?"

"Someone would recognize my pattern. Sometimes, I pass the information on to other organizations to stop the drug shipments. I don't do many interventions like that anymore. I offer a safe space for the women that process the drugs and a landing point for the dealers."

Whew, this is heavier than I expected. I don't know what to do. I rise from my chair and walk through her apartment. Moving shakes some of the nerves, but I don't see anything. I could be walking through a museum or a fire and wouldn't know the difference. I collapse on the couch with Catherine watching me.

"I suggest you start at the beginning. None of this makes sense."

22 · JOSEPHINE

CATHERINE WALKS TOWARD ME and sits on the coffee table before me. I watch her, overwhelmed with my own emotions. She doesn't touch me, but her closeness reminds me of every time she did. She took such good care of me. It feels entirely at odds with her trafficking.

"My father is a mafia don in Spain." Well, that's a bomb I didn't expect. "When I was eight, men broke into our house looking for him. Instead, they killed my mother in front of me." I gasp, covering my mouth with my hands. I'm supposed to be angry at her. Instead, my chest aches. "My father sent me to the States to live with relatives. They weren't in the mafia. He thought I would be safe. He didn't know they were involved with the mob. I watched for years as they conducted illegal business. Guns, money laundering, drug trafficking. They did it all. I learned the ins and outs of their business.

"At 18, I applied what I learned from my family and worked my way in with different cartels. Despite my involvement with the family business, I never saw the impact on people. It was always just business to me. No different than a department store selling shoes." She looks at me, pain from decades of a problematic life shining through. I realize for the first time she isn't wearing makeup. She's completely exposed. It's hard to be mad at her like this. I don't move, frozen as she explains everything.

"Once I was established as a middleman, I made contacts on my own. My focus was making money. I wanted to make enough to escape this life. Like every naïve person, I believed I could work my way out. After several years, I realized I wouldn't get out. I changed my plan and established myself as a vital point in Kansas City. I opened the warehouse, giving them a place to process and then move the drugs. It wasn't until a few years ago that I learned my father has an extension of his mafia here in the States. And I work with them." My mind spins when she stops talking. She told me many times she led a dark life. I never would have guessed this.

"That's why you don't have partners." She nods, wringing her fingers together.

"I didn't want to get close to you. I didn't want to risk you being involved or associated with me beyond the fashion business. But I couldn't stay away, Jo. You... you're special." She opens her mouth like she'll say more but stops herself. My mind wishes she would call me 'baby girl' again. This morning, I wanted nothing to do with her. I debated leaving Marzanna, and now I want her to call me the nickname she gave me. My mind tumbles over the loops it's taking. I look away from her as the tears stream down my face.

"The photos you received yesterday are from my father." Before I can ask the question, she is already answering it. "He wants me to go to Spain to take over his business. He's old and dying and wants to keep the mafia in his family. He thinks using you will get me to go over there. He's been harassing me for months."

"I'm sorry." It escapes before I can stop it. I don't know what I'm sorry for. Her terrible childhood, her difficult life, her dangerous father. I don't know, but it all hurts. Catherine shakes her head, dropping it down. Her hair, longer now than it used to be, hides her face. The movement causes her shirt to ripple, drawing my eyes to her chest. The eye tattoos are visible through her shirt, large and bold against her pale skin. I sit up, and she raises her head to watch me. Slowly, I reach out. My fingers graze her shirt over the tattoos on her chest.

"To see everything," she explains quietly. I trace my fingers over the lines. She always sees everything.

"And your back?" It's a whisper. I have a hunch about that one. I don't want her to say it, and I don't want that answer, yet I ask anyway.

"People I've killed or put in jail. I've dropped an anonymous tip a time or two when I didn't want to deal with them."

"And there's a new one?" She nods. She watches as I step around her. My fingers trace over the bold knife tattoos. Thirty-nine knives in neat little rows on her back. She stays covered to hide her secrets. She etched them on her body, a visual reminder of all that she has done. A sob escapes from my chest as tears blur my vision. I cover my eyes, overwhelmed with everything. Catherine rises and wraps her arms around me, but I push her away. I hold my stomach, ready to leave. Instead, I turn back to her.

"Why did you kill him in front of me?" She takes a deep breath, meeting my gaze.

"I wish I could say it was only to protect you, but that's not true." My breath hitches at her answer. "I've wanted him dead for a long time. He's a rapist. When he pointed the gun at you, I took the opportunity. I wouldn't risk your life, but it wasn't purely noble reasons either." Her words feel honest. This isn't a lie. Nothing she has said today feels like a lie. It all feels raw and honest. I don't think Catherine has ever outright lied to me. She omits the truth. A lot of the truth.

"I need time." I turn to leave her apartment. I need time away from her to process this and decide what to do next.

"Wait, please stay here." I give her a skeptical look. Why would I stay here after everything she has just told me? "I have a spare room. I don't know what my father is doing, but I want you to stay safe. He doesn't know about my condo. I'm trying to figure out who is following us and if they still are."

"Am I in danger?" I cross my arms over my chest. Her request isn't unreasonable. I haven't had any problems since she left, but they know where I live. They have been following us.

"I'm not sure. I don't think my father would hurt you, but he is far more violent and ruthless than I am." Her tone is more of an answer than her words. I may be in a lot of danger. Since she hasn't had partners before, she can't be sure how they would use one against her. This whole situation is so fucked up.

"I don't have any clothes."

"I have some you can use." Her words are wary. We aren't the same size, not even close. Even with some of her oversized clothing, it would still be too small for me. She had these clothes already.

"How long have you had them?"

"I bought them when we returned from Minneapolis." I fight back some tears, turning to look around. "I'll get some dinner going. You can rest in the spare room." She points in the direction of a door cracked open. "It has a bathroom, and I can bring the clothes in there if you want to shower and change." I don't say anything but walk in that direction. I want to lay down now. I'll shower and change later.

"Jo, wait." I turn back, arms wrapped around my waist. I can't take any more information at this point. "Please open these gifts. I bought them for you. I can't do anything with them or return them. I want you to have them." I take the bag from her absently. I don't have it in me to argue now. A gift may distract me and lift my spirits. My mind is reeling over everything. I need a distraction from the confessions, violence, and risks to my life. I can't handle all of this. How does one cope with the knowledge a lover and boss are involved in the mafia?

Pulling out the three boxes, I place the bag on the spare bed. One is a square box, one is a smaller rectangle, and the third is a flat, thin box. I open the largest box first; it was the first to arrive. Inside is a hoodie from the fashion show. I didn't have time to go to the merch stand. After learning how well my design did, I regretted that but couldn't do anything by then. I don't know how she managed to get the hoodie, but I can't deny how happy it makes me. Other branded items are in the box: a keychain, bags, stickers, and a water bottle. I appreciate the thought. A soft smile tugs at my cheeks. My appreciation for the gift further entangles all my conflicting emotions.

I slide the box aside, grabbing the rectangle one. Something is wrapped in tissue paper. A note on top says, "When I can't be there, baby girl." A fresh wave of tears spills down. I need to finish my drink from earlier before I get dehydrated. I pull the tissue paper off a box with a toy inside. It's a weird shape, some toy I have never seen before. It has two balls and a long flat part. I don't know how it works. I wonder when she got it for me. Did she have it before everything went to shit? Or was this an attempt to win me back? I toss it aside, unwilling to think about sex.

I pull the final gift over, nervous about what could be in here. After the thoughtful merch and the sex toy, I don't know what this one could be. This was the last gift to arrive at my apartment. It was close to Valentine's Day when it showed up. She never said anything to me about any of them; she just had them delivered.

I pull the wrapping off slowly, finding the gift wrapped in cardboard. It's not a closed box, just wrapped for protection. Two frames are between the cardboard. I tug them slowly, laying them side by side on the bed. One is a sketch of my design, one of the first I drew. Marzanna has cloud storage; anyone can access our designs or files that are loaded into it. She printed it off and framed it for me. The second frame holds a photograph of me standing on the runway beside the model wearing my dress.

She printed and framed these pictures for me. I can display them in my home and always see my best accomplishment. She gave me that. She gave me the opportunity, pushed me to create it, then celebrated my achievement at a time when I wouldn't talk to her. My emotions overwhelm me, and I drop to the floor, sobbing into my hands. I lean against the mattress, unable to support my own body anymore. This whole day has been too much.

I can't handle all of this. The way she cares for me is so obvious. Her tender treatment, thoughtful gifts, the insistence that I take care of myself and stay safe, it's all because she loves me. But she's in drug trafficking. She uses her business to sell illegal drugs. She murders people. Sure, they're bad guys, drug dealers, rapists, whatever. Does that make her any better, though? She's also a drug dealer. What if someone kills her? My heart clenches at the thought of her lying in a pool of blood on the floor of the warehouse. A loud wail rips from my chest.

"Jo? Are you okay?" Catherine opens the door and rushes over to me. Her arms wrap around me, pulling me into her chest. I let her. I need the stability and comfort, even if it is from her. I can't stand the thought of losing her permanently.

"I'm so sorry, baby girl." She speaks against my head, kissing my hair several times. I savor the gentle touch. I don't know what I want to do about this situation, but at this moment, I need her. "I'm sorry," she whispers against me. I hold her tightly, crying into her chest. Her top is sheer. It won't absorb my tears. Each one drops down her chest, rolling over her eye tattoos. The ones that represent her need to see everything, to know everything.

It's hard to hate her with everything she has told me. She does terrible things, but does that make her a horrible person? She also does good things, like destroying the guns and offering the women safety in their dangerous jobs. Until the warehouse, she was the best thing that ever happened to me. Even after, she still cared for me, even with the distance I demanded. I can't process anything as my consciousness wanes.

It's dark around me when I wake up. I don't remember falling asleep or getting in bed, but I'm here. My body is sore, and a dull ache spreads through my head. I blink a few times, taking in the space around me. The spare room slowly forms. Dark shadows fill the corners. I don't know how long ago I fell asleep.

"Kitty?" My words are quiet and scratchy.

"I'm here, baby girl."

Swirling emotions settle as Catherine moves to the bed. She strokes her fingers over my face, pushing my sweat-soaked hair back. I take her hand, holding it still. My mind is calm, the stories and pain from earlier stored in the back of my mind.

"Do you want something to eat?"

"No, just a drink and pain relievers."

She stands from the bed but pauses. Catherine turns and leans in slowly. She presses a soft but lingering kiss on my temple, then leaves the room. My body tenses but relaxes at the comfort she brings. I can't let her go. I want to stay with her. I need to find a way to reconcile her secret life. Does occasional vigilantism make murder and trafficking better?

Catherine returns with the items I asked for and several snacks. She turns on the bedside light for me. I take the medicine and sip the drink, glad for the relief. She stands, watching me. She wants to sit with me but doesn't know if she should. Her indecision brings a smile to my face. That's not the woman I know, but I love seeing this side of her. She has put on wide pants and an oversized cardigan. Her apartment is cool, but the bed is warm.

We spend the rest of the night in her spare room. She brings her tablet to work. She gives me a spare, letting me download the software to work on some designs. This bed is warm and soft. Thoughts of this situation skirt my mind, but I mostly avoid them. I don't want to think. I've been thinking so much lately. Everything needs consideration. Every detail needs to be known. At some point, I want to live, feel, and experience things without analyzing every little piece of information. It was working before I walked into the fucking warehouse. Can I get that back again? Maybe not the naivety, but the joy, the ignorance, the bliss? I could live that way again, right?

Catherine won't sleep beside me. She holds me while I sleep, but every time I wake up, she is in the chair beside the bed, usually awake. She spends the day sitting next to me, but not as close as she used to be. I miss her warmth, her smell, and her comfort. I understand her hesitancy; I haven't been easy on her. And I'm not going to be. That doesn't mean I don't want her close. She enters the room, walking to the chair.

She is giving me space to process everything. It's heavy. I should put more effort into considering what it means. For me, for my future, for my career. I need to consider whether I want to continue this relationship. Could I not take her back? Can I go back to Marzanna and avoid her like I have been? It will take me time to accept everything she has told me. I need to know more to understand. But deep inside, I know. I don't want to live without her anymore.

I slide over and lift the blankets, holding them open for her. She hesitates for a moment, then climbs in next to me. I rest my head on her shoulder, wrapping my arms around her waist. Her arm drapes over my shoulders, squeezing me gently. In her arms, everything becomes clear. I know what I want to do.

"I want to be with you." Her grip tightens on my arm. "But I don't want you to keep secrets from me. I want to know what is happening with your father, when you are traveling for illegal business or making shipments. I want you to tell me." She wraps her other arm around me, kissing my head. I feel so warm and safe in her arms. She will do anything to protect me. I don't have to worry about anything with her.

"I want all of you, Catherine."

"You have it," she whispers, "but I don't want you there. I'll tell you, but you can't be involved." I nod my head. That's fine with me.

My hand slides down her side and across her abdomen. I'm not looking for sex right now, but I want her to understand how serious I am. I find the waist of her pants and slip my fingers against her skin. I don't push lower than the hem. My fingers slide back and forth over her smooth skin. Her muscles tighten with anticipation and nervousness. Her chest stops moving, frozen beneath my touch.

"I want everything, Kitty."

I lift my head from her shoulder. She looks at me, fear etched in her wide eyes. Her hand slides to my cheek, cupping my face gently.

"Everything," she whispers. Her lips find mine. Her kiss is gentle, promising, loving. I pull my hand from her pants and slip it into her hair. Our lips, our hands, our bodies meld together. We fit perfectly; we belong in each other's arms. I'll learn to accept her dark side, and she'll learn to share it with me. It's not going to be easy, but we will do it. We will get past this and learn to be what each other needs.

"You know," I pull back from the kiss, resting on her shoulder again. "I loved you before you made me an accomplice to murder." I tease, but her grip tightens around me. "I was so angry, so hurt, but I don't think I ever really stopped caring." She strokes my arm, remaining quiet. "You never did, either. Did you?"

She shakes her head, fingers dancing over my skin. "Tell me," I whisper. She loved me before all of this went down. She still does. I can feel it in the air around us. She knows exactly what I want to hear.

"Jo, I..." she pauses, uncertain. "I..."

"You can't say it, can you?" I glance up at her, humor filling me for the first time in months.

"Of course I can say it," she snaps back. "I..." She hesitates again.

"Here, I'll help. Just repeat after me. I." She sighs but indulges me.

"I."

"Love."

"Love," she repeats through gritted teeth.

"You."

"You."

"Good, now all together."

"I..." She still can't say it. I kiss her cheek as I chuckle.

"It's okay. I, too, Kitty." It's close enough. Love and something else shine on her face. Is it relief? Instead of focusing on that, I kiss her again, this time more passionately. My hands slide over her body, finding her breast. I cup her soft flesh, caressing her nipple with my finger. It hardens under my touch. I delight in the sensation I haven't had before. Excitement rolls through me at the thought of enjoying her sexually.

"You need to rest, baby girl." She breaks our kiss, resting her forehead against mine. She's right. My body is worn out, mind distraught. Arousal is an easy emotion that fills the space temporarily, but it won't help or change anything. Instead, Catherine guides me into a prone position, pulling me against her chest. She holds me tight as my body falls quickly into sleep again.

Her expensive perfume fills my senses, bringing comfort I didn't expect. I didn't want to come here and take her back. I came here wanting to hate her. I didn't want this. But now I don't want to give it up. The past months have been miserable without her. No other breakup has hurt this deeply or this long. Most were amicable. Even the more dramatic ones weren't this impactful. Catherine is different. I don't want to let her go. I want to stay with her despite everything she has told me. I'm not ready for this to end.

23 · CATHERINE

She's back.

I have never known relief like I experienced when she said she wanted to be with me. The past few months have been terrible. I don't know how to live without her. I couldn't breathe, couldn't think straight. I would walk through the break room and smell her perfume and citrus hair products. It took all my control not to grab her and demand she listen.

I didn't expect her to be okay with my other businesses. I didn't expect her to break up with me, though. I didn't consider how much of a risk shooting Peter in front of her would be. All I could see was red when he pulled a gun on her. Any other time, any other person, I wouldn't have reacted so rashly. Not with Jo, though. Peter honestly wasn't even a real threat. He wouldn't have shot her. In that moment, though, I could only see her fear.

I'm hesitant around her now, waiting for this bubble to burst. How fragile is our relationship now? We haven't had time to recover from everything. The fear of losing her again tightens my chest. She's snuggled in my arms now, but could that be snatched away again? I don't think I could lose her a second time.

One of my alarms goes off, alerting me it's time to get ready for work. I shift gently to sit against the headboard. Jo is settled beside my legs. I shut off the alarm, scroll through my messages, check the news, and give Jo more time to sleep. I love waking up next to her. I love having her in my apartment. I love everything about her. I can't say it to her. Anxiety grips me; my muscles seize; fear ripples through me. I want to tell her what I feel. When the words bubble close, I see my mother's face, bruised and broken. Indecision rips through me. I don't want that for Jo. Reconciling having her in my life is hard.

"What time is it?" Jo says groggily. She rolls against me, covering her eyes with her arm.

"About five a.m."

"Oh, gross." She groans, burying her face between my thigh and the bed. I chuckle, stroking her side. "Jesus, Kitty," she mumbles. "Are you really 'wake up before the sun' old? Do you also go eat supper at five p.m.? Do you need to get that early bird discount, or do you get an AARP discount everywhere?"

I would laugh out loud if I were willing to give in to her teasing. Instead, I tickle her ribs, making her squeal and rip away from me. I pursue her, climbing on top of her as she squeals her objections. Under normal circumstances, I would stop at her objections, but not this time. She winds up on her stomach beneath me while I straddle her. My hands smooth out, caressing instead of tickling. I haven't touched her in months. It's long overdue now.

"Is that how you want to start the morning, baby girl?" My words are husky in her ear. She doesn't respond, but her quickening breath and blushing cheeks answer for her. I swing my leg over her body, kneeling at her side. One hand splays across her upper back, holding her in place. My other hand glides over her lower back, across her luscious ass.

"Mmm, baby girl," I whisper against her ear. Her ass pushes into my hand. Any hint of hesitation would stop this, but she is willing. Oh, so deliciously ready. I slip my hand under her sleep shorts, under her panties, and grab her ass. I squeeze it roughly, eliciting a gasp from her. I spread my hand across her, teasing my middle finger between her cheeks.

"If I move lower, will I find you wet?" I nibble on her ear. "Ready for me?" I kiss her neck. "Needy?" She doesn't say anything again, just moans deeply. I slide my hand lower. My middle finger follows her center, teasing her. As I reach her pussy, I pause, tracing my thumb over one plump ass cheek.

I hesitate, worried this is too soon, too much. What if Jo isn't ready for this? What if she isn't wet for me? We only rekindled Saturday. It's been less than two days since she said she wanted to be with me again. We have yet to discuss what this means for us.

"Kitty," her hips lift into my hand, "please."

That's enough for me. My hand drifts lower, grazing over her opening. She's so wet. She wants this as much as I do. Relief washes over me, nearly causing me to sigh into her neck. I restrain that reaction, nipping her shoulder instead. Her leg shifts wide, giving me better access to her aching cunt.

"Good girl," I whisper against her ear. She shudders, skin pebbling across her body. I rest against her side, glad for the connection to our bodies. One finger glides through her soaking core. Her groan vibrates against my chest, driving me to plunge inside of her. She is so wet and soft. I want to taste her. I want to feel her. I want to keep her in this bed and make her come so many times she forgets who she is. Unfortunately, we need to work. I have business to tend to today.

"Kitty, fuck, please." She squirms beneath me while my finger slips in and out slowly. "I can't handle this. Please let me come." Under normal circumstances, I wouldn't tolerate those kinds of demands. I understand today. If I continue to prolong this, we won't be going to work.

I add a second finger, then slip my thumb in also. Jo wiggles beneath me, making it harder for me to touch her the way I want.

"Stop moving, or you won't be coming." She freezes, following my directions so well.

My thumb swirls several times, gathering moisture. I kiss her shoulder, where her neck meets her ears. Her sweet scent exhilarates me. I slide my thumb out and thrust the other two in deeply. While I stroke her smooth walls, my thumb presses between her cheeks, finding her tight hole. She gasps, but it turns to a moan as I press against her ass. Using my thumb to stabilize her, I pound my fingers deep into her wet center. I savor the feel of her walls clenching around my fingers.

I massage my thumb around her back hole, not pushing through but increasing the pressure. She groans beneath me, cursing and pleading. My fingers inside her cunt swirl around her slick walls as they glide in and out.

"Come for me, baby girl," I whisper, my lips brushing against the shell of her ear.

I push against her tight hole, just breaking through the ring. She cries out loudly, her pussy clenching around my fingers.

"That's it, baby girl. Come like a good girl." She shudders beneath me as I wring the last of her orgasm from her. As her body calms, she twists to face me, kissing me deeply as our arms tangle together. Nothing feels as good as she does. Holding her in my arms, tight against my body, everything feels right. I cup her face with one hand, pulling away from the kiss.

"Not too old to do that," I joke. Jo hums in agreement, nuzzling into my neck. I sigh in relief, unable to mask that emotion around her. Jo strokes my sides, settling against my chest. An odd tingling fills my soul. She's the only person I let get this close to me. I've never wanted to hold anyone like this. Now, I can't imagine living without it.

"Maybe, but it's still too early to be up." I chuckle at her complaint.

"I need to head into the office early. I have a few calls to make." She tenses ever so slightly.

"Undesirable calls?" I pull back, looking down at her with intrigue.

"Is that what you are calling it?" She shrugs. I plant a kiss on her forehead. "No. I need to call some fashion partners on the coast." She sighs, nuzzling against me.

"You can shower and wear the clothes I bought if you want to sleep longer. I'll drive, and John can give you a ride."

Jo shakes her head against me. "I should go home and shower."

"Okay, but let John drive you." She yawns, nodding as she stands. She gathers her things and moves into the kitchen to collect the rest. My chest tightens again. It does that a lot lately. I would be concerned if it wasn't a reaction to her. I know it's her, though. I don't want her to leave. I follow her into the kitchen, standing by the island while she packs things in her bag.

"Stay here with me." She looks up at me.

"You just said you need to work today."

"After." I created contracts to make drug trafficking look legal and keep cartel bosses in line, but I can't ask her a simple question.

"Tonight? Sure, I can come back." She shrugs, pulling the clothes she wore over the pajamas I gave her. "Do you need more time to figure out if I'm in danger?"

"No," she looks confused. "Yes, tonight. Yes, I need more time, but …" She eyes me incredulously. I can't form the words to ask her to stay. I can't tell her how I feel. What is wrong with me?

"Okay. After work, I'll grab some clothes and come back here." I nod. I can't say what I want. Why do I have such a difficult time articulating my thoughts with her? Is it just the serious, committal thoughts I can't voice? She packs her things while I walk into my bedroom. I need to shower and change clothes. Wash away the awkwardness of that conversation. I stare into my closet, lost in my own thoughts.

"Catherine?" Jo sounds timid from her spot in my doorway. I turn to face her. My face is blank, not betraying my self-consciousness. "Were you asking me to move in?" My lips turn up slowly. I open my mouth to respond and remember everything I have said to her this weekend. Instead, I just nod. She bites her lip, looking down at her feet to hide her smile.

"I still have about six months on my lease." I take a step toward her.

"I'll pay for you to get out of it. Or you can keep it. If you want space." She looks up at me as I stop in front of her.

"You think I'll leave again?" I don't respond. I don't want to consider it, but I can't rule out the possibility. My dark secrets aren't going away and won't be secrets from her if she gets her way. Even if she doesn't leave, she may need space. Her hand cups my jaw, thumb tracing over my cheek. I close my eyes, allowing myself to enjoy the intimacy. I don't like to show intimacy, but I will give that to Jo.

"I don't know what we're doing. I know you just returned to me, but I want," I hesitate again. It's easier to speak with my eyes closed, but she deserves better than that.

"Ask me, Catherine." Her voice is soft but firm. I open my eyes but stare at the ground. I can't bring myself to meet her gaze. Maybe I can say the words if I'm not looking at her.

"Move in with me, Jo." My words are a whisper. Nothing like the commanding voice I use during sex. Nothing like the controlled tone I use for business calls. It's not exactly weak, but it sounds nothing like me. Before I look up, Jo's lips brush against mine.

"I'll bring food and clothes over after work. We can move the rest later."

"I have food." My eyes peel open, finding humor in hers.

"I know. I do, too, but it will go bad if I don't bring it." I pull her into my arms. Emotions roll through my body. Happiness, joy, and excitement make me feel lighter than I have in a long time. I kiss her head, squeezing her soft body.

"I..." The words still escape me.

"I, too, Kitty." Fuck, this woman is perfect for me.

THE WEEK HAS GONE smoothly. Jo is staying with me now. She goes back to her apartment after work each day. She leaves before me, grabs a few things, and is at my apartment when I get there. She has her own keycard, and the guards know her. She has access to the garage with all my vehicles but insists on taking the bus. The only reason I let her is the bus stop is close. She doesn't want to ride with me. We haven't told anyone about our relationship. We aren't ready, and the topic has yet to come up.

I'm staring out the window in my living room. Everything is grey and dreary, and it's nearing the end of winter. In a few weeks, things will start to warm up. Spring will be here soon, but not soon enough. I don't mind winter, but it always starts to drag around March. I'm ready for spring, warm weather, and green. Gloomy grey is dull. Let's brighten things up, Mother Nature.

Jo comes into the apartment, and everything brightens. The gloomy grey fades away as her aura fills the space with faux sunshine. She's bright and colorful today, looking every bit of the spring I want. The color of her hair changed a couple of weeks ago. Instead of the fading yellow and red, she now has a vibrant blue that fades to green. Soft beach waves settle across her shoulders, reminiscent of a mermaid basking on a rock in the sun. She wears a gorgeous orange midi dress, dark tights, and flats that match the color of the dress. She isn't always so color-coordinated, but fuck she is beautiful.

I walk over to greet her, gently kissing her wind-blistered cheek. Her body settles against mine. For a brief moment, everything is right in the world. No darkness enters our space. We are two souls united in peace and harmony. Ribbons of light swirl around us as fate pushes us together, binding us.

As soon as the feeling hits, it's gone as she steps away. Does she feel that? Does she feel the completeness her soul offers mine? Or is my soul so stained that any bit of intimacy would bring it to life? She unloads her bags, putting away more groceries and items she got from her apartment. I watch her move with ease and comfort. I rarely feel anything. She has made this space her home. She's talking to me, but I barely hear the words.

"I told her that is ridiculous, that she can't..." Jo's words drop off as she stares at something behind me. I'm not positive what she was saying before, but I did hear the last sentence.

"Can't what, Jo?"

"What is that?" I turn to look at her question, not finding anything out of the ordinary. She walks past me, focused on whatever she sees. She crosses the living room, stopping in front of the couch. I hung the two photos of her design above the sofa. It's a central spot in the living room, seen from the kitchen and bedroom, and on full display in the apartment.

"You hung them?" Jo turns back, eyes blurry with tears. I nod to her, unsure what the tears are for.

"Yes, I hope that's okay." She lives here now. The photos should be displayed. She rushes over to me, wrapping her arms around me and claiming my mouth. Her fingers tangle in my hair. It catches me off guard. I haven't had a partner touch me like that since I was young. Unwittingly, I moan into her touch. Her kiss, her hold, her body becomes more desperate. Before I realize what is happening, she's tugging me into the bedroom. It feels foreign to have someone drag me to a bedroom, but I don't hate the feeling.

She pulls me to the bed, hands roaming my entire body. I try to caress her back, but every time I make a move, she shifts her arms to block mine. I'm not positive what her goal is here, but I don't like not being in charge, not leading this experience. We snuggle on the bed, but she has me on my back. She's on her side, leaning over me. My body tingles with nervousness and anticipation. She has wanted to touch me since the beginning, and I haven't let her. This is why I hire people for sex. They don't push issues like this.

"Baby girl…"

"No, it's my turn."

Her fingers glide over my stomach, touching lower, lower, lower. I grab her hand instinctively as she reaches the top of my boy shorts. Hesitation and fear coat my body. Her hand stills under my touch, thumb stroking my abs. Her other hand strokes my hair, offering comfort.

"You've been so good to me. Let me be good to you."

Her eyes are pleading but soft and kind. I can't deny this girl anything. She leans in slowly, kissing me deeply. Her lips on mine offer solace in my raging storm. I release her wrist, dropping my hand by my side slowly. Her tongue swirls languidly around my own, slow and casual. A caressing touch, assuring me everything is fine.

Jo dips her fingers beneath the hem of my shorts. My body tenses, and I try to relax under her touch. It's been so long since I have let anyone touch me like this. Let anyone touch me intimately. I've been resigned to handshakes and whatever touches I give my sex workers. I'm not on the receiving end of familiar touches. I battle off the rising anxiety, fear of the unknown, the uncontrollable.

"I want to make you feel good," Jo whispers. I'm so tense with anticipation that I didn't realize she stopped kissing me. My eyes are closed tight, every nerve in my body focused on her fingers cresting my pubic bone, sliding lower, lower, lower, sliding toward a place no one goes, a place no one has access to, a spot I keep reserved.

"You're safe with me, Kitty." Her whispers don't comfort me as her finger glides along my slit. Images of my mother crash through my mind. She said that exact phrase to me many times. My mind blasts images of the last time I saw her. That's not what I need right now. Jo's finger swirls my clit. Sensations course through my body. A tangled mess of anxiety and a ghost of pleasure. My pleasure comes from control, not my own body.

"Kitty," she murmurs again.

"Don't call me that," I seethe, seeing my mother again. I realize how harsh the words sound when her fingers freeze. "Not now." She nods against me, kissing my cheek, ears, and neck. My mind wants it to feel nice, but my body is tense, unsure of what is happening.

I turn my face, burying into her neck and hair. I breathe deeply, letting her scent wash over me. The crisp citrus smell always brings me comfort. It relaxes me enough that when she slips one finger inside me, I don't rail and jerk against her. I grab her arm, holding her wrist tightly.

"You're still in control, Catherine." Jo's soft words settle in my chest. She'll stop if it's too much for me. I'm still in charge. I have the control I so desperately need, just not over her finger that is slowly stroking up and down my opening. The tip of her finger presses between my lips. Not even penetrating, just parting them.

This is supposed to feel good. I've seen it; I've made people feel good doing this exact thing. Just this morning, I was teasing Jo like this, her body shivering beneath mine with need and ecstasy. I can't muster that same feeling. Only fear and anxiety fill me. My body is tense with concern, worry of losing control, of being vulnerable, of having everything taken from me. In my mind, I know I shouldn't feel this way. Jo is my person. She is the one person I trust with everything. Why is my body betraying me now?

Jo swirls my clit, massaging it the way I have to her so many times. I could make this same motion to make her come within minutes. My traitorous body is only filled with dread. Prickles cover my skin. On any other person, it would be a sign of pleasure, of an impending orgasm. This is what Jo thinks. Her circles increase over my clit, flooding my stomach with trepidation.

"That's it, Catherine. Let me see you come."

Rage floods me at my own body's betrayal. This should feel good. I should be close to climax. Instead, my stomach is clenched with anxiety, and my muscles tense with apprehension. The faster Jo moves her finger, the faster my doubts swirl inside. Every opposite reaction to what I should experience tears through my body. Nothing about this experience is euphoric for me. It doesn't look like it to Jo. She only sees my backstabbing body as reacting in a typical way.

I need this to stop. I can't continue with this. My mind is tight with pain, and my muscles tense with anxiety. Do I fake an orgasm? I've seen enough, and I know how to do it. Will Jo know it's disingenuous? She doesn't have any fingers inside me. She won't realize my cunt isn't clenching for her. She doesn't notice the lack of moisture between my legs, which is the only indicator that this isn't working for me. If I fake an orgasm, will she want to do this again? Subjecting me to this torment? Could I stand that? Would it get easier if we do this more? How long could that take?

"Jo," I whisper in a raspy voice. That does nothing to dissuade the notion that I am on the edge of orgasm. I'm far closer to an anxiety attack. Would that look like an orgasm if I let it happen? Her fingers don't stop their ministrations against my clit, only pressing more anxiety into my body. I wrap my fingers around her wrist again, squeezing tightly this time.

"Please stop."

Jo freezes, not moving for a moment. Her hand slides out of my underwear, and relief washes over me. Then regret. I shouldn't feel this way. I keep my face buried against her neck, embarrassed, angry at myself, and worried Jo is angry or hurt. I don't know why this happens. It's probably my own doing. I haven't let anyone this close in decades. Jo scaled the wall around my heart. Apparently, there is another wall around my clit, even higher than my heart. I never really thought I was unique, but who the hell has a wall around their sex?

Jo drags her hand along my arm, not my chest, until she reaches my neck. Her fingers trace over my jaw, tugging me ever so softly to look at her. Dragging the remaining bits of my unaffected consciousness, I look up at her. Her eyes are soft, not pitying but concerned. She is not angry or hurt but worried for me.

"Do you want me to leave?" I shake my head. I don't want her to ever leave. I need to hold her now. She's my anchor. Her hand strokes my arm, offering a small comfort.

"Do you want to talk about it?"

Yes. No. A small part of me wants to turn into her chest, bury my face in her to hide from my discomfort. The rational part of my brain knows that will only make these feelings worse. Instead, I roll on my side and adjust our arms so she is in my chest. She's pliant, letting me take the position I want. Her arms wrap around my body, soothingly rubbing my back.

"I haven't done that in..." Do I say decades? Do I tell her the whole truth? That I haven't come or tried to in ages? Possibly before she was even born. Do I tell her the last time I orgasmed, I was filled with so much dread after that it prevented me from trying again until this moment? That this moment could seal the deal for the rest of my natural life? Before I can answer, she speaks again.

"Did it not feel good?" Jo isn't upset. She isn't filled with self-deprecation. She isn't worried that she did something wrong. I thank all the deities for that tiny relief.

"It..." I pause to search for the right words. "When you touch me," I speak softly, my chin against the top of her head, "It fills me with dread. The goosebumps were from anxiety. The quick breathing was panic." Jo's arms tighten around me, pressing her body into mine. I close my eyes, savoring the sensation.

I worry for a moment that she will apologize for something she did wrong, for something that is wrong with me. She doesn't, though. She holds me, calming my distressed body. We stay like that for several moments, holding, comforting, touching.

"Do you want me to stop calling you Kitty?"

"No." My answer is harsh and quick. "No," I start more softly. I pull back, tracing her jaw. I lift her to look at me. She does, so willing in my hands. Unable to avoid it, I press a soft kiss on her forehead. "My mother called me Kitty. I love that you do it, too. At that moment, all I could see was her." I release a soft chuckle. "Not the image I want while you touch me." The corner of Jo's lip rises in a half-hearted smile.

"Did that cause you to spiral?" I shake my head, pulling her back into my chest.

"No, baby girl. That would have happened either way."

"Did you know it would happen?"

"It's happened before, but I hoped it would be different this time." We hold each other tightly, drifting off to sleep far earlier than we should, but unable to face anything else right now.

24 · JOSEPHINE

I DIDN'T KNOW HOW to react after trying to give Catherine an orgasm. Things seemed to be going so well until she asked me to stop. I'm glad she asked, but I felt wrong for pushing her to that point. It was selfish. She told me she hadn't done that in a long time, but I wanted it. I shouldn't have tried. I didn't know she would feel that way. She doesn't seem upset now that a few days have passed, but she hasn't given me an orgasm either. We've kissed and cuddled but not gone any further. Maybe she is just teasing me again.

I knock on her office door and enter without waiting for a response. She takes one of her illegal calls when the door is closed. No one else can waltz in when the door is closed, but I'm not anyone else. She's on the phone, and I plop in one of the chairs. She motions that she'll be a minute, and I nod. I'm not in a rush at this point.

I take the time to look over Catherine. She's so freaking stunning. Her hair is longer now, dusting the tops of her shoulders. She still keeps it in a bob, just longer. The dark color of her hair contrasts with her pale skin, making her look almost porcelain. An oversized beige sweater with a turtleneck covers all the secrets she permanently marked on her upper body. Her dark brown pencil skirt does nothing to conceal her long, lean legs. The skirt barely covers her knees, highlighting how tall she is. Fuck I love those legs.

A cough breaks my attention. Catherine caught me staring. A few months ago, I would have shied away with embarrassment. Not today. I grin at her, letting heat flood my face, my intentions fully displayed.

"Did you come in here to ogle me?"

"Of course. Why else would I come in here?" Her devilish grin is playful, but she doesn't say anything else. Is she keeping a count of my missteps again? Is that why she hasn't touched me? She's been counting my bad behaviors? If that's the case, I'm in danger. That thought doesn't stop the shiver of arousal coursing through my body, slamming into my aching clit. I wiggle in my seat, trying to relieve some of the increasing pains. Catherine catches the movement, knowing precisely what I am doing.

"Um, tonight is trivia night with my friends. Do you want to go?" I change the topic before she admits she's counting, and I have to start begging.

"I can't. I have a shipment tonight." Oh.

This is the first one since we got back together.

"Maybe I shouldn't go," I start, trying to dampen the rising nervousness. "I can wait at your apartment."

"It's our apartment, Jo." She uses my name to emphasize her point. "Go out with your friends. It will be late before I get back." Catherine shuffles a few papers around on her desk. My mind floods with images of her bleeding and sobbing in the bathroom. She said that night was different, not a shipment, but that doesn't comfort me. The shipment I walked in on still ended in a murder.

"We normally spend time at someone's apartment after, eating and drinking more. I was going to see if you wanted to stay at my place with me." My voice is soft, laced with anxiety and doubt. I've moved many things to her place, but not everything. I have yet to tell the landlord or my friends. I'm holding back for now; not quite ready to make anything permanent. We just rekindled this. I feel confident in the relationship but am not ready to make the final leap official.

Catherine rounds the desk, propping herself in front of me. This is a favorite position of hers. Standing against her desk, looking powerful and sexy and so domineering.

"Go out with your friends, baby girl." Her fingers wrap around my jaw, forcing me to look at her as she leans in. "I'll come to your place after. Then we can pack up more things before we leave." She gently kisses my lips, calming some of my fears. "I've been doing this for ten years, Jo. I'll be fine." She's right. Obviously, she is. I know that.

"Come on. Let's head out. I'll give you a ride to your apartment. I'll be there later. Don't wait up for me."

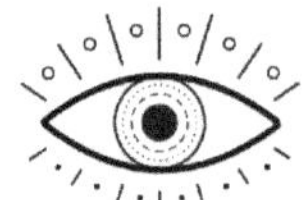

THE BAR IS MORE crowded than usual. Trivia has become more popular, and we have to fight to get a table now. I pretty much hate it. I love being with my friends and drinking and playing trivia, but fuck, there are so many people here. We may need to find a new bar or pick a different night.

"Jo!" Ben yells as he walks up with beer for everyone. "I wasn't sure you would come tonight. When was the last time you even stayed in your apartment?" I haven't actually told anyone that I've been staying with Catherine. I haven't admitted out loud that we are living together. Ben is observant, though. Guess now is a good time to rip that bandaid off.

"It's been a few days. I'm staying with Catherine." Everyone gasps. No one knows what happened, but they all know it was terrible. They saw me at my lowest. They comforted me and brought me food. Made sure I left the apartment in those first few days.

"You're back with her?! Jo..." Amara says my name sympathetically, and I hate it. I can't explain what happened, why we made up, or why it's not as big of a deal as before. Maybe I shouldn't have taken her back. Even explaining the whole situation still sounds bat shit crazy.

"I had to talk with her recently." I try to keep my words hushed, but it's hard in this crowded bar. They lean into the table to hear better. "She...um," I can't exactly say her father is using me to blackmail her, and that's what got me to talk to her. I also can't say she sent me a gift because they know I haven't been opening the gifts she sent me.

"I thought you were avoiding her at work." Ben's response could work to my advantage.

"Yes, I was. It became too difficult. I wanted to talk to clear the air and find a solution we could work with. But she started talking and explained everything that happened. I shouldn't have avoided that conversation for so long." I take a long sip of my beer, hoping the alcohol will kick in quickly.

"What did she say? You never actually told us what happened." Amara reminds me frequently that I won't tell her what happened. And I never will.

"She explained her side of the story." I shrug, leaving it at that. "You guys saw how torn up I was. I couldn't really stay away forever. There's something about her. I can't give up on that." Ben rolls his eyes at me.

"Please." His sass causes all of us to giggle. We've downed enough of our beers that I'm comfortable offering to buy the next round. I leave the table, glad to get away from that conversation. It's not one I want to have. While waiting at the bar, I check my phone out of habit. No new messages. Not that I expected Catherine to message me. She rarely does. She's so weird with technology. That makes more sense now.

Checking my phone only leads me to think more about her. Is the truck there? Are there a bunch of people? How many guns does Catherine have on her at this exact moment? Definitely more than me. My brain floods with questions and concerns. When the drinks arrive, I take a massive gulp of mine and order another immediately. Since we're returning to Ben's tonight, I'm not worried about getting plastered and not making it home. They'll get me there.

Trivia starts as I bring our drinks to the table. They eye both of my drinks but don't say anything. This is why they are my friends. The announcers are going over the points for the month-long tournament. Teams can play for the night, but scores are also tallied for the month. The top winner gets an even larger prize. We aren't competitive, but it's fun to see our score. We are currently in second place. We're laughing and having a great time; only every other thought is of Catherine's safety.

After my double order at the bar, Amara and Ben don't let me get drinks again. I give them money, but they only buy me one drink at a time. This is fine by me. I have a good buzz going; now, only one in three thoughts is of Catherine's activities, so that's an improvement.

"It is time for the game to begin." The announcer draws everyone's attention. "Here's the first question. In the mafia," oh shit. That lands like a rock in my stomach. A reminder I don't need or want. "The middlemen are called capos. What does capo stand for?"

Three months ago, I wouldn't have known that answer. I would have thought capo was just what they called them. Unfortunately, around that time, my life changed. I watched a capo get his brains scattered across a warehouse. Granted, I only learned this weekend that he was a capo. I kinda went psycho girlfriend and researched all kinds of shit. Catherine has no digital footprint outside of a handful of photos about Marzanna Fashion. She's largely off the radar. So, I researched the mafia. And learned so much more than I ever wanted to know. Ever needed to know. Probably still don't need to know, but here I am, about to win some points at trivia for us.

Ben and Amara are making wildly incorrect guesses, also believing capo was the full term. I interrupt them, hoping that other teams are struggling the same way.

"Caporegimes," I answer. Both looked at me, stunned. This isn't an answer I should have. I shrug, "I got really into The Godfather recently." They laugh out loud at me.

"And you tell me this on the day of my daughter's wedding." Ben uses a husky voice, incorrectly quoting the movie. He laughs at himself while I roll my eyes. Amara writes the answer on our card, glancing up at me.

"Alright, let's make them an offer they can't refuse," Amara adds, using the same deep voice Ben did. I give her an unimpressed look, but my friends are nearly falling out of their seats with laughter. It's contagious, and I join in.

After the announcer has all the answers and tallies the points, he shares them with the bar. Most of the teams got that answer correct. We play the rest of the game, have a few more drinks, and thoroughly enjoy ourselves. By the time trivia ends, only a quarter of my thoughts are for Catherine's safety.

We head back to Ben's apartment for pizza, more beer, and, entirely unironically, The Godfather. Even though it's a three-hour movie, we manage to stay awake for the whole thing. A feat on the best of nights. We laugh far more than we should during a drama, repeating quotes in a husky voice. Pretending we are capos. At one point, they discuss what their crew would look like. It's toward the end of the movie, so my silence is taken as sleepiness instead of wariness. Once the movie ends, I go to my apartment. I check my phone once. No new messages. Then I collapse on the bed.

My dreams are addled with gunshots and trench coats and Italian men with gold chains. Then, they slowly shift. It's not so stressful. Now, my dreams are warm and fuzzy. My body tingles with delight. Everything feels right except for my stomach. That bitch is nauseous. Not enough that it drives me from bed, but enough that I know it's happening.

Warmth radiates from my pussy. Tingles spread across my body, leaving me feeling light and free. I shift, trying to roll over to settle my stomach, but something stops me. I didn't have a pillow along my body. Am I tangled in the sheets? As I become more aware of my surroundings, I realize someone is in bed with me. My mind is still cloudy when I jerk awake, rising quickly. I inadvertently knee Catherine in the face as I try to move.

"Holy fuck," I breathe, rubbing my eyes. "Oh my god. I didn't know you were here. Shit! Are you okay?" She doesn't rise from her spot or grab her face where I hit her. Her smile is snakelike as if she just slithered into my bed and will continue to slither, taking what she wants. My core heats again, and I realize she was eating me out. That was what shifted my dreams: her tongue in my cunt. My body relaxes with that realization. She doesn't say anything, just pushes my legs apart, returning to her feast. I didn't realize I stripped entirely before bed, but I'm glad I did.

Catherine's tongue is on my core again. I moan, collapsing against my headboard. Her hands stroke up and down my thighs, using her nails to get my blood flowing. Her tongue makes lazy strokes across my opening, leaving me panting. I shift slightly, sitting up more and dropping my legs wide. Her eyes meet mine as she devours me. It's so fucking hot. Her eyes are brown and huge, solely focused on me. I can't breathe under her stare. It's burning.

Her hands trail up my sides, never breaking eye contact with me. Her fingers reach my nipples and twist them. Hard. I cry out, bucking against her face. She sucks my clit into her mouth. She pops it out with the most sexy fucking noise I have ever heard. Her tongue is instantly inside of me, and I erupt. Every nerve ending is burning, tingling, shining for her. White bursts behind my eyes while my body convulses. She continues working me, bringing me down slowly.

Catherine crawls from between my legs to my side when my body calms. She kisses me deeply. I can taste myself all over her, and why is that so fucking hot? Holy hell, this woman is fantastic. I cling to her, holding on with everything I have.

"Did you have a good night?" She asks when she breaks the kiss. I settle in her arms, resting my head against her chest. She is still fully clothed, but the clothes aren't thick. I can hear the steady beat of her heart through her top. I take a deep breath, fighting off a wave of nausea.

"Mmhm," I mumble. "Did you?" I tense momentarily, remembering what she was doing last night.

"Everything was fine." She kisses the top of my head, squeezing me reassuringly. I know why I was so angry at her, but at this moment, it's hard to remember. Being in her arms is heaven.

"I thought we could pack a few boxes and grab breakfast on the way back to our apartment." I love the way she says, 'our apartment.' I'm still not used to it, but it sounds so good. I want nothing more than that. I open my mouth to respond, but my stomach lurches. Instead, I groan, grabbing my middle and burying my face into her shoulder. She shifts slightly, then chuckles.

"Did you drink a lot, baby girl?" I nod against her, closing my eyes tight. "I'll grab some medicine. Why don't you get the shower started? You still have some clothes here?" I nod again. I have moved most of my clothes to her place. No, our place. I have yet to get all of them, though. I have a lot.

We move around the apartment: I attempt to shower, and she packs and checks in frequently. It doesn't take long, but it feels like forever when she decides we have enough. She filled two boxes and a couple of bags she could carry. I inwardly swoon at the way she is helping me. She takes excellent care of me. How she shows me she cares means more than words she can't speak. A small smile spreads across my face at that thought. While I would love to hear her say those three words, I also love having our own little phrase.

I open the door for her since I have the lighter load. Before I do that, I kiss her cheek, meeting her gaze.

"I, Kitty." The sweetest smile spreads across her face. I wish I could capture it to see forever. It would surely fade if I tried to grab my phone.

"I, too, baby girl." She leans down to kiss me again. As much as I want to deepen it, my stomach rolls over. I need to eat. Soon. I break away, grabbing the door before returning to get my box.

"What is that?" Catherine asks eyes focused on my door. I turn and find a bouquet of roses on the doorstep.

"Did you send that?" Catherine's face answers my question. Confusion and anger written across it. "Maybe it's Ben playing a joke. He does stuff like that." I cautiously grab the vase. A large card is sticking out of the top. Far larger than is normal for a bouquet of flowers. Catherine steps behind me as I open it.

"Look forward to meeting you" is written on the card, with two tickets behind it. Catherine mumbles a curse as I try to understand what I am looking at. It's too early, and I'm too hungover for this. I see the letters MCI and BCN on the tickets. My name is on one, with Catherine's on the other.

"What is this?" I hold them out for her, unable to process this. My mind is at half capacity at best. Between the alcohol, nausea, orgasm, and the shock of finding flowers on my doorstep, I can barely think. Catherine sighs, looking over the cards. Her face shifts from annoyance to anger.

"Looks like we are going to Spain."

25 · CATHERINE

THE FUCKING AUDACITY OF my father. He must be desperate to send Jo flight tickets instead of me. He knows I won't actually come visit him. I haven't seen him since he shipped me off to the States as a child. He didn't talk to me. He sent cash to my relatives, but that was the extent of his communication. He didn't call or send cards. No birthday gifts. Not even the slightest hint at achievement, and I've had plenty.

I finally find a girl I am crazy about and now he wants to speak with me. He refuses to talk over the phone. I've spoken to him once or twice in the past year. I tried to dissuade him of this notion that I could come in after more than thirty years and run his fucking regime. He refuses to let it go. I'm honestly surprised he didn't remarry and try for a son.

I've kept tabs on my father since I was old enough to find the information. My intel is better now than it has ever been. He's been with other women and even had a couple of women stick around for a few years. He never remarried and never had more children. Not even illegitimate ones. I haven't found the reason for that.

There are no medical records indicating any issues or surgeries. Not that there would be. I refuse to believe he actually loved my mother enough to still mourn her. He loved her, but not enough to never remarry or have children.

None of that matters now. What does matter is that he is dying slowly. He wants me to take over his business. He wants me in charge of a vast regime of men I haven't met. A few have lasted since my mother's death, but who knows if they actually remember me. They certainly don't know who I am now. My father has men here in the States. That irritates me more than anything. They followed Jo and me but stopped when we broke up. I need to figure out why he has restarted his efforts now.

I requested Jo stay at our apartment or work. My bodyguard, Liam, or I will accompany her if she needs to go anywhere else. I don't use Liam frequently. Until I know more about my father, I won't risk Jo's safety. She's scared enough that she agreed to my request. I stay close to her as often as I can to offer comfort. Overall, she is handling this situation better than I thought she would. My baby girl is a champ.

My fear since Jo came back into my life is unparalleled. For the briefest moment, I wanted to believe the danger wasn't real. That she could be happy and safe with me. That was always a pipe dream. I knew better. Stupid fucking hope. I held out. I wanted to believe. Then the roses showed up. Anger swirls through my body.

"Hey, Kitty."

Jo wraps her arms around my waist as she presses against my back. I release a deep breath as her body warms me, settling the raging emotions. We are packing for our trip to Spain. I altered the tickets my father booked us. The cheapskate booked us in economy for a Transatlantic flight. I understand being frugal, but I'll be damned if I'm flying coach for twelve or more hours. We're flying in first class with all the bells and whistles.

I did cut costs by staying with friends. Because of my ties to him, I have formed relationships with people near him. I haven't been to Spain since I was a little girl.

I have yet to meet all of my connections in the area. The ones we are staying with came to the States several times over the years. I have met them and tracked them. I trust them. Enough to stay with them for a few days anyway.

Jo's hands roam over my body, bringing me back to the present. I haven't dealt with my childhood in years. My father doesn't reach out. I have no other ties to the area. It was easier to squash everything than to continue to focus on it. I should have dealt with it through therapy. Then, I could keep my head in the present. Therapists aren't exactly known for working within mafias, though.

"How long until we leave?" I glance at my watch to answer Jo's question.

"About fifteen minutes. John should be waiting downstairs for us."

"Hmm," Jo taps her finger against her chin. "Guess that's not enough time for you to get me off then." She shrugs as I spin in her arms. Her face is playful and bright. A quick glance over my shoulder ensures I have enough packed to deal with my baby girl.

"No, probably not." We both know I only need a few minutes to get her off. "But there are other things I can do." Jo is wearing loose cotton pants with a crop top and a sweater over them. Perfect for spring, travel, and easy access. Before she can object, my hand plunges into her panties, finding her warm pussy. I drag my fingers through her opening. Her eyes widen in surprise, then settle into hooded lust.

"It's going to be a long flight, baby girl." She groans, twisting her body to give me access while leaning against me. Her head rests on my chest. One arm wraps around my back while the other braces my arm. Jo always knows exactly what I need. I need a distraction. I need control. I need her. I swirl my fingers along her length, moisture coating them more. She relaxes into me, giving herself to me completely. I slip my fingers out of her, licking them off as she watches with desire burning through her eyes.

"Time to go," I say, and she groans, adjusting her clothes. She grabs her bags with a huff and stomps to the elevator. She's been extra playful and bratty since she came back. I will never tell her, but I love it. I love her playful attitude. I love the quiet, reserved girl I saw initially, but I love the spirited Jo, too.

The ride to the airport is quiet. We watch our city, our home, pass by as we ride to the airport. Once there, we find our terminal and wait for our flight. We arrive the requested three hours early for an international flight. We sit near a window, and I whisper dirty things to her. She squirms in her seat, casting me glares because I only keep my arm around her shoulders. We're traveling for more than thirteen hours. There will be plenty of time to touch her.

The first leg of the flight is uneventful. We eat snacks, drink cheap wine, watch a movie, and I endlessly tease Jo. She may kill me before we ever make it to Spain. Or she may die from desire, as she likes to remind me. I will give my baby girl anything she wants, except an orgasm when she is acting out. The second leg of our flight is longer, over the Atlantic. Jo takes the window seat, staring out at the ocean below us. I convince her to sleep for a few hours. We'll be jet lagged by the time we get to Barcelona.

She closes her eyes, resting her head on my shoulder. Her touch makes every-thing else disappear. I can focus on her. Nothing else matters. All of the lights are dimmed in the cabin. Only enough to see the walkways. Jo sighs, settling into a comfortable position. Now seems like a good time for a bit of punishment.

I slide my hand over her stomach, under her top, into her bra, and stroke her breast softly. A low moan emits from her chest. I kiss her forehead, tweaking her nipple between my thumb and index finger.

"You gotta be quiet, baby girl," I whisper against her forehead. "This flight has close to 300 people on it. I won't share your sounds with them." She bites her lip, shifting just enough to get closer to me. She tugs the small blanket she has higher, covering my arm. It's long enough that it covers her thighs, too. My hand pushes to her other breast, repeating my movements there. She squirms beneath me. I debate whether I want to tease her for the entire flight or let her off now. It would be wickedly delicious to tease her for eight hours, but I do want her to get some rest.

My fingers trail away from her breasts and slip under her pants. Sliding lower, I don't find the hem of her panties. I search for another moment before grazing the patch of soft curly hair above her cunt.

"Jo, what happened to your panties?" I whisper against her forehead, keeping my voice as soft as possible. While most people are wearing noise-canceling headphones, not everyone is. She shrugs beneath me.

"Wanted to give you easier access." Indecision roils through me again. Oh, this girl…

I plunge my fingers inside her. I only have a moment or two before she is too wet, and it will make too much noise. The plane isn't overly quiet, but still quiet enough to make out the sound of fucking someone's wet cunt. As the moisture pools, I draw my hand back, circling her clit. She twists beneath me, arching to get a better position. I'm not in a great spot to give her more, but I am ruthless against her clit. Jo tenses and twists beneath me as her first orgasm rips out of her. She bites her lip, working to keep her breathing quiet.

My fingers slow as she comes down from her orgasm. She gives a soft sigh, then my fingers start again. She gasps out my name as I pinch her clit. She fights to keep in the moans, to be still, to stay quiet. Her body shudders, twists, and jerks beneath me. Her fingers claw at my arm. Both trying to stop me and push me further. It doesn't matter what she wants. I'm taking what I want right now.

Another orgasm crashes through her body. She buries her face into my neck, trying to stop the sounds she wants to make. She's always been loud, especially when I force multiple orgasms. She's huffing and clenching beneath me, but this time, I don't stop my fingers. I keep up the same relentless strumming of her clit. She should have kept her panties on. Her cunt is dripping. I work her through one more orgasm. She barely contains the moans. Any more orgasms, and we will be discovered. I don't want to be on the no-fly list.

After the third orgasm, I let Jo settle down. She drifts off to sleep quickly. She's resting against my arm. I want everything to feel right in this moment. It doesn't, though. Knowing we are going to see my father keeps the never-ending pit of fears alive and well in my stomach. Breathe in, breathe out. I try to settle my fears. These are so different from the ones I had last year before I met Jo. Even though these fears are more concerning, I wouldn't trade them for anything.

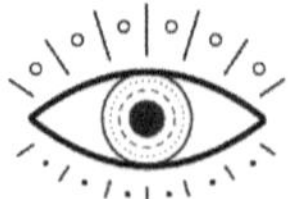

WE DROP OUR BAGS at my friend's house and head out to do some sightseeing. Due to the nature of this trip, there won't be much time for exploring. Our return flights are in three days, so we aren't staying long this time. We could come back one day, but it likely won't be soon.

I take Jo to the zoo. The zoo has excellent exhibits, is easy to get to, and has lots of shade and seating. We walk through the animal enclosures, pausing to look at the animals, occasionally discussing random facts about them. Even though the displays have English descriptions, I read some in my rusty Spanish. I haven't spoken Spanish since I was young.

She's quiet. She holds my hand as we walk but doesn't say much or look at me. We pause in front of the kangaroo exhibit. She leans against the rail, propping on her arms. I step behind her, rubbing her back gently.

"Are you tired or worried?" I ask. She glances over her shoulder at me.

"Both." I nod, leaning in to kiss her cheek.

"We can head back to the house. I need to shower and change." She nods, standing up. I wrap my arms around her. "It'll be okay, baby girl." Her lips curl up in a soft smile. She nods again, and I guide her out of the zoo and to my friend's house.

I have her take a shower with me, but only wash her. She isn't happy about that, goading me to touch her. It's hard to say no, but I need to for now. Once out of the shower, she pulls out more lounge clothes while I put on my business clothes.

"Oh, do I need to pick a different outfit?" She holds up the leggings and oversized shirt she was going to wear.

"No, baby girl. That is fine." She frowns as I put on my crew-neck, long-sleeve body suit and wide-leg trousers over it. She gasps when I put on a gun holster over my chest.

"Kitty, what the fuck is happening tonight?" Her tone is angry and scared. I didn't tell her the schedule for this trip. I didn't want her to be worried. I told her we are having dinner with my father, then need to visit one other house before we leave. I didn't tell her the days those are happening.

"Tonight is my dinner with my father." Her mouth is wide with shock but drops to confusion.

"Your dinner?" Her question is accusatory. I did lie to her about this. I didn't think she would be happy with my decision, but I needed her to go along with it.

"Yes, my dinner. I don't want you there."

"What the fuck? Why didn't you tell me? Am I just supposed to stay here by myself?" I take a deep breath, in and out. Time to rip off the bandaid.

"Yes, but not just that." She eyes me suspiciously. "My friends have a safe room I want you to stay in. I'll bring you out when I get back." Her eyes go wide. Wide enough, I'm sure they will burst out of her skull.

"You want me locked away?"

"Yes, just for a few hours." Her laugh is dry and sarcastic. This is why I didn't tell her earlier. I knew she wouldn't take it well. I get it. It sounds terrible, but it's the only way to ensure her safety. "Baby girl, my dinner with my father will end in death. I will not leave without resolving this issue. I don't have any concrete proof yet, but I believe he wants to take you to use as leverage against me. I need to know you are safe while I deal with him. The room is set up nicely. A large couch for you to rest on. TV with lots of movies, fridge with snacks. You can rest while I'm gone."

"You're taking guns. How am I supposed to rest with that knowledge?" It occurs to me I should have waited until she was safe to don all my gear. It's too late for that now.

"They are only a precaution, Jo. I don't plan on using them." She crosses her arms over her chest, not meeting my gaze. I step closer to her, but she waves me off.

"Show me to this room you are locking me in."

I sigh and motion for her to follow me. I lead her through the house to the safe room in the back corner. I punch in the code, and the thick door swings open. The walls are dark. A sizeable purple couch is against one wall, opposite a large TV with a DVD player beneath it. A small fridge is on the wall between the couch and TV, stocked with snacks inside and on top. A security system is stationed beside the door.

"These screens," I point to a few, "are feeds from around the property. If you see anything suspicious, use that phone," I point to a landline on the desk beneath the monitors, "to call me. I also left my friend's phone numbers if I don't answer immediately. You'll be safe here and won't need to call anyone. Don't use this line for any other reason, though."

"Why did you even bring me if you are just going to lock me away?" I step up, pulling her into my arms.

"Many reasons, baby girl. I want you with me. I want to spend this time with you. We can still go visit a couple of places before we leave. I want you close to keep you safe." I squeeze her tight, knowing my last reason may anger her. "And my father has been watching us for months. He would know something was up if he saw me traveling without you. Then he would have his men in the States take you. And they wouldn't fly you first class over here." She shudders in my grip, understanding the reality of the situation. I hate to put her in this position again. This is my life, though. She nods against me. I tip her chin up and kiss her gently.

"I'll be back in a few hours." I kiss her deeply, holding her tightly. A small voice reminds me this could be the last time. There's a chance I won't make it out of my father's house. While I'm confident in my plan, people can be unpredictable at the best of times. There's no accounting for how they will act.

26 · CATHERINE

I DRIVE MY FRIEND'S car through Barcelona, heading to the outskirts of town. My father has a large mansion on an expansive property. It's my childhood home. The place where my mother was murdered. The place where he still operates his business. From the intel I have gathered, he locked off the room where she died and doesn't use it anymore. I wonder if he knows one of his men reports to me and updates me on my father's activities. I don't think his henchman even realizes I am using the intel for nefarious reasons.

When I arrive, I'm waved through the gates. This dinner was scheduled; they know who I am. I park in front of the house as a butler greets me. I don't know this one. My father treats his personal staff as more indispensable than his foot soldiers. He's missing out on the benefits of long-term employees. He's honestly missing out on a lot.

The butler starts to guide me through the house, but I dismiss him, remembering the way myself. When he gives me a concerned look, I remind him this is my childhood home, and I plan to take over this outfit when my father dies. That does the trick. He lets me walk through alone. I don't need to be alone, but it will send a message when I walk into my father's office without an escort.

My father was never a kind man. He loved deeply, but he didn't know how to share that. His form of love was keeping everyone at arm's length. Guess that apple didn't fall far from the tree. Jo is the only person I have let close. It is a dangerous game we play. We can't risk the lives of others for our personal benefit.

I pass the room where I last saw my mother. The space where we had breakfasts and dinners. She would take me outside for lunch during nice weather. Or we would find a different space when it was raining or cold. She made up for everything my father couldn't give. She loved fiercely and knew how to show it. Despite growing up in a mafia family, she was taught to love and care. Some mafia women are cold and jaded by life. Not my mother. Giuseppe never deserved her. How did he even win her? Was it an arranged marriage? They never told me.

I shake those thoughts as I walk into my father's office. It's exactly as I remember. Dark mahogany wood. What is it with these rich mafia types and their mahogany? So many other types of wood exist. Let's mix things up. Books that have never been touched are stored on shelves. A single photo is on his desk, facing him. Without seeing it, I know it's one of my mother. Which one? I have none of her. Maybe I'll take it when I am done here.

My father swivels in his chair at my sudden entrance. He hasn't weathered the years well. His hair is thin and grey. Skin freckled with spots. His suit is still perfectly tailored, every bit of wealth on display. He looks lean and sallow. I haven't been able to ascertain medical records to indicate what is wrong with him.

Gabriel steps closer to my father. He also hasn't aged gracefully. I wonder if that is the mafia life or something lacking in their personal lives. Gabriel is my father's most trusted guard, but my father never gave him a position in the organization. Gabriel is always by his side, occasionally running errands. He is not officially associated with the mafia. He holds no power, and I don't understand my father's reluctance to give him any.

"Catherine," my father swoons. "You are early! I hope your travels went well." His accent is thick and muddled. My father grew up in Italy but moved to Barcelona after realizing he couldn't progress in the regime he was with. He started his own and built an empire near the coast. His most significant business is imports. Primarily drugs, but also guns. His business is bloody and dirty and constantly under surveillance from the law.

Everyone knows who he is. He is notorious for his brash punishments and retaliations. Building a respected mafia in a new location is challenging without being deadly. That is every bit who my father has always been. He cycles through guns faster than he does underwear. Ammunition and knives in every single room of the house. No more than five feet between weapons.

"I expected my butler to walk you down. You can help yourself to a drink." He waves toward a bar on the side wall, not rising from his seat. I file this bit of information away.

"I dismissed the butler. I don't need someone to show me around my home." My words are intentional. I would never refer to this mansion as my home under any other circumstance. I make no move to get a drink. When my father notices, he tells Gabriel to get one for me. I don't tell him I have no intentions of drinking.

"Where is your friend? She is beautiful."

"She'll be here later. Jet lag left her exhausted. She'll arrive for dinner after our business is done." My father nods, looking ecstatic. I take the drink Gabriel offers and watch as he moves to my father's side. Despite his aged appearance, Gabriel is still fit enough to battle. It isn't evident at first glance, but with closer inspection, I can see the muscles shift beneath his suit.

"Do you have the documents?"

"Straight to business. You've learned well, daughter." I maintain a cold mask at his words. Inside, I burn at his endearing term. I'm no daughter to him. I nod in response as he grabs a file with papers. I sent him a request for documents after we received the flight tickets. "What made you change your mind after all this time?" His voice is raspy, affected by whatever ails him. It's probably cancer from smoking or some other lung disease.

"I realized I have been stagnant. With your business, I can expand Marzanna and go international. I can run your business and mine together. Increase my wealth exponentially." He beams at my response. I'm almost surprised by his eagerness. Does he not see through my lies? Is he that eager to have me here? I take the documents from him, sit in a chair, and look them over.

"Everything you requested. My will, naming you as beneficiary. The deeds and titles to all my possessions. Ownership transfers for my legitimate businesses. Gabriel even created a dossier of the men I work with directly. You will meet with them in the coming days." Gabriel tuts by my father's side. Smart man. He knows my father shouldn't hand over everything at once. My low profile has spared me. My father can't understand why I wouldn't want more, want everything. He sees my life as lacking. He doesn't realize my value is higher than his.

"I also made arrangements for you to meet Michael. He is my underboss's son. He could help you run this regime when my time is up. You two would make a handsome couple and have beautiful children. I took the liberty of including a marriage contract in your documents. It could be beneficial for all involved. And Michael is discreet. He wouldn't deny you having an outside relationship. As long as it remains secret."

I fight the urge to glare at him, to display my disgust. Arranged marriages are practically unheard of today, even in mafia families. Of course, they happen, but no one talks about it. I didn't officially come out, as it wasn't something I wanted to share with anyone. I hide my relationships, especially Jo. I was careless when I was younger, learning what I like in less conspicuous manners than I use now. Many people know I'm bisexual, but not my preferences beyond that. I take my time reading over the documents. I need them to squirm, to feel uncomfortable with me. Everything is exactly what I want.

"Is everything there?" My father asks cautiously. I nod to him, taking a pen from his desk. I sign all of the documents, even the marriage contracts. I need him to think I am along for the ride and get his guard down. He has already signed. Gabriel signs after me as a notary. That's always a good person to have in your pocket. Once the documents are signed, I tuck the folder into my bag, securing it safely.

"Congratulations, Giuseppe. You have an heir to take over your regime. To expand your legacy. If you don't mind, I arranged a small token of appreciation with your butler earlier today." The last part is spoken as a question. Despite that everything is in my name upon my father's death, he is still in charge until then. He gives me a hesitant look but phones his butler anyway. Gabriel shifts uncomfortably. A little voice inside me cheers that these men don't understand the depth of my darkness.

"You never told me what ails you." I take the drink I was given earlier, swirling it around in my hand as I lean back in my seat. I appear comfortable and in my element. I'm not, but I am familiar with this position, this game.

"Emphysema. The doctors tell me I don't have long. I don't need oxygen yet." I nod, remaining stoic.

"Will you continue working when you need oxygen?"

"I hope you will take over before that." Gabriel rustles again. "Go sit down, Gabriel. You are making me nervous. We are celebrating!" My father flaps his hands, happy with how this evening is going. His butler walks in, placing a tray on my father's desk. He glances at my father, then at me. I nod to dismiss him. Even though that should be my father's job, he doesn't hesitate to leave the room. My father eyes the tray with intrigue and delight.

"Have you ever tried puffer fish, Giuseppe?" His gaze is curious. He expected me to walk in here and call him daddy again. It's been more than thirty years since I saw him in person. He is a stranger to me, and I to him, which is why this plan is going smoothly.

"No, I can't say that I have." His raspy voice reminds me of his condition. If I had waited much longer, I wouldn't be able to understand him between his muddled accents and harsh voice.

"It's a delicacy in Asia but has to be prepared just right. In my preparations for the visit, I learned that a highly sought-after chef serves this dish in Barcelona. He was willing to prepare the dish for the infamous Giuseppe Marzanna and his daughter. Despite his willingness, he still charged an exorbitant rate. He assured me that is the discounted price. Please," I motion toward the plate with sliced fish on it. My father takes a plate, staring at it with intrigue and enthusiasm. While he receives many desirable gifts for his business, the more lucrative ones have always drawn him. He's a sucker for unique, shiny, different.

I take a plate, passing it to Gabriel, before gathering my own. I lift my piece, nodding toward both men before taking a bite. The fish is soft and spongy, with a delicate flavor in my mouth. I've never been a huge fan of sashimi, but my father always enjoys expensive gifts. I swallow my bite while the men watch me with suspicion. This fish isn't poisoned. I ensured this was safe to eat.

"Please," I motion toward my father's plate. "This dish cost me two grand a piece. Let's celebrate before dinner." With that, my father takes a large bite, and Gabriel does the same, but with wary caution aimed at me. Now, it's time for the dangerous part of my plan. I rise slowly, still swirling my drink in my hand.

"I am excited to meet your men and Michael and see the empire I am gaining from you. You have built quite a legacy in your time here." My father beams at his praise. Always a sucker for admiration. I walk behind Gabriel, patting him on the shoulder. "You have good men in your ranks, trustworthy men." Gabriel glares at me. I know a few secrets about this man that will help me tonight. I circle back to my bag, taking out a separate file.

"I have one more gift for you, Giuseppe." This time, he eyes me warily. Gabriel stares at me with distrust. My father has good reason to keep him close. I walk behind my father's desk and step behind him as I place the file in front of him. "Open it." I keep my eyes on Gabriel as my father opens the file, flipping through the pages. He glances up at Gabriel, then back to the stack.

"What is this?"

Gabriel's face flashes with a brief flash of fear. My father eyes him again, but before either man speaks, I intervene.

"Gabriel has been planning to take over the regime after you. I would never receive anything. Your consigliere has been scheming with him to overthrow you. They are planning to kill you after making you look weak." With my now gloved hand, I slide several photos of Gabriel and the consigliere aside to a transcript. It's dated about a week ago and is entirely fictional. I typed it out on Word. It's not even fancy. It just looks like a transcript. My father scans it as Gabriel starts protesting.

The gunshot silences him. My father jumps in his seat, startled by the noise next to his ear. Despite the suppressor on my gun, the sound is still painfully loud. The rest of the staff are far enough away from this room that the sound shouldn't be alarming. Gabriel slumps in his chair, blood dripping from his head. Brain matter scattered across the mint condition books behind him. My father looks at his personal guard, who has been by his side most of his life. Tears well in his eyes at his loss. The exact emotion I wanted.

A sob escapes my father as I jam the needle into his neck, injecting the serum that will end him. He gasps but doesn't move. I lean down to whisper quietly in his ear. "You know your birthday is next week. Gabriel wanted to surprise you with something special. I reached out to him a few weeks ago and mentioned this pufferfish, knowing you would be a sucker for the delicacy." My father's eyes shift to the plate then back to Gabriel. The effects of the serum are taking hold of him.

"You feel that tingling? The numbness starting in your extremities? That is your demise." I rise, placing the needle on the desk beside his plate. "Gabriel did reach out to that chef and placed an order for your birthday. I reached out to the same chef and changed the date to tonight, having it delivered before I got here, in Gabriel's name." I place the gun on the other side of the file I gave my father.

"If it brings you solace, Gabriel didn't betray you. Those are photos of them discussing the soccer team. I created the transcript on my laptop. Very easy to create." I chuckle as I walk toward my bag. My father is paralyzed now and can't move. I pull a plastic bag out of my purse then perch on the desk so my father can see. He only has a few minutes before the poison takes him. I won't be sad if I don't finish my speech before then. He'll be dead even if he doesn't know the truth.

"That syringe contained tetrodotoxin, the neurotoxin from the puffer fish that is so deadly. The reason only certain chefs can prepare the dish. Thankfully, the chef Gabriel hired isn't certified and probably doesn't know what he is doing." I pull a small food container from my bag, removing the other parts of the fish. "Did you know most of the neurotoxins are contained in the ovaries? Quite ironic that I should use those to kill you. While you probably ate enough of the fish to not raise suspicions about the source of the poison, let's take an extra precaution." I shove a small part of the fish into his mouth, forcing him to swallow. With his muscles paralyzed, it's more challenging than I would like. At least he can't fight back.

Once I'm satisfied, I pat my father's head and place the rest of the fish on his plate. Then, I collect the syringe and my plate with the uneaten fish and store them in the bag. I toss the alcohol from my glass into the empty fireplace and add it to the bag. No traces of me staying longer than a few minutes will be left.

My final act is to wrap my father's fingers around the gun. I duck behind his chair, firing again into Gabriel's chest. Now, gunpowder will be sprayed up my father's arm. The scene will look like Gabriel poisoned my father, and my father caught wind of his betrayal. The butler delivered a Manila envelope earlier in the day. It contains all the documents I showed made, but without my fingerprints. I pull it from my father's desk and press his fingers over several of the pages. Everything should be accounted for now.

My father's lifeless eyes stare at Gabriel's bleeding body. I gather the rest of my items, noticing the photo on my father's desk. It is one of my mother and me. I was young, maybe around four. We played in the sand on the beach as waves crashed behind us. I don't remember that specific trip. For a moment, my heart squeezes, wondering if I made a mistake. I squash it.

I was never going to take over my father's mafia. Once he is discovered, I can sell off all his properties, leaving the mafia in the hands of his underboss. I'll even sell him the properties at a discount. No one will suspect me and I will be done with this famiglia.

Before I leave, I ask the butler if Giuseppe saved any of my mother's things. He nods, guiding me to the dining room where she was murdered.

"He stored it all in here and locked it away."

My body freezes as he unlocks the door. A room that contains so much trauma and heartache and memories. He steps aside, holding the door for me.

"Giuseppe received a call from his underboss and wants privacy for it. We settled our business early, and I won't be staying for dinner." I speak absently, staring into the dark room. The butler nods and scurries off toward the kitchen.

I walk into the room, flicking the lights on. The carpet was never cleaned. Dark brown stains from blood pooled so long ago are still there. Even my tiny footsteps from running away are still there. I bet if I opened the door, I would even find my socks.

I move past that, opening the boxes on the table. I will never leave this house if I stay and fixate on the memory. Inside the boxes, I find clothes and trinkets. I spot one box that has jewelry. I take a small ring box and slip it into my pocket. In another box, I find a photo album. I flick through quickly to find a photo of my mother and me. Once I see one I like, I slip it in with the file I took from my father. I lock the door and leave the mansion, fighting the memories, the emotions.

This almost feels too easy as I walk from the mansion with my documents and fish in my bag. My father was in his late seventies, and Gabriel was only a few years younger. I didn't expect a gunfight, though I was prepared for one.

I drive the rental back to my friend's posh neighborhood. They decided to head out of town this week. I didn't tell Jo about that because I wanted her to feel secure. My mind settles into a restless calm I'm not familiar with. After my shipments, I usually have an adrenaline high. I don't feel that now. Everything went smoothly. My plan was flawless, and it didn't feel right. No hiccups or anything. I'm not used to this feeling.

At the house, I call the phone inside the safe room. Jo answers with a hesitant voice.

"Hello?"

"Hi, baby girl."

"Oh, fuck, Catherine." She sighs with relief. I tell her how to open the door and let me in. Once the door is open, she rushes into my arms. I hold her tightly, breathing in her scent. She settles everything within me. None of the concerns about my plan going smoothly matter anymore. She is safe. I'm free of my father. Everything will be fine.

"I was scared you wouldn't come back."

"Me, too." She jerks back from me, staring at me.

"You said you would be safe!"

"Well, I wasn't wrong," I tease. Jo jabs my rib hard enough to leave a bruise.

"I was worried!" Her voice is loud and angry.

"I know. But it could have gone wrong, and I need you safe." She huffs at me.

"Are you going to tell me what you did?"

"Not now." I shake my head at her. I'll tell her when things settle, knowing it won't blow back on me. "For now, we need to grab our things. We're going to Marseille, France, tonight." Her eyes grow wide with excitement, then trepidation.

"Are we running? Are we on the lam now?" I laugh at her questions.

"No, silly girl. We're going sightseeing." I shrug. "Grab your things. It's a five-hour drive ahead of us." I kiss her head as we gather our bags. I'm not worried about my plan going forward, but my body feels unsettled. I'll feel better in a few weeks when everything has settled. I just need to know that everything worked. That Jo is safe. I need to get out of my father's territory. I want to go back home, but I don't want to rush away so soon. That would look suspicious. Driving to

France looks like we are sightseeing. We need to appear happy and normal now. I can do that. I can be happy and normal.

I tuck the documents from my father and my mother's ring into my suitcase, changing out of my clothes. I add the jacket to the bag with the syringe and other items I took from my father's house. A brief longing at what I have done passes over me for the second time. My biological family is gone. I have no further ties to them. It feels both light and heavy. Before I can process it, Jo slips against me, kissing me softly, breaking all thoughts and feelings.

"I, Kitty."

"I, too."

27 • CATHERINE

THE ROADS ARE DARK as we drive toward the French border. I have a hotel booked for us, and we can sleep as long as we need. Our flights are in two days. Plenty of time to sightsee. I imagine we will be asked to return to my father's house once he is discovered. I haven't decided if I will do that or not. Jo sits in the passenger seat, her hand resting on my thigh. She recognizes the mood I am in but doesn't say anything.

My thoughts wander over what I have done, over my mother, over everything. After my mother's death, my life has been marred by darkness. Murder and illicit business, abuse and mistreatment. Jo's hand squeezes my thigh when my mind spirals deeper, bringing me back to this moment. She is my anchor, my point of reality. She is my light in the darkness. I can't lose her. I can't risk her.

We stop to refuel and grab drinks just over an hour before we reach the hotel. I'm exhausted and need something to get me the last couple of hours until I can sleep. I pull Jo close as we walk inside, kissing her forehead. She leans into me for a moment, and I find her lips. I love this woman with everything I have. She walks off to the bathroom while I grab things for us. I grab an energy drink for myself, a soda, and a bag of candy for her. I don't want any food at this point. My stomach is unsettled. Probably not the best idea to drink an energy drink, but that won't stop me.

The cashier rings me up as I count the cash. Jo hasn't come out yet. This cashier is taking a long time to ring up my three items. My senses go on high alert. Maybe I am just paranoid or still off from my earlier activities. I feign reaching into my pocket for more cash. The cashier is watching me now, not even pretending to do his job. I place my hand on my gun as something in the back crashes. I glance that way, and that look nearly costs me. In my peripheral vision, the cashier reaches under the counter. I don't hesitate. I pull my gun and fire into his chest.

He drops, and I rush to the back. Several boxes have been knocked over. The bathroom door is open with the lights off. The back door is swinging on its hinges. It crashes into the wall then slings wide in a telltale sign that shit is terrible. I rush through it, gun in hand. A dark van is speeding off as the side door is slammed shut. Just before it closes, I spot Jo. A man holds her, and terror fills her eyes. They took Jo, my baby girl. I fire at the tires, but the bullets go wide. I'm a good shot, but this situation affects my vision and nerves. The need to retaliate, to stop this, is powerful.

I rush through the shop and out to my car, not even glancing at the groaning cashier on the ground. Serves him right. I start it and race after the van. I catch up to them quickly. My heart hammers in my chest. My father must have put this plan into motion. He didn't expect me to cave so quickly. He thought I would fight him. He ordered them to abduct her as a bargaining chip. I killed him before he could call off the order.

Anger boils beneath my skin. These men are dead. I've never been one to torture. That's not an area I want to delve into. But these men... I'm suddenly angry I gave my father a quick, painless death. He didn't deserve that. I swerve between cars, staying on the tail of the van. Not many vehicles are on the road at this late hour, but there are enough that we need to shift lanes every now and then.

Suddenly, the van turns off the road. It's traveling so fast that it nearly tips over. Red blurs my vision. My girl is in that van. I will get her out. My car can handle these fast turns. It struggles more on the dirt road. I push it as hard as I can. The van gains just enough distance from me that when it pulls into a large warehouse, the door has enough time to close before I get there. I debate rushing it, but I don't want to risk our only means of escape. I also don't know what's on the other side. I don't want to endanger Jo any more than I already have.

Before I let that thought settle, I pull off to the side and turn the car around to leave quickly. I grab my bag, digging through for whatever ammo and weapons I have. I left the tactical bag at my friend's house. It was their guns. I only borrowed them to take to my father's house. I kept one gun and two magazines. I wasn't planning on trouble. I didn't expect my father to put out a hit on my girl. I hope this is just an abduction and not a murder. I will be responsible for the demise of every single man in his regime if they hurt my girl.

I sneak around the building, looking for cameras, snipers, guards. I don't find any. Either they are hidden well or didn't expect me to follow. They don't know what I am capable of. My father may have had us tailed, but his men weren't thorough. They wouldn't agree to this abduction if they knew what I was capable of. I find a door propped open, probably from a cigarette break. I'm almost appalled at their indolence. I am insulted by their doubt in me. It is time for them to learn who I really am.

The building is shrouded in darkness and shadows. I creep through crates, listening for anything. It's completely silent, with no lights. I tiptoe through slowly. Before we left Barcelona, I changed into black leggings and a sweatshirt. Jo gave me hell for the casual clothes. I wasn't preparing for an attack. Some part of my brain knew it was a possibility—not the part that would bring extra guns.

The van entered this building. I don't understand why it is so quiet and dark. I turn through shelving, heading in the direction of the van. This is taking longer than I want it to. What are they doing to Jo? Are they hurting her? Is she still conscious? I stop myself before the next thought enters my brain. I can't even entertain the idea that something worse has happened.

Just as I lose hope, I spot a light leading down a set of stairs. Fuck, that isn't a good sign for me. I creep down as quietly as I can, watching for anyone. All the lights are off in the basement except for one room at the end of a hallway. All the doors are closed. I debate, opening them to check and know who I am up against. With the quiet down here, I would make my presence known. I take the risk of not knowing and walk down the hallway.

"I love fucking fat girls," a man's voice sounds from the room. "Always more to hold onto." The sound of a zipper and rustling material sends me into reckless abandon. I slam the door open, taking in the sight. Jo is on a mattress, bound and gagged, clothes ripped open. Her body is completely exposed. Only one man is in the room, his cock in his hand, already hard. Before he has the chance to grab his gun, I fire a single shot into his head. I rush over to Jo, pulling my small knife from my boot.

"Diego! I heard...Fuck!"

Another man rushes into the room, pants unbuttoned, with a hard cock pushing against the zipper. He turns and runs as I fire after him. A bullet grazes his hip, but he gets away. I let him. I'm not worried about him at this point. I turn my attention back to Jo, ripping the rope and gag away from her. She sobs, wrapping her arms around me.

"Baby girl, are you hurt? Can you run?'

Jo nods her head, and I pull her up. I don't say anything else. I hold her hand, and she tries to keep her clothes over her. It's a useless effort. They shredded her clothes to get to her body. As much as I hate that, I must get her to the car. We have more clothes there. Again, I shove more thoughts into a box that is already full. I have to focus on getting her safe. I can't think about what they were going to do. What would have happened if they had taken her quietly. What they would have done to her...

No, I shove all of those thoughts deep down. I guide her through the path I took to get here, knowing it's open and will lead to my car. We don't come across anyone else. The two men must have been working alone. My father seriously underestimated me.

I shove Jo in the car, jump in the driver's seat, and then speed to the main road. Jo is frozen in shock, staring out the window in her tattered clothes.

"Jo," I say softly. She turns to look at me, but she is a ghost. I reach out to grab her thigh, but she jerks away from me. Fuck, I don't know what they did to her. She wasn't alone long, but it was enough. "Your bag is in the backseat." She glances down at her clothes and nods. She twists to get the bag; her movements are slow and labored. A few scratches cover her body. They clawed her. I don't see any more serious injuries. Many will be hidden, bubbling at the surface, waiting for a chance to explode from her.

I drive to Marseille as she changes into sweats. The ride is long and silent. My gun stays by my thigh. I'm on high alert, watching for any signs of being followed. Jo stares out the window lifelessly, and my chest burns. Every one of my fears surfaces. Once in the city, I forgo the hotel I booked. I circle several blocks, ensuring we aren't being followed. When I am satisfied, I find parking for a different hotel.

I pause for a moment, watching Jo. She hasn't moved since she got dressed. I fight the wave of nausea, the discomfort growing in my chest, the fear, the anger. I gently touch the top of her hand, not wanting to startle her but hoping to bring her to the present. She slowly looks from my hand up to me. Neither of us shows any emotions.

Her blue and green hair is rumpled, knotted, and disheveled from her experience. Her cheeks are tear-stained and red, and her eyes are swollen and hollow. I squeeze her hand. I want to take her into my arms, hold her tight, and assure her everything is fine and she is safe. It's not true.

"We should go inside. I'll get us a room, and we can sleep."

Jo nods, but I doubt she will sleep much. I won't. Sleep will evade us both, overwhelmed by adrenaline and fear. I stack our bags and wheel them together in one hand. My gun is holstered under my jacket, within reach but out of sight. I hold Jo's hand, not willing to let her go again. While I am sure the man didn't follow us, he likely alerted others. My father's regime doesn't stretch to Marseille, but that doesn't mean his men won't travel.

At this point, Giuseppe should have been found. How quickly will that information be disseminated? Will they piece together my plan? Will my quick departure show my guilt in his death? Will they assume my counterattack on the abductors to be just that, a counterattack? Could the two be tied together? I don't know my father's underboss well enough to see if he will realize my involvement. I planted enough doubt around Gabriel and the consigliere that it shouldn't look framed. I don't know how intelligent my father's men are, how observant. They may notice. Maybe they won't.

I book a room for us using one of my aliases. If Jo notices, she doesn't react. I don't drop her hand at all. I would rather risk the suitcase with all my secrets than risk her again. She floats through the hallways with me like a balloon floating down to earth as it deflates. More emotions than I have experienced in a long time crash through my body. How could I let this happen to her? I took so many precautions only to slip up at a fucking gas station.

She stands by the dresser in the room, staring at the beds. Her arms wrap around her middle, but that is all the reaction she shows. I place our bags on one bed and step in front of her. She doesn't look at me, staring at one spot, completely lost in her thoughts.

"Why don't we shower and rest, baby girl?"

Her eyes finally meet mine. She nods but doesn't attempt to move. I step away from her, gathering everything we will need to shower. I place it in the bathroom and then start the shower. I glance at myself in the mirror. I look worn, tired, older than I am. My hair is also disheveled, not as bad as Jo's. Dark, puffy bags stand out under my eyes. I drop my head; disappointment in the evening weighs heavy on my body.

Mustering strength from inside, I walk back to grab Jo. She is still staring off, not really present. I touch her elbow, and she jumps but settles quickly when she realizes it's me. I pull her into my arms, but she stays tense. I sigh, realizing I can't give her the comfort she needs now. I guide her to the bathroom, where steam fills the room.

Any other day, I would undress her. That isn't a wise choice now. I tug off my clothes, dropping them haplessly. The gun thuds against the tiles, and Jo jerks at the sound. I hate how jumpy she is.

"Baby girl," my voice is barely above a whisper. I tell myself I don't want to scare her. The truth is I can barely muster the words because of my own insecurities. I am the reason she was taken, nearly raped. Her clothes were open. While they didn't have time to get a dick inside her, they likely had time to do other things. That thought has my teeth grinding. Breathe in, breathe out. This isn't what Jo needs now. "Do you need help undressing?"

Jo looks up at me slowly, recognition finally showing through. Tears well in her eyes as she nods again. She hasn't spoken since I found her. I'll learn sign language or get her a whiteboard if she never wants to talk again. I'll do anything for her. I speak softly, narrating my movements to her. I want her to be prepared for what I am doing and able to stop me. I grab the hem of her shirt, moving slowly and intentionally. As I tug up, she raises her arms, letting me remove her clothes. I drop them with mine, covering the gun still affixed to my pants.

I take her hand and guide her into the water. I keep her back in the spray, letting it soothe her aching body. I want to caress her body, rub her softly, bring her back to life. I'm worried about scaring her, hurting her. Instead, I grab a washcloth and add some soap. I start at her wrist, working my way up slowly. By the time I reach her chest, she begins to heave, and sobs take over her body. She crumples, but I catch her. I hold her close as she cries into my chest. Her arms wrap around me, squeezing me tightly.

She cries for a long time while I support her. She doesn't say anything, doesn't scream, just weeps. When she settles down, I resume washing her body. She's more pliant this time, letting me clean her easily. I massage her scalp with shampoo, gently working out the tangles. Her eyes close, tears slip free, almost unnoticeable, with the water streaming down her cheeks.

Once she is clean, I quickly clean myself. I dry her first, tugging on the lounge clothes I pulled out for her. After I dress, I guide her to the bed. I'll pick up our items later. Now, she needs to rest. I pull the blankets back for her, but she collapses on top of them before I can get them out of the way. She lays on her back, staring at the ceiling. I crawl into the bed beside her, watching her the whole time. She is still a ghost of the girl I knew. I need to find a way to get her back. I can't live with having ruined her forever.

I slide close to her, wanting to wrap my arms around her, but she pulls away from me. I have occasionally cried after a difficult shipment or takedown when the adrenaline wears off. I haven't cried over another person since my mother died. I hardened my heart, not letting anyone in. When Jo pulls away, my heart breaks. It shatters into a million pieces. My eyes sting as a single tear slips down my face. It's such a foreign feeling, crying not from adrenaline but from emotions.

I roll onto my back, staring at the ceiling. The entire night runs through my head. The moment I locked her in the room. When I arrived at my father's house. The way his eyes looked without life, staring at Gabriel's dead body. The room where my mother's blood still stained the carpet. Jo in my arms after the safe room. I had her in a fucking safe room for hours only to lose her in a gas station bathroom.

My mind repeats the gas station and warehouse over and over. What I should have done. What I could have done differently. How did this happen? How did this night turn from smooth to one of the worst cases? And why did it have to go to shit over Jo? Why couldn't the night have gone to shit earlier? My friends knew she was in the safe room. I had a plan in place in case I didn't return. She would have been safe. But no. everything went smoothly. I planned for that. I didn't prepare for an abduction.

I usually don't let myself sink into doubt and uncertainty. Tonight, lying beside my girl who is struggling, I let those feelings wash over me. All the pain I have caused. All the fear. The realization that I can't keep her safe. I can't protect her. I can't...

28 · CATHERINE

I DON'T NOTICE THE paint on the ceiling, the ornate light fixture, the dance of light from the city bursting through the curtains. The soft thuds of people moving through the hotel go unheard. Other people start their day by preparing for work or a day of leisure. None of those register in my consciousness.

The only thing that matters is the girl lying beside me. She's quiet, eyes open, staring at the ceiling. Her body radiates heat. I can feel her warmth and stillness. I don't know what she is thinking. No emotions are on her face. If her eyes weren't open, I would think she was sleeping. Hell, I'm not convinced she didn't fall asleep with them open. Except it's hard to sleep after a night like that.

She was locked in the safe room for hours. She hadn't fully grasped the danger of coming here until that moment. She understands some of the risks of my life. I didn't sugarcoat things for her, but I didn't explain everything. I still want to keep her sweet and innocent. I don't think she will be either after tonight. I did that to her. I ruined her.

My chest is jumbled, like a box of Christmas lights nobody bothered to untangle before storing away. Everything is looped and knotted and tangled, doubtful if it will work again. I'm angry I let her out of my sight. I'm fucking scared that it isn't over. I'm upset for her. Those men... the things they would have done to her.

Part of me knows I shouldn't focus on things that didn't happen. A quick glance at Jo tells me she still hasn't moved. Still frozen with shock or anger or whatever emotions she is feeling. For a moment, just a brief moment, I let my mind run on the what-ifs. Just a moment, then I'll stop it. I just need to feel it to process it.

What if she hadn't caused a scene, made a ruckus to alert me as she was dragged out? I wouldn't have known she was taken. I would have figured it out soon enough. It could have been several minutes. That much of a lead could have stalled me. I might have found the tire tracks and caught up with the van. Perhaps I wouldn't have. Maybe I would have needed to track her down through my father's men. Then, I wouldn't have stopped the men's grubby fingers, their dirty cocks.

"Do you always use a gun?" Jo's soft voice breaks my thoughts. I blink several times to clear the vision of Jo on the mattress. I've gone far enough down the 'what if' rabbit hole. She's speaking to me now. I need to focus on her.

"No." I don't know where she is going with her questions. I don't want to give her more information than she needs. She doesn't move. She lays still, staring at the ceiling.

"Do you torture them?"

"No. I don't like to prolong those situations."

She turns to look at me. A dark fire burns behind her eyes. I'm not sure what she is feeling. Hatred? Need for revenge? Anger? Whatever she is feeling, she isn't the sassy, bubbly Jo I know so well. She's consumed with darkness. I stare at her, trying to process what she is feeling. She was so bright, hidden from the wickedness of the world. My own lust and need forced this on her. I never should have pursued her.

"Can you find him?"

I pause at her words. Of course, I can find him. I can probably find him in the next few hours. Between my own abilities, Harpo's, and some local friends, we can find the man who wanted to hurt her, who abducted her. Do I want to give her that, though? She can come back from what has happened. I know she can. While it is terrible, it's still possible to recover from that. What she is asking for, you don't come back from that.

Her eyes bore into mine. She knows I can give her what she wants. She knows I am hesitating. She knows me as well as I know her. I slide my hand over the sheets until I find hers. I trace my fingers over hers, but she doesn't move or react.

"Can you find him?"

Her words are the same as before. She's not bitter or sad. She is asking a question she wants an answer to. She could have asked about the weather, what time a movie starts, or if I could pass the salt. She didn't ask those mundane things, though. She asked me to find her attacker. So she can deal with him.

"Yes."

"Find him."

It's all she says. She turns to look back at the ceiling. Her hand stays still under mine. Her chest rises and falls with steady breath. She is in a calm state. I wish I could feel that relaxed. I'm not familiar with being the emotional one. I can be steady. Breathe in, breathe out. I repeat my mantra, not moving from the bed to find the man. I need rationality before I answer.

I give Jo everything she wants, everything she needs. I will always do that. Even if she leaves me, I'll protect her from a distance. She is it for me. I dragged her into this life. Do I want her in it with me? I thought I could keep her separate. I thought I could keep her safe. Would she be safer with me? In the darkness, learning how this world works? I could teach her to protect herself. But do I want to start that with revenge? Without proper time to think this through? We only have a couple of days left. Time isn't on our side to consider this. The repercussions, the effects, how this will play out.

"I don't ask for anything, Catherine. Give me this."

Her voice has an edge to it now. She is angry I haven't caved immediately.

"You shouldn't make a rash decision..." She interrupts me before I can explain why this is a bad idea.

"You shot a man in the head in front of me for pointing a gun at me." She turns her gaze on me. Pure hatred is splayed across her face. It's not aimed at me, but I still feel it deep in my soul. "The man that took me, that touched me..." Her words fade out. My heart burns, realizing the extent of what they did to her. I turn on my side, pulling her hand to my lips. I'm going to give him to her. As much as I want to keep her from going down this path, I just can't. I squeeze her hand in mine. She doesn't exactly return the squeeze, but her fingers tighten to hold mine. It's enough for now.

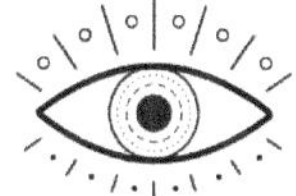

It's our last day in Marseille. We leave late tonight. I called Zed and told him we won't be back this week. We planned to return to work in two days and finish the week. With the way this trip has gone, I don't want to go back, let alone have Jo there that soon. As much as I want to leave France, I'm not ready to return to our day-to-day life.

Jo has been silent and removed. We did go sightseeing one day, keeping up those appearances in case anyone was watching. She barely reacted to anything we visited. I tried to cheer her up. She didn't leave my side. Even in the bathroom,

I followed her, hovering outside her stall. If she is upset by my overprotectiveness, she doesn't say anything.

Lawyers called earlier today, informing me my father is dead and the estate is mine. I'm not surprised they waited so long to call. I was wondering if they would sweep the whole thing under the rug. I watched my father's men with the eyes I already had on them. His consigliere has disappeared. Either my plan worked, or they are playing along to keep things manageable. Doesn't matter to me. After the lawyers called, I spoke with my father's underboss. He was willing to buy the entire estate for a discount. The paperwork has already started. I didn't even ask for anything from the house. I took what I wanted when I left. It will take a few weeks for the process to finalize. A few more weeks until I am finally done with my father and his mafia in Spain. If I never visit this country again, I won't be upset.

I haven't told Jo where we are going. We drive through the city in the new rental car I acquired. The men saw my other rental. I don't know what contact the one man made with the mafia after he got away. I found his location about an hour after Jo asked. He was far too easy to find. I didn't tell her right away, though. I needed to assess the situation and ensure I could get him away quickly and quietly.

My father has an extensive regime, but their focus is on drugs and guns. They don't worry with abductions or personal squabbles of other men. They don't get involved in each other's lives. They don't work together or protect their brothers. They primarily operate independently. My father had a group of trusted footmen to do his dirty work, but they weren't overly loyal. They do the job, take their pay, and return to their lives. My father was an idiot. I've spent an unreasonable amount of time trying to understand how my father built this empire from the ground up.

The city expands to suburbs. Spanish-style homes grow larger. Yards are filled with flowers and bushes and long driveways. Fences become more prominent and more ostentatious. Jo watches out the window in silence. My hand on her thigh absorbs the heat between us. I turn into a driveway, waiting as the gate opens for us to enter. As I near the house, Jo turns to look at me. I give a soft smile, unable to draw a whole emotion.

Jo has a question glaring through her eyes but doesn't say anything. She hasn't said much in a few days. She hasn't asked for an update on her attacker. She hasn't checked in. I debated whether she had changed her mind. Even if she has, I will do the job for her. This scum doesn't deserve to live anymore. I guide her into the house quietly. Neither of us speaks.

My friend greets me in the foyer. One benefit to watching my father is knowing who I can trust. I made several connections while stalking him. This one is glad for my father's demise. He kisses both my cheeks and turns to do the same to Jo. I tug her closer, stepping between the two. No words are exchanged, but he takes the hint. He nods, telling me the basement is ready.

I pull Jo along, winding my way through the house. I've never been here. I found the layout online and know exactly where to go. I lead her through a sitting room, a kitchen, a mud room, and finally to the basement. We walk down the stairs, stopping in the large room. The floors are concrete, but the space has tables, chairs, and a couch. A fully stocked bar is on one side. A shelf containing playing cards and poker chips hangs next to one of two doors. One door leads to the bathroom. I guide Jo to stand beside the other door.

The air is crisp and cool from being underground. The room is silent—nothing can be heard from the room or the rest of the house. The soundproofing is top-of-the-line, a necessary feature. This room is used for meetings for the mafia. It's secure and private. I paid the man more than I would have in any other situation.

I remove my gun and knife, leaving it in the sheath. I press them both to Jo's chest. Her hands wrap around them, but I don't let them go. I don't immediately meet her eyes, staring at the weapons instead. My finger traces the outline of the knife. I won't change my mind, but I don't want to give her this. I hesitate in hopes she will change her mind. She doesn't speak, though.

"If you get in there and can't do this," I finally look at her, "I will do this for you. You don't have to go through with it." I finally release the weapons to her. Her breathing is steady. She has thought of nothing but this since she asked. She will follow through. I grab her shoulders, not letting her go. I press my forehead against hers. I've tried to kiss or hug her a few times, but she always turns away. It's like salt in an already deep wound. Every little rejection is another shake.

"Baby girl, I..." I take a breath, not entirely sure what I want to say. Do I want to talk her out of this? Tell her how I feel about her? I can't even admit it to myself. How the hell am I supposed to say it to her?

"I, too, Kitty."

My breath catches, a more visible reaction than I have ever given. I lean back, meeting her gaze. Her hand tangles in my hair. I close my eyes, tipping my head into her touch. It takes everything I have not to moan at her. She pulls me close, pressing her lips against mine. I wrap my arms around her, deepening the kiss. What I would give to keep her here, out of that room, in my arms where she belongs.

The press of the weapons between us pulls her back from me. I don't want her to go in there. I want to stop this. I keep my arms around her tightly. I wish to every deity or power that this will stop, but it won't. I know that. She needs this. She's a big girl.

"Kitty..." her voice is sure, unwavering.

I nod, pulling back from her. A quick glance at her face tells me she wants this; she's ready. I open the door and step inside. She follows, and I close the door behind her. The man I shot in the hip is tied to a chair in the center of the room. He is gagged, blood caked on his face and hair. His head is drooped, eyes closed. He's been in this chair for twelve hours. His clothes are disheveled, ripped, and covered with drips of blood. He fought as he was taken. Unfortunately for him, I'm more thorough than my father. I paid for the best. He never stood a chance at getting away.

Jo circles him, walking around the back. She moves like a hunter preparing for a kill. She stalks around him, taking in every inch. She wants to know her prey, to know where to strike. Is she debating torture? How far will she go? I stay by the door, watching. As much as I hate it, something is thrilling about watching her. She looks to be in her element. Her dark side is showing, and it's enthralling.

Jo rounds his side and stops. He hasn't moved at all. A small table is in the corner, and Jo gently places the gun and knife down. The room is silent. Only her attacker's labored breathing can be heard. She steps to his side, rears her arm back, and lands a solid punch on his hip, the exact spot where I shot him three days ago.

His ear-piercing scream breaks the silence. I wince at the shrill noise, but Jo remains steady. She walks around, entering his vision. His eyes widen when he sees her. He starts shaking, mumbling over the gag tied around his head. He jerks the chair, hoping for any opportunity to escape. He's not leaving this room alive, though.

Jo tilts her head, then walks to the weapons she placed on the table behind him. He spots me and attempts to plead for his life. I don't react at all. He sealed his fate when he touched my girl. I may have let the abduction slide, but knowing his grimy fingers touched her... His time is limited.

She returns to his front with my knife in her hand. The knife is sharp, ready for whatever she has planned. She leans close to him, still a reasonable distance back but meeting his eye level. She raises the knife to his face with a steady hand. If I didn't know her, I would assume this isn't her first rodeo. The blade rises to his cheek. The man closes his eyes, trying to lean away from her. His fear is palpable. His breathing quickens as she slips the blade between his cheek and the gag.

With a quick tug, the gag falls away. A bead of blood spills from his cheek where she nicked him. He whimpers, eyes shut tight, leaning away from the girl with blue and green hair. He underestimated her, too.

"What is your name?" Her words are dark and venomous. The man glances between us, pleading, begging for help.

"S-Santino."

"Who sent you after me?" His eyes dart again but with fear.

"I didn't know," he says to me in a thick accent. He didn't know I was Giuseppe's daughter. He didn't know Jo was mine. It wouldn't have made a difference, though. He's a soldier. He would have done it. Jo presses the tip of the blade into his cheek. A small bubble of red grows from the spot.

"Who?"

"Giuseppe."

I already knew that answer, and I assumed Jo did, too. Maybe she just wants confirmation. She doesn't look back at me, and I suspect she would lose her courage if she did. She stands upright and walks behind the man. She pauses at the table, looking down at the weapons.

"Please," he cries, "I have cooperated. I won't do this again. Giuseppe is dead. He won't be a danger to you again." His pleas go unheard. Jo rounds the room, both weapons in hand. When Santino sees her, his cries grow louder, and he is on the verge of weeping. She pushes the gun into my holster and pulls me to her. Her lips crash against mine. I cup her head, returning the kiss. I don't know what she plans, but I can't deny my burning desire to watch her handle this man.

"I'm sorry!" His repeated shouts are unnecessary. One of us will end him tonight. Jo pulls back from me, looking up at me, resolve in her eyes.

"Is the knife important to you?"

I shake my head at her. I've had it for a long time, but it's nothing special. She walks back to the table and sets the knife down. Above the table is a shelf with extra supplies. She grabs a pair of gloves and a bottle of liquid. She pours it over the knife as the scent of alcohol fills the room. The man whimpers again, shaking the chair to get free. Jo replaces the bottle. I watch with intrigue as she moves around the space. I've never been one for torture. The few murders I perform are quick, quiet deaths. Watching Jo, I'm not positive this will be the case.

The sound of the table being dragged across the floor is ominous. It's loud, drowning out Santino's muttered prayers in Spanish. She drags it next to him, bumping it several times to make the legs squeak against the floor. She's spent far too much time planning this exact moment. Jo walks back to the shelf and grabs a strand of rope. She cuts a small piece, then ties her attacker's bicep to the chair. I watch with interest, leaning against the wall.

Jo is in a dark place, but I'm impressed with her actions. She couldn't have planned for all of this. I didn't tell her anything about the man or the room. Some of this she is doing on the fly, but it's clear she has thought about it. Once his arm is secured, she walks around to his front. She stares down at him in a menacing glare. He meets her eyes, chest heaving, but silent. He hasn't accepted his fate but isn't fighting it either.

"Google said it takes 2-5 minutes to bleed out from a severed carotid artery. It's right here," Jo drags the blade down the column of his neck, over his artery. She traces the artery up and down a couple of times. The man watches her, daring her to stab him. It's hard to tell if he's ready to die or if he still thinks he can get away. Jo stops the knife at the base of his neck, aiming the tip to cut him. She pushes ever so softly, just breaking the skin. Blood trickles down to his stained collar. His eyes focus on hers. She doesn't look away from him as she puts her weight behind the knife and shoves it violently. He jerks backward, yelling in pain. Blood sprays from his neck, replacing the scent of alcohol with the tangy metallic smell.

Jo jerks the knife out of his neck and walks around his back. He begins gurgling as the blood oozes from him. She slices the rope around his wrists and pulls his free arm to the table. She rounds the table so she is in his view. His eyes are glazed over, a sign of his imminent death. With his hand unmoving on the table, Jo raises the knife high in the air, then slams it down into his knuckles. A crunch of bones is quickly met with the thud of the knife embedding in the wood below. Santino winces at the pain, head drooping as blood continues to coat his chest.

She stands and looks at me. Her eyes are wild, blood soaking her clothes. Santino's wheezing stops as he stills, lifeless. She tugs the gloves off, dropping them on the table. She walks before me, and I stand straight to meet her. I wrap my fingers around her neck, watching her for a second. I know what she needs now.

I kiss her gently as our lips meet, then forcefully. She moans beneath me, and I pull her closer, not concerned about the thick layer of blood on her front. I need her; I need to consume her. She's so fucking brave and beautiful and mine. Her tongue swirls in my mouth, taking what she needs from me. I give her everything. Everything I have, every bit of me, everything she needs and wants. She will always get everything from me. There will be no more hesitation. She's stronger than I thought. I underestimated her, too.

29 · JOSEPHINE

Her lips melt me like butter, washing away the tension and stress of this trip. I never expected my first trip to Europe to be so life-changing. I knew it would be impactful. Any major travel would have an impact. But this trip? This one changed my core. I'm not the same girl I was last week, last month, last year. So much has changed since I met Catherine. Some of it is good. Some of it is much, much darker.

Catherine breaks the kiss, pulls my hand, and leads me out of the room. She guides me to the couch, grabbing a duffel bag. Of course, she has a duffel bag. This isn't her first abduction and murder. She's accustomed to this life. She knows what she needs. Now, she knows what I need. I'll know that soon, too. First note: always be prepared. I search the bag and find clothes and a double-ended dildo?

I hold the toy up to Catherine. She shrugs nonchalantly. As if murdering someone then finding a double-ended dildo is an everyday occurrence for her. Hell, it probably is. She has as many weapons as she does toys. Why wouldn't she carry a toy to a hit? Don't they always say near-death experiences make you horny? Is it just near death or any death? Based on the wetness growing between my thighs, it's definitely the latter.

"Who were you going to fuck? Me or him?" I nod back toward the room we left the body in. She stalks to me, grabs a fistful of my hair and jerks my head back.

"Always you, baby girl."

If the death experience didn't already have me heating up, that would. I moan as she slams her lips into mine, forcing her tongue into my mouth. My knees nearly give out, causing me to grab her back to hold myself up. She pulls away, grabbing my shirt to tug it over my head. Once it's gone, she covers one nipple with her mouth. Her hand grabs my other breast, tweaking my nipple between her fingers. I groan, rubbing my legs together to get some friction where I want it.

She pushes my pants and underwear to the ground, leaving me wholly exposed before her. Her eyes ravage my body, lust, and desire filling her gaze. She wants me desperately. Her hands slide across my stomach, my breasts, my waist. Fuck, I love the way she touches me. Her fingers are exploring, memorizing, claiming, possessing. Her fingers slide between my legs, spreading me open for her. She drags a finger through my core, finding out how much the death experience affected me.

"How do you feel, baby girl?" Her words are soft and concerned, not matching the heat in her eyes.

"Like a sausage casing waiting to be stuffed." Her laugh is loud and gleeful. It startles me. She doesn't laugh like that often.

"There you are, baby girl. My little sunshine hidden by rain clouds. Even when surrounded by darkness, you burn bright at your core." She kisses me before I can react to her words. Her kiss is passionate, as if she's worried she won't get to do this again. I have been reserved for the last few days, but that's to be expected. Surely, she didn't think I would always be like that. I may not be back to my usual self, and probably won't be for a long time, but I do feel better knowing those men are dead.

Her arms pull me tightly against her chest. Her clothes are rough against my skin, rubbing my nipples almost painfully. I grab at her shirt, tugging it to get at her soft, inked skin beneath. Maybe I should ink my body count too. I have one of my own. Can I count the others since their death was because of me?

I'm distracted from those thoughts as Catherine pulls away to remove her shirt. Her chest is impressive. Her breasts are small, but the ink makes them gorgeous. I trace my fingers across the tattoo, down to her nipples. She watches with a blank face. She hasn't mentioned whether she enjoys this touch. She may not like being fingered, but that doesn't mean this is a problem. If it is, she doesn't stop me.

Catherine lets me explore with my fingers. She doesn't stop me when I lean in to wrap my lips around her budding nipple. Her hand tangles in my hair, holding me while I swirl my tongue over her soft skin. I do the same to the other, enjoying her taste. She pulls away from me and guides me to the couch behind us. She grabs the double-ended dildo then plops down on the couch. She motions for me to lean in, keeping her eyes on me the whole time.

"Open," she instructs. I part my lips, and she slips the shorter, curved end into my mouth. I close my lips around it, swirling my tongue around the short length. She hasn't explained her plan. I don't particularly care. I have pent-up energy that needs to be let out. I trust she'll do that for me. She always gives me what I want.

She slips the toy out, turns it around, and shoves the longer part in my mouth. She doesn't go slow or ask if I can handle it. It bumps the back of my throat, and I barely manage not to gag. She twists it around before pulling it out. Instead of putting it back in my mouth, she brings it to her hips, where her pants are already undone. Without removing them, she slips the toy inside, twisting it and pressing it into her own pussy.

The image of her putting a toy that was just in my mouth into her cunt sends a wave of pleasure through my body. Bumps break out across my skin with arousal. She inserted a toy covered in my spit into her cunt. A shiver of anticipation rolls across me. My core clenches with need. I want her so badly.

"Ride me until you come."

I don't need to be told twice. I climb on the couch and straddle Catherine's thighs. The dildo stands straight from her hips, waiting for me to sit on it. Her hand reaches my pussy, slipping two fingers inside. She knows how wet I am; she doesn't need to check. She does anyway. I close my eyes as her fingers wiggle inside me. It feels so good, but it's not enough. Her fingers hook my pelvis bone as she guides me over the toy, wet with my own saliva. She positions it at my core, letting me lower onto it. She's giving me control here. She's letting me set the pace. After everything I have done, she's giving me her power.

I lower myself onto her. In this position, our size difference is glaring. She's much thinner than me. Even though she is taller, she looks much smaller beneath me. A brief concern about hurting her flashes through my mind. The only people I have ridden like this were bigger, big enough I wasn't concerned about breaking them. She looks so fragile beneath.

"Move, or I will," she demands, sensing my hesitation. She would know if she's at risk of getting hurt. My worry is she would get hurt for me. She would do anything for me. Catherine is giving up her control for me. She would surely take an injury to give me what I want.

A slap to my ass breaks my train of thought. It's not hard, but stings enough that I jerk. The toy inside me rubs against a sensitive spot, and my eyes roll back in my head. That's enough to silence all my worries. I bounce on her, rising and falling on the toy, on her hips. Her hands settle on my waist, giving a small, reassuring squeeze. I move harder and faster. Pleasure coursing through my body. My toes, hanging off the edge of the couch, clench together. I lean into Catherine, crashing my lips into hers.

As our tongues mingle and dance, her hand moves to my breast, squeezing painfully. I moan into her mouth, the pain driving my pleasure. I switch to grinding, rubbing my clit against her pants that have shifted around the toy. The sensation is delicious. I pull back from her, arching backward. The toy rubs inside me as the fabric caresses my clit.

I don't notice her breathing increase until she moans. I open my eyes to look down at her but don't change my pace. Her hands on my body tighten as her eyes clench. For a moment, I'm worried she's not enjoying this and is suffering for me. Then, her head pushes back on the couch. Her stomach clenches and releases. Her eyes fly open, and a silent scream rips through her. Her body lunges forward, landing on my chest. She inhales deeply then shudders. Her arms hold me tightly as her breathing settles.

"Did you just…"

"Come for me," she interrupts.

I slowed my pace to watch her. I'm still trying to figure out if I just saw her orgasm when she leans back just a bit. She sucks her finger, then wraps her arm around me again. Her fingers spread my ass apart as the one she just sucked on presses into my ass without any warning. The sensation stings but feels so fucking good. I groan as I thrust on her again. She stays close to my chest, keeping her finger inside me as I grind on the toy. Her other hand rubs my clit, sending me over the edge.

My body shakes with my orgasm. Bright lights burst behind my eyelids. A loud whine escapes. Every inch of me trembles. It's only my body soaring through pleasure as Catherine whispers praise into my chest.

I collapse against her body. My head rests against her shoulder, my breath heavy against her chest. She slips her finger out of my ass, bringing the other around to cup my cheeks. She massages my butt softly as we both calm down in each other's arms. My body is coated in a small layer of sweat. She is, too. I'm not used to Catherine breaking a sweat. The only time she has during sex is when I fingered her. That didn't end well. I lean back to ask her about it. Then, remember the toy is still inside me. I curse as it rubs against my sensitive pussy. I climb off her, settling on her side.

"Did you come too? Or was that uncomfortable for you?"

Before she answers, she wraps her arms around me, holding me tight at her side. She's preparing me for a letdown. I don't want to think that was uncomfortable for her. She can't put herself through that for me. It's not fair to her and doesn't make me feel better. We need boundaries for that. The last thing I want is to hurt her.

"It was the first orgasm I have had in a long time."

Her face is calm and relaxed. A settled happiness shines through her eyes. I worried she lied when she spoke, but seeing her face, it's obvious it's the truth. I can't stop the grin that spreads across my face. I rest against her shoulder again, snuggling into her more. Pride fills me. I gave her something only a few people have. She came because of me. I trace my fingers over her chest, where her heart would be. That belongs to me. I'm the only one that holds it. Confidence settles inside, knowing my importance to her.

We sit like this for several minutes, soaking up the intimacy and joy. I open my eyes, the door glaring at me. The man I murdered sits behind it. His body growing cold, drained of blood, restrained to the chair he sits in. Dread seeps in. I killed a man. A person with a life I know nothing about. A crime so severe I could be extradited. As if sensing the change, Catherine speaks.

"I paid my friend to take care of the body. It won't come back on us."

I lean back to look at her. Catherine cups my cheek, trying to comfort me.

"He was a bad man. He had no family and worked for a drug lord. His whole existence was ruining the lives of others. This wasn't the first time he assaulted someone. It wouldn't have been the last. You did what the law couldn't."

Her words soothe some of the dread, but the reality is I still killed a man without much of a second thought. It was intentional. Not self-defense. She informs me we must get dressed and leave to catch our flight on time. Negative thoughts still swirl in my mind, but having a task will make that easier. I rise, taking clothes from the bag she has. It doesn't take her long to get dressed.

Catherine is tinkering around with a wood-burning stove in the corner. When I smell smoke, I turn back to her. I ask what she is doing. The fire is burning strong now. I'm impressed with her fire-starting abilities. I don't start many fires, but it usually takes a few minutes to get a good bonfire going. Have I been that distracted?

"I'm burning the evidence."

Her grin is almost evil as she holds up my blood-soaked clothes then shoves them in the stove. Knowing there isn't any physical evidence linking me to this crime is comforting. I cleaned the knife then wore gloves. Now she is burning my clothes. More of that dread from earlier fades away. The last bit will take time to go away. Maybe it won't ever go away. Knowing Catherine has killed dozens of men and is still walking brings me peace.

The flight from Marseille to Kansas City is long and arduous. I'm still jumpy, glancing over my shoulder as if the cops will appear and put me in cuffs. Catherine switches between teasing me and reassuring me. I never know what she will do. It helps distract me more, not knowing if I am about to be teased, comforted, or aroused. She does plenty of sexual teasing on the plane.

At her apartment, we shower and settle in. She straps on a giant dildo and fucks me senseless. The size and edging she has done for the past eighteen hours give me a mind-bending orgasm. I fall asleep before I have even fully come down from the orgasm. I awake later, with darkness draping the bedroom. Only a soft glow fills the room.

It takes me a couple of minutes to get my bearings. It was morning when I returned from the airport. I have no idea what time it is now. Catherine is propped against the bed, working on her laptop. I groan, sitting up. The change puts pressure on my full bladder. I stumble to the bathroom to relieve myself. It occurs to me I am wearing clothes now, my preferred crop top and shorts sans underwear. I was naked from fucking when I fell asleep. At some point, Catherine dressed me. My chest flutters at the realization. Shock fills me at how heavily I was sleeping to not even notice.

I slip into the bed, sliding next to Catherine. I wrap my arm over her legs, burying my face on the bed beside her hip. She drapes one hand over my shoulder, continuing to type one-handed. Is there anything that is unimpressive about this woman?

"What time is it?" I mumble.

"About four a.m."

"Shit," I groan, letting my eyes drift close again. I'm not exactly sleepy, but overly tired from sleeping so long. I feel both aches from being in bed for so long and wanting to sleep more. I need to get up and move, but it's warm here, and Catherine smells good.

"What day is it?" She chuckles at me. Between the vacation, time changes, and sleep, I have no idea when it is. It could've been a year for all I know.

"Friday." She rubs my arm, both soothing and rousing.

My friends are doing trivia tonight. I told them I would be there. They are excited to hear about my vacation. Thank god Catherine took me to enough places. I have stuff to tell them about. I can't exactly say, "I stabbed a man in the carotid artery and watched him bleed out" in the middle of a bar. Probably also shouldn't go with, "I hid in a safe room for hours while my girlfriend killed her father, only to be abducted from a fucking gas station bathroom and nearly raped." It's not really bar talk. A shiver runs down my body.

"It's bar trivia night. Do you want to go with me?"

"No, you should go by yourself." The thought of being away from her makes me nervous. She hasn't left my side since she found me in the warehouse four days ago. Five days? A lifetime? I don't know. It's been long enough that I feel uncomfortable about her not being there. "I can send Liam with you if you are worried."

Liam. Her bodyguard. The only person she would trust to protect me if she can't. He's good at his job and staying discreet, but not perfect. I spotted him several times while we were broken up. Maybe he wasn't meant to remain hidden. I wanted to believe he was in the same place as me, but that's not true. She had him watching me.

"Do I need him?" Fear creeps in. Would he stop cops from arresting me? Would her father's mafia come after me again? Could they get me back to Spain, or would that not be their goal?

"No. You're safe."

I release a heavy breath. That dread settles to the small bit that won't go away but is manageable. I am safe. Catherine won't let me be taken twice.

"Okay. I'll go alone. Can I take John?"

"Of course, baby girl. I'll be here." Her hand raises to caress my cheek. I close my eyes, savoring the soft touch. "I want to take you to the gun range tomorrow."

"What?" It's too early for all this talk. Sleep and dread fill my mind, and I can't comprehend much else.

"I want you to learn to shoot. Carry a gun. Protect yourself if I'm not there." I breathe out deeply. It's a good idea. Obviously, I'm going to do it, but the reality brings that sense of dread to life. "Except for the men in Spain," Catherine explains, "the only people I have taken out were involved in trafficking. I killed them during parties or business meetings. I don't take that lightly and don't expect you to. It's unlikely you'll need it for self-defense, but I want you to have it."

I nod against her thigh, letting her words sink in. Her words don't suppress the dread, but it makes sense. I haven't been in danger here. She hasn't indicated that level of danger is in Kansas City. It was all from her father, who has been dealt with. The dread swells over that situation. Is it dealt with? Will the mafia continue his pursuits? Catherine doesn't seem to think so.

"Why don't we get some breakfast? We can chat more about what I want for you or talk about something else." I nod, sitting up slowly. She catches my face, offering me a soft kiss. I can't help but melt under her lips. Her lips are like butter: soft, warm, silky, and so tasty.

30 · JOSEPHINE

CATHERINE RUSTLES AROUND THE kitchen, grabbing pans, eggs, and vegetables from the fridge. She moves gracefully through the kitchen, preparing breakfast for both of us. I watch with intrigue as she cooks. My parents taught me how to cook, and I can make a lot of meals, but it's the bane of my existence. If I could get food without cooking it myself and it still be moderately healthy, I would take that opportunity. My budget doesn't allow for a personal chef, though. I'm not poor, but I'm not personal chef rich.

"I didn't think you'd be the type to cook," I say, popping a piece of bell pepper into my mouth. She dices an onion expertly like she's had training. "I figured with you being so loaded, you'd have someone do it for you." She shrugs casually, adding the onion to the bell peppers and grabbing some mushrooms. This omelet is going to be amazing.

"I had a chef for a while." She glances at me hesitantly as I steal another bite. She watches without saying anything, then returns to cutting.

"What happened to them?"

"I... had some free time a while back. So I took a cooking class, which became my new hobby." Her words are calm but filled with hesitance. Why wouldn't she want to tell me that? I watch her face, but Catherine stays focused on the mushrooms. Then it dawns on me. She had free time when I left her. I bite my lip, unsure what to say now. An odd sensation swirls inside me. I needed that space, but knowing how deeply it affected us both is still weird.

"Um, do you like cooking?" She adds the mushrooms to the other vegetables and meets my gaze. She stares at me, assessing my reaction. Part of me feels bad for running off and having no contact with her for so long. If I had spoken to her, it might have eased some of my fears and concerns sooner. However, I needed that time away from her. I needed to reconcile my own feelings before talking to her again. Not that I had dealt with my feelings when I did speak to her. Catherine finally prepares the eggs.

"I do, but I don't always feel like it during the week. Sometimes, I am too busy or forget to prep for those nights." She adds the vegetables to the warm pan, and a soft, searing sound fills the quiet between us. I'm not used to this kind of silence. I always have music or TV on in the background. I'm rarely in a quiet space.

"Why don't you hire a chef for those nights?" I grab a pepper that dropped on the counter, but she swats my hand with her spatula this time. I grab my hand, holding it to my chest, and feign outrage. Catherine looks at me with a sideways glance. I act offended but drop my hands back to the counter. She returns to cooking as she answers. This is a casual, playful, comfortable act. A heavy darkness still lingers beneath the surface.

"I haven't gotten around to it. With the traveling, I didn't want to hire someone only to leave." That makes sense. I prop my chin on my hands, watching removes the vegetables and pours the eggs in. She's so sure in her movements. I always feel like I'm doing things wrong. Worry about burning it or over seasoning or undercooking makes cooking stressful for me. And don't even get me started on meal planning and actually buying the food.

"Now that I'm here, we could split that chore. Make it easier on both of us."

Catherine puts a couple of slices of bread into the toaster as she adds the vegetables to the eggs. She glances at me quickly, assessing me again. She's good at making me squirm with just a stare. This isn't the squirming I prefer, though. Now, I feel a little uncomfortable.

"Is it a chore for you?"

"Yes. I don't particularly like cooking. It probably won't be so bad if I'm not doing it daily."

She nods, considering my words as she removes the first omelet from the pan and starts the second.

"I could hire someone for your nights. You don't have to cook."

This time, I feel uncomfortable about her spending that money on me. I have no idea how much a chef would cost, even for just a few nights a week, but it's still too much. I could never afford something like that. I don't want to mooch off of her. I can pull my own weight.

"You don't have to do that. I can cook.," I reply.

"I'm loaded, remember?" She smirks at me, sliding a cup of coffee with my favorite creamer. I nearly moan as the warmth hits my senses. I close my eyes, inhaling the smell before drinking, forgetting about her words. Damn, I love this woman. After the first sip warms my insides, I respond to her.

"Sure, but you don't have to spend that on me. I can hold up my end of the chores."

Catherine walks around the bar, placing my breakfast in front of me. It smells as divine as the coffee, and I can't wait to dig in. Before I grab the fork, Catherine wraps her arms around my waist. I lean back into her. She kisses my neck, whispering into my ear.

"Baby girl, I can hire someone to do every chore for us, and it wouldn't make a difference to me." Fuck, this woman. It doesn't matter what she says to me when she whispers against my neck. She could tell me about the vaccine scientists are creating for koala chlamydia, and I would still groan as arousal courses through my body. She chuckles behind me, her chest vibrating against my back. She grabs my phone from the counter before sitting in the chair beside me.

"Eat," she nods to my plate. She unlocks my phone, already knowing the code somehow. I don't question her at this point. I dig into my food. It's delicious, as I knew it would be. Having a chef wouldn't be the worst thing. I've never had any luxury like that. Maybe I should allow her to hire one. I've also never murdered someone before we went to Spain. Why not? New year, new me, or whatever they say. Even though it's almost May.

Before I can say anything to Catherine, she turns my phone to me. "I downloaded our banking app." Our? "Your card will be in tomorrow. You can transfer money to your account if you need money before then." What? I take my phone and look at the app she is showing me. It's a banking app for a bank I'm not familiar with. Then I notice the number in the account.

I choke on my food, coughing and spitting everywhere. I would feel bad about spitting eggs all over the counter, but that number is more than I have seen in real life. More than I earn. I didn't know you could have that much in an account at one time. Catherine rubs my back as I calm down, still staring at my phone.

"What..." I gasp, trying to catch my breath. "What do you mean, 'our account'?"

"It's yours. Everything I have. Whatever you want." I stare at her, too stunned to comprehend what she is saying. Sure, she's told me she would give me anything I want, but this?

"I can't take this. I can't spend your money." I shove my phone back in her hand as if she could take it away.

"Why not? I have more money than I could spend in one life. I want you to have that." She says all of this so casually. As if it's obvious I would have access to her immense wealth. Immensely massive and entirely unreasonable wealth. We haven't been together for a year. The time we have been together hasn't even been consistent. "Even if you leave, I still want you to have this." My breathing shallows. I don't know what to think.

"You're still getting paid through Marzanna, and you have your own apartment as long as you want. But you're it for me, Jo. There's no one else. You don't have to spend this money, but you have access to it. It's yours." I meet her eyes, terrified of what she is saying. I'm not sure exactly what I'm scared of. Why would that many numbers in a bank account be so scary? It feels that way, though.

Catherine takes my hand, pulling it to her lips for a kiss. She's serious. I'm her end game. I don't know how to feel about that. I've never been that for someone. It feels daunting, but she knows who I am. She knows everything about me and still wants me. My eyes sting with tears. She slips out of her chair and pulls me into her chest, wrapping her arms around my back. I chuckle against her chest, laughter being the only expression I can manage now.

"You're mine, baby girl." I hug her back, letting her words settle in my soul. She's mine, too. I would do anything for this woman.

"Kitty, I..."

"I, too, baby girl." I laugh at our inside love joke. I have no qualms telling her, 'I love you.' But shit, I love saying it that way too.

"I was going to say, 'I don't know what to say,' but I guess that works too." She laughs at me, cupping my cheeks. She tilts my head up and gently kisses me. It's a sweet kiss. She's not trying to arouse me. That does nothing to stop the ache in my core. Catherine affects me like no one else ever has. I guess that's what she means when she says there is no one else for her. I could find someone else to be happy with, but it wouldn't be the same. No one could have the same impact as her.

She pulls away and returns to her chair to eat her food. I watch for a moment, too stunned to eat.

"What if I bought a mansion with all of this money? Paid cash, spent it all." Catherine shrugs.

"That money will accumulate again in a few months. We can move into that house together. I could sublet this one. If you need more cash, I have some stocks

I could sell. I have a few other accounts from which we could pull cash, too. This account is just what I keep readily available to use. I can add more if you need it."

I gawk at her. No person could ever need that amount. Maybe Kanye, but I'm just a middle-class girl from Minnesota. What am I going to do with that kind of money? She is entirely unfazed by this conversation, as if money has never been a concern for her—with this kind of cash, it never has been.

"What about my money?" I ask in a way that makes me feel stupid. As if my measly account could hold up to her wealth. I may as well be homeless compared to her.

"I can help you invest it. You can keep it in your own account, add it to mine, or whatever you want."

"Fuck, Kitty."

My mind is swirling. How is this my real life? I went from suburban to mafia millionaire life in less than a year. Or is it billionaire? If there are other assets, it may be in the billions. Catherine grew up this way. She is comfortable with this lifestyle. Not me. I grew up on hotdish and ice fishing and a disappointing football team. They'll win next year. We had a good season. That's the motto. Fuck, I bet she has enough money we could buy the damn team. Holy hell.

My mind swirls for the rest of the day. Catherine called Marzanna for us, but she still works on her laptop. Whenever I open my drawing app, I see dollar signs instead of clothes. At this point, the only design I can come up with is one made of cash. That's been done before and looks terrible. I try to watch a movie, but money is my only focus. I try to listen to music, but my app starts with Wu-Tang Clan's song Cash Rules Everything Around Me.

Time passes at a weird pace. Some periods drag while others go quickly. Before I know it, I'm getting ready to go to the bar. Catherine offers me some cash, a ridiculous amount. I refuse it. It's enough knowing I have access to it online. I want to avoid walking around with that kind of cash. John gives me a ride to the bar where my friends are already waiting. They already have drinks. I decide to test out this new account. I open a tab and use my phone to pay.

"I opened a tab. Tonight is on Catherine, apparently."

My friends cheer, offering a salute with their drinks. The familiarity distracts me from my new and profound wealth. I forget about my mafia affiliations and my new murderous personality. I get to be myself and fall into the person I was a few months ago. It's nice and comforting.

We rack up several hundred dollars in drinks and snacks. No one asks what the total bill is. We each know how much we spend on a night out but haven't sat down to figure out what all of it adds up to. It's a substantial amount or would be for my personal account. It's barely a drop in Catherine's.

John drives me back to the condo, where I drunkenly amble through the lobby and elevator. I'm on cloud nine right now. Drunk enough to be giddy but not blackout drunk. I'm not thinking about the money anymore. Now, I get to be happy. Once in the apartment, I kick off my shoes, toss my bag on the floor, and shed clothes as I walk through. We haven't discussed cleanliness. I won't leave them past morning, but I'm making a mess for now.

Catherine is in bed with her laptop. Working, always working. I imagine that amount of money requires a large amount of work. Or maybe she's watching porn. That's what I would do at this time of night. My head spins with the alcohol as I meander toward the bed.

"What happened to your clothes, baby girl?" I can't tell if that's an admonishment or intrigue. I glance down at my body, only in a lacy bra and a mismatched thong. Shock fills my face as I lean against the wall.

"What the hell? Where did they go?" I look around the room as if I hadn't tossed them all in the entryway. Catherine slowly closes her laptop, keeping her eyes on me. Her look is full of hunger and intensity and lust. That look could bring the strongest to their knees. Unfortunately, based on the wetness pooling between my thighs, I am not among the strongest.

Catherine stalks toward me, a predator on the prowl. Her hands cup my cheek briefly, then trail down my neck. Her touch flits over my breasts, leaving goosebumps in its wake. She slides over my waist, my rolls. Her hands wrap around my thighs, then cup my ass. She hoists me into the air, pressing me against the wall as if I'm not a big girl. She holds me securely, making me feel as light as a feather.

"Fuck me," I gasp, caught off guard by her lifting.

"That's the plan, baby girl," she whispers against my neck, peppering it with kisses. I moan, grinding against her as I wrap my legs around her small waist. She's surprisingly strong for how small she is. I wonder how often she goes to the gym, but just as that thought appears, Catherine's thigh presses between my legs, giving me the perfect spot to grind on.

"How do you want to be fucked?" Her breath against my neck sends me spiraling in arousal. "Do you want me to get a strap-on and fuck you on the bed? I could bend you over and eat you from behind. I can hold you here while you grind against me until you come. We can get in the shower, and I can finger you until you are dripping down your thighs." She scrapes her teeth over the base of my neck, and my eyes roll into the back of my head.

"Yes," I moan. I want it all. Everything. Anything. Just the promise of orgasms has my body tingling. Catherine spreads my ass cheeks apart, slipping a finger near my hole. Just spreading me like that has me grinding harder against her leg. I can't quite get the friction where I want it, but that doesn't stop me. My hands are on her shoulders, barely holding on as she drives me higher.

Catherine spins suddenly, carrying me to the bed. I groan as she lowers me to the mattress. She places me near the edge, propping my legs wide open for her. I look down just in time to see her staring at my pussy, still covered by my thong. The cloth is soaked with my arousal. She can see that with the light-colored material. Her eyes catch mine briefly then she grabs my hand.

"Touch yourself until I get back." She grabs my wrist, pulling my hand to my cunt. Usually, I'd feel awkward about such a command. The alcohol coursing through my veins squashes that feeling. I rub my clit, dragging my fingers through my wet opening. I apply the pressure her thigh couldn't, making me moan and twist my head with delight.

She returns a few moments later. Her hair is pulled back in a bun, exposing her exquisite face. Her hair normally shadows her high cheekbones, dark eyes, and sharp jaw. With her hair pulled back, she looks even stronger than usual. Her crop top hides her strong shoulders but highlights the muscles in her arms. She wears her favorite high-waisted boy shorts with a strap on over them. I freeze when my eyes make it to the dildo.

It's massive and has ridges all over it. I've only heard of toys like that. It's bright and colorful and big. It's not so big I can't take it, but it will be a stretch. A delicious stretch that has my core clenching already. I lick my lips, looking up at Catherine.

"Is that ribbed for her pleasure?" I tease in a drunken, slurred voice.

"Let's find out," is all she says before she shoves my shoulders back. I collapse on the bed, letting her ravage my body. Even if I wanted to, I can't move my arms to touch her. Her hands are on my sides, my thighs roaming and scratching, driving me crazy. Her lips are on my chest, neck, jaw, anywhere she pleases. I can only writhe and groan beneath her. She tugs my bra down, letting my breasts spill across me. Her mouth is over my nipple, sucking and biting. Gods, that feels so good. Shivers run down my skin.

Catherine presses her hips against mine, rubbing the colorful, ribbed cock against my aching cunt. I can feel each little bump and can't wait for it to be inside me. My hands finally move, reaching between us to get it lined up. She swats my hands away.

"Patience, baby girl," she admonishes. "I'm savoring your body right now."

That gives me pause. No one has ever told me they are savoring my body. I swell with warmth, glowing at her words. I drop my hands, letting her do as she pleases. And fuck, does she do what she wants. She nips all over my breasts, hands roam my sides and thighs and belly. With anyone else, I'd be self-conscious. Not with Catherine, though. She ensures I feel good in my own skin.

Her hands cup my ass, pulling me apart in a way that feels exposed but so good. Her finger drags across my ass, pressing against my tight hole. She massages it as she watches my face. I watch her for any awkwardness, but she continues her touch. Her eyes are glazed with desire, as mine are.

"Have you ever been fucked here?" My eyes go wide, concerned now about the size of the dildo.

"N-no." I haven't been, and while I want to be, I need to work up to the size she is wearing.

"We will one day." Her lips find mine in a deep, reassuring kiss. That sounds perfect. Her fingers continue their trek to my pussy. She sinks two in deep, moaning into the kiss over my wetness. Her tongue dances with mine, and her fingers withdraw. I grunt at the emptiness, but she quickly puts lube on the dildo, then lines up and pushes in slowly. She breaks the kiss to watch me. My head tips back, enjoying the stretch and edges moving through my cunt. Her hips bottom out against mine. She pauses, watching me for a reaction to the size. It's sinfully good.

Catherine strokes my belly, grabbing my legs. She hooks my knees over her elbows as she pulls out and thrusts deep inside me. I groan, grabbing fistfuls of bedsheets. She pounds into me, my body soaring with ecstasy. She slows her pace when I think I am about to come. I whimper at the evil smirk on her face. Shit, this woman could probably make me come with her facial expressions. Not that she would ever let me get off that easily.

Her hands move teasingly slowly up my thighs. The colorful cock only half inside me in an infuriating position. She rubs my legs, tugging my ankles up in the air. The new position makes the dildo feel even more prominent. My ankles are propped on her shoulders, held in place by her tight fingers. She pushes the dildo back inside me so agonizingly slow that my body arches off the bed. I need more. I need her to fuck me hard.

Before I can say anything, she pulls out and slams into me. It's such a forceful impact that I shift further up the bed. She continues her relentless pounding. My cunt tightens around the massive toy inside me. I have adjusted to the size, and the ridges are divine against my inner walls. I'm on edge again, about to tip over into a mind-blowing orgasm when she freezes.

I scream in frustration. I did not agree to be denied tonight. I just want to be fucked. Catherine knows that. She doesn't care. She takes what she wants. As long as I get an orgasm tonight, I don't care what she takes. If she leaves me unsated, though, we gon' fight.

She fiddles with the waist on her shorts, pulling something from it. I watch in confusion, frustration momentarily forgotten. Is she about to get naked, too? She clenches her fist and then drives deep inside me again. Her actions are hidden with desire. She pounds several times, hard and fast and so fucking exquisite. I'm so close to orgasm again, and I fear she won't let me come. Before my fears take over, she presses a small bullet vibrator against my clit, between my clenched thighs.

I scream again, this time because my orgasm rips through my body. I tense and arch off the bed. Pleasure slams through my body, but Catherine doesn't stop thrusting. She increases the speed of the vibrator and shifts her hips. The dildo hits a new position, and my fading orgasm swells again.

I might be crying. Maybe I'm screaming. Maybe I've died and gone to another world where only ecstasy exists. Unrivaled pleasure spirals through my body. Nothing else matters. Clouds surround my body. Rubbing my sides, my thighs, my shoulders. My body drops, settling into fluffy, warm sheets. It's only when a cool cloth strokes my cunt that I am brought back to reality with a gasp.

"Sorry. I thought I was being gentle," Catherine murmurs against my forehead. I can barely process the words. Something is wrapped around me, and I'm warmly enveloped. I sigh, snuggling into the expensive magazine perfume I'm familiar with. I slowly drift off to sleep, happier than I have been in a long time. The dread that normally lurks deep in my chest is buried under orgasmic bliss.

31 · JOSEPHINE

I AWAKE AGAINST CATHERINE'S chest. Her breathing is slow and steady beneath me. I don't think I've ever awoken before her after a regular night. She is still wearing her crop top, the material soft against my cheek. Her breast is just below my mouth. I part my lips to suck on her nipple when a pounding in my head causes me to groan. Her grip tightens around me as she is startled awake.

"Sorry. My head is pounding." She kisses my forehead. I roll away from her, heading to the bathroom. I sit on the toilet, feeling the soreness from the toy last night. A smirk spreads across my face as I think about how she looked. Standing above me, fucking me, staring at me like I'm the only thing in the world. She owned me in the best possible way. Catherine is beautiful, and every inch of her oozes power and strength. Even if she weren't physically strong, she still looks strong.

"What are you thinking about?"

Her words are swoon-worthy as she hands me a few pills and a glass of water. I clean myself gently, rising to take the medicine from her.

"You," I respond playfully before brushing my teeth. She steps behind me, stroking her arms over my body. I realize I'm naked as her fingers tighten around my waist. A niggling feeling pulses in my mind until I look in the mirror. She watches her fingers glide over my sides. I see my body the way she must. Beautiful, soft, pliant. The stretch marks and lines don't remind me of all the times I tried to exercise for weight loss or ate a salad instead of the burger I wanted. Instead, they look like me.

"Do you feel like going to the gun range today?"

Her words catch me off guard. Her hands are still caressing my body, not in a sexual way. In a content way that shows how much she appreciates how I look. If I had met her sooner, I might have learned to love my body instead of hating it. Though, more than five or six years ago, our relationship would have been indecent, bordering on illegal. The age gap is only acceptable now because I am not a child.

Catherine's hands pause, and she looks at me in the mirror. I've been staring at her hands on my body this whole time. I still don't know what she actually said to me. She assesses my face. She doesn't speak as I finish brushing my teeth. I turn in her arms and wrap my arms around her shoulders. Hers settles on my waist as I kiss her. It's a sweet kiss as our bodies press into each other. She pulls back from the kiss, looking down at me.

"Do you want to learn to shoot today?"

I nod. "After breakfast." She steps away from me, swatting my butt gently to get me out of the bathroom. I sift through the closet, unsure what to wear to a gun range. Is a dress appropriate? Should I wear jeans instead? Do I want to wear jeans? I finally settle on a loose tunic and a pair of jeggings. I wear a pair of red sneakers that match the flowers on my top. I pull my hair into space buns, ready for brunch and guns.

AT THE GUN RANGE, I let Catherine make all the decisions. My father took my sister and me to a range a few times when we were younger. I'm familiar with guns, but not enough to be comfortable with them. Catherine knows what she is doing, so I let her do her thing. She books a lane for us at the end of the range. She gets the guns and ammo and lets me pick a few targets. I go for the papers with bullseyes instead of people. I know the purpose of learning is to shoot people if need be, but I still feel uncomfortable practicing on them.

She guides me to the lane and then shows me basic gun safety. Her skills are impressive. She explains how to clear the gun, load the ammo, hold it, and aim. She tells me we won't break down these guns, but eventually, she'll show me how to clean hers. She goes over how to hold it and where to point it. Never put my finger on the trigger unless I am ready to pull it. She emphasizes that point a few times. I already knew that from the lessons with my dad, but I still heed her word.

Finally, after what feels like thirty-two hours, we step up to shoot. Her hands rub against my thighs, spreading my feet apart. She may be widening my stance for stability, but it feels awfully sexual. Her hands slide up to my arms, lifting them until they are level with my sight. She pushes my ear protection just behind my ear and whispers how to use the sight to aim. I don't know why I didn't expect this to be so sensual.

She whispers how to wrap my finger around the trigger, what kind of recoil to expect, and where to aim. All the while, her hands slide over my shoulders, my back, settling at the top of my ass. Instinctively, I press back into her.

"Mmm, baby girl," she hums, "we're here to shoot, not fuck." She nibbles on my earlobe then covers it with my earmuffs. She steps away from me, leaning against the wall. I can still see her in my peripheral. She's so fucking casual as if she didn't just intentionally turn me into a damn horny waterfall. I take a deep breath, intending to fire after my exhale. When all the air is out of my lungs, pleasure slithers through my arms before I can squeeze the trigger. Catherine didn't move, but my body reacted all the same.

She smirks as I shake out my shoulders, taking a deep breath again. This time, I fire the gun. After the first shot, the next few are easier. I empty the magazine, clear the weapon, and place it on the shelf. Catherine presses the button to pull in my target while I load the magazine again. I hit the center once, but my other shots went to the side. Catherine explains what I was doing wrong. Of course, she explains this with her body pressed against my back. Her words whispered against my ears. Her hands caress my body to reposition me.

"I could probably aim better if I wasn't so fucking horny," I sass to her. She steps back a solid foot from me, and I regret saying anything. She waves her hands before returning to her spot against the wall. That was a stupid thing to say. I silently reprimand myself for saying anything. I take a deep breath and aim at the next target. Instead of shooting at the center, I aim for the top corner, opposite where most of my shots were last time. I empty the magazine again, and she pulls in my target.

My shots are closer together but several inches away from the target. She raises an eyebrow at me but does not say anything.

"I think I was wrong earlier. I'm probably better if I'm horny."

Her laugh is sweet, like honey. Smooth and luxurious. She steps behind me again, and I melt against her. I love her standing behind me like this. It feels right. This is where I belong, in her arms, letting her protect me. I settle into a comfort I haven't known before.

Catherine continues her instructions the way she started, pressed against my body seductively. By the time we pack up and leave, I'm a gooey, wet mess. My shooting did get better with her guidance. I'm no marksman, but I'm not bad and can probably hold my own.

She guides me back to the Chevelle. I slide into the middle beside her. Her hand wraps around my thigh, stroking the inside. Her fingers drift closer to my core, then back away, teasing me as she drives. She leaves the city, heading out into the farmland beyond. She turns off the road, driving through a thicket of trees.

"Where are we going?"

"On a picnic."

Her words are so casual like that's the most obvious answer. It is a nice day for a picnic. It's not terribly hot, and there are enough clouds in the sky that the sun hides intermittently. She drives through the trees until she turns off on a dirt road. We drive for a few more minutes until she stops at an opening. Nothing is in the cleared space. An empty fire pit is off to one side, but the area is bare, surrounded by trees.

Catherine climbs out of the car and walks around to the front. I join her, but she doesn't have food or a blanket. It's quiet here, hidden from the road and people. A soft breeze rattles the leaves, and birds sing from the trees. It's so peaceful that I'm briefly distracted by the fact that she hasn't brought anything for a picnic. As I'm looking around the trees, she steps around me and pulls my phone from my back pocket. I don't question her as she opens it. She stands by the car door, fiddling with my phone momentarily. She props it on the hood as soft, long notes pour out. I recognize the song when a man's quiet voice begins to sing. I raise my eyebrows at her as Here I Go Again by Whitesnake fills the area.

"What are you..."

"Get on the hood," she demands. I hesitate for a second, but when she stalks toward me, I move back until I am sitting on the hood. She walks up to me, pressing between my thighs. Her lips find mine while her finger caresses my jaw, back into my hair. Her fingers tangle in my hair, jerking me back from the kiss.

"You like my car so much, I'm going to eat your pussy on it."

A gasp slips from my lips. Her other hand slips between my legs, rubbing over my core tantalizingly. I groan, resisting the urge to rub against her fingers. She can feel my wetness through my jeggings. Her fingers caress harder as she finds my lips again. The kiss is searing, her tongue diving into my mouth.

She breaks the kiss by tugging my hair back. This time, she guides me until I am lying on the hood. The song starts over, playing on repeat from my phone above us. Her fingers hook the waist of my pants, tugging them down.

"Where are your underwear, Jo?" The way she says my name distracts me from the fact that she didn't call me baby girl. I bite my lip, ready to answer, but she plunges a finger deep inside me. She flicks my shoe off with one hand. That hand replaces the one in my core then she flicks off my other shoe. She pulls her hand away from me to remove my pants altogether.

I'm bared to her on the hood of her sports car. My pussy is dripping, so ready for her tongue. This wasn't what I envisioned when she said we're having a picnic, but this is much better. She spreads my legs wide, dragging another finger down my opening. She stares at my cunt with admiration. A strong sensation pools deep in my gut. I bite my lip harder than I intend, breaking the skin. A tiny bit of blood touches my tongue as she slowly leans into my cunt, never taking her eyes away.

I lick the cut as her tongue licks my length. I drop my head back, moaning as she glides across my aching pussy. I look down to find her staring at me. The image of her eyes above my cunt is absolutely gorgeous. I commit it to memory as her tongue swirls just inside my opening, teasing and light.

"Please, Kitty," I beg. "I need more."

I can feel her grin between my thighs. Her lips wrap around my clit, sucking the swollen bit into her mouth. I cry out as she slips a finger inside me. She doesn't fuck me as hard as she did last night. This is more gentle, more loving, but still so good. Her tongue flicks against my clit, driving my pleasure higher. I reach down to grab her head but feel unstable. I use one hand to grab the top edge of the hood while the other holds her head.

She pulls her finger out as her tongue returns to my opening, licking long and deep. I moan and start grinding against her face shamelessly. She doesn't stop me. Her hands grab my hips, pulling me closer to her. She wraps one hand around to press against my clit while her tongue laps inside me. I shove her head tighter against me.

"I'm...I'm gonna..." Before I can finish that, though, my orgasm rips through me. Glorious and delightful. My skin tingles as my body lights up with ecstasy. It's less powerful than last night but no less enjoyable. She pulls her hand away from my clit but doesn't stop licking me. Her tongue slows down, guiding me back from the orgasm. Whitesnake continues playing in the background.

She just fucked me on the hood of her car, and I fucking love it. I've been fucked inside a car plenty of times, but never on the hood like this. She slowly rises, gliding over my body.

"You are so fucking sweet."

Her lips are soft and wet from my orgasm. I groan beneath her, tasting myself on her lips. She breaks the kiss and walks around the car. She returns with a few pieces of cloth, handing me two.

"I didn't plan for you not wearing panties. So, I don't have new pants for you. You'll have to wear the wet ones." A devious glint shines in her eye. She has a cloth to clean up with and a pair of panties. She planned this whole thing. I slide off the hood, clean myself, and slip on the underwear. She wipes the car's hood down, making me feel awkward. She notices and explains.

"John doesn't say anything about the car when I use it, but I don't want him to clean up after something like this." She smirks and moves to the trunk. This time, she returns with a soft cooler and a blanket. Catherine thinks of everything. I follow her to a spot where she sets up the picnic. Sometimes, I don't know how I got so lucky with her. She is amazing. Even though she can't say 'I love you,' she shows it in many ways. All the kind thoughts and actions.

I join her on the ground, eating fruits, vegetables, and dried meats like a less formal charcuterie board. It's delicious and perfect. After the food is gone, I lie down, resting my head on her lap. She strokes my head, causing my eyes to close. I revel in her touch. It's soothing. With the calmness around us, the soft breeze, animals scurrying, and the rustling of leaves, I drift off.

I don't know how long I sleep, but I roll over and glance up at Catherine. She is just sitting, watching the forest around us. I'm surprised she doesn't have a tablet or phone to work on. I've never seen her utterly idle like this.

"Sorry, I didn't mean to sleep."

She glances down at me with the sweetest look. She pushes my hair away from my face, giving me a soft smile.

"I have something for you."

I sit up, watching her. As if she hasn't already given me enough stuff, I'm still excited to see what it is. She pulls a small box and holds it out to me. She isn't hesitant but looks unsure about something. I love seeing her torn, knowing I am the reason for that. She is so confident in everything she does until it comes to me. At moments like this, I enjoy that little bit of knowledge.

I take the small box from her, but she doesn't say anything; she just watches. It's a black ring box. My breathing hitches. Is she about to propose to me? Does she want to marry me? Do I want to marry her? I know I'm her end game, and she is mine but is marriage what I want? Not that I don't want to be with her. Whew, my mind is running away from me.

I flip open the box, exposing a ring inside. It has a simple gold band with three small diamonds on one side of the gem. The gem looks like it contains fire inside it. It's orange and glimmers in the light. It has an octagon cut with round edges at the corner. The gem isn't large, but so beautiful. I'm mesmerized by the ring, and Catherine's voice breaks my gaze.

"It belonged to my mother," she says, pulling the ring from the box. She grabs my hand, slipping it over my ring finger. It fits perfectly. I've never seen a picture of her mother. Catherine only mentioned her once and didn't describe her appearance. I question whether she was the same size as me. With Catherine's slim frame, I doubt she was a large woman.

"She never promised it to me, but it was the one ring I always wanted. She had several, but this one was my favorite. She wore it on special occasions. My father gave it to her to represent the fire inside her." Catherine stares at my hand, the ring set against my pale skin. Her face is unreadable, though. My breathing is shallow, unsure what to say. This is such a special gift she is giving me. All the other things pale in comparison to her mother's ring.

"I..." she hesitates. I don't know what she wants to say. I don't know what I want her to say.

"I, too," I whisper and lean in before she can stop me or say anything. I press my lips against hers, cupping her face with my hand, now wearing the ring. Her kiss deepens into a desperate act. Both of her hands frame my face. She pulls from the kiss, pressing her forehead against mine. Her eyes are closed. I watch her as she speaks, her breath warm on my lips.

"I do love you." Her voice is almost a whisper. "I'm so scared of losing you." My heart aches for her. She has experienced so much loss, so much damage. I wrap my arms around her, moving my head to her shoulder. No words would help right now. Instead, I hold her. I can't assure her nothing will happen to us. Hell, if the past few months are an indicator, life won't be easy for us. I'm along for the ride, though.

32 · CATHERINE

THE BREAK ROOM IS warm. Early morning sun shines through the windows, casting a comfortable heat across the tables. Today is my monthly meeting with Diane, my head designer, Jenny, the head collaborator, and Zed. We meet to discuss needs, goals, and plans for Marzanna. Diane is the closest thing I have to a best friend. Zed is, too, but our relationship is mainly work-related. He likes to comment on my personal life, but he typically doesn't get involved. Jenny has been with me for several years and delegates all the other jobs of Marzanna. We wouldn't function without her, without any of them.

Jo rode in with me this morning. I love waking up next to her every morning. It's more than I ever dreamed of. She is perfect. No one compares to her. Instead of hanging in the shop, she went to her favorite café to get coffee. She'll come back later when her shift officially starts. I'm staring at my screen with reports, emails, and numbers, but my thoughts are on the girl with the colorful hair.

"Why does Catherine look so dreamy?" Diane's words are whispered, but it is the loudest possible voice a person can manage without speaking. Before I can respond, Zed speaks up.

"Because she's in *love*." He sings the last word, and I glare at him. While it's true, I have no intentions of discussing my personal life at this meeting.

"Oooh, with who?" Jenny asks.

"Jo," Diane answers quickly. Jenny gasps, covering her mouth and looking to me for confirmation. I say nothing and switch my tablet to the reports to start the meeting. I'm not entirely surprised Diane knows it's Jo. As far as I know, she's never caught us, but it's possible.

"How are things going with marketing, Jenny?"

"Oh no, we are not switching away from this. You are in love with Jo?" Jenny questions instead of responding to my question.

"She has been since Jo started here," Zed supplies. This fucker. If he wasn't so vital to me, I would fire him. I give him a look that says as much, but he smirks at me. He knows I won't fire him.

"That long?" Diane interjects. "I knew recently, but she was hired in September. That's," she counts on her fingers, "eight months ago!" Jenny stares in disbelief.

"You knew?" Jenny looks at Diane, then to Zed, "And you?" I knew we weren't hiding it well, but a small swell of satisfaction that Jenny didn't notice builds inside me. Zed huffs a laugh.

"How did you not? They ride together. Jo brings her coffee now. They sit as close as possible at lunch without being at the same table. They stand closer than anyone else during Catherine's rounds. Honestly, I'm surprised you haven't caught them kissing. They are always sneaking out for a quick rendezvous." I sigh, resigning myself to this conversation.

"They're having quickies at work?" Jenny gasps again, scandalized by this situation.

"No one is having quickies at work," I state, stopping that line of thought. Jenny is a few years younger than me but surprisingly sheltered. "Yes, Jo and I are dating. We..." I pause. I can't say we've been together since September because that isn't true. I don't want to admit we broke up, though.

"Something happened before Christmas, right?" Diane looks at me suspiciously. "You were more ornery than I have ever seen. What happened?" Diane leans in, her long grey hair falling in her face. She doesn't bother to push it away, exhilarated with the thought of drama. I love the woman, but she sometimes gets too giddy over gossip. It's fun when it's not me, but I could do without this pressure now.

"I don't know the answer. It was serious, though. Jo was a fucking mess. And, well," Zed waves his hand at me as if the answer is still shining on my face. The anger written there is apparent. I am good at schooling my features until it comes to Jo. I can't hide anything about her.

"Yes, something happened. We broke up. Then reconciled. We are dating now, and everything is fine. Can we continue, please? Diane, how are the designs for the summer line going? Have we started on the fall line yet?"

"Oh!" Jenny starts. "That's why Jo missed so many meetings. I was worried she was sick and needed to see a specialist or something. She was just lovesick," she coos. I want to slap the swoony look off her face. Her face ticks through several more emotions before she speaks again. "But she's a lot younger than you. And your employee. How scandalous." The last word comes out with pure glee. She leans on the table, propping her face on her hands. I sigh, rubbing my hand over my face. The front door chimes as someone walks in.

"Speak of the devil. Jo!" Zed calls to her. She smiles and waves, placing her bag down. Zed sits across from me with Diane and Jenny on my sides. All three watch with intrigue as she walks over. When she steps closer to Zed than me, their faces drop with disappointment. She notices and gives curious glances to all of us.

"Hi," she offers a slight wave to everyone, "is something wrong?"

"You're dating your boss," Diane supplies.

"What is the age difference? Twenty years?" Jenny adds, returning to her propped position on the table. Jo looks petrified. To her credit, she looks to Zed instead of me.

"What? What..." she stammers, unsure what to say.

"It's only fifteen years, Jenny. Honestly." I sigh again as Jo turns her attention to me. She's stunned, caught entirely off guard by this conversation.

"Oh, this is adorable," Jenny swoons.

"You were heartbroken!" Diane exclaims and slams her hand on the table. She turns to face Jo. "That's why your designs were so dark over the winter. It all makes sense now." Diane looks like she solved the greatest mystery of our time, assessing Jo with a new set of eyes.

"They know about our relationship," I inform Jo. She probably already pieced that together. I offer her an apologetic look. This conversation is a lot for me this early. Jo must be entirely thrown by it.

"Oh, okay. Um," she turns back to her workstation. "Well, I'll get to work then?" Her question is adorably awkward. I nod to her with a small smile, and she walks away.

"Can we get back to business now?" I look at everyone sitting at the table, but they watch Jo. Jenny's face lights up with a realization.

"Oh my gods, she made an amazing design when she started working here. Were you her inspiration? Aww." Her voice is gushing again, and I try to suppress the irritation. A tiny hint of pleasure pops inside my gut.

"No, she came up with that on her own. Please," my voice is stern as they turn back to me. "Marzanna." I tap some papers Diane placed on the table. Jenny gives me an infatuated look as if this is the best love story ever. Zed looks pompous. Diane looks impressed like it's impossible that I could fall in love. It takes them all a long minute to recover. I do everything not to think about the girl rustling around her desk, setting up for the day. Jo walks over, looking far too nervous to be approaching us.

"I, um, got you coffee," she says meekly, placing the large, hot beverage in front of me.

"I'm so sorry," I offer.

"Kiss her," Jenny whispers.

"Kiss the girl," Zed adds. Jo chews on her lip but leans in and kisses my cheek. I can't help but close my eyes as her warmth brushes my face. Fuck, we're not getting through this meeting today. I grab Jo's hand by my side, giving a gentle squeeze. Jenny coos in the background, and Diane claps. Jo straightens with bright red cheeks.

"Shall we have this meeting over lunch?" I question, trying to draw the attention away from Jo.

"Only if Jo stays, and we can talk about you two." Diane's eyebrows wiggle, and I want to slap her for the first time in our friendship.

"No." I rise from the table, gathering my things. I place my hand on Jo's back as I guide her to her workstation.

"Fuck, that was awkward," she mumbles as the others rustle behind us, starting their day.

"You weren't here for most of it," I state. She nods, looking at me softly. "I have a shipment tonight. Why don't we go out for coffee this afternoon? I likely won't make it back to the condo." Her eyebrows furrow for a moment.

"Can I come with you?"

"To coffee? Yes," I'm confused by her question.

"No, to the shipment." My stomach knots at her statement. She's said she wants to be more involved, but we agreed she wouldn't be present. I tell her about my meetings, and she stays behind.

"Can we talk about it after work?" I ask, hoping to prolong the answer. Maybe I can come up with good reasons to tell her no. I don't want her involved, even if she wants to be. Even if I prepare her for the worst outcome, I don't want her there. She nods at me, rising up to kiss my cheek again. It is less comforting than the one a few minutes ago.

I need good, convincing reasons Jo can't go tonight. She won't take a no easily. I have to think of reasons she can't. She won't accept her safety as a valid reason. She hasn't done that any other time. After her abduction, I doubt she'll be convinced to stay anywhere but my side. The shipments aren't dangerous, though. We have to maintain a low profile.

That's it! Her colorful hair would be too recognizable. She can't change her hair by this afternoon. I can't risk her being identified by the crew. It might be traced back to her if they talk about a girl with blue and green hair.

It's a weak argument, but it's all I have now. I need more reasons. I can't let her go. I don't want her involved with these businesses. I spend the rest of the day distracted by the shipment tonight. I can't focus on work. Even the meeting during lunch doesn't distract me. Jenny, Diane, and Zed assume I am thinking about Jo. It's true, but not in the sense they believe.

A second idea hits me. Orgasms. I'll distract Jo with sex, make her wait for me. I don't honestly know if that will work, either. I've got two half-assed ideas to keep her from the warehouse tonight. I've never felt so pathetic as I do now. I've always been good at coming up with alternative plans. I have what appears to be a legal drug trafficking business. But I can't come up with a reason to keep Jo away.

I've been staring at my tablet, unable to process the information for twenty minutes. A slight knock breaks my stare. Jo walks in, closing the door behind her. Work is over for the day, and I assume most people have already left. Only a few employees stay late other than me. She crosses the room with quiet confidence. I turn my chair to face her as she leans against my desk. I'm out of time to prevent this. I only have two weak ideas.

"You can't come tonight."

"Why is that?" She knows I don't have a good reason. I don't know why she thinks that. There must be a legitimately good reason she shouldn't go.

"Your hair," I try to keep my voice steady, but even I can hear the anxiety in it. "You're too recognizable with the bold colors. If someone talks to the cops, they could trace it back to us." She glances at her hair, then back to me, considering.

"I'll wear a hat," she shrugs like it's the most obvious thing in the world. It is. I knew it was a weak argument, but I had to try. Time for my second attempt. I grab the toy from my drawer, sliding closer to her. She wore a dress today. The weather is finally warming up for summer. That means more sundresses. Jo looks stunning in the dresses, and they give me easy access.

I place my hand inside her thigh, just above her knee. The toy vibrates against her skin as I slide it higher. I lean against her chest, closing my eyes and hoping this works. Her hand drapes over my shoulders. I don't look up at her. I don't want to see my failure on her face. I can't accept defeat.

"I want you a sopping mess in my bed tonight. I'll be back early in the morning to give you what you need." I am almost at the apex of her thighs when her hand grabs my wrist.

"I love your attempts, but I'm going to the shipment with you."

She gently pushes my hand away. I toss the toy onto the desk haphazardly. I rise from my seat, unable to stay still. I pace the room, feeling her gaze on me the whole time. I can't look at her. My resolve will break. I'm still running through any reason she can't go.

"Kitty."

Her soft voice breaks my resolve. I collapse on the couch, unable to hold myself up any longer. I've tried so hard to separate her from this part of my life. I only gave in while in Spain because I could see the pain in her. I wanted to give her that closure. I didn't want to, but she handled the situation better than expected. Maybe having her there wouldn't be the worst thing. No, I can't have her there.

She stands in front of me, pulling me against her stomach again. I embrace her body, trying to find solace in her warmth. I breathe in her warm honey scent, letting it soothe my raging mind.

"What are you scared of?" Her words are soft, nearly a whisper. Her hands rub my back and my head, comforting me.

"Losing you. You getting hurt again. A whole myriad of dangers in working with the mafia. What if they take you again? We were lucky last time." I stop there. I can't go back down the road of what-ifs.

"What if you let me go and nothing happens? What if you have someone to share this burden with?" I squeeze her tight. I've occasionally thought about what it would be like to have a partner. To have someone that knows all of my secrets. Jo knows them all. She knows everything about me. She has offered me comfort I didn't think I could have. She's held me as much as I have held her. We do work well together. Letting her go with me feels different. It's terrifying, but is it really that different?

Her fingers massage my head and back, letting me work through my feelings. My feelings. Aside from sexual desire, I never let myself feel things. I push down the anger and hatred and joy and love. When was the last time I truly enjoyed something before Jo came into my life? Aside from my brief appointments with Brayden, what has made me happy?

My hands tighten on her back. She still doesn't speak, as if she knows the turmoil I am struggling with. Maybe she does. She requested her attacker in Spain. It's not quite the same, but it's not that different. She came to terms with loving me and being involved in my life. I need to come to the same terms. I can love her, but I can't keep her at arm's length from myself. I've tried that, and it only resulted in more pain.

"Okay," I start softly. Her hands slow against my body. I look up at her; we both have neutral faces, unsure how to react to my proclamation. "But you have to follow some rules." She nods obediently but doesn't react.

"You have to cover your hair. You have to stay by my side. And you can't get close to the crew. Don't tell them your name; don't ask for theirs." She nods again, agreeing with me. Before I can lean against her again, she slides onto the couch next to me. Her arms wrap around me, holding me in the way I need. I've never been held and comforted like this. I don't hold or comfort other people. All of this is foreign to me.

Jo leads me through locking up the shop and to her favorite coffee shop. We grab large drinks to get us through the night. Then, we walk silently to the warehouse. She keeps her hand in mine. I marvel at the connection. It feels so natural and disarming at the same time. She is the only person I hold hands with.

I lead her into my office in the warehouse and talk her through the evening, what will happen, and what to expect. I sit behind the desk, talking while she looks around. I startle when she starts removing her clothes. I glance at the clock. I have enough time to get her off, but it would push it. Is she really in the mood right now? I was just telling her how a drug trafficking shipment works. Is she more depraved than I thought?

She smirks at me and pulls gym clothes out of her bag. She slips into black leggings with a black crop top, keeping her bra and thong on. She pulls her hair up, wrapping a pink headband around it. I chuckle at her as she walks over to me. She leans over my chair, stopping mere inches from my face.

"Nice to know where your mind is at."

She presses in the rest of the way, planting a gentle kiss on my lips. I soak up every bit of pleasure I can from this single kiss. She pulls back, standing straight to fuss with her hair.

"I don't have anything to cover the rest of it."

I'm momentarily distracted by her body. With her arms above her head, her breasts are pushed out. I want to wrap my lips around her nipple, taste her, lick her. Her shirt rises to expose skin above her leggings. I want to bite it. Not enough to break the skin, just enough so she knows how desperately I need her. I want to cover her body with my lips. My fingers twitch at the possibility of trailing her skin, feeling it pebble beneath my touch. My tongue licks over my lips at the thought of her body. Her arms drop by her side, and I envision leaving a line of nips and kisses from her wrists to her collarbone. How delectable she would taste, writhing beneath me.

"Holey fucking cheeses, Kitty," she breaks my concentration. "You're going to burn me with your eyes if you don't stop." She chuckles, standing in front of me, straddling my thighs. My mind clears from the haze of lust. And I was just wondering how she could be horny at a time like this. I'm like a goddamned teenager.

"Did you just say 'holey cheeses'?"

"Yeah. It's not offensive but sounds like it is." I laugh loudly at her explanation. I wrap my arms around her body, pulling her against my chest. She settles in, chuckling with me. I kiss her forehead.

"I, Jo."

"I, too. Kitty."

She hasn't actually said 'I love you' outright to me. I don't actually care. I never thought anyone would say it to me. I didn't think I could say it to anyone. Having Jo in my life has been better than anything I could have imagined. She makes my life brighter and worth living. Jo is like waking up to the shining sun in winter. The warmth penetrates my cold body and offers me hope of brightness. She is everything worth living for.

A car horn draws our attention. Time to get into action. I find a black scarf for Jo to wrap around her hair. I change quickly as Jo goes to open the garage door for the truck. When I walk out, the large truck is backing in. It doesn't block the image of the sedan in the lot. I curse as Robert exits the vehicle, walking through the garage door with complete disregard for the truck backing into it. He hasn't been here in months. I don't know why he is here now.

33 · JOSEPHINE

"CATHERINE!" A MAN IN a nice suit walks through the garage door beside the reversing truck with reckless abandon. I'm scared for him. I don't even like driving beside semi-trucks. No way would I walk beside a reversing one. This man has bigger balls than I can even conceive. He enters the warehouse, stopping in front of Catherine. I close the garage once the truck has come to a close.

"Who is this?" He glares at me. I struggle not to cringe or cower at his words. I don't know who he is, but I don't like him.

"This is Mae. My assistant. She'll be around more often." I don't know what shocks me the most. She used my middle name. She also said I'll be around more. I didn't think she'd let me come back. Or at least wouldn't agree to it this quickly. Her demeanor is stern, the one she uses for business. It's almost startling to see the change. From the lust she exhibited a few minutes ago to this cold aloofness. Meanwhile, I'm probably giving her heart eyes.

"Getting ready to retire on us?" The man jokes. His hands wrap around his belly as he laughs. He's not particularly fat; it just looks like he's had a few too many beers or tacos over his life. His greying hair betrays his attempts to appear youthful with sunglasses, nice suits, and impressive accessories. It's an odd look, but it also works for him.

The men climb down from the truck's cab, walking to the back to open it. I stroll over to Catherine's side. Robert sees me momentarily but turns his gaze to the crates now being carried off the vehicle.

Catherine opens a side door. The women I saw last time enter and head down the hall. They strip off their clothes and enter the back room while the crates are unloaded and bricks are carried back. My insides are twisted, and I am more nervous than I thought I would be. I didn't anticipate to feel this anxious here. I was scared last time because I didn't know what was happening. I know now.

An odd, removed confidence settled over me while we were in Spain. I knew what I was doing to the man, but it didn't feel like it was me. It was as if someone controlled me. I don't regret what I did to him, but that tiny sense of dread lingers inside me. The dread grows larger now that I am here and involved with this. The truck roaring to life startles me.

"Robert, let's go into my office for a drink." Catherine begins walking, knowing he will follow. She didn't say anything to me. I debate staying here with the crew. Do I want to talk to them? She said not to. I follow behind Robert, closing the door behind us.

Inside her office, I take a spot against the back wall. She has a shelf there, and I lean on it. She gathers a few glasses, mixing drinks for all of us. Catherine passes a drink to Robert, who has settled in the chair before her desk. He accepts with a nod, and she turns to me. She holds the drink out, looking directly into my eyes. She's searching for something, anything that would bring this to a halt. I take the drink, hoping my eyes convey more confidence than fear.

"You haven't been here in a while, Robert." Catherine settles in her own chair, taking a swig from her glass. I take a small sip, trying not to cough at the burn. I'm not unfamiliar with scotch, but my stomach is a tangled mess. The alcohol hits harder than I expected it to. I suppress the cough, but my eyes water the slightest bit with effort.

"Yes, I thought I would check in." He swirls his drink, not taking a drink from it. "Seems I should have come sooner. You didn't inform me there would be more people." He casts an evaluating glance in my direction. I don't move, unwilling to make myself look larger or smaller in his gaze. I'm entirely unaffected by him, or I hope that's how I look.

"This is her first night. It was a last-minute decision. She has been learning more of the business side and wanted to see a shipment in person." He eyes me suspiciously, swirling his drink again but still not bothering to try it.

"I want a girl tonight." His voice is almost threatening.

"No." Catherine is confident without being rude. She drinks again, but her focus stays on him.

"They are mine. I can do with them as I please."

"Not in my warehouse," she retorts.

"You have beds and showers. I want to use them. I plan to fuck one of them tonight, and you won't stop me." He is angry. His cheeks flare red as his fists tighten.

"Those are for them to use after their job. I have a connection to a good pimp in the area if you want a girl. I will even pay as a peace offering." He takes a deep breath, running a hand over his face. Catherine didn't mention anything like this happening. The urge to move closer to her is strong. But I won't be some weak, simpering girl. I can hold my own. I also have a gun hidden under my crop top. While my aim isn't great, I don't think I would have any qualms shooting at this man if it comes to it.

"You know, I'm pretty sure you drugged me last time I was here." I struggle to hide the shock this time. Catherine is entirely unfazed by his comment. I need to ask her to teach me whatever she does to hide her emotions.

"Why would I do that, Robert?" She sips her drink as casually as if they are discussing the Royals game.

"You don't want me to fuck my girls here."

"That is true." Her voice is so calm. I glance between them, overwhelmed by this interaction. I'm frozen with curiosity, fear, discomfort, and intrigue. Where is all of this going? Robert stands, leaving his untouched drink on the edge of the desk.

"Maybe I won't fuck one of them." He stands in front of me, calculating something. "Maybe I'll take her." This won't bode well for him. Or for me helping Catherine again. I'm going to make sure she can't use this to stop me.

"I wouldn't do that if I were you." My voice is surprisingly steady. I mustered confidence straight out of my ass. I'm more capable than I thought.

"Oh? And why is that?" He takes a step closer to me. His cheap cologne hits my nose, almost overwhelming me. It wreaks of terrible drugstore scents.

"You'd have two bullets in your brain before you could unzip your fly." I shrug, watching his face dance with glee. "You can try if you want." His smirk grows to a laugh. He turns to Catherine, nods, then takes his seat again. He grabs the drink, downing the entire thing at once. I sip on mine as he points at me.

"I like this one." He nods, a broad, toothy grin still on his face. "I won't fuck her. But I will take you up on your offer." Catherine makes a call and pours him another drink. She offers me one, but I decline, not even halfway finished with mine. She adds more ice to hers and refills it, but it's less than she did last time. Her sips are tiny, barely enough to get anything into her mouth. She looks like she is drinking without actually taking anything.

A young woman in a long jacket with skimpy clothing underneath shows up. Catherine guides them to a room in the back I never knew existed. She mingles with the crew for a few minutes, then motions me into her office. As soon as the door is closed, she wraps her arms around me, kissing me repeatedly.

"I didn't know he'd be here. I wouldn't have let you come if I'd have known." I chuckle at her concern, which is so at odds with her demeanor just a few moments ago.

"You wouldn't have stopped me. I'm fine, Kitty." I kiss her cheek, hoping to reassure her. She sighs, pressing her forehead to mine. She holds me like that for a long time, hands cupping my face, reminding herself I am safe. She kisses me quickly, her business face returning.

"We're almost done here," she nods to the door, and I follow her out. Another truck rolls inside, and the back is open. The women leave the room and tug their clothes back on. The men grab the smaller bags with drugs and load them into the crates with the secret compartments. Everything is loaded onto the truck, and the crew leaves through a side door. The truck drives off as Robert comes out of the room. He tips the girl. I'm surprised he does, knowing Catherine is paying her fee. He doesn't seem like the type to tip.

Robert thanks Catherine and nods respectfully to me. He walks out the door, and it closes with a loud sound, echoing through the empty warehouse. I jolt, remembering the last time I was here with her flashing in front of me. I gasp loudly enough that Catherine notices. She's instantly in front of me, cupping my face. She offers comforting words, but my eyes find the spot where the man fell with blood oozing from his brain. Peter. That was his name. A capo for the mafia.

"Jo," Catherine's voice is almost frantic. I pull my gaze from the spot to look at her. Reality slowly returns to me. She's so close I can't see much around her. My eyes dart back to the spot where his body once was. She realizes what I am looking at and takes a small step to the side, preventing me from seeing it.

"You're safe, baby girl."

I glance at her and nod. I know she will keep me safe. She will kill for me. She has killed for me. She will do anything to keep me alive. A small smile spreads on my face as the flashback fades. I release a deep breath, leaning into her touch. Her warmth soothes me.

"I know," I whisper.

"Cleaners will be here soon." She releases my face but leans in to kiss me deeply. I grab her back, holding her tight; we are desperate for each other. This night has been challenging but feels important for us. With all our trials, this feels like a real turning point. We can handle anything together. Seems odd, after all the murders, that a simple transaction like this would seal us together. She finally pulls away from me.

"What do you do while the cleaners are here?" I ask, looking up at her.

"Run," she answers simply. "But I need something else from you tonight." I nod, knowing I won't say no to anything. No matter what it is, it will be better than running. I despise running. Before I can answer, her phone buzzes, and she walks toward a different door. She opens as a few women with buckets and mops walk inside. None of them acknowledge me as they get to work. They clean the snacks from the tables and stack the chairs the crew used. A couple walks into the back rooms to clean them.

Without a single word uttered the entire time, Catherine motions for me to follow her into her office. She closes the door and turns the lock behind me. I wait patiently, unsure of what she needs. When she faces me, her eyes convey desperation and lust. Her jaw clenches, but she moves to her desk and opens a drawer. She returns with a toy, stopping in front of me. The look she gives me has my body heating. It's different from the look she gave me when I changed. There's a hint of something like fear.

"Take your shirt and pants off."

I obey instantly, tossing my clothes near my bag. I stand in my thong and bra with the gun holster strapped in the middle. She had me practice removing the gun in her condo several times to ensure this fit would be comfortable for me. I reach to remove it.

"Leave it."

I drop my hands by my side as she stares at my body. Her fingers graze my chest with such a light touch I'm sure I'm imagining it.

"Take your thong off."

I wonder if this is what subs feel. The world has faded around me. Catherine is the only thing here. I want to do everything she says. I don't even want to push back against her. I want to please her. I push my thong over my hips, letting it fall to the floor. She watches the action but has stopped touching me. A soft caress of air hits my dampening pussy. I nibble on my lip as arousal floods my body. She plucks my lip from my teeth with her thumb. Her eyes trace the movement.

"Sit."

The toy is pressed into my palm as I return to the chair the man was in earlier. She sits across from me, eyes never leaving my body. Her gaze is full of heat as confusion fills mine. Why is she sitting in that chair? It's far enough that she can't reach out and touch me. It could be a million miles away. Why is Catherine so far?

Her eyes leave my body for the first time in what feels like ages as she grabs her phone. She flicks through several screens as I sit in front of her, exposed. She is still fully dressed in athletic gear. Her outfit was similar to mine, at odds with what she wears at work and home. I'm not surprised to see her in workout clothing. She obviously exercises. Her looks are just so different. Her eyes meet mine as the toy springs to life in her hands. She gives a slight nod, leaning back in her chair.

She means to watch me. It doesn't seem like something out of Catherine's wheelhouse, but it's certainly out of mine. She doesn't say anything as I consider what she wants. I masturbate a lot, but never with an audience. I stare at the toy in my hand, debating whether I can overcome the awkwardness.

Catherine bumps up the vibrations, and I look at her. She isn't impatient; she is just watching. It's like she knows I'll do this. She is giving me the time to get there. She always gives me time. She gives me everything. She let me join her tonight. She could have locked me away. She has a safe room in her condo. She could have forced me to stay in there, but she didn't.

With that thought, I spread my legs, hooking my knees over the armrests. Her eyes shoot to my cunt, where she will find it glistening with desire for her. I will give her what she wants. A small ask compared to everything she has given me. The gun pokes into my belly. I shift it slightly, making it more comfortable and ensuring the safety is still on.

I finally bring the toy to my opening, sliding it through my lips. I keep my eyes on her. She glances between my gaze and my exposed pussy. I slide the toy up and down, chills running through my body. I circle my clit just enough to tease before guiding the bulb vibrator over my core again. Pleasure swirls inside me as I finally pull it to my clit and let it sit. I tip my head back and move the vibrator back and forth over my clit, giving a delightful sensation to the area.

My hips thrust against the toy, pulling extra sensation from the movement. A low groan escapes as my orgasm nears. It's so close my eyes shut tightly. My breathing is heavy. Then, the toy stops. I jerk, looking at Catherine, worried the battery died.

Her smile borders on wickedness. She wouldn't have a toy with a dead battery. She stopped it! I glare at her, angry that my orgasm was denied. The toy slips down as I prepare to use my fingers. I prefer a toy, but I will use my fingers when desperate. Just as I cover my clit with my index finger, the toy jolts to life against my pussy. I groan, rubbing it over me again.

I slip the toy inside me, letting my orgasm build slowly again. As much as I want to, I don't rush this. The vibration increases as the toy rubs across my G-spot. In this position, it's intense. I mumble a few curses and tug the toy in and out. My cunt clenches, so close to orgasm again. The toy is pushed out of me with my clenching muscles. Instead of trying to force it in again, I bring it back to my clit, circling it quickly. I rub it hard against my clit. Oh, it feels so good.

My body tightens, my breath quickens, and my pleasure surges higher, so close to an orgasm. Right as the peak hits, the vibrator shuts off again. I cry out as my body jerks. I whimper, nearly sobbing with the sting of the orgasm I didn't get to have. This is so much worse than the previous one. Catherine didn't just deny my orgasm. She fucking ruined it. I was on the edge. I was about to explode, and it stopped. My body convulses with need and an incomplete orgasm. I curse several times, but the vibrator starts up again.

It's on my clit in an instant. She won't stop me a third time. I think. She apparently knows my body better than I do. She knows when to stop it and how to drive me higher. While I may be the one moving the toy, it's clear she's in charge of my pleasure. I'm almost violent in my movements, thrusting the toy up and down over my clit. It burns with the friction, but in the best possible way. My head rolls back as I let my body build closer and closer to rapture.

I'm on the edge again. I want to open my eyes and watch her. I want to see if Catherine is stopping this again. But I can't. My eyes refuse to open. They are sealed shut with passion. I can't control my body. I'm barely able to keep the toy moving against my cunt. My toes curl as I get closer again. My body tenses with both anticipation and fear. I may literally die if she stops again. I'm breathing deeply. My chest heaves. My body burns, sweat coating my skin. My mouth opens to yell as my orgasm is ready to rip through me.

Then, the toy stops.

I scream in anger. I glare at her, but she returns a look of pure carnal wickedness. My body shakes in front of her. Clenching from being so close to an orgasm only to have it ruined. I throw the toy on the ground, staring at her as I do. She keeps her eyes on me. My fingers move to my clit, rubbing quickly. But I can't achieve the pace I need now. She's fucked with my body too much. My clit is over-sensitive, and I can't get what I need with my fingers alone. I whine, throwing my head back as I groan.

Catherine slides out of her seat, grabs the toy, and inches toward me. Part of me wants to kick her away, angry for denying me. The more reasonable side knows I need her to get off now. I cannot possibly return to everyday life without an orgasm. I will rip this office apart, looking for more toys I know she has hidden. Surely, she has some that aren't Bluetooth enabled.

Before I do anything drastic, she is between my legs, licking me up and down with a wide tongue. I could cry with pleasure. Maybe I am. I don't know. Her tongue slips inside my opening, and I tighten around her so close to the edge. She presses the toy against my clit, rubbing it back and forth in smaller motions than I used. It's perfect, though. My chest rises and falls quickly. Bumps pebble across my skin as white flashes behind my eyes, so close to the orgasm I desire.

Catherine slips two fingers inside me, rubbing my G-spot. I groan, feeling myself clench. She keeps her fingers inside me, pushing against my tightening cunt. I can feel her eyes watching me. She pushes the toy harder against my clit, and my orgasm finally rips through my body. It's as intense as the time she edged me for four days. I yell, twisting and jerking in the chair. Catherine's movements guide my body through the orgasm, driving me higher and easing me down.

I whimper and shake as her hands still. She turns off the toy but keeps it against my clit. I jolt as it stops, thankful she didn't pull it away. Her fingers slip out of my pussy, and I shake more. She leans in, pressing a kiss to my belly. I chuckle and grab the back of her head. I can't open my eyes, can't fathom anything beyond the pleasure I am feeling. She removes the toy with another thrust of my own hips. I groan, but she tugs me down into her lap.

I'm a blubbering, soaking pile of goo in her arms. She holds me tight, kissing my damp forehead. She doesn't care about the sweat. Catherine strokes my arms, soothing my tense muscles. We stay on the floor for a long time. I don't know how much time passes. Maybe I fall asleep. A knock on the door startles me, though. She kisses the top of my head, sliding me off her lap. Her sweater is wrapped around my shoulders. I don't know when she got it.

I stumble over to the couch and climb up on it. I plan to sit but wind up on my side, lying down. Catherine speaks softly with the person who knocked. I don't hear what they are saying. The door closes softly. Catherine moves around the office then a blanket is draped over my body. It's warm and soft. She lifts my head, sliding onto the couch so I am resting on her lap. She strokes my hair, sending me right back to the sleepy state I was just in.

"Thank you," she whispers. She shifts and rests on the couch. She settles in for a few hours of sleep before we need to get back to Marzanna for work.

"I love you," I mumble. I enjoy our other method of expressing that, but this feels like a moment to say the whole phrase. A lot has happened in the past twenty-four hours. Our coworkers found out about our relationship. She agreed to let me come to a shipment. She let me stand my own ground against Robert. Not to mention the mind-blowing, agonizing orgasm.

"I love you, too, baby girl," is the last thing I hear before drifting off.

EPILOGUE

Josephine • One Year Later

"Why can't he put his dick inside me?"

"Because that's not what we do."

"That's not what *you* do," I emphasize. We've had this argument a few times now. Catherine usually gets her way, not letting Brayden fuck me.

"Why do you want him to fuck you?"

Catherine walks around her office, organizing papers, cleaning shelves, and rearranging pictures. She's just keeping busy at the end of the work day. Brayden will be here soon. We changed her routine morning appointments to afternoons with him. We don't meet weekly, but a couple of times a month. We don't need him in our relationship, but it's fun to have options. Brayden is amazing at what he does, and neither of us wants to cut ties with him. We only play with him together.

"Because it's a waste of that beautiful cock."

Catherine cringes at my crassness. She's used to it by now but hates when I do it at work. We've settled into a good routine at work. We ride in together. If she needs to stay late, I'll wait at the coffee shop or one of the other stores nearby. Things were awkward when everyone first found out we were dating. Everyone is cool with it now. Catherine doesn't show any favoritism.

I haven't had a piece do as well as the first piece I created, but working at Marzanna has been excellent. I still create gorgeous outfits. While I prefer to work on high-end or avant-garde, I enjoy pieces for local events. We do quarterly fashion shows. I attend two a year, and Catherine always goes with me. I love traveling with her, and not just because plane rides mean mile-high orgasms.

We haven't been international since we went to Spain. We don't bring that trip up much. The unease of what I did there still hides in my chest, resurfacing in nightmares and random panic attacks. They are less frequent than they used to be but still cause issues. Catherine is quick to help with that. She has more experience dealing with it. I haven't killed or tortured anyone since. Some days, I think it's been too long...

I have been working with some of the bosses more. Catherine won't let me do anything alone. She is present for everything. Her decision is as much about control as it is about my safety. I don't argue with her. At the end of the day, I don't particularly want to deal with mafia and cartel bosses by myself. I may need to one day, but not any time soon. Catherine has added my name to her legal documents, making me a co-owner of most of her ventures. Marzanna Fashion is in Diane's name, but mine is on everything else. I didn't know Catherine had so many dummy corps.

The phone rings. I'm sitting behind Catherine's desk while she tinkers around the room. I grab the phone and answer it before she can even turn. She glares at me again. She doesn't like when I answer her phone, but that doesn't stop me. I speak in my most cheerful voice.

"Marzanna."

"Ah, Mae, my favorite entrepreneur." I roll my eyes, meeting Catherine's gaze. She turns to face me, leaning against the shelf. Her arms are crossed, and she places one ankle on the other. She oozes power and sex. My pussy dampens at the sight of her. She still wears long sleeves with high necklines to cover her tattoos. She knows how to pull off the look, though. The tightness of the shirt fits her athletic body. Even knowing what is underneath, I want more. She is wearing a miniskirt today in anticipation of Brayden's appointment. My cunt clenches at that thought.

A noise from the receiver draws my attention back to the conversation.

"Ah, Robert, my most onerous partner." Catherine shoots daggers at me, unhappy with my response. Robert is a pain in my ass. Hers too. I don't care if he knows it. His loud guffawing forces the receiver away from my ear.

"I like you, Mae. You are special."

"I am." He's buttering me up. I know it. I'm not going to pass up praise, though.

"I have a favor to ask."

"Oh, I know Robert. There is still a week in the month, and you have used all your allotted shipments. Now you want to add another one for this week? Is that the favor?"

"How did you know?" A playfulness masks his desperation.

"Because you are the only one to call and ask for extra shipments. Every. Single. Month." I emphasize the words to drive home my point.

Catherine watches with her patented blank face. She's given me some pointers on hiding my emotions, but I am terribly inept at that skill. I wear my heart on my sleeve. I can't help that. I try, especially when dealing with the shipments. I go to the warehouse with her for every shipment. If Catherine is there, I am too. We work together, ensuring everything goes smoothly.

"Mae, you are a mind reader! So fantastic. Your skills are unparalleled." More praise. I smile, letting his words soak in, ignoring the thinly veiled condescension.

"Oh, say more like that." Catherine scoffs, but Robert continues to compliment me. After a couple of minutes, he stops, waiting for my response.

"Those are the kindest words I've heard from someone other than Catherine all week. Thank you. My answer is no."

"What?!" I knew his response would be loud, but I wasn't prepared for how loud it would be. I flinch at the sudden noise. "Mae, I need another shipment. I have a big buyer coming in tomorrow. I need this deal."

"How much more is he paying than your highest bidder?"

"That depends on the quality." Hmm, I tap my chin, considering what to do. We don't always turn Robert down. The first answer is always no, but sometimes we'll take extra shipments for him.

"You can ship three containers; we take 75% of the profits." The sound of surprised horror is loud enough that even Catherine hears it. She raises her eyebrows at me, encouraging me to be cautious. Unfortunately, that's not how I work.

"Fifteen, and you take 25%."

"Robert, that offer is so insulting that I won't even counter it. Try again, or I'll hang up."

"No, you can't hang up. I need a shipment through you. I don't have time to find the quality you provide from elsewhere." I hum into the phone. "Okay, Mae. Just for you. Ten and 40%." I stay silent momentarily, letting him think I am considering his offer. I'm not. I already know what I will ask for next. I just want to drag this out for him.

"Seven and 50%. Final offer." He pauses, considering whether to counter.

"Fine."

"I want sales receipts. If you try to lowball us, you'll be done, Robert." We've never explicitly told him what that threat means. He assumes it means the business will end. We intend to take him out entirely. He's already a problem for us, frequently trying to break his contracts. We tolerate it because he is our biggest shipper.

Robert agrees, and we end the call. I add a few notes to our calendar about his shipment. I glance up at Catherine, who is staring at me with admiration. I give her a curious look, turn the tablet off then tuck it away. Brayden will be here shortly, and I no longer want to think about work.

"Do you remember," Catherine starts softly, "bar trivia the first time? When you asked me to come into your apartment while you were drunk and horny and barely knew me?" I nod, remembering with embarrassment how desperately I wanted her to go into my apartment with me. She left me with a forehead kiss. "If I had known then that this is what would be the outcome," she waves her hand in my direction, "I would have taken you inside, told you everything, then fucked you senseless that night."

Her face is still calm, but her eyes burn with desire. The afternoon sun peaks from the clouds, making her gaze even more intense. My mouth is suddenly dry, all the moisture settling between my legs.

"I wouldn't," I lick my lips, trying to speak with a dry mouth, "I wouldn't have taken it well then. I wanted to fuck you but wasn't in love with you. I could've still left at that point." She nods, understanding my response. I wouldn't have believed her if she had told me then. If she had shown me, I would have run. It's a lot to accept, even learning everything over months. I know and am involved now. I wouldn't change anything, but it was a lot to take in.

A knock at the door breaks our conversation. Catherine calls out to Brayden, who walks into the room, greeting us warmly. I ran into him once at a grocery store. I assumed he wouldn't be as cheerful outside of work, assuming his demeanor is part of his job. I watched from behind him as he greeted one of the grocers in the same friendly manner despite them being out of whatever product he needed. He is genuinely a good guy, even when not being paid exorbitant amounts to fuck people.

He doesn't dress up for our appointments. He doesn't need to. We usually have him strip right away. Today, he wears his signature tight jeans and a fitted grey shirt. Even with the shirt on, I nibble my tongue at the thought of what he looks like beneath. Catherine draws the shades to her office as Brayden drops his bag against the wall. It suddenly occurs to me that Catherine and I never finished our conversation.

"Brayden, how often do you put your dick inside of clients, not oral?" Catherine tuts at my vulgarity, but Brayden shrugs.

"More than half of my clients prefer that. The others usually want companionship. You two are the only sexual clients that limit me to oral." I raise my eyebrows at Catherine, trying to make her see my point. "Is that something you want today?"

"No," Catherine responds at the same time as me.

"Yes." I stare at her, then back to Brayden. "Yes, I want that. She wants to peg you, see the skirt." I wave my hand at her. She is standing with her hands on her hips, watching me. "I want you to fuck me while she has the vibrating dildo." He smiles between the two of us.

"I have condoms," he adds casually.

"See? He has condoms!"

Catherine drops her arms to her side, not entirely willing to concede. Brayden walks over to the couch, and I approach Catherine. I place my hands on her hips, tugging her close to me. She watches me but doesn't wrap her arms around me. She's only a couple of inches taller than me. I rise just a bit to kiss her cheek.

"You still get to be in control," I whisper against her skin. She sighs and places her hands on my arms.

"Fine, but you owe me." I nod excitedly. Owing means orgasms. Whether she takes or denies them, it's a win-win for me. One of her hands tangles in my hair, tugging me to her. She kisses me deeply, exerting her dominance over me. I glide my hands up her sides, tracing the underside of her breasts with my thumbs. She doesn't get the same satisfaction from being touched, but what it gives me makes up for what she doesn't get.

"Go sit on the couch." I bounce over, plopping down. My short dress flutters around me, barely covering me as I sit. Catherine thinks for a moment, looking between Brayden and me. "Both of you strip." I don't need to be told twice. I tug the dress over my head. The soft leather feels smooth under my exposed ass. I lift my hips, sliding my orange thong to the floor. I unhook the matching bra and toss it, sitting completely bare on her couch. I should have grabbed a towel to avoid ruining it, but I'm already here. Brayden is also naked, standing half-mast between Catherine and me.

"Suck it," she instructs me, pulling harnesses and vibrators from her toy drawer. It's my favorite drawer in her office. Brayden steps in front of me, and I grab his hips. I don't use my hands, just wrap my lips over the tip of his hardening cock. I slide my tongue along the silky skin, closing my eyes as I suck him. His member hardens and lengthens in my mouth, making it more challenging to take it all in. He groans as I swirl my tongue around his length.

Fingers brush my cheek. I open my eyes to find Catherine peering down at me. She is standing behind Brayden's arm, watching me suck his massive cock. I shift just a bit, letting his dick fill that cheek. Her fingers dance over my stretched mouth, memorizing how I look. She nods her head sideways.

"Lay down."

I do as told, lying on my back on the couch. She instructs Brayden to lick me. She knows I'm already soaked. She's maintaining her control by telling us what to do. Despite wanting nothing more than to be thoroughly fucked, I have no qualms about letting him lick my pussy. He climbs on the couch, wasting no time finding my aching core. I groan as his tongue licks between my lower lips, teasing my clit. He licks up and down several times.

I open my eyes when Catherine clicks a bottle open. I watch her lube the vibrator she is wearing now. The image is so erotic, my pussy clenches as Brayden's tongue slides inside me. Catherine's lip twitches up, knowing what she does to me. She loves to loom over me, stroking her false dick. It's such a power move. I keep my eyes on her as she steps behind Brayden. Her hands drag over his ass, teasing his hole playfully. He tries to hide it but groans slightly, sending vibrations across my opening.

She instructs him to grab a condom and then place it on the couch. He does as instructed, returning to my cunt. His fingers slip inside me as he flicks his tongue lightly against my clit. I can't see her, but she is prepping to peg him. My thighs shake with anticipation. She pulls his shoulders back, raising him up straight. Catherine whispers in Brayden's ear, but I can't hear despite our proximity. He nods and puts the condom on. Before I can react, he slams deep inside me. I moan loudly. Brayden is hovering over me, thrusting roughly inside me. My pleasure builds, and my body tingles with an impending orgasm.

Just before my release, Catherine stills Brayden. I know when she enters him because I can feel the vibrations inside me. It's muted, but it's still there. Catherine begins fucking him, and he's fucking me. It's awkward initially, the two finding the right pace that works. Once they find it, it's glorious. The vibrating, the thrusting, the fullness. The only thing that could make it better is clitoral stimulation.

As soon as I think it, Brayden has a small bullet pressed against me. I cry out. My body tenses and then, all at once, releases. My orgasm crashes through me, sending me soaring. White flashes behind my eyes as the relentless pounding continues. Just as I return to my body, another orgasm reaches its crest. As it tears through me, Brayden shudders, releasing his load in the condom. I groan, grabbing onto his shoulders to stabilize myself. He rests his shoulders against my chest, heaving deep breaths to settle himself. Peace and joy descend through my mind and body. My life isn't perfect, but hell, it feels like it right now.

Some shuffling happens, and Brayden's rugged body is replaced with Catherine's warm one. She lays beside me, squeezed between the back of the couch and me. She's rubbing my arms, cooing soft words as I savor her presence. Brayden sits on the floor beside us with his clothes on. He says he doesn't care about aftercare, but I don't like letting him just leave after fucking us. With him beside us, Catherine and I rub his shoulders and chest. He preens under our attention, genuinely enjoying it.

The three of us sit for several minutes, touching and softly chatting. Soon, Brayden leaves, heading out to see other clients. Catherine pulls me up and helps me dress. She can be intense during sex, but she's always soft and gentle afterward. I enjoy the intimacy after as much as I enjoy fucking her.

We ride in the car silently. John drives while Catherine works on her tablet. I stare out the window, watching buildings, restaurants, and shops pass. We drive by the stadium and several bars, passing through Kansas City.

"We're having some issues in Texas with our shipments." I glance at Catherine. She's mentioned issues near San Antonio before but hasn't said much to me about it. "What do you think about taking the bike for a long trip? A couple of weeks, just us and the open road?" A twinkle in her eye conveys the excitement she holds. She already has everything planned out. She has a plan in mind to fix the issue, but just like with our other trips for shipments, we plan a variety of activities.

"We haven't taken the bike on a long trip before. Will I die?" We chuckle together at my dramatics.

"No, we'll stop often. The bike will be better for this trip, though."

I don't know what Catherine has in mind or why we need the bike, but I will follow her to the ends of the earth without a second thought. Even if it means a numb ass.

Acknowledgements

Thank you to anyone that has made it this far! I do this for you and wouldn't be where I am without you. If you keep turning the page, you'll see my other books and some totally random facts about me. It's mostly worth it. I promise.

Also, thanks Ben, Stephanie, Emily, Caitlin, Kandace, Nicole, and Stella. You all are excellent sounding boards! lol much love!

ALSO BY

Roommates

James's life is in shambles. When Addy drags him back to her apartment, he can't refuse. He needs to get back on his feet. Addy and her roommates are gorgeous and kind. How can he focus when he can't stop thinking about them?

Roommates is a queer poly romance. There are kinks, alcohol and drug consumption, mild violence, and language.

Sweet Briar Series

A cursed princess must find her true love to save her kingdom. A new edict will bring men to the castle in hopes of breaking the curse. Will she find her true love? Or will she be forced to reign over a dying kingdom? Will she ever learn the truth of the curse placed on her kingdom?

Sweet Briar series is a medieval fantasy romance. The series is completed and contains sexual situations, SA, infertility, violence, alcohol, death of family members, and queer characters.

352

About the Author

April is a non-binary parent living in Minnesota. They are an avid reader, with a special interest in smut. They love collecting random things, such as Funko Pops, posters, graphic tees, scrunchies, and more. They love long romantic trips around bookstores and watching hours of TikTok videos.